THE DAFFODIL SEA

EMMA BLAIR
THE DAFFODIL SEA

LONDON NEW YORK SYDNEY TORONTO

This edition published 1994 by
BCA
by arrangement with Bantam Press
a division of Transworld Publishers

CN 8521

Printed and bound in Great Britain by
Mackays of Chatham PLC, Chatham, Kent

Remember . . .

THE DAFFODIL SEA

Chapter One

'I love you.'

Phoebe Hawkins stopped what she was doing and stared at her husband in astonishment. Such a declaration was rare, very rare indeed. Reynold simply wasn't the emotionally demonstrative type.

He smiled at her. 'I do.'

'Whatever brought that on?'

'I don't know,' he said softly. 'Maybe it's the time of night. Maybe—' He trailed off and shrugged.

A warmth blossomed in her, and she went tingly all over with affection. 'You soft old thing.'

'Not so old!' he protested. 'I'm only thirty-eight.'

'You know what I mean.'

She smiled back at him, thinking he looked tired. It had been a hard day for him in the fields. There again, it had been a hard day for her, too.

He crooked a finger. 'Come here.'

'Why?'

'I want to hold you.'

She noted the glint in his eyes and knew what that meant. A glance at the clock told her it was just after nine-thirty – bedtime. Early to bed and early to rise – that was the way of life on a farm.

'Would you like a last cup of tea before going through?' she asked. The kettle was on the side of the range and would only take a few seconds to boil.

'Would you?'

She thought about it. 'Yes.'

'Then make the tea. But come here first.'

She went over to him, knelt, and slipped into his arms as they enfolded her.

'Do you ever consider how lucky we are?' he queried.

'How so?'

'The fact we have each other and the girls.'

Lucky? She supposed they were. She'd just never thought of it that way before.

He stroked her hair, marvelling at its rich auburn beauty. Her hair had been the first thing he'd noticed about her all those years ago when they'd first met – her hair, then her face. Both had drawn him like iron to a magnet, winning his heart, a heart that had been hers ever since.

Phoebe closed her eyes in contentment and drew the smell of him down into her lungs, the smell of man combined with the deep rich smell of the earth that he worked. It was a satisfying smell.

'Did you get much milk from Daisy?' he asked. Daisy was the oldest of their three cows.

'More than yesterday.'

'That's good.'

'She's getting to the end of her days, I'm afraid.'

'Hmmh,' he murmured. Daisy had been a good cow, now she needed replacing. 'I'll see to her.'

'Soon?'

'Shortly.'

'Pity, that,' Phoebe said.

His hand dropped down to encompass a breast, a breast that drooped where once it had been firm and upstanding. But that was what happened when a woman had children.

'Don't tickle,' she chided.

'Am I?'

'A little.'

He tweaked her nipple, which caused her to yelp, and him to smile again.

'Stop that!'

'What?' he queried innocently.

'What you're doing.'

'You mean this?' he said, and tweaked again.

She broke away from him to squat on her haunches. 'You're a terrible man, Reynold Hawkins,' she admonished.

He gazed benignly at her, thinking of bed and her in his embrace. There had been others when he was young but he'd chosen Phoebe, a decision he'd never regretted for an instant. Lucky – he was certainly that.

'I'll get your tea,' she declared, rising.

Reynold yawned and ran a hand over his face, scratching the bristles that were already appearing. 'I'm hungry,' he declared.

'Get away with you. You ate a huge supper.'

'Nonetheless I'm hungry again.'

'There's cheese and pickles.'

'That might give me indigestion.'

'It never has before,' she stated.

'True. But I feel it might tonight.'

'So what would you like?'

'Cheese and tomato.'

She laughed. 'You daft hap'worth.'

'I don't see what's daft about that.'

'You're just being contrary. Typical of you.'

'No I'm not.'

She knew fine well he was contrary, and a little difficult, but that was her Reynold all over. Never difficult in a big sense, but in small ways, as though he always had to have the last word.

'Cheese and tomato it is then.'

He pushed himself further back into his chair and watched her cut the bread, while the kettle started to sing. When the food was handed to him he wolfed it down, then drank his strong, sweet tea.

'Bed now?' she asked, clearing away his dishes.

'Bed,' he confirmed, coming to his feet.

'You go on through. I'll be with you in a minute.'

He went to her and kissed her neck. 'I'll be waiting, my lover.'

'On you go then.'

He patted her playfully on the bottom, pecked her again, then left the room.

Phoebe paused for a moment, and sighed. She didn't really feel like lovemaking but would never have dreamt of telling him. If Reynold was in the mood she'd go along with him. That was how she was, a totally accommodating wife; how a wife, as she saw it, should be. Not that she was downtrodden or subservient, far from it. She had a mind of her own which she was quite capable of expressing, and a temper which would occasionally flare when she was crossed. But why deny him just because she didn't feel like it? Anyway, despite how she felt she would enjoy it. She always did.

11

She washed and put away the dishes, then extinguished the larger of the paraffin lamps. Picking up the second one, she followed Reynold from the kitchen.

She stopped at the girls' room, following her nightly routine. Linnet, who was sixteen, was closer to the door, her long blond hair cascading over the bedclothes, her face serene in sleep. Roxanne looked a little troubled, her fourteen-year-old brow creased, as though she was having an unpleasant dream.

'Goodnight, maids,' Phoebe whispered.

'Are you coming?' Reynold called quietly from further down the corridor.

She heard the whisper of bats' wings outside, a rustling noise that she found strangely comforting. The sound quickly receded and faded to die out altogether. Some folk didn't care for bats, were afraid of them, but not her.

'Phoebe?'

Later, when it was over, she turned onto her side and he snuggled up against her. She was thinking about the bats when he started to snore.

'How many eggs do you want, Linnet?' Phoebe queried from the range where she was making breakfast.

'Two, Ma.'

'And you, Roxanne?'

'Two for me as well.'

She didn't have to ask Reynold as he had five eggs and five rashers of bacon every morning without fail – and a couple of sausages should there be any going.

'Is it weeding again today, Da?' Roxanne inquired.

Reynold, munching bread, nodded. 'It be, girl.'

Ben, their dog, came snuffling into the kitchen. He wandered round the table before finally settling at Reynold's feet. 'Hallo, my beauty,' Reynold said, reaching down and scratching the top of Ben's head.

'Roxanne, I want you to come home this afternoon and help me to make butter,' Phoebe declared.

Roxanne grinned, much preferring that chore to grafting in the fields which was back-breaking work.

'Aw! Why not me?' Linnet protested.

'Because Roxanne is better at making butter. Don't ask me why, she just is.'

Linnet stared daggers at her sister. 'I make good butter,' she argued with a slight whine in her voice.

'Not as good as Roxanne,' Phoebe repeated. 'You be better at some things, Roxanne at others. That's all there is to it.'

'Horses for courses,' Reynold commented.

'Huh!' Linnet sniffed, while Roxanne could barely contain her delight; any work indoors was a dawdle compared to weeding. Both girls were extremely fond of each other, but the rivalry between them was intense, and had been since they were tiny.

'Breakfast won't be long,' Phoebe declared.

'I'm starving,' Reynold said to no-one in particular, then added, as he glanced out of the window, 'I think it'll rain today.'

'I hope not, I've got washing to do,' Phoebe said, tucking into her meal.

Reynold was only half listening, thinking about the work before him. The cows had already been milked, but that was only the beginning: the chores were endless.

When breakfast was over Reynold left the house first, striding off over the fields, leaving Linnet and Roxanne to follow on.

'What time shall I come back, Ma?' Roxanne queried, half a question, half a dig at her sister.

'I'll fetch you.'

'But what sort of time?' This was merely to spin things out, make as much out of it as she could.

'Afternoon, after dinner.'

Roxanne was disappointed; she would have much rather been summoned in the morning. But there you were, you couldn't have everything.

Linnet and Roxanne left together, heading for the fields and their weeding, which they both found boring beyond belief, but knew that it had to be done nonetheless. They'd realized early on in life that drudgery was the name of farm work.

Roxanne halted to stare at a clump of daffodils which grew close to the house and came up regularly every spring.

'I've always loved daffs,' she murmured.

'I prefer roses myself,' Linnet declared, just to be different.

'Roses are all right, lovely I suppose, but there's something special about daffs. Maybe it's the time of year they appear, when everything's fresh and newborn.'

Linnet inhaled the spring air, thinking Roxanne had a point, but she was certainly not going to agree with her. If Roxanne had said red was red she would have insisted it was white.

'Better get moving,' she said.

Roxanne bent and smelt one of the daffodils which was swaying gently in the wind. Its perfume was light and delicate.

'We'd better get moving,' Linnet repeated a trifle crossly.

'All right, keep your hat on.'

'I'm not wearing one, stupid.'

'Who are you calling stupid!' Roxanne flared.

Linnet skipped away a few paces. 'At least I don't have huge feet!'

'I have nothing of the sort.'

'Absolutely huge. Like boats.'

'Your feet are bigger than mine,' Roxanne countered.

'Bitch!' Linnet hissed.

Roxanne laughed mockingly. 'It takes one to know one.'

'Why I'll—'

Roxanne ran off, knowing she was far fleeter than Linnet who would never catch her.

Linnet gritted her teeth at the continuing sound of Roxanne's laughter.

Phoebe paused to catch her breath. She was carrying a wicker basket containing dinner for her family. She could see Reynold ploughing in the distance. Him or the girls first? Him, she decided.

A solitary swan appeared to wing overhead. It made a curious, quite distinctive sound as it flew by. Phoebe watched it bank, then dive, finally gliding to a halt beside what she took to be its mate.

What elegant creatures they were, Phoebe reflected. At certain times of the year there were lots of them round this part of Devon. How beautiful they were when swimming on the rivers, proud and noble, the aristocrats of the bird world.

Reynold was making good progress with his ploughing, she noted. He'd been working hard, but there again, he always did. There was nothing slack or lazy about her Reynold.

She thought of Linnet and Roxanne, they were excellent workers too – that was when they weren't squabbling. And how they were both growing up. Linnet was quite the young woman, while she'd seen a big difference in Roxanne during the past year. Her figure was filling out, curves were forming where, not that long ago, there had been none.

Both were good looking, if she said so herself. Though, from the way things were shaping, Roxanne was going to be the better looking of the two which would certainly annoy Linnet. Their ash-blond hair and startling blue eyes came from Reynold's family, Devonians like her own people, from time out of mind.

14

The land was all they'd ever known and, as she understood it, all they'd ever wanted to know.

Her ruminations were disturbed by the sudden appearance of a weasel, which stopped to gaze beadily at her for a moment before scurrying off and disappearing into a clump of long grass.

She brought her attention back to Reynold plodding along behind Fern, their Shire horse. Besides Fern they also owned a pony called Barton which was used to pull their cart and trap. Fern did all the heavy work.

She hefted her basket and was about to continue on her way when a sudden thought filled her with sadness. The son they'd lost from flu, aged almost two when an epidemic swept the area, would now have been seventeen. If he'd lived it might well have been him out there ploughing instead of Reynold.

Losing Freddy had been a cruel blow, even crueller than they'd realized at the time as he'd been the only boy born to them. How Reynold missed having a son to carry on his name and line. It was something he never mentioned but she knew how he really felt about the matter.

Besides losing Freddy she'd also suffered four miscarriages, all occurring after the birth of Roxanne. At thirty-five she could still have children, it wasn't impossible, but old Doc Pepperill had been sceptical about her chances of carrying a baby to full term after the last miscarriage. He'd muttered that there was a possibility that her insides were damaged in some way, and on being pressed had suggested she might like to go to Plymouth and consult a specialist. That was out of the question, of course, as it would have cost far too much money and their cash was strictly limited.

So it was up to nature whether or not she produced another son. Nature, and them. Her face lit up in a smile; if she didn't it certainly wouldn't be for lack of trying, Reynold saw to that. He was as active now as he'd been when they'd first got married – a little too active sometimes – but she wouldn't have had it any other way.

'Hurry up or you'll get left behind!' Reynold called out to Linnet and Roxanne who were still indoors. It was market day in St Petroc and he intended selling Daisy and hopefully replacing her with a younger beast. There was also some other business he had to attend to, he thought grimly.

'Are you fully loaded, my lover?' he asked Phoebe, who'd been stacking produce into their cart.

'All finished now,' she declared.

'Proper job.'

Linnet and Roxanne came bustling out, the pair of them laughing at something funny Roxanne had said.

Reynold closed the flap at the rear of the cart, then tied Daisy's lead to an iron ring specifically positioned there for that purpose. Daisy swished her tail, bothered by the flies buzzing round her.

'A good day for it,' Reynold commented as he climbed onto the driver's seat. It was the beginning of June, the early morning sun already blazing down.

'It promises to be a scorcher,' Phoebe said, joining him.

Linnet and Roxanne scrambled into the back of the cart where they sat on boxes of produce. 'Poor Daisy,' Linnet commiserated to the cow, aware of its fate. Within a day or two the animal would undoubtedly be butchered.

'For the chop,' Roxanne said sympathetically.

Reynold often did his own killing, but because they currently had an ample supply of meat in the larder, and with Daisy's yield continuing to decline, he had decided in this instance to sell the beast on.

Daisy gave the girls a soulful look as though she knew what lay in store for her.

'Let's go,' said Reynold, flicking the reins.

The girls chatted animatedly as they progressed along the narrow lane that adjoined the farm, a lane bounded on both sides by six foot banks crowned with hedges. These were an important source of firewood, faggots and useful timber trees when the saplings were left to grow. It was said that some of the hedgebanks in the locality went back to medieval times, others beyond that to the prehistoric era. All were a haven for every kind of wild-life.

'Are you going to the pub?' Phoebe asked Reynold, thinking she wouldn't mind a glass or two herself to hear the latest gossip. The pubs were great places on market days, invariably thronged with menfolk intent on making all sorts of deals.

'I'll definitely be going. There's a man I want to speak with.'

'Oh?'

He winked conspiratorially at her. 'Something I want to arrange. I'll tell you later if I'm able to.'

As they left their lane they joined the main road leading to St Petroc which they could now see in the distance, with a sparkling blue ribbon beyond that which was the sea.

As it was market day the road was busy, by normal standards

16

that was. Other carts and waggons were also en route to St Petroc, filled with people well known to the Hawkins family.

There were the Tutchings whose maid Sally had been at school with Linnet. And over there were the Calcrafts, all twelve of them. Jack Calcraft only had one arm, having lost his left one in an accident with a threshing machine. His arm had been sucked into the feeding hole of the heavy toothed drum while it was rotating at speed, and that had been that.

Sally waved to Linnet and Roxanne who returned her wave. She then shouted something, but was too far away for either of the girls to make out what she'd said. Realizing this, Sally made a gesture indicating that she'd see them in town.

The first house they came to on the outskirts of St Petroc was Snowdrop Cottage which gleamed white under its thatched roof. The next cottage was pink, the one following primrose yellow, all thatched, as were the majority of dwellings in the town.

Now they had arrived in the town proper, where the houses and shops stood on raised pavements. They passed the Hart Inn from which wafted a strong smell of ale; it was already doing a roaring trade judging from the noise emanating from within.

Reynold brought the cart to a halt as sheep burst from one of the many alleyways leading off the high street, a black-and-white collie bounding alongside guiding them towards the centre of town.

'How do, Reynold!' called out the shepherd when he emerged from the alley. He was a small, dumpy man with a grizzled, weatherbeaten face.

'How do, William. They be fine-looking Suffolks you got there.'

William beamed. 'Beauties, one and all. Should fetch a pretty penny, I'm hoping.'

'Are you going to the King's Arms later?'

'I should imagine. I'll be wanting to wet my whistle.'

'We'll have a chinwag then.'

William waved his crook in affirmation, then strolled on after his sheep which were proceeding along the street with the collie well in control of them.

'Nice fat beasts,' Reynold commented to Phoebe, who nodded her agreement.

Reynold started up the cart again, heading for the square where he found a suitable spot for their purposes.

'Linnet, see to Barton,' he instructed, leaping down onto the cobbles.

The square was alive with the noise and bustle of the many

17

animals gathered there to be bought, sold and traded. Milk cows, bullocks and heifers mooed and stamped their feet; chickens squawked; sheep milled, while pigs snorted and squealed in their temporary pens. There were also horses present, all types and sizes from Shires to wild Dartmoor ponies.

Reynold untied Daisy with the intention of seeking out a friend who, he thought, might be interested.

'Goodbye, old girl,' said Roxanne, patting Daisy affectionately on the rump. Daisy's reply was to swish her tail extra hard.

'Goodbye from me too,' added Linnet, patting Daisy as well.

'You're going to the King's Arms then?' Phoebe queried, recalling his conversation with William. He used different pubs as the mood and humour took him.

'That's my plan.'

'I'll probably join you when I get a chance.'

'Make sure you bring some cash with you,' he said, eyes twinkling, half in jest, half in earnest. And with that he left them, Daisy following disconsolately on behind.

Phoebe went round to the rear of the cart and undid the flap. She then climbed back on board and started laying out and arranging the stacked boxes. Like many people there, her intention was to sell and barter what she could, as this was a way of supplementing their income and also acquiring items they neither grew nor produced on the farm. When she had finished she'd transformed the cart into a miniature shop.

'They be nice beets,' declared a potential customer.

'Handsome, aren't they?'

The woman peered at the box of beets, then prodded one. 'What price you asking?'

Phoebe informed her.

The woman pursed her lips in contemplation.

'You won't find none cheaper. And certainly none better,' Phoebe informed her.

'Oh I don't knows about that.'

Phoebe was used to this, certain rituals were invariably gone through before a purchase was made. It was all part and parcel of how things were done.

'Hmmh,' the woman murmured, pretending to be undecided.

'Beans is good too,' Phoebe said. 'Sweet as can be.'

'I saw some nice ones earlier.'

'I'm surprised you didn't buy them then,' Phoebe countered with a disarming smile.

'I might still.'

'What price was being asked?'

The woman named a sum Phoebe knew must be a fib. 'Well I can't match that, I'm afraid. That's just giving them away.'

Linnet whispered in Roxanne's ear, who nodded. They waited till the woman had finally made her purchases and moved off, then Linnet said, 'Ma, can we have a while to ourselves? If you don't need us, that is.'

Phoebe thought about it. 'Not too long now,' she agreed, for she'd want the girls to look after the cart while she went round the market and did a bit of bartering and if she was to go to the pub.

Ann Weeks, an old chum of Phoebe's who lived in St Petroc, came over. 'Hallo me dear, how are you today?' she inquired.

Linnet and Roxanne left as Phoebe fell into conversation.

'Shall we just wander?' Roxanne suggested.

'I want to look in the sweet shop and see the lady with only a head.'

Roxanne laughed. The lady with only a head, a nickname Linnet had given her, was a favourite of theirs. 'All right. The sweet shop it is then.'

They hadn't gone far when they bumped into Sally Tutching who was on an errand for her father. 'There are gypsies here,' Sally informed them.

'That's nothing new, there often are,' Linnet pointed out.

'But one of this lot is a fortune teller. I'd love to have me fortune told, wouldn't you?'

'Oh yes,' breathed Linnet. Having your fortune told sounded really exciting, and a little scary.

'It's all a load of nonsense,' Roxanne declared airily.

' 'Tis not. They gypsies genuinely can see into the future. My ma had hers done once and it all came true.'

'Get away,' Roxanne murmured, round eyed.

'Every last bit of it. I swear.'

'Is she expensive? The one here now, I mean.'

'Don't know. Didn't ask. No point in asking when I've no money. Not even a farthing piece to my name.'

'Us neither,' Linnet stated.

'Where is this fortune teller?' Roxanne asked.

Sally pointed. 'That way. You can't miss her. She's got a caravan with stars and moons painted on the sides.'

'Stars and moons!' Roxanne exclaimed, impressed. Now that really was something.

'I've got to go,' said Sally. 'My Da's run out of baccy and will get in a right old paddy if I keeps him waiting.'

'Maybe see you later then,' Linnet smiled.

Sally winked at Roxanne. 'Mind you don't offend the fortune teller. She might also be a witch who'll turn you into a toad if you do.'

'If she wants someone to turn into a toad I'll give her your name and address,' Roxanne riposted quickly.

'Cheeky.'

'No more than you, Sally Tutching. Don't think you can take a rise out of me cause you're older.'

'I found that out a long time ago,' Linnet sighed.

'Anyway, must dash. Ta ra!'

Linnet and Roxanne watched Sally race off. 'Come on,' said Linnet, dying to see the fortune teller and her fabulous caravan.

As Sally had predicted they found the caravan easily enough, and the raven-haired woman sitting on a stool in front of it smoking a clay pipe. Atop a dark skirt the woman was wearing a bright red shirt and multicoloured bolero with strings and strings of beads and chains around her neck. Her eyes, when she glanced at the girls, were as black as pitch.

Roxanne wondered how old she was. Older than Phoebe, that was certain.

The caravan was as fascinating as the woman herself. Besides the stars and moons there were several suns and what Roxanne took to be a fiery comet sweeping across the heavens.

The woman stood up, ran scarlet-tipped fingers through her shoulder-length hair, glanced at the girls again, then went up the two short steps that led to the door of the caravan and vanished inside.

'Gosh,' whispered Linnet.

'Did she frighten you?'

'Not at all,' Linnet lied.

Roxanne smiled to herself. Linnet had been frightened all right, she could tell.

As they stood staring at the caravan the woman's face suddenly appeared in the window facing them, then the curtains were snapped abruptly shut.

'I wonder what she's up to?' Roxanne mused.

'Perhaps she's gone to gaze into her crystal ball.'

'How do you know she uses one of those?'

'Don't they all?'

Linnet decided to air her superior knowledge. 'They also use

20

special cards while some reads your hand.' She paused for a moment, then added, 'And if I read your hand right now even I could tell you something.'

Roxanne knew it was a tease. 'What?'

'That it's dirty.'

Roxanne liked that, and laughed. Then they both had to move out of the way as a farmer in moleskins and rough tweed jacket led a pair of high spirited, snorting horses past.

'The sweet shop,' said Linnet.

The reason behind the nickname for the lady with only a head was that the female in question, a Mrs Westlake, was so tiny only her neck and shoulders showed above the counter. It was a strange experience being served by her as the customer invariably had to hand her items from most of the counter as she couldn't reach them.

'Oh yum,' crooned Linnet when they arrived at the shop and saw the new display in the window.

'Look at all that chocolate.'

'And toffee.'

Linnet, who had an extremely sweet tooth, licked her lips. 'I'd give anything for some of they.'

'Anything?'

'You know what I mean.'

'Those chocolates there,' said Roxanne, pointing, 'look absolutely scrumptious. And can you see that big marzipan thing? Marzipan's your favourite, isn't it?'

Linnet nodded and wriggled with desire. 'This is torture,' she breathed.

'I know,' Roxanne grinned. 'And I've just been helping torture you.'

Linnet realized that Roxanne was teasing her in retaliation for the dirty hand joke.

'I certainly got you going there, dear sister. You shouldn't really come and stare in this window. It don't do you no good, Linnet.'

Mrs Westlake spotted them and smiled. She waved a thin, scrawny hand at them and they waved back.

'Tell you what,' proposed Roxanne, 'why don't we go down to the harbour? I haven't been there in ages and I love to see the boats.'

Linnet looked undecided. 'Do you think we got time? Ma said not to be too long.'

'We've hardly been gone at all.'

'But the harbour—'

'Taint far,' Roxanne interrupted. 'A hop, skip and a jump. And I so want to see the boats. I find them ever so romantic.'

Linnet sneered. 'What do you know about romantic?'

'You'd be surprised. I know lots of things.'

'Like what?' Linnet was intrigued.

'Oh all sorts,' Roxanne replied vaguely.

'You're daft,' Linnet declared. 'I've thought that for a long while now. Daft with far too much imagination.'

Roxanne smiled knowingly. 'Boats is still romantic, as can be a flower or a sunset.' Then, changing her tone, 'We're wasting time. Let's get down to the harbour.'

They left the square and dived into an alley that led them into Sea Street which eventually brought them out on to the quayside.

There were only four boats currently in the harbour, as the rest were out fishing. The nearest boat was painted duck blue and had a rust-coloured sail which was at that moment being hoisted.

They watched the boat move away from its berth and out through the harbour entrance into the open water beyond. The boat's name, painted in black highlighted in gold, was *Firefly*.

'I always think it's such a wonderful smell round the harbour,' Roxanne said dreamily. 'The salt, and fish, and tar all mixed together into something special.'

'I'll tell you what, it certainly beats the pig shit I have to put up with.' It was one of Linnet's many chores to feed and generally take care of their pigs.

Roxanne grinned.

'Still, despite it all, I'd never leave the farm. Not for nothing.'

'But you'll get married one day, surely?'

'You misunderstand me, Roxanne. Naturally I'll marry, but I'll just be going from one farm to another. The only difference, I hope, that in the one I go to I'll be the mistress with my own kitchen and all.' The 'I hope' referred to the possibility of having to move in with parents-in-law where the kitchen wouldn't be hers until the mother-in-law had passed on.

Linnet glanced at her sister. 'It'll be the same for you, no doubt. In time.'

'I don't know,' Roxanne mused, staring out at the harbour breakwater which was in the shape of an incomplete circle, the stone structure ramped like the walls of a medieval castle. The quayside and breakwater had been built around 1750, making them almost one hundred and fifty years old, as it was 1896.

'How do you mean?'

'I just don't know, that's all. I'd hate to think my life was going to be as cut and dried as that. It seems so predictable somehow.'

'But it is predictable for the likes of you and me. That's how it's always been for us. For Ma, her Ma and her Ma before her.'

'There should be something more, though.'

'Well there won't be. You can count on it.'

A fresh breeze had sprung up causing both girls' hair to dance in the wind. The same breeze was filling the *Firefly*'s sails, now at full sail, and taking it rapidly out to sea.

'What are you thinking about now?' Linnet demanded, for Roxanne's expression had become one of deep introspection.

'That gypsy fortune teller.'

'What about her?'

'I wonder if she really can tell the future, and if she told ours what it would be.'

'I just said. Farm work, marriage and more farm work. All that's missing are the details. Who you marry, how many children, will there be any health problems, will he be a good farmer, and a lucky one. Those sort of things.'

Roxanne suddenly laughed. 'If I have too much imagination then you have too little, Linnet. Don't you ever dream of far away places and the people there? What a totally different life would be like?'

Linnet gazed at her sister in wry amusement. 'What would be the point? Twill never happen.'

Probably not, Roxanne thought. And yet it was nice to dream, and dreaming never did any harm, after all.

'We'd best get back now or we'll be for it from Ma,' Linnet said.

Roxanne reached out and gently touched her sister on the arm. 'Thanks for coming to the harbour with me. I've enjoyed it.'

Linnet was touched by this show of appreciation and affection. 'Twerent anything. I enjoyed it too.'

Together they made their way back up Sea Street towards the market.

As she entered the King's Arms, Phoebe was immediately hailed by Marjery Tregale and Vi Privett who were near neighbours of hers, both women holding half-pints of cider. Phoebe thought Marjery looked a little the worse for wear which was confirmed when she spoke with slurred speech.

'I'm looking for my Reynold,' Phoebe explained, glancing round the crowded saloon.

'I saw him a minute or two agi,' Vi replied.

'Oh he'll be here somewhere,' Marjery said, and hiccuped.

'How you do today?' Vi asked. She and Marjery, like Phoebe, had been selling produce and other items off the back of their carts.

'So so, could've been better.'

'I did well, sold all the material I had on offer,' Marjery grinned. She'd spun and woven the material herself.

'Good for you.'

Marjery winked slyly. 'And got a grand price for it, too. Most of it was bought by someone who wasn't local. A real city lady in fancy clothes, all done up like a dish of fish she was.'

'You were lucky then,' Phoebe said.

'I was indeed. So on the strength of that let me buy you a drink.'

As cash was in short supply they usually bought their own. 'Are you sure, Marjery?'

'Of course I am. Now what'll it be?'

'Cider. Same as yourself.'

'Then cider it is.' And with that Marjery began elbowing her way to the bar.

'She's had a skinful,' Vi commented.

'I can see that. Her Joe won't be best pleased.' Reynold would certainly have had something to say to her if she'd got tipsy in a pub. It was all right for a man in his book, but never a woman.

'Now where is that husband of mine?' Phoebe murmured, gazing around again, trying to peer through, round, and over, the press of bodies.

Marjery was returning with her cider when she finally spotted Reynold sitting at a table deep in conversation with a small, ferret-faced man whose thinning hair was combed straight back from his forehead. The man was a stranger to her. Then she recalled Reynold mentioning that he was going to the pub because there was a man he wanted to speak with, and wondered if Ferret-face was him.

Should she go over or remain where she was? If Reynold was trying to do a deal he wouldn't appreciate her barging in on the middle of things. Stay put, she decided.

Marjery hiccuped again. 'Nothing like cider for making you feel good,' she beamed.

'Or a drop of gin,' Vi added, who adored gin but only occasionally got to drink it because of the cost.

'How's your apple crop doing this year?' Marjery asked Phoebe.

'Fine.'

'That touch of late frost we had gave my Joe a real scare and no mistake. But fortunately no damage was done.'

Phoebe nodded. Frost could wreak all manner of havoc at certain times of the year and was greatly feared by farmers.

'I hear Bess Snelling is expecting again,' Vi said.

'Really?' queried Phoebe. The Snellings already had a large family.

'She's none too pleased by all accounts.' Vi shrugged. 'But what can you do?'

'Very little,' Phoebe answered, thinking of Reynold.

'Bess had a hard time with her last babe,' Marjery murmured, brow furrowed in sympathy. 'I only pray this one's easier. Though tisn't likely, is it?'

'You never know,' said Phoebe.

They were still talking about Bess Snelling when Reynold appeared beside them. 'Hallo you lot,' he smiled.

'I saw you but didn't come over as you looked as though you didn't want to be disturbed,' Phoebe told him.

Reynold nodded. 'That twere the right thing to do.'

'A deal?'

'Not really. I'll explain on the way home. But right now I must be off to pick up the cow I bought.'

'You sold Daisy then?'

'I did, then traded for this new one.'

'Don't you want another drink?'

He shook his head. 'I've had enough. And anyway, I promised to collect this cow round about now. You stay and have another though and I'll meet you back at the cart.'

'I can come with you if you want?' She'd nearly finished her half-pint.

'No, you stay on and enjoy yourself.'

He looked pleased with himself, Phoebe thought. The trade must have been in his favour. 'Was that man you were with the one you said you wanted to meet?'

'He was.'

'Is he from hereabouts?' she probed.

'Not exactly hereabouts, but not that far away either. Now I'll be off. See you in a bit.'

When their glasses were empty the three women went up to the bar for refills.

*　*　*

25

When Phoebe returned to the cart she found Reynold already there and everything packed away. The new cow was tied to the rear of the cart.

'Handsome beast,' Phoebe commented.

'She'll give us plenty of milk I'll be bound,' Reynold said. The cow was a Friesian, same as Daisy.

'Does she have a name?'

'Not so far,' Reynold replied.

'Let's call her Buttercup,' suggested Roxanne.

'Why that?' Phoebe asked.

'Because I like it.'

'She don't look like no Buttercup. I think we should call her Pansy,' Linnet said, disagreeing with Roxanne just to be awkward.

'She certainly don't look like a Pansy,' Roxanne objected.

Phoebe could see a row brewing. 'I'll name the animal myself,' she stated. 'And that'll be the end of it.'

'So what's your choice?' Reynold queried, climbing aboard.

Phoebe thought for a few moments. 'We'll call her Leafy,' she declared, as it was a common name in those parts.

Roxanne pulled a face. 'I think Buttercup's better, Ma.'

'And I think—' Linnet began.

'I said Leafy and Leafy it is,' Phoebe interjected, joining Reynold at the front of the cart.

He chuckled, amused by the interchange. 'Gee-up!' he ordered, and rippled the reins.

Roxanne glared at Linnet who glared right back. Roxanne was furious, knowing full well if Linnet hadn't stuck her foot in, the cow would have been called Buttercup. That was her sister all over, interfering so and so.

'I take it you struck a good deal,' Phoebe said as they left the square.

'I considered it that. I traded an amount of our apples when they're ready plus four of the piglets born last week.'

'And what about the money you got for Daisy?'

He patted a pocket. 'Have it right here, more than I expected.'

'So it's been a worthwhile trip?'

'I should say.'

Phoebe thought about how the money would be used, the things that needed buying which they couldn't make themselves. She would discuss the details later with Reynold.

'You've got me all curious about that man you met. Who is he?'

'Josia Grim, he owns three of the best sportin' terriers in

Devon. He also hates badgers just as much as I do.'

'What have badgers got to do with it?' she queried.

Reynold's lips thinned into a disapproving slash. 'Some of they vermin are living in Natcott Wood and I intends doing something about it. I've organized a hunt for the Sunday after next.'

'A badger hunt!' Roxanne exclaimed, having been eavesdropping.

'That's right, girl. Josia will bring his dogs and we'll do for they badgers before they cause any more harm.'

'Have they already done any?' Linnet inquired.

'Bound to, it's their nature. Vermin and pests, that's what they are. I won't have brock on any farm of mine.'

'A week on Sunday,' Phoebe mused.

'Directly after church.'

'Can I come?' Linnet asked.

'If you wishes to.'

Roxanne wasn't about to let her sister go off on a hunt while she stayed at home. Linnet would have seen that as putting one over on her. 'And me, Da?'

'Of course you can, girl.'

A badger hunt, Roxanne thought. She'd never been on one of those. It would be a new experience.

Phoebe wiped a sweaty brow. She'd been on the go since the crack of dawn, cooking and baking the meal she was expected to provide for the hunters. As a consequence she'd missed church together with Linnet and Roxanne who'd been helping her. Reynold had attended, however, returning home a short time ago and was now getting changed.

There was a rap on the back door and Joe Tregale popped his head round. 'There be a great smell coming from this kitchen,' he stated, smiling broadly.

'I should hope so after all the hard work we've done this morning,' Phoebe declared.

'It'll be good eatins and drinkins then?'

'I won't let you down, Joe. You should know that.'

His eyes twinkled. 'You're a dandy cook, Phoebe Hawkins. None better, with the possible exception of my Marjery, that is.'

Phoebe knew she was a far better cook than Marjery Tregale, but Joe could hardly be expected to admit as much. He had to be loyal after all.

'Can we go and get ready now, Ma?' Linnet asked. 'We're nearly done here and I don't want to be left behind.'

Phoebe paused and surveyed the kitchen. Most of the wicker baskets had been packed, with only a few remaining still empty. 'All right then,' she said.

'How many you expecting?' Joe inquired as the girls hurried from the room. He didn't enter the kitchen, not wanting the bother of taking off his boots.

'Around twenty I'm told.' Once word had got out that a badger hunt was to take place offers to assist had flooded in, all seeing it as a fine afternoon's sport.

Reynold came into the kitchen. 'How do, Joe,' he greeted his neighbour.

'How do, Reynold.' Joe produced an ancient, battered bugle and gave them a toot. 'I'm all set as you can see.'

Voices were heard outside. 'It's Ted Christmas and his son Billy,' Joe informed Reynold and Phoebe. The Christmases were also neighbours.

By the time Linnet and Roxanne reappeared the hunting party had more or less assembled. Josia Grim was the centre of attention, as he held court while his three terrier dogs prowled restlessly around. All three bore the marks of previous hunts. One dog who was Josia's pride and joy, had lost not only an ear but an eye and although he was getting old, he was still as ferocious in the hunt as he'd ever been.

Roxanne was excited at the prospect of what lay ahead and just hoped she wouldn't be expected to do any of the actual digging – not that she was a stranger to manual labour, far from it, but with so many able-bodied men in the company they surely wouldn't want her to participate.

Phoebe, Linnet and Roxanne took the cloth-covered wicker baskets outside where they were seized by members of the party. The atmosphere was festive, everyone laughing and joking with some good-natured back slapping going on. There were ten other dogs present beside Josia Grim's.

Earlier Reynold had placed a number of firkins outside the house which he now instructed be brought along.

'As if we'd leave these behind,' declared Ted Christmas, whose florid face and veined, bulbous nose testified to his love for cider.

Several of the men were carrying guns, the others shovels, picks, mattocks and thick sticks.

'Lead on then, Reynold,' Tom Stoneman cried out, his property bordering that of Reynold's. Both he and Reynold owned their farms, unlike many of those present who were merely tenants.

As they set off Billy Christmas fell in beside Roxanne; the two of them had been close pals since childhood. Billy, who was the same age as Roxanne, was an extremely well-built boy who had the plainest face imaginable. He was a kindly soul though, with a heart of gold, whom Roxanne liked a great deal.

'How are you today, Roxanne?' he inquired.

'Not too bad, Billy. And yourself?'

He grinned at her, a grin that had a slightly slack, foolish appearance about it. 'Thinkin' I'd much rather be here than ploughin' or plantin'.'

She smiled in agreement, as these were her sentiments exactly. 'This is my first badger hunt,' she informed him.

'Me too. Gone shooting rabbits often, but never dug out old brock before. Taint been too many round here for a while. I hear they're right tasty eating.'

Roxanne had heard that as well, but wasn't sure she fancied the idea of eating badger.

'My Da says Mr Grim is famous for catching they buggers,' Billy declared.

'That's what my Da says as well.'

'So we should be successful.'

'What are you two talking about?' Linnet asked, joining them.

'Nothing much,' Billy answered. He wasn't nearly as keen on Linnet as he was on Roxanne. He'd never felt really at ease with the older girl, not that Linnet was ever anything other than pleasant with him, there was just something about her. Perhaps it was the age difference, though he didn't think so.

'I can't wait to get tucked into they baskets,' Billy said, which made Roxanne laugh. Billy was known for his prodigious appetite, and that was among folk who were all hearty eaters.

'And the firkins?' Roxanne teased, for although Billy was only fourteen he drank like a grown up.

'And the firkins,' he confirmed.

Kevern Stoneman, Tom's lad, who was striding alongside his father, glanced back at them. Kevern was one of those quiet chaps who kept himself to himself. His mother had died some years previously, and these days father and son ran their farm by themselves.

Billy, Roxanne and Linnet continued chatting as they strode along path and over meadow. As they walked the dogs ran hither and yon, with the exception of the terrier with only one ear and eye, who never strayed more than a couple of feet from Josia Grim.

When they reached Natcott Wood they plunged inside, shortly halting at the first of the badger holes belonging to the sett.

'Right, spread out and see what other holes you can find,' Josia Grim ordered, taking charge.

Within the space of a few minutes, a total of four more holes were discovered. Men were instructed to group round each hole, and once they were in position, the dogs were sent in.

Linnet and Roxanne stood beside Reynold who was with Josia Grim, the latter's expression now matching his name.

'Brock be home all right,' Grim announced when there was a clamour from within the burrow.

Only his dogs had been sent underground, the others were guarding the various holes with the men. 'Start digging,' Grim called out, and the men fell to with a will.

Earth flew as shovels delved, picks bit and mattocks assisted. Before long the cry went up that they had one of the vermin.

Roxanne had expected the animal to be shot, so she was horrified to watch the young beast being methodically bludgeoned to death by stick and shovel.

'That's awful,' a white-faced Roxanne breathed to Linnet who was also appalled by these savage proceedings. They were both used to seeing animals being killed, but in a fairly humane manner, not in this cruel, barbaric way.

Jack Gifford held up the bloody carcass, and laughed. 'Number one with more to follow,' he bellowed.

Joe Tregale and Dick Metherell, who both had brought along bugles, began blowing them, a curiously eerie moaning sound that sent cold shivers racing up and down Roxanne's spine.

There was a second shout when another badger had been located. The dogs at that hole barked and snarled, nipping in and out of the hole with bared teeth, tormenting their quarry who could now be seen.

This was a big badger who put up a fierce and protracted fight, its claws flashing again and again as it defended itself. The badger was fighting on two fronts, with Grim's terriers behind, the surface dogs in front. One of the surface dogs dashed in to the attack, but its timing was wrong. It screamed in pain as the badger's claws raked its face. Keening in agony it raced away with its tail between its legs.

Roxanne gazed in horrid fascination as the end came for the big badger. Again shovels and sticks rose and fell, knocking the badger this way and that, inflicting horrendous wounds to its head and shoulders. Finally a shovel whistled sideways to catch the beast in the neck, almost decapitating the animal, and it was all over. The badger collapsed in an untidy, bloody heap.

A yell of triumph went up from those men congregated round the hole. One man danced obscenely on the spot, but Roxanne couldn't quite make out who due to the tears blurring her vision. She felt vomit rise in her throat. Turning away she bent over and was violently sick.

'What's wrong, girl?' Reynold demanded, coming to her side.

She tried to reply, and couldn't.

A thoroughly shaken Linnet placed a comforting hand on her sister's arm. She, too, was speechless at the barbarity they'd just witnessed.

'There's another!' Tom Stoneman yelled, and once more the shovels, picks and mattocks went to work.

'Roxanne?' Reynold queried with a frown.

She spat out some pieces of vomit that had stuck in her mouth.

'How could you, Da?' she managed at last in a weak whisper.

'How could I what?'

She gestured towards the still body of the big badger. 'That.'

'They be vermin, Roxanne. Needs dealing with.'

'That's not dealing, Da. That's butchering. Cruel, cruel butchering. I thought you were going to shoot them, not beat the poor creatures to death. Where's the sport in that?'

Reynold straightened. 'You don't know what you're talking about. Now pull yourself together before you shames me in front of the others.'

'Shame!' She saw red. 'It's you and they who should be ashamed.'

'Oh Da,' Linnet whispered, in total agreement with her sister.

Reynold's expression became stony. 'You shouldn't be so soft. Life isn't, you must learn that.'

'Kill them yes, but not like that, Da.'

Reynold's reply was contemptuous. 'Grow up,' he snarled, reminding her of the dogs. Whirling on his heel he strode over to rejoin his cronies.

As Roxanne watched him go something within her withered. She'd always loved her father, believing that he was a kind, considerate man. Today she'd witnessed another side to him, a side she loathed, detested and which filled her with disgust. Their relationship would never be the same again.

Grow up? Well, maybe that's what she just had done.

She glanced at Linnet who gazed back sympathetically. 'Shall we go and lay out their dinner? They'll be finished soon from the looks of things,' Linnet suggested.

'They can set it out themselves for all I care.' And with that Roxanne began the long walk home. In her mind's eye she reran the badger's death and the men laughing as they administered their fatal blows. They'd enjoyed their job, she thought, actually enjoyed it.

'Roxanne! Roxanne!' Billy Christmas, who'd just noticed her departure, called anxiously after her.

She immediately broke into a run.

Chapter Two

'She's here!' Roxanne announced, as she heard the horse and trap pull up outside the front door. Phoebe had gone to the railway station to collect her elder sister, their Aunt Elvira, who'd come from Bridport to visit.

Roxanne, with Linnet close behind, flew to the front door and threw it open; there was Aunt Elvira beaming at them from the trap.

'It's so good to see you again,' Roxanne enthused, helping Elvira down. Elvira immediately swept Roxanne into her arms and hugged her tightly.

'My, how you've grown since I was here last,' Elvira said, holding Roxanne at arms' length and gazing at her out of shining eyes.

'You don't look a bit different.'

Elvira gave a tinkling laugh, then turned her attention to Linnet. 'And how are you, darling?'

Now it was Linnet's turn to be hugged and scrutinized. 'You, too, have changed. What a transformation!'

'It is two years after all, Auntie,' Linnet replied.

'I know. I was so sorry I couldn't make it last summer, but there we are.'

'You are better now though,' Roxanne said.

'Oh completely. Right as rain as they say.'

'Unload Elvira's things and take them into the house, then the pair of you put Barton and the trap away,' Phoebe instructed the girls. She turned to Elvira. 'You must be dying for a cup of tea?'

'I think I could drink a whole potful by myself,' Elvira answered, and laughed.

There were two heavy suitcases in the trap. 'Where shall we put them?' Roxanne asked as she humped hers towards the door.

'Carry them straight to Elvira's bedroom,' Phoebe informed her, linking arms with her sister. 'Now come on through and say hallo to Reynold.'

Reynold rose from his chair when Phoebe and Elvira entered the kitchen. 'From the hullabaloo I thought it must be you,' he said, his tone warm and friendly, reflecting his feelings towards his sister-in-law.

Elvira kissed Reynold affectionately on the cheek. 'How are you, my lover?' she queried, her voice still broad Devon though she'd lived for many years in Dorset.

'I be champion. And you?'

'Never better. Putting on beef, mind.' And with that she patted her tummy.

'Not at all!' Reynold protested gallantly.

'There's more to me than there was before, and that's a fact. Though Ern says he doesn't mind, he says he likes his women on the plump side.' Ern was her husband, who came from St Petroc and who'd moved them to Bridport shortly after their marriage, when he'd landed a good job there. After a few years in Bridport he'd struck out on his own by opening a small pickling factory.

'And how is Ern?' Phoebe asked.

'In the pink. Though getting on now. I see him starting to slow down, which he denies of course, but it's true.'

Elvira had married a man considerably older than herself; Ern was now bordering on sixty while she herself was only forty-nine. She'd always declared that the age difference between them didn't matter a fig. She'd fallen in love with Ern Pennington and as far as she'd been concerned that had been that. It was a true love match, each idolizing and doting on the other.

'I wish he'd come with you sometime,' Phoebe said.

Elvira shrugged. 'He always means to but never gets round to it. I think he believes the factory will burn down or blow away if he leaves it for any length of time.'

Phoebe laughed. 'No-one can ever accuse Ern of not being a hard and conscientious worker.'

'He's that all right, and not the only one,' Elvira said, winking at Reynold.

'So how's business?' Phoebe inquired.

'We certainly can't complain. Last month's figures were the best ever.'

34

'Let me take your coat,' Reynold offered.

Phoebe couldn't help but admire the soft wool coat which was an eye-catching burgundy colour. She thought in dismay of her own 'Sunday best' which had seen better days and desperately needed to be replaced. No doubt it would be some time before they could spare the cash for it.

'What a lovely dress!' Phoebe exclaimed. Elvira's dress was navy-blue and looked as though it must have cost a fortune.

'Bought it in London,' Elvira explained. 'A little treat to myself. It's still nice and stylish even if I have had it for a while.'

Phoebe would have given her eye teeth for such a dress and was suddenly very conscious of her own which was black, plain and workaday. Oh well, she mentally sighed, she was the wife of a smallholding farmer after all, not a successful factory owner.

She wasn't jealous of Elvira's good fortune, and never had been, but on occasion the comparison could be a little hard.

'I'll put that kettle on,' Phoebe declared, and was filling it at the sink when Linnet and Roxanne burst in.

Elvira sniffed appreciatively. 'Something smells good.'

'It's one of your favourites, stargazy pie,' Phoebe informed her. This was a Cornish rather than Devonian dish and consisted of a pie crust through which pilchards gazed heavenwards, their heads just proud of the pastry.

'Stargazy pie,' Elvira repeated with a smile. 'I haven't had that since the last time I was here.'

'Well there you are then.'

Elvira, who was extremely fond of her food, rubbed her hands appreciatively. She was a mediocre cook herself, something she freely acknowledged. She'd never been able to hold a candle to Phoebe in that department. 'And what about afters?'

'Raspberries and clotted cream.'

Elvira sighed in delight and anticipation. There was nothing like home-made clotted cream, especially if Phoebe had had a hand in it.

'And lots of it,' Phoebe added with a laugh.

'Which reminds me,' Elvira declared. 'I'll be back in a tick,' she said as she hurried from the room.

'She looks well,' Reynold commented to Phoebe, sitting down again.

'I was worried about her last year when she was ill. She didn't say in her letters, but I got the impression it was worse than she made out.'

'What was it again?'

'The doctors never did find out. But whatever, it laid her low for quite some time.'

'Anything I can do, Ma?' Roxanne asked.

'The two of you can lay the table. Supper won't be long.'

Linnet and Roxanne were in the process of doing this when Elvira returned carrying two tissue-wrapped items, a brown paper parcel and a bottle of Scotch.

'Elvira!' Phoebe admonished, realizing these were gifts.

'Now not a word, Phoebe. I always brings something with me, after all.'

Reynold eyed the whisky, knowing that was for him. He didn't drink spirits very often, unable to afford them, but always enjoyed them when he did.

'For you,' Elvira stated, handing him the bottle.

'This will go down a treat. Thank you, Elvira.'

'And that's for you,' said Elvira, giving Roxanne a small box.

'And you.' She placed a tissue-wrapped box in Linnet's hands which was a different shape to Roxanne's.

Roxanne gasped, opening her square box for inside was a gold bracelet. 'For me?' she queried, almost speechless at this generosity.

How like her mother she was, Elvira reflected, not simply in looks, but through her mannerisms, gestures and, above all, character, which made Roxanne very special to her. She didn't feel the same towards Linnet, who most decidedly took after her father. She loved them both, but Roxanne that bit more, something she'd never articulated to Phoebe or anyone else.

'Dear me,' muttered Phoebe, coming over and staring at the bracelet which Roxanne had now draped round her wrist. 'Is that real gold?'

'Real as can be,' Elvira declared.

Linnet squealed when she discovered in her box a silver pendant with an amethyst drooping from it. 'Oh Aunt Elvira, it's gorgeous!' she exclaimed.

Elvira was pleased that they were both so excited.

'You're spoiling them,' Phoebe chided, though not unkindly.

Elvira shrugged. 'I don't have children of my own to spoil, so I have to do it to yours.' She smiled at Phoebe to whom, despite their age difference, she'd always been particularly close.

'Eighteen carat,' Roxanne said, peering at the underside of the bracelet.

Reynold was frowning, not at all sure he approved of this largesse. A present yes, but to go to such expense! It also slightly annoyed him because he could never in a month of Sundays have bought them the like.

'Help me put this on,' Roxanne pleaded to her mother.

'And me,' Linnet added.

When the clasp had been snicked shut Roxanne waved the bracelet in front of her where it glinted in the light. 'Thank you Aunt Elvira, thank you,' she said, throwing her arms round her aunt.

With the pendant secure around her neck Linnet also embraced Elvira, both girls simultaneously hugging their aunt.

'Are you sure you can afford this?' Reynold queried.

She waved a hand dismissively at him. 'I wouldn't have bought them if I couldn't.'

'It's too much,' Phoebe said anxiously, at the same time wondering what was in the brown paper parcel that obviously had to be for her.

'Not at all,' replied Elvira.

'I can't wait to show my friends,' murmured Linnet, fingering the amethyst set in a circle of silver.

'Me neither. Won't they be jealous,' added Roxanne. None of her friends had anything that could compare to this latest acquisition.

'Last but not least,' smiled Elvira.

Phoebe accepted the parcel, and stared at it.

'Go on, open it,' Elvira urged.

'I'm almost scared to.'

'Don't be silly.'

Phoebe nervously placed the parcel on the table and began undoing the string. Inside was a cashmere shawl, its colours a combination of grey, dark blue and black.

'Thought it would suit you,' Elvira stated.

Phoebe lifted the shawl free of its wrapping and twirled it round her shoulders. 'I don't know what to say,' she husked.

'Then don't say anything.'

'It's . . . beautiful.'

'I'm glad you like it.'

'Like it! I love it.'

Phoebe pressed a section of the shawl against her cheek where it immediately radiated warmth.

'Not to be worn working round the farm, mind,' Elvira teased.

'As if I would.'

Phoebe took her sister's hands in her own and squeezed them. 'Thank you, El.'

When Elvira tried to reply she found her throat clogged with emotion. 'Now what about that tea? I'm parched,' she managed at last.

Phoebe carefully removed the shawl and folded it up. 'Linnet, will you put this away for me please? Just leave it on my bed for now.'

'Of course, Ma.'

Thinking they might come in handy at some time Phoebe gathered up the tissue and brown paper which she put in a convenient drawer. Beside the paper she laid the string which she'd rolled up and secured with a tie.

'How's Thomas?' Elvira inquired as Phoebe tidied up.

Phoebe shook her head. 'Don't know. Never see him from one month to the next.' Thomas was their brother who was four years older than her.

Elvira's expression became grim. 'I've never understood him. He's always been strange to say the least. Even as a child, he was different to the rest of the family.'

'And the woman he married is even stranger.'

'They Venns were always an odd lot,' Elvira said, referring to Margaret, Thomas's wife's, maiden name. 'Too much of you know what.' The latter was a reference to inter-breeding which the Venns had indulged in throughout the generations.

'What's "you know what"?' Linnet queried.

'Never you mind,' Reynold told her gruffly.

Linnet glanced at Roxanne who shrugged; she was as mystified as her sister.

'I suppose I'll go and see them while I'm here, though heaven knows why I should, they're never exactly welcoming.'

The tea was now ready so Phoebe poured it out. 'You, Reynold?' she asked.

'When did I ever turn down a cup of tea?' he replied with a low laugh.

Phoebe smiled, that was certainly true enough. Still, you never knew. Supper was imminent, after all.

'It's living up in the hills that does it, I think,' Elvira murmured pensively.

'Does what?' Phoebe queried.

'I was thinking about the Venns and how isolated they are.'

Phoebe understood the point Elvira was making. 'Could well be,' she agreed.

The supper which followed shortly was a huge success with

Elvira, who declared the stargazy pie was absolute perfection, so much so that she had two very large helpings, saying as she dug into the second that she shouldn't really but couldn't help herself. She had two helpings of 'afters' as well.

'I feel I might bust,' she declared when she'd finally finished.

'Nothing wrong with enjoying your food,' Reynold commented.

'Maybe, but I don't get the chance to work it off as you lot do,' Elvira replied, as she was a woman of leisure.

'Well you can do some chores while you're here,' Reynold teased.

'She'll do no such thing. Elvira's our guest,' Phoebe protested.

'I'd be delighted to muck in,' Elvira said. 'It's not as if I don't know how. I had the same upbringing as you, don't forget.'

Roxanne suddenly remembered the conversation she'd had with Linnet the last time they'd been down by the harbour. What was it Linnet had said? All that life held in store for females such as them was getting married and moving from one farm to another. Well, that didn't have to be the case; Aunt Elvira was living proof that the pattern could be broken.

'Right, so it's down to the shippon for you first thing tomorrow,' Reynold further teased. The shippon was the cattle house.

'Not tomorrow, and certainly not first thing. Elvira is here on holiday,' Phoebe stated emphatically.

'Twouldn't bother me at all. In fact I'd rather enjoy it. Twould bring back many fond memories.' Elvira flexed her hands. 'Twould indeed, me dears.'

Phoebe gazed in envy at Elvira's smooth, well-cared-for hands. She wondered what it would be like to have long, beautifully manicured nails like Elvira's, as hers were short, unattractive and several of them cracked.

'Speaking of tomorrow, can you spare the girls for a couple of hours?' Elvira asked Reynold.

'Spare them. Why?'

'I'm going into St Petroc, if you'll lend me your pony and trap that is, and would like to take them with me.'

Roxanne and Linnet glanced at one another; this was promising.

'And what do you want with them in St Petroc?' Reynold queried.

'Now don't take offence Reynold, I knows fine well how prickly you can be, but I wish to buy them some clothes.'

Neither Linnet nor Roxanne could hide the excitement which blazed from their faces. New clothes!

'You can't do that, Elvira, you've already spent a small fortune on them,' Phoebe said.

'As I mentioned earlier, I intend spoiling your children as I haven't been blest with any of my own. Anyway, don't tell me they couldn't use new clothes?'

'I can provide what they need,' Reynold declared, a stubborn, slightly injured tone in his voice.

'Of course you can, my lover,' Elvira replied placatingly. 'No-one could deny that you are a good provider, Reynold, but I want to treat them. And what girl, or woman come to that, wouldn't like new clothes?'

'I don't know,' Reynold murmured. It would certainly be a help, no doubt about that, and a big saving to him.

'I'll be very disappointed if you don't allow it,' Elvira said, cajoling her brother-in-law whom she knew of old to be a proud man, and sensitive where that pride was concerned.

Reynold looked at Phoebe, whose expression told him that she wanted him to give his permission. She dropped her glance to stare at the empty bowl in front of her.

'Nothing fancy then,' Reynold capitulated. 'Everyday togs is what's required.'

Elvira stifled the smile of satisfaction that nearly came onto her face. She'd always been able to twist Reynold round her little finger. It was simply a case of how you approached him, always being reasonable, and never head on. Her Ern wasn't quite as malleable, but she usually got her own way with him too.

'Now what time would be best, Reynold?' Elvira went on. 'I'll naturally fall in with whatever you say.'

They agreed the details to the great delight of Roxanne and Linnet.

'And stockings, two pairs each I think,' Elvira said to the shop assistant whose name was Betty.

'Silk or lisle?' Betty queried.

Silk? Roxanne held her breath.

Elvira considered the question. She would have liked to buy them silk but knew Reynold wouldn't have approved. 'They'd better be lisle,' she replied to Betty, who nodded.

While Betty was fetching the stockings she said to the girls in a low voice, 'There's no use upsetting your Da, and that's all that would happen if I bought you the silk ones. Maybe another time when you're both older.'

'We understand, Aunt Elvira,' Roxanne replied, disappointment clear in her voice.

So like her mother, Elvira thought yet again. How she'd missed Phoebe since moving to Bridport. The chats and confidences they'd shared, the mutual support they'd given one another. For Phoebe wasn't only her sister but also her closest friend, always had been and always would be. There was nothing she couldn't talk about to Phoebe, or vice versa. If there was one regret she found in her present circumstances it was that they now lived so far apart. Still, they had their letters, and she did manage to visit once a year; with the exception of the previous summer, that was.

When the stockings had been seen and agreed upon they were added to the pile of clothes already on the counter. 'Is that all?' Betty asked.

'I believe so,' Elvira murmured, casting her eyes round the shop to see if there was anything she'd forgotten.

'New hats,' she declared. 'For going to church. And then that'll be it.' Reynold could hardly object to those, she reasoned, as he was a devout churchgoer and believer.

Roxanne chose a sort of velvety pancake with a lilac bow on top, while Linnet set her heart on a smaller affair that had trailing ribbons at the back. Finally, everything was wrapped up, leaving Elvira to pay for her purchases.

The girls carried their parcels out to the trap where they were safely stowed.

'Is the Christmas tearoom still open?' Elvira asked Linnet. The Christmas bakery and small, adjoining tearoom was owned and run by relatives of Ted and Billy Christmas.

Linnet nodded. 'It is, Auntie.'

'Then what do you say to some tea and cakes?'

Both girls were thrilled, as they had never been in the tearoom before. There was no money for luxuries like that.

'Please!' they chorused in reply.

They climbed aboard the trap and urged Barton into a walk, as the tearoom was further along Fore Street. When they reached their destination Linnet jumped down and tied off the pony.

A bell tinged when they opened the door and their noses were immediately assailed by the most mouth-watering smells.

'Hmmh,' murmured Roxanne, thinking this was heaven. She gazed about her, enthralled to be in this place which she'd passed countless times.

There were only six tables, but the tearoom did a small but consistent trade with the better-off members of St Petroc. At Roxanne's suggestion they chose a table by the window, so that if any of her friends and acquaintances passed, they would see her there.

Hilda Christmas, a stout jovial woman, bustled up. 'Hallo, Elvira,' she said, as the pair of them had known each other all their lives. 'And how nice to see you girls.'

Pleasantries were exchanged after which they ordered coffee for three and a large plate of cakes.

'How many can we have each?' Roxanne asked Elvira when Hilda Christmas had gone.

'As many as you like, me dear.'

'Proper job!' Roxanne exclaimed gleefully.

'Just don't make yourselves sick, that's all,' Elvira warned.

'We'd better not mention this to Da, he'd think it a foolishness and waste of money,' Linnet counselled.

'It's my money and I'll spend it as I see fit,' Elvira retorted. Then, on reflection, added, 'But perhaps you're right. What he don't know won't hurt or upset him.'

'Da can be very funny about some things,' Roxanne said.

'Oh I know, darling, I know.'

The girls exclaimed in delight when Hilda Christmas returned with their plate of cakes. Roxanne eyed a chocolate eclair which she promptly asked if she could have.

'But I want that,' Linnet pouted.

'Too bad. I asked first.'

'Taint fair.'

'Girls,' Elvira admonished. 'The only solution seems for us to have two eclairs. Is that possible, Hilda?'

'It be. Another eclair coming right up.'

While they were waiting, Elvira poured from a tall, elegant, silver plated coffee pot. 'You just get started,' she instructed Roxanne, who immediately removed the eclair from the plate.

'Ma and I were talking this morning and she said you've been to London,' Roxanne said after she'd bitten into the eclair.

Elvira nodded. 'Several times. And a big city it is too. A most exciting place, you take my word on it.'

'It must be wonderful there?' Roxanne went on.

'Oh it can be. And the shops, quite glorious.'

Roxanne tried to imagine what such shops would be like, and failed. It was simply beyond her experience and imagination. 'I'd like to go there sometime,' she declared.

'Not me,' said Linnet.

'Why not?' queried Roxanne. 'Think how exciting it would be.'

'Far too exciting for me. I think I'd be quite overcome.'

'I wouldn't,' Roxanne stated vehemently. 'I'd love every minute of it. The lights, the glamour, all those people, thousands and thousands and thousands.'

'It isn't all bright lights and glamour,' Elvira smiled as Linnet's eclair arrived. She thanked Hilda Christmas, then went on. 'There are many poor parts to London, a great deal of poverty. But there are also some grand areas with houses like palaces. I must admit the first time I drove through Mayfair, it quite took my breath away.'

'Mayfair,' Roxanne repeated, awed. She'd read about it in the newspaper. 'Tell me everything you know about London. Please?' she urged. 'Everything you know and everything you've done there.'

Elvira laughed. 'You are keen, aren't you?'

'Oh yes,' Roxanne breathed, at the same time fishing another cake off the plate having finished her eclair.

'Well now . . .' mused Elvira. 'Let's see.'

Roxanne listened entranced while her aunt spoke about London, every so often interjecting with questions or requesting elaborations. To her London sounded a magical place, an Aladdin's cave of wonders. What she would have given to have gone there herself.

'My goodness, look at the time!' Elvira exclaimed, glancing at the clock. 'I'll catch it from your father for keeping you away so long.'

Linnet wiped the corners of her mouth with her white napkin. 'That was lovely, aunt, thank you very much.'

'Yes, thank you,' Roxanne echoed, her mind whirling with thoughts of London.

They rose and made their way to the cash register. 'You girls wait for me outside, I'll only be a moment,' Elvira said, opening her handbag.

Lingering on the pavement a poster in the bakery window caught Roxanne's attention. She was studying it when Elvira appeared beside her.

'What's this about?' Elvira queried, peering at the poster.

'It's a concert coming to St Petroc this Saturday,' Roxanne explained.

Elvira read the poster, which made her smile. It appeared a

Mr Barnett would be singing 'The Sensible Girl And The Boy Romp'. Below that it proclaimed: Comedy Duets, Mrs Forde & Mr C Parker, Charity School & Sister Ruth, as originally sung by them.

'Looks interesting,' Elvira murmured.

Linnet had now joined them and was gazing at the poster over Elvira's shoulder. She giggled to read that Sambo Sutton would be singing 'The Old Nigger Man'.

'I wonder what Boleno's Celebrated Dissolving is?' Roxanne frowned. This was an act listed at the bottom of the bill.

'Well there's only one way to find out and that's go and see,' stated Elvira.

'You mean us?' Roxanne queried.

'All of us, including your Ma and Da.'

Roxanne shook her head. 'Da would never go to anything like that. And he certainly wouldn't allow us to go.'

Elvira regarded Roxanne steadily. 'Would you like to see it?'

'If I could.'

'And you, Linnet?'

'Oh yes, auntie. It looks fun.'

Elvira couldn't have agreed more. She thought for a few moments. 'When was the last time your Ma went out?'

Linnet and Roxanne considered that. 'Dunno,' Linnet answered eventually.

'Last harvest supper, I think,' Roxanne ventured.

The previous autumn, Elvira reflected. Now it was well into the following summer. 'I'll have a word with your Da,' she declared softly.

'His answer will be no,' Linnet stated, as certain of that as Roxanne.

'Maybe, maybe not,' Elvira said in the same soft tone.

As they drove back to the farm Elvira planned her line of argument.

Elvira lifted her eyes from her darning and gazed at Reynold opposite. She'd offered to help Phoebe with this task, so the three of them were sitting grouped round the range.

'How about a nice cup of tea before bed?' Phoebe suggested.

'Have you any cocoa in the house?' Elvira inquired.

'Sorry.'

'Then tea's fine by me.'

Reynold grunted that he would join them, his mind focused on the next day's work. There were potatoes that needed digging up – he and Linnet would do that while Roxanne got on with other jobs. Phoebe could also help after she'd finished her early morning chores in the house.

'There's a concert on at the town hall this Saturday,' Elvira said.

'Really?' Phoebe replied, putting her darning aside and rising.

'I thought we might all go.'

Phoebe hesitated, and glanced at Reynold, doubt showing on her face.

'I'll pay, of course.'

Reynold roused himself as what she'd said sunk in. 'Concert? What concert?'

'At the town hall this Saturday. It should be most entertaining.'

'I've never been to a concert,' Phoebe murmured.

'Nor ever will be if I has anything to do with it. Waste of time they things,' Reynold snorted.

'Have you ever been to one?' Elvira asked innocently.

'Me! Never.'

'I have. And thoroughly enjoyed them. Plays too, they can be fascinating.'

'Plays and actors!' Reynold sneered. 'They's not for the likes of us.'

'I don't know how you can say that when you know nothing about either,' Elvira replied quietly, thinking this was exactly the response she'd expected. It was typical of Reynold's small-mindedness about certain things.

'I knows all right,' Reynold declared defiantly. 'They actors are all degenerawhotsits.'

Elvira thought of the Venns, and smiled inwardly. What could be more degenerate than sleeping with your own daughter, then bringing the resulting child up as your daughter's brother?

'Phoebe hasn't had a night out since last harvest supper, I believe,' she went on.

Reynold shrugged. 'We don't socialize much. No time for that.'

'Yes, it's hard work running a farm,' Elvira agreed sympathetically. 'All the more reason to get out once in a while. All work and no play—' She trailed off with a smile.

'Would you like one of they scones I baked this afternoon?' Phoebe asked her.

'Please. That would be lovely.'

'And raspberry jam.'

'I'll have a couple as they're going,' Reynold said.

'I understand many of the town notables will be attending,' Elvira continued smoothly.

'Notables? What notables?' Reynold queried.

'Bob Widgery for one.'

Reynold stared at her; Bob Widgery was the mayor of St Petroc. 'Where did you hear that?'

'In town today,' Elvira lied.

Reynold cleared his throat. Bob Widgery? 'Who else?' he demanded.

'Important people, those of standing in St Petroc. They'll all be wanting to be seen supporting the event, doing their bit for the town.'

'Doing their bit,' Reynold mused.

'Landowners, naturally.'

'I'm a landowner,' Reynold reminded her unnecessarily.

'And one of the important people round here. You count for something in St Petroc after all, Reynold. As you've pointed out, you're not merely a tenant, you *own* your farm.'

Flattery was a weapon she'd decided earlier to use, something to which he'd always been susceptible, together with the fear of not being there to take his rightful place amongst his peers and betters.

Phoebe laid out the scones and jam, well aware of what her sister was up to, although Elvira had said nothing to her. She knew Elvira of old. In the circumstances she judged it best to keep quiet and only contribute if asked directly to do so. Elvira was far better at these matters than she.

'It should be quite an occasion,' Elvira said.

Reynold found himself tempted. He most certainly didn't approve of attending the concert, but there was a side to him that didn't want to be absent if the élite turned out. His might only be a small farm but as an owner he considered himself to be a definite cut above the majority of other farmers in the district. Looking thoughtful, he wrestled with his conscience.

Elvira delivered the blow she knew would hurt most. 'And if you don't go you realize what they'll say, don't you?'

He almost glared at her. 'What?'

'That either you're too mean to pay for tickets or else can't afford them.'

'Mean! Can't afford . . . !' The words exploded from his mouth.

Phoebe turned away to hide her smile.

Elvira nodded. 'That's what they'll say,' she repeated.

Reynold was appalled. Prudent yes, careful if you like, but never mean. Weren't all farmers prudent? The sensible ones anyway. A man was a fool who didn't watch his money. But for it to be said that he couldn't afford to go, and all that implied, that simply couldn't be borne. The humiliation would be awful. No matter that it wasn't true, there would be those who'd believe it. And there would be no point him protesting to the contrary, should he lower himself to do so, only sly winks and nodding of heads. For it was a curious phenomenon that people liked to think the worst of their neighbours, and in so doing feel themselves superior.

He suddenly felt trapped, knowing now he would have to attend whether he wanted to or not. The alternative just wasn't acceptable.

'We'll go,' he growled, capitulating, as Elvira had been sure he would.

'But it's my treat, I insist,' Elvira stated.

'No, I'll—'

'I said I insist. And I'll have no further argument on that score.'

Phoebe decided to break her silence. 'Can tickets be bought in advance or do you have to buy them at the door?' she queried.

'You can do both according to the bill I read,' Elvira informed her. Then, realizing what Phoebe was getting at, continued, 'I intend going back into St Petroc before Saturday so I'll pick up ours when I do.'

That satisfied Reynold, who would have refused to let Elvira be seen forking out cash on the night.

When Elvira shot Phoebe a surreptitious, triumphant look Phoebe could almost hear the mental purring that went with it.

Elvira knew her luck was in when almost the first person they spotted outside the town hall was Bob Widgery, the mayor.

Reynold, hair slicked down, tugged at his stiff, detachable collar which seemed tighter than usual. 'How do, Bob,' he smiled when their party came alongside the Widgerys.

'How do, Reynold,' Bob beamed back.

Phoebe and Elvira had a brief conversation with Stella Widgery as they moved inside. Stella was looking extremely handsome in a flowing dark green dress which was highlighted by bands of black velvet round its collar and cuffs.

Elvira had offered to lend Phoebe one of her dresses for the evening, but sadly none fitted. There had been a time when they were both the same size, but no longer. Elvira's dresses had simply drooped on Phoebe.

Roxanne spotted Billy Christmas with his father, and waved. Billy waved back.

'Quite a turn-out,' Bob Widgery commented to Reynold, glancing round the foyer which was jammed with the good citizens of St Petroc. The air was abuzz with chatter and laughter, as everywhere people greeted friends and neighbours.

'Squire Palfrey's here,' Phoebe whispered to Reynold who unconsciously straightened up and squared his shoulders.

Linnet stared at Henry Palfrey, the squire's eldest son, who was at Oxford University. What a handsome chap, she thought, hoping he might notice her and smile, although they didn't know one another. She was disappointed when he did glance in her direction, for he stared right through her.

Roxanne was aflutter with excitement. She still couldn't believe Reynold had agreed to their coming. What a miracle worker Aunt Elvira was!

She and Linnet ran into Florie Newcomb, Doll Pomeroy and Annie Littlejohns who were pals of theirs. 'Isn't this a giggle,' gushed Doll, and promptly giggled.

'Lots of lads here,' Florie commented, eyeing Dickie Webber whom she fancied like mad.

'I'm told he's got a "thing" as big as a bull's,' Doll confided in a whisper, and giggled again.

'Told or know?' Linnet jibed. Being country girls they all possessed an earthy sense of humour and were quite matter-of-fact about sexual matters which they witnessed every day on the farm.

Doll giggled again. 'Taint saying,' she teased in return.

Roxanne regarded Dickie with new interest. Big as a bull's? Well, well.

Tom Stoneman clapped Reynold on the shoulder. 'Good to see you here, man.'

'Just doing my bit for the town,' Reynold responded. 'Supporting the event so to speak.'

Elvira glanced at Phoebe and winked; both of them had overheard Reynold's reply.

'Fortunately for you Bob Widgery and the like are here,' Phoebe whispered to Elvira.

'That's me all over. If I fell down in a shippon I'd come up smelling of roses,' Elvira answered with a low laugh.

Reynold visibly swelled when he was addressed by Squire Palfrey who inquired how he was.

Snob, Elvira thought, meaning Reynold.

Mrs Westlake, the lady with only a head, squeezed past Linnet and Roxanne; she was with her daughter Edie who was considerably taller than her mother.

Phoebe noted that the Tregales were there, as were the Tutchings, Giffords and Calcrafts. Their neighbours were out in force.

'I can't wait to hear Sambo Sutton,' Linnet said to Roxanne, thinking his name a great hoot.

Eventually they all went into the hall itself where the Hawkins secured good seats near the front. En route Elvira had bought three programmes; one for herself, another for Phoebe and Reynold, and the last for Linnet and Roxanne. Reynold thought it was a terrific waste of money.

Once they were settled Elvira produced a large box of chocolates from her handbag, opened it and handed it round.

Shortly afterwards, to a rustle of anticipation, Roxanne held her breath as the concert began.

Later that night Roxanne lay in bed staring at the ceiling, her mind still buzzing with thoughts and images of the concert. What a completely different world she'd been transported to, one that had both dazzled and enraptured her. The songs had been glorious, the costumes a riot of colour. She smiled remembering the three women who'd danced an Egyptian number, how splendid and stunning they'd been. As she'd watched she'd wished with all her heart she'd been dancing with them.

Even her Da had thoroughly enjoyed himself, admitting as much to Elvira in the interval. During the drive home he'd been just as full of it as the rest of them.

Magic, she thought. The performance had been sheer magic. Her only regret was she couldn't go again the following night, and the night after that, and the night after that . . .

She sighed with pleasure, not the least bit tired as her mind continued to whirl and turn. She'd pay for this in the morning, she told herself, having to be up at the crack of dawn. First the cows had to be milked, then the chickens fed, then . . .

She made a face. Cows, chickens, how dreary compared to what she'd witnessed earlier. How utterly, utterly dreary and stultifyingly boring.

She imagined herself as part of the troupe, but what would she do? Dance perhaps? Except she didn't know one step from another. Sing? That was more like it. She had a good voice, which the vicar had once remarked on, and often sang in the shippon when milking. The cows liked it when she did and it helped keep them quiet and peaceful.

Yes, it would have to be singing. She alone, every eye in the hall fastened on her, listening to her, she the centre of attention.

She sighed again. Thank goodness they'd gone and she hadn't been forced to miss it. What a tragedy it would have been to have missed *that*!

She started with the first act, Mr Randall singing 'Red Rover', and began reliving the acts one by one.

'Da?'

Reynold glanced up from his supper at Roxanne. 'Yes?'

She took a deep breath. 'Would you mind if I used the barn to put on a concert?'

He stared at her in astonishment as did Phoebe and Linnet. Elvira, on the other hand, looked amused.

'A concert? What kind of concert?'

'Sort of like the one we saw.'

Reynold threw back his head and laughed uproariously which caused Roxanne to colour with embarrassment. 'It's not funny,' she muttered.

'Well I think it is,' he choked, wiping tears of mirth from his eyes.

'Reynold,' Phoebe admonished gently, thinking, rightly, he was being both unkind and insensitive.

'I think it's rather a good idea myself,' Elvira stated mildly.

'Who's going to be in it?' Linnet queried, wondering why her sister hadn't discussed this with her. She was somewhat piqued.

'There are quite a few people our age who can do things. Sally Tutching can play the mouth organ, for example. I shall be asking her.'

'And I suppose you plan to be in this concert?' Linnet said a trifle bitchily.

'Of course.'

'Doing what?'

'I'll sing.'

'She's got a nice voice,' Phoebe informed Elvira.

'You're being ridiculous, maid,' Reynold said to Roxanne. 'You can't do no concert. Taint got time for a start.'

'I'll make time, Da,' Roxanne replied stubbornly. 'And don't worry, I won't neglect my jobs. Promise.'

This had taken Reynold completely by surprise. He didn't know what to think. His first reaction was to refuse out of hand.

50

Phoebe, realizing this, said, 'You can at least consider it, Reynold. Twouldn't do any harm after all. And it would give the girl an interest.

'I quite agree,' Elvira declared.

'Am I to be in it?' Linnet inquired.

'Naturally. If you wants to be, that is. I was hoping you'd help me organize everything.'

Linnet brightened on hearing that, though heaven knew what she'd do on stage.

'It would be a bit of a lark,' Phoebe smiled.

'And a good excuse for you men to get together and share a few flagons,' Elvira said, matching Phoebe's smile.

Now that did interest Reynold, as Elvira had known it would. 'Hmmh,' he murmured, running a hand thoughtfully over his face.

'When would you have your concert?' Phoebe asked Roxanne.

'Sometime in the autumn, after harvesting. I thought we could use bales for the audience to sit on.'

'And we'll invite all the neighbours and such,' Linnet enthused, now extremely keen.

'I don't know,' Reynold prevaricated, rubbing his chin. How would this reflect on him? Was it really a good idea?

'Look how everyone enjoyed the town hall concert,' Phoebe pointed out. 'So it's bound to be a success.'

'A laugh if nothing else,' Roxanne added.

Reynold remained unconvinced. 'Needs thinking on,' he declared and, with a sideways chopping motion, indicated the subject was closed.

Elvira glanced at Roxanne, and winked. A wink that said, leave it up to me. She'd work on Reynold until he came round.

Phoebe and Elvira were in the farm dairy scalding milk, which would be turned into cheese and clotted cream. The whey from cheese making would go to the pigs.

Scalding was a process which needed due care and attention as the milk mustn't be allowed to come to the boil, for if it did it would be useless for clotted cream.

Both women were standing before the cream oven. Phoebe was intently watching the milk in the copper pan on top of the oven. As she'd been taught by her Ma the milk had reached the right temperature when tiny bubbles started to appear on its surface.

'This brings back memories,' Elvira said, thinking of the innumerable times in the past when this had been her task.

51

'Must do,' Phoebe replied.

'There,' announced Phoebe a few seconds later and, hands encased in cloths, she removed the pan from the top of the stove and placed it on a cold late shelf. The milk would remain there till it was cold, by which time it would have formed a delectable yellow crust, the clotted or 'clouted' cream.

Phoebe then busied herself tidying up, only stopping when she found Elvira standing at the dairy door staring pensively out over the farm yard. When she saw Elvira's wistful expression she frowned.

'What is it?' she queried softly, joining her sister.

Elvira roused herself. 'Sorry. Just daydreaming, that's all.'

'Can I ask what about?'

Elvira gave Phoebe a strained smile. 'They girls of yours actually.'

'Linnet and Roxanne?'

'What fine, upstanding girls they be. A credit to you Phoebe, the pair of them.'

Phoebe knew her sister better than that. 'And?'

Elvira shrugged. 'Nothing really.'

'Oh yes there is. Can I help?'

Elvira gave Phoebe another strained smile, but this time there was a film of tears in her eyes. 'I'm just being an old fool. Should know better.'

Phoebe put her arms round Elvira's shoulders and gently squeezed. By now she'd guessed what was bothering her sister. 'The good Lord dealt you a hard hand there, didn't He?' she stated.

'I came to terms with it a long while past. But there are still moments when I think, wonder—' She trailed off.

'It's easy for me to say, but if tweren't to be tweren't to be, and there's nothing you can do about it. Just as there was nothing I could do about losing Freddy, or having they miscarriages.'

'I so wanted a child of my own, Phoebe. I ached for one, years I ached. But nothing ever happened.'

'I know,' Phoebe sympathized.

'At least I got two grand nieces to be proud of. And proud of them I am.'

'There's also Thomas's children.'

'They're not the same. No, it's yours I'm close to.' Particularly Roxanne, she thought.

Elvira sucked in a deep breath. 'I must stop being so

daft. There's a lot in life I have to be thankful for. Ern most of all.'

'I suppose we can't have everything, eh?'

'I suppose not,' Elvira agreed. 'Now let's get on, shall we? What do you plan to do next?'

'Put the kettle on. How does that sound?'

Elvira sniffed, then laughed. 'Exactly what was running through my mind.'

'Come on then.'

They went outside, Phoebe shutting the dairy door behind them. When they reached the kitchen Elvira was quite her old self again.

'I've finally persuaded the Pipe twins to do their juggling act,' Roxanne said to Billy Christmas as they entered the Hawkins' barn.

'Have you! That's tremendous.'

'They were most reluctant, but eventually I talked them into it.'

Billy hung up the lantern he was carrying and Roxanne did likewise. The light the lanterns threw out cut through the darkness, casting long shadows over the straw-strewn floor.

'So have you been practising as you promised?' she queried.

Billy nodded.

'Then let's hear you.'

He hesitated. 'I wouldn't do this for anyone but you, Roxanne. I mean, standing up in front of all they folks. I'll be unnerved through and through.'

She laughed. 'No, you won't, Billy.'

'Oh yes, I will. Shaking in me boots no doubt. It's one thing doing it in the kitchen and the like, but this!'

'Well, if you'll be nervous, so will we all. And what you must remember is it'll only be friends and neighbours here. No-one to be frightened of.'

'Just the same.'

She eyed him coldly. 'You're not trying to back out, are you, Billy Christmas? I'll never forgive you if you do.'

'Oh Roxanne,' he mumbled wretchedly. He adored Roxanne, although it was a hopeless adoration, of which he was well aware. He knew there could never be anything other than friendship between him and Roxanne. She'd never be interested in a lad like him, just twasn't on. And luckily he had the sense to realize it.

'You're going to be a big success, Billy. I knows it,' she told him.

His face lit up. 'Do you really mean that?'

She made several quick gestures across her chest. 'Cross my heart and hope to die. You'll see I'm right.'

'I don't want to show myself up, that's all.'

'You won't, Billy. I wouldn't let you.'

He believed her. But there again, he'd have believed anything Roxanne told him. 'All right then.'

'So, on you go.' And with that Roxanne sat on a bale of straw and smiled expectantly.

Billy's song was a comic one about old Devon which he delivered slightly off key with lots of hammy gestures and risqué innuendo.

Roxanne thought he was terrific and knew their potential audience, whose humour could be extremely basic, would lap it up.

Roxanne peeped out from behind the curtain that had been strung up to shield the performers from the crowd. She was more nervous than she'd ever been in her life.

So far everything was going splendidly, each act received with enthusiasm and given a good hand at the end.

The interior of the barn was festooned with lanterns and lamps, the audience bathed in soft yellow light. There were shadows everywhere which added to the atmosphere.

Her Ma and Da were seated near the front, Reynold clutching a flagon of cider which he occasionally passed to Joe Tregale who was sitting on his right.

Elvira was beside Phoebe, the two of them exchanging whispers from time to time. Everyone appeared to be thoroughly enjoying themselves.

The Pipe twins came off and now it was Billy's turn. She would follow him, bringing the first half to its close. Sally Tutching would be opening the second.

Linnet wasn't appearing after all, for the simple reason that she had been unable to come up with an act. She'd been a marvellous help otherwise, however, and done wonders with the costumes.

'Good luck,' Roxanne whispered to Billy, who smiled back tentatively. 'You'll be fabulous,' she assured him.

'I hope you're right.'

'Of course I am. They're only friends and neighbours, don't

forget. Just pretend you're at home in your kitchen, go out there and give it big licks.'

Good advice, she thought. She only hoped she could take it herself when her time came.

She crossed her fingers as Billy strode out onto the stage and listened with bated breath as he announced the number he intended singing. A murmur of expectation and appreciation went round the audience – this was an old favourite.

'It's going well, I'd say,' Sally Tutching whispered to Roxanne. 'I think so.'

'No doubt about it. Mind you, the cider they men are throwing down their throats – tain't doing no harm.'

Roxanne smiled, that was very true. But it was not only the men from what she'd witnessed. Marjery Tregale for one, sitting apart from her husband, wasn't being restrained where the cider was concerned.

Billy's song was a great success just as Roxanne had predicted. Billy delivered it with gusto and energy, clearly revelling in the response he was receiving. His face broke into a huge, amiable grin when some of the audience started singing along with him.

Then Billy was finished and it was Roxanne's turn. She swallowed hard as Billy came off, closed her eyes and offered up a quick, silent prayer, before she stepped out from behind the curtain. Initially her nervousness intensified, her heart banging like fury, then strangely it melted clean away, leaving her cool, calm and very much in control.

She opened her mouth and began to sing. She'd worried that her voice might seize up, but that didn't happen. Instead the notes emerged clear, pure and strong, winging their way to the back of the barn.

A hush fell over the audience as she sang for she didn't simply have a good voice, but a glorious one, a voice fully on form that night.

The song she'd chosen was a popular piece and, although the audience knew the words, no-one dreamt of joining in. That would have been sacrilegious.

Halfway through the number you could have heard the proverbial pin drop, the audience mesmerized by what they were hearing. This was in a different league to what had gone before, and was even better than some of the professional offerings in the town hall concert.

And without any accompanying music, Elvira marvelled. She was as knocked out as everyone else.

All too soon, not only for Roxanne but those listening, it was over. As she curtsied everyone in the audience, even a stunned Reynold, came to their feet to clap. The applause was thunderous.

Roxanne was filled with exhilaration as waves of adulation washed over her. Cheers went up, and loud shouts for more. She felt . . . She didn't know how she felt. But it was the most wondrous sensation. She was positively glowing as she took a second curtsy, and a third. Nor would they let it go at that. A fourth followed, and a fifth.

Later, everyone agreed she'd been the hit of the evening.

Chapter Three

Roxanne groggily woke up, roused from a deep sleep by a persistent tapping. She rubbed her bleary eyes, wondering if she was dreaming. Then, as her senses returned more fully, she realized she wasn't. The tapping was at her window.

She shivered as she slipped from her warm, cosy bed into the cold night air, and hurriedly reached for her dressing gown. The low, urgent tapping continued as she put it on.

'Billy!' she exclaimed softly when she saw his face pressed against a pane.

He grinned at her and motioned she should raise the window.

'What is it?' she demanded when she'd opened it. She shivered again as an icy blast swirled round her, for it was now the following February, in the year 1897.

'Ship's run aground in the fog and the crew's gone ashore,' he announced gleefully. 'Me and a few others are going to see what we can lift.'

'Are you indeed,' she responded, digesting this news. Glancing past Billy she noted wisps of fog floating past. 'Don't seem too bad,' she said, referring to the fog.

'It is away from here. Fair thick she be in parts. And must be bad at sea for a ship to run herself on to the rocks.'

'Whereabouts?' she demanded.

'At the point.'

Roxanne thought about the ships that had run aground at the point before, although the last one to do so had been before she was born.

'Any loss of life?' she asked.

He shrugged. 'Dunno. But the crew have abandoned her and

gone for help, that I do know. The police shouldn't be along for a while yet, depending on how long the crew takes to make contact with them, which could be morning, as they don't know the area and are hindered by the fog.'

'What's the ship's cargo?'

'Dunno that either. But there's bound to be something worthwhile to lift if we're nippy about it.'

Billy gave a low laugh. 'I thought of you immediately when I heard. Doing a bit of "salvaging" is just the sort of thing you'd enjoy. A real adventure, like.'

Roxanne wrapped her dressing gown more tightly round herself, not for modesty's sake but because she was getting colder by the second. It was freezing outside.

'Can Linnet come? She might enjoy it as well.'

'I suppose so,' he replied none too enthusiastically. He'd envisaged taking Roxanne on her own.

'Wait there.'

Roxanne padded through to her sister's bedroom where she found Linnet as sound asleep as she'd been.

'Uhh!' Linnet muttered when Roxanne shook her. 'What—'

'Sshhh,' Roxanne warned, placing a hand over Linnet's mouth.

Linnet struggled up into a sitting position. 'What's going on?' she asked when Roxanne removed her hand.

In a quiet voice Roxanne quickly told her.

'A wreck?' Linnet breathed.

'At the Point. Run aground in the fog.'

'And Billy wants us to go with him?'

'Should be exciting. I've never seen a wreck. Who knows what we may find.'

Linnet frowned, pondering the situation. 'I don't know,' she murmured at last.

'Not scared, are you?' Roxanne taunted.

'No, I'm not. But that's stealing.'

'No, tain't. Not really. Finders keepers.'

'The cargo isn't lost. It's where it's supposed to be, right there in the hold of the ship.'

'But the ship's wrecked,' Roxanne argued, beginning to get exasperated.

'Nonetheless, if we take anything we'll be looters, and that's against the law.'

'Lots of folks round this coast does it when they gets the chance. You know that.'

'Maybe so, it's still against the law. And what if you're caught? Have you thought of that?'

'We won't get caught. You'll see.'

'Sez you.'

'I think you are scared, Linnet Hawkins.'

The accusation annoyed Linnet for the simple reason it was true. 'Pa would be dead against it,' she declared. 'He don't agree with looting. We've both heard him say that many a time.'

'He doesn't need to know,' Roxanne retorted. 'And what he don't know won't worry him.'

'But what if he did find out. What then?'

'He won't.'

'But what if he *does*?' Linnet persisted.

Roxanne could see it was no use, Linnet wasn't interested. She should have known, she told herself. This reaction was typical of her big sister.

'Well, I'm going,' Roxanne declared defiantly.

'I don't think you should. I really don't. Apart from anything else it could be dangerous.'

'Billy will look after me. Not that I need looking after, I'm well capable of taking care of myself.'

Now it was Linnet's turn to be exasperated. Why did Roxanne never listen to her! She was older, and wiser, after all. 'You're far too headstrong, Roxanne, too much for your own good. It'll land you in real trouble some day, you mark my words. And this could be it.'

Roxanne climbed off Linnet's bed. 'If you want to stay here that's fine by me. Just don't ever say you weren't asked. Now go back to sleep.'

Roxanne was about to leave the room when Linnet quietly called out, 'You will take care?'

'Of course I will.'

Roxanne squeezed out through the window and was helped to the ground by Billy who was delighted Linnet wasn't accompanying them.

'I hope you're well wrapped up,' he fussed, looking at what she was wearing.

'You sound like an old mother hen,' she teased, causing Billy to blush.

'Didn't mean to,' he mumbled, abashed.

She reached out and touched his arm. 'Only joking, Billy. I've got two cardis on under this heavy coat so I should be warm enough.'

'Should be,' he agreed, thinking how wonderful she smelled. He found her natural scent intoxicating.

'Then let's get a move on.'

They hurried along side by side to the lane where the others were waiting. The loitering party consisted of Dickie Webber and the Pipe twins, Stanley and James.

'How do, Roxanne,' Dickie grinned.

'How do,' she smiled in return, then exchanged a few pleasantries with the twins.

'Quicker to cut across the fields rather than go by land and road,' Dickie proposed, to which the rest of them immediately agreed. If Dickie hadn't made the suggestion Roxanne had intended doing so.

Luckily for them the Point was this side of St Petroc, otherwise they would have been in for quite a hike. As it was, their destination, by crossing the fields, was only about a mile off.

They'd all brought lamps with them, but as yet these remained unlit as they all knew every foot of the ground between there and the Point.

Within a short distance the fog worsened, till eventually they could see no further than about a yard in any direction. The lamps would have been more or less useless anyway.

Roxanne heard a rustle in the undergrowth and wondered what kind of animal had made it. Reaching William's Wood they plunged inside, the trees eerie, and somehow threatening.

An owl suddenly hooted, a lonely forlorn sound. Then there was a flap of wings, but no-one in the party saw the bird as it flitted from one branch to another.

'All right?' Billy asked Roxanne.

'Fine.'

'Want to hold my hand?'

'What for?'

He grinned sheepishly at her. 'It might help if you're frightened.'

'Well I'm not, so I don't need to.' Then, because she knew his gesture hadn't been an attempt to be intimate or an overture of any sort, she added, kindly, 'But thanks anyway.'

'Christ, it's cold,' complained James Pipe.

The closer they got to the sea the colder it became.

★   ★   ★

60

Linnet was sitting up in bed fretting, her shoulders draped with a large knitted shawl. She'd tried to get back to sleep and found she couldn't.

How long would Roxanne be? she wondered, worrying a nail. Hours yet. She hadn't been away all that long.

'Damn the silly bitch,' she murmured. Roxanne should never have gone. It was far too risky. Should their Da ever find out all hell would break loose. God knows what he'd do to Roxanne. He might even take his belt to her which he hadn't done for ages.

Linnet screwed up her face as she remembered the last time Reynold had whacked her across the bottom with his belt. She'd had an angry red weal for days afterwards. He was a heavy-handed bugger who at times didn't realize his own strength.

Not that he was cruel in any way, far from it. But he wasn't a man to take lightly, and could be a devil when crossed, something both she and Roxanne had discovered at an early age.

Linnet sighed. She was going to pay for this interruption in her sleep the next day. And heaven knew what state Roxanne would be in having been out all night. Serve her right too, she thought bitchily. She was such a fool.

'Not far now,' Billy said to Roxanne.

'Tide turned a few hours back which should make things easier,' Stanley Pipe informed them.

Roxanne glanced up but there wasn't even a hint of sky, only dense fog. This was a real pea-souper and no mistake.

They came to a small hillock, which they skirted round, then resumed their original direction. They all started when there was a sudden movement beside them, but their fear subsided as Dickie laughed softly when a sheep materialized from the fog to regard them quizzically.

'Baaaa!' mocked Billy.

The sheep's response was to turn and amble away, quickly swallowed up again by the fog.

Roxanne rubbed her hands together, glad of the woollen gloves she was wearing. Her fingers would have turned to icicles without them.

A little further on they paused as they heard voices, others heading for the wreck they correctly surmised, and wondered to whom the voices belonged.

Then they were at the beginning of the Point, a narrow strip of land that jutted out into the sea and was surrounded by rocks.

It was a treacherous area for boats and only navigated by the locals when visibility was perfect.

'Look!' exclaimed Dickie a matter of minutes later.

The outline of the ship was just discernible from the peep and glimmer of a number of lights.

'We'd better make sure the police aren't here before we light our lamps,' Dickie counselled, to which there was a murmur of agreement. Stealthily they made their way towards the wreck.

A figure appeared out of the fog pushing a wheelbarrow piled high with goods. It was Jack Gifford.

'Who's that?' Jack demanded, setting down his barrow.

'Dickie Webber and some friends,' Dickie replied.

Jack grunted in relief. 'You gave me quite a start there.'

Roxanne decided to hang back a little. The fewer people who knew of her presence the better. Remembering she was wearing a scarf she pulled it up so that it covered the lower part of her face.

'Are there any police about yet?' Dickie asked anxiously.

Jack shook his head. 'Not so far. And I reckons there won't be for quite some time.'

'What have you got?' Stanley queried, peering into the barrow.

'All sorts,' Jack replied with undisguised delight. 'Bottles of Spanish brandy, a roll of lace . . .'

'Is she a Spanish ship then?' Billy inquired.

'No, Greek. Name of the *SS Katina*.'

'Greek,' Billy mused.

'Out of Piraeus according to what's painted on the stern.'

'What's that?' James asked, pointing at a wooden box.

'Cigars. I'll enjoy smoking they,' Jack beamed.

Quite an assortment, Roxanne thought, wondering what else the *Katina* was carrying.

They spoke for a few more minutes, then Jack continued on his way, the others hurrying towards the wreck.

The *Katina*, firmly impaled on the rocks, was leaning on one side. It had a great gash at the front and had partially broken in the middle. It was high and dry, for the sea had already receded beyond it.

With Dickie in the lead they scrambled down on to the wet sand and rocks, swiftly reaching the side of the dead ship. Four rope ladders dangled from the deck.

'Right,' declared Dickie, grasping the nearest ladder which he began to rapidly ascend.

'You go in front of me,' Billy instructed Roxanne.

'Isn't this fun!'

He nodded, watching Stanley Pipe haul himself up another ladder with James close behind.

Roxanne was halfway to the deck when her feet slipped, causing her to spin out of control and bang against the metal hull. She hung on grimly as she tried to get her feet back on a rung. Then Billy caught one foot which he replaced for her, after which he guided the other.

Roxanne swallowed hard. What a nasty moment! Thank goodness Billy had been below to help her.

'Ta!' she whispered.

'On you go.'

She hauled herself aboard where she took a deep breath. 'Thanks again,' she said when Billy joined her.

'Don't mention it.'

'What happened?' Dickie asked.

'Nothing,' Billy answered. 'Let's get below and see what's what.'

'First the lamps, it'll be black as pitch down there,' Dickie replied, reaching for the lucifer matches he'd brought with him.

When the lamps were lit they traversed the sloping deck and plunged into an open hatchway which brought them into a narrow corridor. Instantly Roxanne's nose was assailed by the rather stale smell peculiar to ships, which would get stronger as they went deeper down.

A light appeared ahead of them and two men carrying a crate with their lamps on top came into view. One of the men said something and his companion laughed.

'Here we are,' said Dickie, having discovered a companionway which took them down a level.

They all gazed around, wondering how to get to the hold. They found another companionway and were about to descend when someone appeared at the bottom and stared up at them.

'Who's that?' a voice demanded.

'Dickie Webber and friends,' Dickie replied.

'Don't know you,' the man snarled, and vanished.

'Charlie!' the man's voice called out, receding into the distance. 'Where the fuck are you, Charlie!'

'I wouldn't mind some of that Spanish brandy,' Stanley commented to his brother as they clattered down the steps.

'Me neither.'

'Or cigars.'

'I'd feel like a lord in his castle smoking such as they,' James laughed.

They were striding along another corridor when Dickie came up short with a gasp. The others crowded round to see what was the matter.

The man lying crumpled in the passage was clearly a member of the crew. His eyes were open and staring, his head at an odd angle to his body.

'Must have broken his neck when the ship hit,' Dickie said.

Roxanne stared in fascination at the corpse. 'He probably didn't feel a thing. Not if he broke his neck,' she murmured, a slight tremor in her voice.

'Poor sod,' Billy declared sympathetically.

'Amen,' James added.

'Well, there's nothing we can do for him, so let's get on.'

On the next level down, they bumped into Kevern Stoneman whose father's farm adjoined the Hawkins' property. He was carrying a bulging sack slung over his shoulder.

'How do, Kevern,' Dickie greeted him.

'You'd better hurry up, they're like vultures down there,' Kevern replied.

'Where's the hold?'

'There are three of them, but two are filled with coal. It's the hold right at the front you want.'

'Thanks,' Dickie acknowledged.

The ship gave a loud groan which made them all pause, and wonder. 'You don't think she's going to topple over, do you?' Stanley asked nervously.

'Shouldn't think so,' Kevern replied. Then, added with a sardonic smile, 'There again, you never know.'

'Christ,' swore James, anxiously.

Kevern's eyes swept over the little party and he frowned when he noticed Roxanne whose lower face was still covered by her scarf. Recognition dawned, and he gave her a curt nod which she returned.

'Good hunting,' he said, and went on his way.

'Funny lad that, never taken to him,' Billy commented quietly to Roxanne when Kevern had gone.

Although Kevern was one of the Hawkins' neighbours, Roxanne didn't really know him very well. He'd always been quiet and rather standoffish, preferring his own company. She didn't think she'd spoken to him more than half a dozen times in her entire life.

Soon they found number three hold which was stacked high with crates and boxes, many of which had been pulled down and broken open. Discarded debris littered the floor.

'Wow!' Dickie exclaimed, taking in the busy scene. At a rough estimate he'd have said there were about twenty people already there. There were many faces he recognized, others he'd never seen before.

'Let's get to it then,' James urged.

Billy was wishing he'd had the foresight to bring along a sack like the one Kevern had had. But maybe he'd find one, or something as useful in the hold.

Stanley picked up an iron bar lying on the floor and attacked a large wooden crate that had words in Greek stencilled across the side nearest him.

'How do, Dickie!' Ted Back called out, and waved. He and Dickie were old chums.

Dickie returned the wave. 'How's it going?'

'Only got here a minute ago myself. Ain't this terrific!' And without waiting for a reply Stanley resumed what he'd been doing.

The crate Stanley was attacking split open, James and Billy eagerly grasping the shattered wood and ripping sections of it away.

'Books,' Dickie proclaimed in disappointment. 'Sodding books.'

'Trust us,' muttered Billy.

Roxanne thought that funny, and smiled.

They fared better with the next crate they opened, because it contained bottles of brandy similar to those in Jack Gifford's barrow. Stanley let out a whoop when he saw the crate's contents.

'Well you got your wish,' James grinned at him.

'I certainly did.'

After a while Roxanne was in despair because she felt that she would never find anything for herself. There was certainly plenty to be had, an abundance of spoils, but nothing she could take home with her. How on earth would she explain Spanish brandy, for example? Not that she wanted any. Then she had an idea, perhaps she was looking in the wrong place.

'Billy?'

He turned a flushed face to her.

'I'm going back up to search through the cabins. All this is useless to me.'

Billy had found a cardboard box into which he'd crammed his choice of loot. 'I'm nearly finished here anyway. Want me to come with you?'

She thought about that. 'I'll be all right on my own. I'll meet you up on deck.' She clutched his arm. 'Just don't leave me behind, that's all.'

'I promise,' he assured her.

'By the ladder we came up.'

'I'll be there.'

Holding her lamp in front of her she retraced their steps. When she reached the first level again she went exploring.

The initial cabin she found contained nothing of interest: clothes, gear of various sorts and some dirty cups and saucers which had somehow survived the ship running aground.

She momentarily mused on the irony of the latter. The cups and saucers had survived where a crew member hadn't. Life was strange.

The next cabin was larger and better furnished. She had just stepped inside when there was a sudden blood-curdling screech and something dashed between her legs.

Roxanne went rigid from a combination of fright and shock. Her heart was pounding wildly.

'Miaow!'

She relaxed, laughing with relief. A cat! A damn cat! When she looked out into the corridor she saw a large, ginger tom staring back at her, its yellow eyes gleaming in the darkness.

'Hallo puss, locked in were you,' she said, her voice shaking.

With a disdainful flick of its tail the cat turned round and stalked haughtily away.

Smiling broadly, Roxanne returned to the cabin and gazed about. Bolted to the floor was a desk, covered in paraphernalia including several marine charts. A silver-framed photograph stood on it of a middle-aged man and woman, he with his arm round the woman's shoulders. The background clearly depicted a foreign country which she presumed to be Greece. They appeared a happy couple, she thought, wondering if they had any children. The question was answered a few moments later when she happened upon another photograph, this in a walnut frame, of two girls a little older than herself and Linnet.

The bunk was dishevelled with a battered trunk underneath. Pulling out the trunk she tried the catches only to find they were locked.

She then rummaged through the desk drawers, realizing in the process that she was in the captain's cabin, but there was nothing of any interest to her.

She discovered and opened what transpired to be the ship's equivalent of a wardrobe, filled with an assortment of clothes, civilian and otherwise.

She paused then, thinking that what she was doing was wrong. It was pure and simple thieving. It was one thing stealing cargo from an abandoned wreck, quite another pocketing personal effects. However, she hadn't taken anything yet.

She shrugged. She was just going to have to put the night down to an exciting adventure, that was all. The others would have trophies to take home, not her. She'd better be getting back on deck, she thought. Billy would be waiting for her and no doubt they'd all be impatient to be away. Coming to search cabins had been a stupid notion anyway, she told herself, and didn't know what she'd been thinking.

She started to leave when she noticed a box file lying on the floor, which had obviously tumbled off the shelf on impact. She was about to ignore it, when curiosity got the better of her. Crossing to the file she bent down and flicked it open.

Inside were various official forms and reports, a few of which bore the crest of *SS Katina* on top. There was also a small chamois bag, tied round the top with an attached leather thong. When she shook the bag it chinked.

Her face dropped in astonishment when she opened the bag and, using her lamp for illumination, looked inside.

Linnet burst into Roxanne's bedroom, still pulling on her clothes. Phoebe had shouted for them to get up only a couple of minutes before. It was 5 am.

'Well?' Linnet demanded.

'Well what?' Roxanne teased in reply.

Linnet frowned in annoyance. 'Don't "well what" me. How did you get on? I hardly slept a wink worrying about you. I was awake for ages after you'd gone.'

Roxanne reached for her black skirt. 'We had a tremendous time.'

'And?'

'Billy and the others got masses of stuff, so much so they could hardly carry it all back. Still, they managed.'

'What kind of stuff?' Linnet queried, eager for the details.

'Spanish brandy, cigarettes, coffee, Greek wine—' She

shrugged. 'There was so much there they found it hard to choose.'

'And what about you? What did you take?'

'I didn't take any of that as I could never have explained it to Da. So I left the cargo alone.'

'You mean – you came away empty-handed? So what was the point of going in the first place?'

'It was an adventure,' Roxanne explained patiently. 'And one I wouldn't have missed, not for anything.'

'You're ridiculous,' Linnet said caustically.

'Am I?'

'Well, I think you are. Imagine not taking anything.'

'I didn't say that,' Roxanne replied quietly.

'So you did bring something back?' Linnet was now eager again, dying to know what the something was.

'Nothing from the cargo. But I did manage to pick up a little memento.'

'What?'

Roxanne regarded her sister steadily. 'If I show you, you must promise to keep it a secret between the pair of us. If you don't I won't show you.'

'I promise,' Linnet snapped.

'Your word of honour?'

Linnet sighed with impatience. 'My word of honour. Now *what*?'

Roxanne reached under her pillows and pulled out the small chamois bag. 'This.'

'What's in it?'

Maddeningly slowly, which was her intention, Roxanne undid the leather thong, then tipped the bag into her hand. Linnet gasped when five golden sovereigns dropped out.

'They were in the captain's cabin,' Roxanne explained. 'I'm certain they weren't his, though, but belonged to the ship, which made them the same as cargo as far as I was concerned. I wouldn't have pinched them if they'd been his personal property.'

'Why the ship's?'

'Because of where I found them.'

'Five sovereigns,' Linnet breathed. 'Just think what they could buy.'

'An awful lot,' Roxanne agreed. She gazed down at the coins. 'Do you know this is the first real money I've ever owned. All I've had in the past were farthings, ha'pennies and pennies. And once a sixpence from Aunt Elvira.'

'Now you're got five whole pounds,' Linnet declared enviously, wishing they were hers.

'It's unbelievable. A fortune. And all mine.'

'I wish—' Linnet broke off, and bit her lip.

'That you'd gone along? Well, it's your own fault you didn't.'

'Can I help you spend it?' Linnet asked, thinking that would be the next best thing to having the money herself. And if she was with Roxanne surely her sister would treat her.

Roxanne curled her hand slightly and shook the sovereigns back into the chamois bag. 'No,' she replied as she retied the leather thong.

'Oh, come on, Roxanne, don't be rotten.'

'The answer's no.'

'But why?'

'Because I'm not going to spend them, that's why. I decided that on the way home from the wreck. I'm going to hide them for the future.'

'That's daft,' Linnet declared, seeing her treat disappearing.

'I don't believe so. Rather than frittering the money away I'll keep it for something I really want. And don't ask me what that's going to be, I have absolutely no idea. Anyway, if I started spending sovereigns in St Petroc, Da would be bound to hear about it and want to know where I'd got them from. So hiding them is the sensible thing to do for now.'

'Where are you going to put them?'

Roxanne gave a soft, mocking laugh. 'Wouldn't you like to know.'

Linnet glared at her sister. Then the glare changed to a friendly smile. 'What about giving me one? Just one, that wouldn't hurt you, would it?'

Roxanne considered Linnet's request. 'No,' she answered eventually.

The glare swiftly returned. 'I wouldn't spend mine, I'd hide it as well.'

'No,' Roxanne repeated firmly. 'I don't trust you. The temptation would be too great. You'd be in the shops before the week was out. Besides, why should I give you one? It was me who took all the risk while you stayed safely tucked up in bed.'

Linnet was furious. 'If it was the other way round I'd share.'

'Hah!' Roxanne retorted, knowing that was most unlikely.

'If you don't I'll tell Da.'

Roxanne rose and stared her sister straight in the eye. 'Do that,

Linnet, and I'll never forgive you.' She paused, then repeated with emphasis, '*Never.*'

Linnet shrank back from Roxanne's fierce gaze, the younger girl's strength of character dominating her own, making her wilt mentally as well as physically.

'You're mean,' she whispered.

'Linnet! Roxanne!' Phoebe cried out from another part of the house.

'We'd better get moving,' Roxanne declared, slipping the chamois bag into her skirt pocket. There was a loose brick in the shippon behind which she intended hiding the bag, certain it would never be found there.

Later, that was what she did.

The chickens fussed noisily round Roxanne as she gave them their morning feed. It was a month since the *Katina* had run aground and the public hullabaloo that had followed its looting had died down. The ship had since been patched up, refloated, and gone limping off to Plymouth for repairs.

The ship's captain, whose name was Smyrnas, had gone on record as saying he was deeply grieved by the looting, declaring that: 'These people cannot be English, for I could always trust the English.' The latter remark had caused great merriment and mirth in the St Petroc pubs where it had been quoted over and over again.

Roxanne glanced up at the sound of approaching feet, surprised to see Kevern Stoneman coming towards her. Now what did he want?

'How do,' he said awkwardly, stopping a few feet away.

'How do,' she smiled, continuing to feed the chickens.

'My Da's sent me over with a message for your Da. Is he in?'

Roxanne shook her head. 'He's out in the fields. Calico Meadow, if you know which one that is.'

'Over yonder,' Kevern said, pointing.

'That's right. Just keep going that way and you can't miss him.'

Kevern stared at Roxanne, thinking how incredibly beautiful she was. He'd always thought of her as a youngster until the night of the concert in the Hawkins' barn when he'd had a real eye opener. Now, face to face, just the pair of them alone, he found that beauty disconcerting in the extreme. It made him nervous and very unsure of himself.

'Did you do well out of the wreck?' he asked, as that was the last occasion he'd seen her.

'All right. You?'

He nodded. 'I must say I was surprised to see you there.'

'Were you?'

He nodded again.

'I'd be grateful if you didn't mention it to my Da, he doesn't know.'

'I won't,' he assured her.

'Thank you.'

He suddenly realized his face was reddening, which mortified him. She must think he was a proper fool.

Roxanne was amused by his heightening colour, correctly presuming she must be the cause. His voice had gone all peculiar too, becoming croaky as if he had a bad cold coming on.

Kevern shifted from one foot to the other. Part of him wanted to be away from Roxanne, another part compelled him to linger. He'd never experienced a girl having this effect on him before.

'I thought you sang marvellously at the concert,' he said, mentally cursing himself when he stumbled over several of the words.

'It's kind of you to say so.'

'No, I mean it. You were wonderful.'

'I really enjoyed myself that night. Everyone agreed the show was a great success.'

'I certainly thought so.'

He had an almost overwhelming desire to reach out and touch Roxanne. He went even redder when he wondered what it would be like to kiss her.

'Think it'll rain?' he queried, glancing up at the sky.

That amused Roxanne further. Of course it was going to rain, he could tell that as well as her. 'Oh, I imagine so,' she replied casually.

'Won't go amiss.'

'No,' she agreed.

He wished the ground would open up and swallow him. But still he couldn't bring himself to leave. 'They chickens look healthy enough,' he said.

She wanted to laugh. Chickens now! 'They are. And fine layers.'

He cleared his throat, and shifted his feet again. He wanted to ask her out, but didn't have the guts to do so. Simply being in her presence had turned him to jelly inside, making him despise himself for being weak and lacking courage. She could only turn him down, after all, but still he couldn't bring himself to utter the words he so dearly wanted to.

'Where's your sister?' he asked.

'With Da. She's helping him.'

'Ah!'

Silence fell between them as they both watched the chickens scrabbling for their feed.

'Right,' he mumbled at last. 'Pleasant talking to you, Roxanne.'

'And you.'

'See you about.'

'I suppose.'

He gave her a feeble smile, then strode off in the direction of Calico Meadow. Roxanne stared at his retreating back, thinking she didn't like Kevern Stoneman. Why? She didn't know. There was just something, something she couldn't quite put her finger on.

With a mental shrug she dismissed him and went on with the job in hand.

Kevern came up short when he saw Roxanne ahead of him gazing into a shop window. It was a Saturday, market day in St Petroc; the square, which he'd just left, was jam-packed as usual.

Here was the perfect opportunity, he thought. All he had to do was say hallo and ask her to go for a walk or whatever.

God, she was beautiful! That hair, those eyes, her figure. The most gorgeous maid he'd ever come across.

He retreated into a doorway and continued watching her from there.

Go on, he urged himself as she moved along the street to stop at another shop. She won't bite you for goodness' sake. Say hallo, and take it from there.

Kevern closed his eyes and counted to ten. When he reached ten he'd make a move, he promised himself.

Nine . . . ten.

He stayed where he was.

'Shit,' he swore.

Then he moved, not towards her but back down the road he'd just come up.

When a friendly dog came snuffling round it took all his self-control not to kick it.

Chapter Four

It was a fine day for harvesting. Reynold and others had been out since dawn scything starter tracks for Fern. These tracks were made round the perimeters of each field and the big Shire would plod along them while Reynold guided the reaper. Starter tracks were dug by hand so that none of the precious crop would be trampled on and destroyed.

As was the custom, all the neighbours were present to help bind the cut oats and barley and stack the results into stooks. When the Hawkins' harvest was in they'd all move on to the next farm where the Hawkins would repay the favour. This went on from farm to farm, until the entire harvest in the immediate area had been cut and stooked.

Roxanne paused and ran a hand over her streaming brow. Her back ached abominably as did her calloused hands.

'Don't get no easier, do it?' Sally Tutching grumbled.

'You can say that again.'

'I can't wait for the eatins and drinkins later on.' As again was customary, at the end of each day's harvesting the farmer's wife laid on a huge spread for all those who'd toiled in the fields.

Roxanne glanced up at the sun and roughly gauged the time. 'Hours to go before that.'

'I know,' Sally sighed, deftly binding the stalks she'd just gathered.

Roxanne spotted Cory Vranch in the distance. He was the young man she'd been seeing for a year now and who was madly in love with her. He was a nice lad, very personable, and he could certainly make her laugh. The only trouble was that she wasn't in love with him.

He was a handsome bugger, with that auburn moustache and twinkling green eyes. Quite a catch hereabouts, and popular with the maids, most of whom would have given their eye-teeth to be in her position.

She thought of the previous Sunday evening when she and Cory had been alone in the barn, snuggled up like babes behind some bales. There had been lots of kissing and cuddling, then Cory had spoiled it all by wanting to go further, pleading with her to sleep with him.

Many girls did before marriage, there was nothing dreadful about it. But if a maid fell pregnant, that was that. The banns were called and the lad did his duty by her.

However, Roxanne had no intention of marrying Cory and didn't want to put herself in that position. Fun and great company he might be, but how could she marry a man she didn't love? Which she'd have to if he got her in the family way.

She should have given him up before now, she told herself. Going on as they were tweren't fair on him, she was being totally selfish and leading him up the garden path. She'd set off to meet him with the intention of breaking it off several times, and somehow she always baulked when it came down to it.

The thing about Cory was that he brought lightness and relief into what was otherwise an unremitting, seemingly endless slog.

'What you daydreaming about?' Sally demanded.

Roxanne wiped more sweat from her brow. 'Just thinking, that's all.'

'I can see that. About what, though?'

Roxanne shrugged. 'Nothing much. Just how bored I am, I suppose.'

'I don't get bored. No time to.'

'Well, I do.' Roxanne gestured all around. 'I hate all this you know. It's so . . . tedious.'

Suddenly, there was a brown flash as a rabbit raced from the still uncut oats, only to be quickly pounced on by Ben, the Hawkins' dog. He'd been lurking, hoping for just such an event. The rabbit died in a flurry of movement as Ben sunk his teeth into its throat.

'Another for the pot,' Sally commented. Lots of rabbits were killed that way during harvesting.

A second rabbit scampered from the same spot, and died as well, this time with an anguished squeal, when Ben pounced again.

'Proper job,' Sally breathed, nostrils dilated, eyes gleaming, referring to Ben.

Roxanne didn't bother to hide her disgust at her friend's reaction, although the disgust was completely lost on Sally.

Cory's face was flushed; he'd drunk a considerable amount of cider. Ambling over to Roxanne he slid an arm round her waist.

'Your Ma sure is a fine dandy cook,' he slurred.

'Good eatins and drinkins then?'

'No complaints, and that's a fact.'

Joe Tregale, sitting nearby, pushed his bottom into the air and loudly broke wind which raised a laugh from the others round about. It was typical of farming humour, at least farming humour thereabouts. Roxanne looked on in dismay.

'Want to go to the barn?' Cory whispered in her ear.

'I can't. Too much to do here. I've got to help Ma with the clearing up. That'll take ages.'

He squeezed her waist. 'Afterwards then? I can hang around. Won't be no problem that.'

'No, Cory,' she insisted. 'It just isn't possible.'

'Of course it is, my lover. If you wants it to be.'

He was irritating her for once. In her present mood the last thing she wanted was a rendezvous. 'I'm far too busy for the barn,' she lied. 'Now don't go on so.'

Disappointment filled his face. 'Have I done something wrong?'

'Nothing,' she assured him, putting on what she hoped was a disarming smile.

'Are you sure?'

She removed his arm from her waist. 'Very. Now trot off and have some more cider. There's still plenty left.'

Roxanne could be a real puzzle on occasion, Cory thought. He never really knew where he was with her. But wasn't that one of the things that attracted him? He had to make the running, which wasn't the case with other maids.

'This Sunday again then?' he queried hopefully.

'Perhaps. I'll see.'

He winked salaciously at her. 'I'll be there same time as last week. Ready and waiting.' Having said that he left her and strolled away.

Would she go? She didn't know. It would all depend on how she felt on Sunday evening.

She watched Cory stop and chat to Sally who, she knew, fancied him like mad. Sally wouldn't have hesitated to meet him in the barn or to sleep with him. For Sally wasn't a virgin like herself, having already been with two lads. They'd giggled together when Sally had described in graphic detail what it was like, doing 'it'.

'Roxanne,' Phoebe called out, 'come and give me a hand here, girl.'

Putting all thoughts of Cory and Sally from her mind, Roxanne hastened to obey.

'A grand day. A grand day,' Reynold declared from a chair by the range. He, too, had imbibed heavily of the cider during the meal.

Phoebe stared lovingly at him from the dresser where she was putting away the last of the crockery. 'Going to bed soon, me dear?' she queried.

Reynold knew from the tone of her voice what that meant. Phoebe was in the mood.

He tossed aside a newspaper that someone had left behind, which he'd only glanced at. He'd been thinking how tired he was just before she'd spoken. Now he didn't feel quite so tired any more.

'I was about to go through,' he said, rising and stretching.

'I won't be long after you,' Phoebe smiled.

Reynold hoped he hadn't drunk too much cider as he made his way to the bedroom.

Roxanne sank into the chair her father had been occupying as Phoebe closed the dresser doors. If she'd agreed to meet Cory it was now she'd have been sneaking off.

Dear Cory, she thought. Dear, sweet Cory. He'd make someone a marvellous husband – but not her. She decided she would meet him the following Sunday and break it off. Twas the only decent thing to do.

Definitely break it off, she promised herself, although sad at the thought, for she did like him tremendously. But she knew that liking wasn't loving and would never be so. He was going to be hurt, of course. But he'd get over it in time.

Was she being callous? she wondered. She didn't mean to be. She didn't want to hurt Cory, but knew there was simply no other way.

'Where is it tomorrow?' Linnet asked, sitting across from Roxanne.

Roxanne roused herself from her reverie and focused on her sister. 'The Christmas farm. That right, Ma?'

Phoebe was hanging up the white, well-starched apron she'd been wearing. 'That's right,' she confirmed. 'And the Tregales after them.'

'I saw a rat today that was the biggest I've ever seen. Huge he was, black all over.'

Roxanne shivered. She loathed rats. You'd have thought being born and brought up on a farm she'd have got used to them, but she never had. She was as afraid of them now as she'd ever been.

'Good night then,' Phoebe said.

'Good night, Ma,' Linnet and Roxanne both replied.

'It's early yet,' Linnet commented, glancing at the clock on the mantelpiece. It was another hour before she normally took herself off to bed.

Roxanne picked up the newspaper her father had discarded to discover she hadn't read it, although it was several days old. She began to flick through the pages.

'Are you going to read or talk?' Linnet queried, eager to have a natter.

'Read.'

That annoyed Linnet. 'Suit yourself then,' she sniffed and, getting up again, flounced out of the room. She'd had a juicy bit of gossip to tell Roxanne which she'd now keep to herself. Serve Roxanne right!

Moments later Roxanne's attention was caught by a half-page editorial on the London music halls, the article highlighted by a clever and witty drawing.

When she'd finished the piece, which had been even cleverer and wittier than the drawing, she leant back in her chair and sighed. What a wonderful life the music hall sounded, and how completely different to her own.

She thought of the concert that had taken place in St Petroc Town Hall, and how glorious that had been. It was three years now, back in 1896, since that concert and the one she'd organized in the barn.

She smiled at the memory, reliving her own performance and the adulation that had washed over her at the end. Adulation that had made her feel so . . . full inside, so alive. She began humming the song she'd sung, then softly broke into the words.

Strangely, despite its success, she'd never organized a follow-up concert. She'd thought about doing so on several occasions but, for one reason and another, thinking was as far as she'd gone.

Maybe she'd do so this autumn. It would be tremendous fun. Her mind began whirling with potential plans and possibilities.

'That twere lovely,' Phoebe crooned as Reynold rolled off her.

He encircled her neck and drew her to him, as she snuggled up close. The cider hadn't affected him at all, he thought with relief and pride.

'Twere indeed,' he agreed.

Phoebe drew in a deep breath. She was satiated from their lovemaking, beautifully relaxed and at peace with the world. She ran a loving hand down Reynold's hard thigh.

'You don't want more, do you?' he teased.

'Any more would be too much of a good thing.'

'Can never get too much of that,' he joked.

'Of course you can. Too much spoils it. At least for me it does.'

He wasn't sure he entirely agreed with her, but refrained from saying so. 'I was thinking earlier about Roxanne,' he said instead.

'What about her?'

'She's been seeing Cory for quite a while now. I think we might expect an engagement soon.'

'Nice lad, Cory. Good looking, too.'

'They be a fine match those pair. Well suited I'd say.' Reynold highly approved of Cory whose father was one of his close cronies. If he could have hand-picked someone for either Roxanne or Linnet it would have been Cory Vranch.

Phoebe thought of grandchildren, and smiled, hoping at least one of them would be a boy, a boy she might even persuade Roxanne to call Freddy after the son she'd lost. She would be very appreciative of that.

'They could stay here,' Reynold mused, for the Vranches were chock-a-block at home, as there were seven children. Cory might get a place of his own, of course, but in time surely, in time. Meanwhile if Cory was to live with them, he could give him an extra hand about the farm and he wouldn't be losing Roxanne. 'We got plenty room,' he added.

'Plenty,' Phoebe agreed, thinking it would be lovely as she'd have her grandchildren at home with her rather than elsewhere.

'I'm sure it's a match,' Reynold further enthused, already envisaging Cory hard at work for him. A big strapping lad was that Cory.

'But I don't think we should interfere, mind,' Phoebe cautioned. 'Let them get round to things in their own time. Nothing worse than parents interfering.'

'I wouldn't interfere,' Reynold protested.

'Oh yes, you would. Well, you shan't in this instance, hear?'

'If you say so, my lover.'

'I do. In their own time.'

Another man on the farm, Reynold thought, delighted at the prospect. What a right proper job!

During the middle of that night, Roxanne woke, her eyes snapping open in surprise, the idea fully formed in her mind. Forget the concert in the barn. She would go to London and get herself taken on by one of the music halls. That was what she'd do, the new life she'd craved for so long. She'd become a professional entertainer.

Excitement gripped her. She was amazed at her own audacity in even contemplating such a notion. 'London!' she breathed the word aloud, trying to imagine the noise, the bustle, the general to-ing and fro-ing, the smells.

She laughed softly. There would be no cow and pig smells in London, that was certain. Horses of course; the capital must be teeming with horses pulling all manner of vehicles.

And the lights, bright lights. Night-time in London; the sheer glitter and glitz breathtaking to behold. She could, would, be part of it.

Then her euphoria faded as doubts assailed her. Did she have sufficient talent for the music hall? Competition must be fierce if not downright cut-throat. Why, there might be hundreds, if not thousands, trying to break in at any one time. What made her think she could do it? And if she tried, and failed, what then? Crawl back to the farm and St Petroc with her tail between her legs? What a humiliation that would be! How they'd laugh – Linnet, Sally, everyone.

But the temptation to try at least – oh, that was very great. If you never tried you never got anywhere. What was the alternative? The same old chores and routines – feeding the chickens, milking the cows, making butter and cheese, morning till night. She couldn't bear to think about it.

Not that she was afraid of hard work, no-one could ever accuse her of that. She could hold her own with the best of them – plough a field, sow a crop, dig potatoes, pull and top mangolds, cut and pack broccoli.

But all boring, boring to distraction. She craved something else, something London and the music hall could most certainly provide.

Was she good enough even to try? That was the big question. And did she have the gumption to set out on her own? Cut her family ties and leave the only place she knew? She'd never been further afield than about ten miles from her own doorstep.

She'd be the original country bumpkin with extremely limited experience. Could she cope? Or would she be an innocent stepping into the lion's den to suffer who knows what fate?

Courage, Roxanne, she told herself. That's what you'll need, courage and determination. And it wasn't as if she was stupid, far from it. She had a decent brain in her head. Why, hadn't she learnt to read and write at almost the same time as Linnet who was two years older? Her teacher had remarked that she'd taken to book learning like a duck to water.

Nor was it just book learning; she was quick at figuring things out, solving problems. Nor did she panic as Linnet did. Give Linnet a crisis and her sister went completely to pieces, fell apart at the seams. Not her. Roxanne remained cool, calm, rational and *thought*.

But London. Would that be too much for her, simply overwhelm her?

Then she recalled how she'd felt at the end of her number in the barn – the tremendous exhilaration, the internal sunburst of joy. Imagine that night after night, and being paid for it, too.

She had to think this through, she told herself, really through. It was far too big a step to be taken lightly.

And then there was Ma and Da. What would they say to such a proposal? They would hardly be encouraging.

Sleep on it, she counselled herself. Sleep on it and then look at it from every conceivable angle.

'London,' she whispered, tingling all over, '*London*.'

'Roxanne's broken with Cory Vranch,' Linnet announced across the supper table.

Reynold's fork stopped halfway to his mouth. 'What?'

'Is it true, dear?' queried Phoebe, frowning.

'Oh, it's true all right. Isn't it?' Linnet smirked at Roxanne.

Roxanne happily could have slapped Linnet. It wasn't her sister's place to make such an announcement, but hers, if it was going to be made at all. 'Yes, it's true,' she said.

'She's mad, gone cuckoo,' Linnet went on, still smirking. 'All the girls are after Cory and my silly sister goes and breaks it off with him.'

Roxanne gave Linnet an ice-cold stare. She'd wipe that smirk off her face. 'At least I had a lad to break it off with. Which is a lot more than can be said for you.' She smiled thinly when she got the reaction she'd anticipated.

'Just because I'm between lads,' Linnet shrugged.

'It's a long between,' Roxanne retorted. 'When was the last one? Ages ago. Ages and ages in fact.' It was an odd thing about Linnet, although she was extremely good looking she simply didn't attract the boys. Or if she did it never lasted long. She just wasn't popular with them, which was the complete opposite to Roxanne.

'Why?' Reynold demanded angrily.

Not knowing anything about his plans for Cory, she wondered at his response. Why should her Da be so upset? 'I liked him well enough, but that was all. Twasn't fair to keep on seeing him.'

'We thought it was a match between you pair?' Phoebe said.

Roxanne shook her head. 'Certainly not on my part.'

'I hear he's real upset,' Linnet declared.

Roxanne glared at her sister. Why didn't she just shut up? She knew Cory was upset. On the Sunday night she'd told him there had been a terrible scene in the barn and several frightening moments when she'd thought he was actually going to hit her. So much so that in the end she'd walked away, leaving him there.

'You won't do better than Cory,' Reynold said through clenched teeth. Since his conversation with Phoebe about Cory he'd quite convinced himself that Cory would be his son-in-law and working on the farm before long.

'She should be thankful he was interested in her,' Linnet bitched.

'Maybe you should reconsider, Roxanne?' Phoebe suggested.

'Nothing to reconsider, Ma.'

'We thought the two of you would wed,' Phoebe went on.

'Well, you thought wrong.'

'Enough of your impertinence!' Reynold fumed, banging the table with his fist. 'You'll show your Ma respect or you'll get what for.'

'I didn't mean to be disrespectful.'

'I should hope not, girl.'

'But Cory just isn't for me, Da. He's a farmer and—' She trailed off, realizing what she'd said.

'And what's wrong with being a farmer?' Reynold queried.

'Nothing, Da.'

'Roxanne has aspirations beyond farming. She's told me that on a number of occasions,' Linnet smiled sweetly.

Roxanne was now angry. 'So what if I have?'

'Delusions of grandeur. She thinks she's something special, that's what,' Linnet sneered.

'I'm something special compared to you. Certainly when it comes to the lads. You're a complete flop in that department, aren't you sister, dear?' Roxanne riposted, smiling sweetly back.

'That's a lie!'

'Facts speak for themselves.'

'What's this aspirations beyond farming?' Reynold demanded.

Phoebe was intrigued. She knew nothing about this.

Roxanne took a deep breath. She hadn't meant to speak to them about London yet, intending to choose her time and place carefully. Suddenly, she decided, what the hell! Get it over and done with, take the plunge.

'I want to go to London,' she stated.

Linnet's face fell as she gawped at Roxanne. Reynold was thunderstruck, Phoebe horrified.

'London,' Reynold croaked.

'And become an entertainer in the music halls.'

There, it was out, Roxanne thought, staring from one face to the other. She found their expressions so comical that, in other circumstances, she'd probably have laughed.

Reynold laid down his knife and fork. 'Is this some kind of joke?' he queried, voice tight from shock.

'No joke, Da,' Roxanne informed him.

'An entertainer in the music halls,' he repeated.

'That's right, Da.'

'Jesus Christ!' he swore softly.

Linnet giggled, this was really too daft for words. Roxanne was fibbing, she had to be pulling their legs.

'Shut up!' Reynold snarled at Linnet who immediately complied. He then fixed Roxanne with a jaundiced eye. 'I've never heard anything so ridiculous in my entire life.'

'London,' Phoebe breathed. Her Roxanne going to live in London. It simply wasn't on. What had got into the girl?

'I want to try, Da. I think I can make a go of it.'

'I suppose you think we're not good enough for you any more? Next thing you'll be saying is that you're ashamed of us.'

'That's not true, Da.'

'Oh no?'

She shook her head.

'Well, you listen to me, girl, and you listen good. I absolutely forbid it, you hear?'

'It's utter nonsense. I've never heard the like,' Phoebe said.

'I don't want to stay on the farm, Da. I want more out of life than what farming has to offer,' Roxanne explained.

'*More*,' Reynold repeated caustically. 'And I suppose that's why you broke it off with Cory. He wasn't good enough for you, either.'

'It wasn't a case of that, Da. I don't love Cory, and he's not what I want.'

'What sort of entertainer?' Linnet inquired, hoping she wasn't going to be told to shut up again.

'A singer.'

'They concerts,' Reynold nodded, the penny dropping. 'The one in the town hall and other in barn. They're behind this I'll be bound. I knew we should never have gone, I knew it. Damn Elvira!'

'Reynold,' Phoebe admonished. She wouldn't have her sister spoken of like that.

'Well, it is her fault, isn't it? And mine, for letting her talk me into going. You can see the result!'

'Still,' Phoebe mumbled, biting her lip, in as much shock as Reynold.

'Please, Da?' Roxanne pleaded.

'Please, my arse. You're going nowhere, Roxanne, least of all London. And do you know why?'

She shook her head.

'Because I forbids it, but also because you got no money and I sure as hell ain't giving you any. So what do you say to that?'

Roxanne held her breath waiting for Linnet to chime in, betraying her secret. But Linnet didn't.

Roxanne dropped her gaze to the table, her lips narrowing to a thin, hard line. What else had she expected? Hardly for her Da to be supportive. Or her Ma, come to that.

'Nowhere,' Reynold repeated.

He suddenly thrust his chair back and stood up. 'I'm going out for a bit. I need some air.'

'What about "afters"?' Phoebe asked.

'Sod "afters".'

As he left the kitchen Reynold banged the door behind him.

'Now look what you've done,' Phoebe said reprovingly to Roxanne.

'I'm sorry, Ma.'

'And so you should be, my girl.'

'But I meant what I said. The farm isn't enough for me, and never will be. Nothing can change that.'

'Roxanne!' Phoebe snapped. 'You should just thank the good Lord for what you've got, which is more than many.'

'Maybe so, Ma. But that doesn't mean it makes me happy.'

'Ungrateful,' Phoebe said tightly.

Linnet regarded her sister intently, realizing this wasn't a joke, Roxanne was in deadly earnest. An entertainer! What an extraordinary idea!

'You've really upset your father,' Phoebe told Roxanne. 'God knows how long before he'll calm down again.'

'And what about me?'

'What about you?'

'Doesn't it matter what I think or want? I'm my own person, after all, not just yours and Da's daughter.'

'You're being cheeky again.'

'Well, I don't see it that way. What's so wrong about going to London anyway? I know it's different, but surely that doesn't make it wrong?'

'To become what? A painted woman, that's what. A tart. It's well known females who go on the stage are that. And I'll not have you become one of those, not while I have breath in my body,' Phoebe declared vehemently, a hint of tears in her eyes.

Roxanne's face coloured. A tart! What did her mother take her for? That was not only unkind, but cruel and most unjustified.

'I think I'd better leave,' Linnet said, white-faced.

'No,' Roxanne husked. 'I will.'

'The washing-up needs doing,' Phoebe stated.

'I'll do it, Ma. Let Roxanne go.'

Roxanne rose. 'Thanks,' she mumbled to Linnet.

Linnet shot her sister a sympathetic look as Roxanne left the kitchen.

Roxanne eased the brick from the wall, then set it aside. The cows were restless, perhaps picking up her mood. Tails swished and feet rustled as she reached inside.

The chamois bag was damp, which didn't surprise her. A little green mould had grown just below the leather thong. She found that she was shaking as she undid the thong and shook the five golden sovereigns into the palm of her hand.

Money – *her* money which neither Ma nor Da knew anything about. As she stared at the coins she wondered why Linnet hadn't spoken up at the previous evening's supper table. Had Linnet forgotten the sovereigns? The shipwreck had been a couple of years ago after all, sufficient time for something to slip to the back of her mind. Why, months on end went by, without her even thinking about them, so why shouldn't Linnet forget when they were never mentioned?

Five pounds, five whole pounds – enough to do all sorts. Certainly enough to take her to London and get her established. Well, hopefully that was, for she was only too well aware how unworldly she was about financial matters.

Roxanne sat down in the straw covering the floor of the shippon, money in one hand, chamois bag in the other. What was she going to do? Run away of course. She couldn't, just couldn't, stay on at the farm; and all that meant. For if she did she'd regret it for the rest of her life. It would always be there, what might have been.

Well, it wasn't going to be what might have been, but what would be. She might fall flat on her face, come a cropper. But surely that was better than never taking a risk and staying at home full of resentment. She would run away, as soon as possible.

No, she thought, not as soon as possible. Let things die down, cool off. Let this episode seem to be forgotten. Then she would make her move. When the time was ripe and no-one would be watching, suspecting anything.

Now did she keep this to herself or tell Linnet? Keep it to herself, she decided. Why involve her sister when she didn't have to? Apart from anything else, could she trust Linnet to keep her mouth shut? She wasn't sure she could.

And another thing, if she did confide in Linnet and it came out afterwards that Linnet had known then Linnet would suffer as a consequence. It was best, for her sake and Linnet's, that Linnet remain in ignorance.

Run away? Her heart hammered at the thought. But run away she would. She was determined about that.

She returned the money to the bag and the bag to its niche behind the wall. Not too long though, she thought, not too long.

'Autumn Fair this Saturday,' Phoebe said, knitting needles clacking. She was making a new pullover for Reynold.

'So it be,' he nodded, and smiled, thinking of the St Petroc pubs. Cider and ale would be flowing.

'Can I have something to spend, Da?' Linnet asked.

He glanced over at her. 'For what?'

'To enjoy myself. Maybe have a go at one or two of the stalls.'

'Waste of money, girl.'

Roxanne, who'd been well aware that the fair was coming up,

kept silent. The day of the fair was the day she intended leaving. There was a Plymouth train shortly after 2 pm which she planned to be on.

'Aw, Da!'

'Money's too hard come by to be chucked away on silly things like coconut shies and the like.'

'You gave us something last year,' Linnet persisted.

'Did I?' he queried, pretending to have forgotten.

'A penny piece. Each.'

'Can't remember that,' he lied.

'You did, Reynold,' Phoebe said, knowing he was having Linnet on.

'Must have been mad. Tain't like me to go spoiling they girls with penny pieces.'

'We works hard enough for them,' Linnet declared in a rare bout of assertiveness.

Reynold stared at her. 'You complaining, girl?'

'No, Da, but—'

'You gets your keep and everything else,' he interjected. 'You're no hired hand but a member of this family. You works for your living and that's that. Money don't come into it.'

Roxanne was tempted to join the discussion at that point, but decided to remain silent.

'Reynold?' Phoebe smiled.

'Well, it don't,' he repeated.

'Aren't you taking this too far? She's only asking for a penny piece and tis Autumn Fair.'

'The Steam Circus is going to be there, I hear,' Linnet said. 'Would dearly love to go on that.' The Steam Circus was a merry-go-round powered by locomotive-driven electricity. The engine used was called the *Empress of the West*.

'You're too old for they shenanigans. That's children's stuff,' Reynold sneered.

'Nonetheless,' Linnet shrugged, suddenly embarrassed. 'Twould be nice. Children's stuff or no.'

'The boys would laugh at you,' Reynold taunted.

'No, they wouldn't,' Roxanne declared, breaking her silence. 'They'll think it fun.'

'And are you an expert on boys now?' Reynold jibed sarcastically.

She gazed at him, thinking how easy this made things for her. Any qualms she might have had were rapidly disappearing. For some reason she remembered the badger hunt, though why she should think of that after all this while eluded her. That dreadful day when they'd – She shuddered at the memory. No, it was right for her to go, as right as could be. She didn't belong here any more.

'Hardly,' she answered.

'There then,' he smiled triumphantly.

How stupid he was, she now realized, seeing him for the first time as a man and not her father. Stupid and limited. A sense of shame swept over her at the thought.

'You'll give them both a penny at least,' Phoebe said, thinking Reynold's little joke had turned sour and was needlessly upsetting both girls.

'I suppose,' he conceded.

How could she get her few possessions to the station? Roxanne wondered. It was a problem she still hadn't resolved.

Roxanne watched a heron wing its way past the farm. What an elegant bird, how graceful it was. She would miss herons, and swans, and otters, and—

'What you doing?'

Roxanne caught her breath, fearful her face might have been betraying her emotions. She turned to smile at Linnet. 'Nothing. Why?'

'You're looking gormless, that's why.'

'I was just watching that heron. Nothing wrong in that, is there?'

Linnet regarded her sister quizzically. 'Since when did you take to watching herons? Tain't ill, are ee?'

Roxanne laughed. 'No, I'm not ill. I simply thought . . . well, we see these things every day and take them for granted. And we shouldn't. They're beautiful.'

'Sometimes I worry about you,' Linnet declared quietly.

'Worry? There's no need for that.'

'But I do. You been so strange recently. Withdrawn, quiet. All into yourself, like.'

'Have I?' Roxanne queried innocently.

'As if you weren't there. Or here, or whatever.'

'You're imagining things.'

'No, I'm not. At least—' Linnet hesitated, 'I don't think I am.'

'Well, you are,' Roxanne lied. 'Now why don't you get on with your chores and let me get on with mine.'

'You weren't getting on with anything. Just standing there staring. Like you was moonstruck or something.'

'Moonstruck!' Roxanne laughed.

'Moonstruck,' Linnet repeated.

Roxanne gazed out over the fields and meadows. She was going to miss this place for it was all she'd ever known. She'd found happiness here, well, happiness of a sort. And now she was going to give all that up for who knew what?

Frightened? Yes, she was. She couldn't deny it. Frightened, but also, excited, excited beyond belief. This time tomorrow, all going to plan, she'd be on the train en route to Plymouth and then London.

London, the word thundered in her brain. London and the music hall. The unknown, the total unknown.

'Why you shivering?'

'Am I?'

Linnet sighed with exasperation. 'Of course you are. I wouldn't have said so otherwise.'

'Perhaps someone just walked over my grave,' Roxanne joked.

'That tain't no laughing matter. You wouldn't hear me saying something like that.'

No, Roxanne thought, you wouldn't. But how different she was to her sister. Chalk and cheese. 'Autumn fair tomorrow,' she said, changing the subject.

Linnet's face brightened. 'I'm looking forward to that.'

'Me, too,' Roxanne declared, meaning something quite else.

The heron reappeared to glide overhead, its long grey wings motionless as it scythed through the air.

'Me, too,' Roxanne repeated.

Reynold jumped down from the cart and tied up Barton. He was impatient to be off as he'd arranged to meet Joe Tregale and Dick Metherell. He couldn't wait for that first pint of cider.

'You go on while we get sorted out here,' Phoebe said, knowingly.

'You certain, lass?'

'I'm certain all right. And I'll hopefully see you later.'

'Right.'

'Da?' Linnet reminded him.

'What is it, girl?' he queried, well aware of what she was after.

'You promised.'

'Promised?'

'Stop your teasing now,' Phoebe told him.

Roxanne glanced at the gaily decorated Steam Circus which was mobbed by young and old. She saw Billy Christmas with

Bessie Burrow whom he'd recently started taking out. Bessie was a fat girl with legs like treetrunks and a face as plain as Billy's. They were a good match, however, and got on well enough.

Billy spotted Roxanne and gave her a wave. He was someone she'd miss, she thought, waving back. Good old Billy, the salt of the earth. There were lots of people she'd miss, mind you, and the animals – Ben their dog in particular.

'Here,' said Reynold, holding his hand out to Roxanne.

She accepted the penny. 'Thanks, Da.'

'Now I'll be off.' He winked at Phoebe. 'You'll find me in the King's Arms.'

'Roll up! Roll up!' shouted the coconut-shy man. He wasn't local, but there, like many of the stallholders, for the occasion.

'Tis busy,' commented Phoebe, as she undid the cart's back flap, thinking she should do good trade that day.

Roxanne and Linnet began sorting out the stacked boxes while Phoebe issued instructions on how she wanted them and their contents displayed.

'Hallo,' said Doll Pomeroy, stopping by the cart.

'Not helping your Ma?' Phoebe queried.

'I have been, but she's given me some time to go round the fair and see what's what.'

Linnet glanced hopefully at Phoebe. 'Not yet,' Phoebe said, correctly interpreting the look. 'You can go gallivanting later. In the meanwhile you're staying put.'

'Sorry,' Linnet shrugged to Doll.

'I'm going to try the lucky dip. And maybe play a game of skittles after that,' Doll informed them.

'See to Barton's feed, Linnet,' Phoebe instructed her.

'I'll do that,' Roxanne said quickly. She'd hidden the few belongings she was taking with her in the bottom of the feed bag; it was the only place she'd been able to think of to do so. As a consequence she didn't want anyone else handling the bag.

'There,' she declared, attaching the bag. She hoped Barton wouldn't get down to the bottom of the bag and start eating her clothes.

'How do, Phoebe,' smiled old Doc Pepperill, eyeing the produce already on show.

'How do, doctor. Enjoying the fair?'

Phoebe and the doctor chatted for a bit, during the course of which he made some purchases.

Roxanne glanced up at the church clock. It was hours before

her train was due to depart; the trick was going to be getting away and on it.

'Look!' exclaimed Linnet, pointing.

It was the first hot air balloon Roxanne had ever seen. She stared at it in fascination as it floated over the square.

'Imagine going up in one of they contraptions,' Phoebe mused, shaking her head.

Roxanne wondered about the people in the wicker basket. What a view they must have, able to see for miles.

'I wouldn't mind going up in it,' she said.

'You wouldn't?' Linnet queried incredulously.

'Sure. Twould be fun.'

'Not me. Not in a million years or for all the tea in China,' Linnet declared.

'Or me,' Phoebe added.

'Scaredycats,' Roxanne teased good humouredly, before her attention was claimed by a customer interested in their broccoli.

Mr Boal, the stationmaster, gazed at Roxanne in astonishment. 'For yourself, Roxanne?' he queried.

That was the trouble with a small town, Roxanne thought. Everyone knew everyone else and was nosey about their business. 'I'm going to visit my Aunt Elvira. She hasn't been well,' Roxanne lied smoothly. This was the explanation she'd previously worked out.

'I'm sorry to hear that,' Mr Boal sympathized, dealing with her ticket.

Roxanne handed over one of her precious sovereigns, then accepted both ticket and change.

'Ma and Da not seeing you off?' Mr Boal asked.

'They're busy. So's Linnet. Anyway, I'm a big girl now. I don't need no seeing off.'

Knowingly, he smiled; he had a lass the same age at home. She too liked to assert her independence whenever possible. 'Another five minutes to go. The train's bang on time.'

She was pleased to hear that. The last thing she needed was a delay.

She thanked Mr Boal and picked up the brown paper parcel at her feet containing her belongings. She then headed away from the ticket window and out onto the platform.

It had been difficult removing the parcel from Barton's feed bag without being seen, but eventually she'd managed it when Phoebe had gone to the lavatory and Linnet was busy with a customer. She'd then hidden the parcel amongst some rubbish.

Getting the parcel away from there had been easier than she'd envisaged. Linnet had decided to go off with a couple of pals, which enabled Roxanne to decline the invitation to join them, saying she preferred to be on her own.

And now here she was, at St Petroc station, all set to embark on her huge adventure.

Should she have left a letter? she wondered for the umpteenth time. For better or worse she'd decided not to. The family would soon work out what she'd done anyway. It shouldn't be too difficult for them to put two and two together.

Momentary panic almost engulfed her as the cream and brown liveried train puffed into view. It wasn't too late, she hadn't yet committed herself. There was no reason at all why she couldn't just turn round and return to the bosom of her family.

'No reason,' she heard herself mutter.

The train clanked to a halt amid exhalations of smoke and steam. Doors were opening, others closing.

'All aboard!' Mr Boal cried out.

Her hand was trembling as she reached for the brass handle in front of her; her senses reeling, her throat constricted. As if in a dream she climbed into the carriage and shut the door behind her.

A whistle blew, and the train shuddered into motion.

She'd done it, she thought. She'd done it.

The train was pulling away from the station when she saw the balloon again, soaring high in the sky. How gloriously free it looked, as free as she herself now was.

'Free,' she said.

Then she laughed. For en route to the station she'd spotted Cory Vranch arm in arm with Sally Tutching. It hadn't taken those two long!

For some inexplicable reason that dispelled her fears and trepidation. She watched the balloon getting smaller and smaller in the distance.

'Free,' she repeated as the train entered a tunnel and the balloon was lost to view.

'Where the hell is that girl?' Reynold raged. He and Linnet had already been round the square twice searching for her.

'This isn't like her at all,' Phoebe frowned. 'She's been gone ages.'

'Probably met some boy and forgot the time,' Linnet sniffed.

'Well, I'm damned if I'm standing here any longer. I'm going back to the pub,' Reynold declared.

Phoebe would have liked to accompany him, but felt she shouldn't in the circumstances. 'I'll stay on till Roxanne turns up,' she said.

'I'll do that, Ma. You go and have a drink with Da,' Linnet offered.

'I don't want the cart being left alone, mind. There are lots of strangers around today. Things could take a walk.'

'I won't leave it, Ma. Promise. And I'll send Roxanne to get you at the pub when she reappears.' Roxanne was in for it, Linnet thought. Her Da was furious.

'Bloody girl,' Reynold snarled, stamping off.

Phoebe hurried after him.

'That's it,' announced Reynold, placing his empty glass on the bar. 'There are animals needing to be fed and watered, so it's home for us. The girl can walk.'

Phoebe didn't blame Reynold for his anger. This was unforgivable of Roxanne. Unless . . . 'You don't think something's happened to her, do you?'

He barked out a short laugh. 'In St Petroc? Highly unlikely.'

'Still, you never know. And tis fair day with strangers about. Gypsies too, I saw a band of them earlier.'

He considered that. 'I doubt she's come to any harm. No, she's up to some sort of high jinks, you mark my words. And I wouldn't be at all surprised if it was with a boy as Linnet said.'

He reached down and touched his belt. She wasn't too old for a taste of that, by God. To keep him and her Ma waiting like this. Simply disappearing off without a by your leave.

Phoebe hoped they'd encounter Roxanne on their return to the cart, or find her there.

But they didn't. And she wasn't.

'I really am getting worried, Reynold,' Phoebe said. It was way past their usual bedtime and there was still no sign of Roxanne.

Reynold crossed to the window and glanced out. Could he be wrong and was something amiss? He couldn't believe that. It was just so unlikely.

'She's probably out there this moment scared to come in,' he declared.

Phoebe joined him at the window. That was a possibility. Roxanne must realize how cross her Da would be with her.

'We'll go to bed and I'll attend to her in the morning,' Reynold said, thinking she'd probably give them plenty of time to get to sleep before sneaking in. Well, that wouldn't do her any good, only prolong the confrontation.

He'd warm her arse when he got hold of her. The maid wouldn't be sitting down again in a hurry; he promised himself that.

He put a comforting arm round Phoebe. 'Don't you worry now, my lover. Tain't no more than high jinks on her part.'

'I pray you're right.'

'You'll see I am.'

Phoebe gave one last anxious glance out the window before turning away.

When Phoebe entered Roxanne's room the next morning, she found the bed hadn't been slept in. She stared at the bed in dismay, not knowing what to think.

'Where is she?' Reynold demanded, coming up behind Phoebe, belt dangling from his hand.

'She . . . doesn't seem to have been in all night,' Phoebe answered in a tight voice.

Linnet, wearing her dressing gown, appeared in the doorway. 'Ma?' she queried on seeing her parents' expressions.

'It's Roxanne,' Phoebe replied. 'She's stayed out all night.'

'*All night?*' Linnet breathed, wide-eyed.

'Oh Reynold,' Phoebe mumbled, now extremely worried.

He crossed to the bed and gazed at it. It definitely hadn't been slept in – unless she'd risen early, made it and gone out again. Could that be the case?

'Something's wrong. I know it,' Phoebe said.

Was it? Reynold wondered. Had he been mistaken? Was this more than high jinks?

Linnet glanced round the room. 'That's funny,' she commented.

'What?' queried Reynold.

'Her bracelet's gone. The gold one Aunt Elvira gave her. It's always there on the dresser.'

'Did she have it on yesterday?' Reynold frowned.

'No Da, I'm certain of that. She only ever wears it to church and on special occasions.'

''Twas fair day yesterday,' Phoebe pointed out.

'But Roxanne was working at the cart. She'd never wear it when she was working in case it got scratched or damaged in some way. She loves that bracelet.'

93

'Try the drawers. See if it's in any of those,' Phoebe instructed.

Linnet tried the drawers but didn't find either the bracelet or its box.

Why should the bracelet be missing? Phoebe asked herself. Could it have been stolen? Had there been a burglary?

'Go check your pendant,' she said to Linnet, as that was the only other item of real value in the house, except her wedding ring, which had never been off her hand since the day it had been put there.

Phoebe had a sudden, horrible thought. Walking swiftly to Roxanne's wardrobe she threw open its doors and peered inside.

Linnet returned clutching her pendant. 'Here tis, Ma.'

Phoebe glanced at Reynold. 'Some of her clothes are gone, her good dress for one.'

Reynold was baffled. 'Why should she take her clothes? I don't understand.'

'I think I'm beginning to,' Phoebe replied weakly. 'Her bracelet, her good dress. Her not coming home all night, just vanishing—' She broke off and swallowed hard. 'She's run off, Reynold.'

'Run – Don't be silly, woman. Why should she run off? And to where?'

'London,' Linnet stated suddenly. 'Could that be it? Remember the conversation about her wanting to be an entertainer in the music halls?'

Reynold was aghast. This was dreadful. Appalling. It couldn't be so. 'But how would she manage to run off? She had no money other than the penny piece I gave her yesterday.'

Linnet's hand went to her mouth as, with a blinding flash, she recalled the five golden sovereigns, something she'd completely forgotten about. The night of the wreck seemed so long ago, after all. And Roxanne had never mentioned them since.

'She had money, Da,' Linnet said quietly.

'What are you talking about?'

'Five pounds, Da.'

'Five—' He stared at Linnet in astonishment. 'How did she come by five pounds?'

Linnet told them then about the wreck, how Roxanne had gone off with Billy Christmas while she'd remained at home fearing her father's wrath.

Reynold's face was thunderous as he sat on the edge of Roxanne's bed. He was stunned.

'I could be wrong,' Phoebe said hesitantly. 'Perhaps there are other reasons for all this. Another explanation.'

'That maid was always too headstrong for her own good,' Reynold hissed. 'And now this. An . . . entertainer.'

He gave Phoebe a stricken look. 'Think of the shame and embarrassment if this gets round. What will people say? I'll never be able to hold my head up again. The disgrace.'

Phoebe knew that was true. She could already hear the sniggers and quiet guffaws. Her neck reddened at the thought.

Reynold started to shake. 'It don't bear thinking about, Phoebe, it just don't. We'd never live it down.'

'How could she?' whispered Phoebe vehemently. If Roxanne had been there, and it was true, she'd have taken Reynold's belt to her herself.

'Being on stage is no better than being a common prostitute,' Reynold choked.

Phoebe shuddered. Her daughter, *that*.

'She must have caught the train,' Linnet mused. 'Which she could easily afford if she'd taken five pounds with her.'

'Or perhaps someone gave her a lift,' Reynold said. 'There were plenty there yesterday who'd come from a distance. She might have gone with one of they.'

'You must try the station,' Phoebe told him. 'For if she went by train Jim Boal would have seen her.'

Reynold came to his feet. 'Good idea. I'll go there straight-away.'

'I'll get your breakfast first.'

He shook his head. 'I couldn't eat a thing. Not a morsel.' It was the first time in their entire married life that he'd refused breakfast, a reflection on his emotional turmoil.

'Jesus Christ,' he muttered as he left the room.

'Well?' Phoebe demanded the moment he stepped through the front door.

He nodded. 'She took the train all right. Told Jim Boal that her Aunt Elvira was ill and that she was going to help out.'

'Did you tell Jim otherwise?'

'No, I let him go on believing that was true.'

Phoebe's shoulders slumped. What a huge relief! If Jim had been aware of the true story it would have been all round St Petroc by now.

'No-one must ever know, especially that she plans to be an entertainer,' Reynold declared.

'No,' Phoebe agreed.

'We must keep up the pretence that she's gone to Elvira's.'

'And if she don't come back?'

He ran a hand through his hair. 'I suppose we can only say she likes it so much there she's decided to settle with your sister.'

'Folks will think it queer that she never visits though?'

'We'll think of something,' Reynold said heavily.

The tears Phoebe had so far held back now oozed from her eyes. Their good name and standing in the community had been saved, there was at least that. But her baby, her darling baby whom she loved so much, had gone, perhaps for ever. The thought that she may never see Roxanne again, or never touch her, proved too much. Phoebe staggered, and would have collapsed if Reynold hadn't caught her and held her tight.

'My baby,' Phoebe whimpered, face now awash.

Reynold did the best he could to console his distraught wife.

Chapter Five

'That's a funny accent you've got.'

Roxanne recognized the speaker as Harry Bright. He was part of the line-up currently appearing at the Angel Inn, Islington, where she'd found employment as a barmaid. 'No funnier than yours,' she riposted quickly.

Harry threw back his head and laughed. '*Touché*! I like a woman who can give as good as she gets.'

A woman! A little thrill of pleasure ran through her to be called that – not girl, not maid, but woman. 'I can certainly do that all right.' She wondered what *touché* meant.

'So where are you from?'

'I'm a Devon dumpling.'

He waggled his dark eyebrows at her. 'There's nothing of a dumpling about you. Not from where I'm sitting, there isn't.'

That too pleased her. 'You're a Londoner from the way you speak.'

'Hackney, born and bred. A Cockney through and through.' He pronounced it frew and frew.

He had a sip of his pint, regarding her over the rim of his glass. 'How long have you been in the big city?'

'Two months now.'

'Enjoying it?'

She nodded. 'I think it's wonderful.'

'What you expected?'

'Better.'

'Best city in the Empire. The whole world come to that. Cities don't come better than dear old London town.'

He was very personable, she thought, easy to talk to and good looking with it. Not as good looking as Cory Vranch, but good looking nonetheless. How old? That was difficult to judge. She suspected he had a face older than his actual years.

She took in his appearance. Neat grey suit, striped tie, an immaculate white collar. She noted that he had the typical London pallor, a complete contrast to her own healthy, country complexion.

'I'm Harry Bright,' he said suddenly, extending a hand.

'I know. I watched your act the other night.'

He gave her a dazzling smile. 'And?'

'You were very good. I think I laughed at all your jokes.' Harry was a combined singer-comedian.

'I'd be disappointed if you hadn't,' he mocked, eyes twinkling with good humour.

'Don't be vain.'

'Vain. Me!' He pretended outrage. 'I can never be accused of that, Miss . . . ?' He trailed off, and raised his eyebrows.

'Hawkins. Roxanne Hawkins.'

'Can I call you Roxanne, or would you consider that too forward?'

'Roxanne, of course. The other barmaids are called by their Christian names so I can hardly expect to be any different.'

'Ah, but you are different. You're special.'

What a charmer, she thought. But there didn't seem to be any harm in him. 'Why special?' she asked coyly.

'You have quality, it shines out. I noticed it the first time I looked at you.'

'Quality,' she mused. 'But I'm only a farm girl.'

'Your background has nothing to do with it. Quality is something you're born with. And you have it.'

She'd have loved to believe him, but warned herself it was probably only flattery.

'A pint of mild, darling!' a man requested from further along the bar.

'Excuse me,' she smiled to Harry, and moved away.

He produced a gold cigarette case, removed a cigarette, tapped one end on the case, then lit it with a gold lighter. While doing this he studied Roxanne.

When she'd finished pulling the pint and ascertained there were no other customers waiting to be served, Roxanne wondered whether to stay where she was or move back to Harry. Her dilemma was solved when he drained his drink and held the glass out to her.

'Where are you staying?' he inquired as she took it.

'Upstairs. I live in.'

'Nice room?'

She shrugged. 'It'll do.'

So it wasn't so nice, he thought. 'What are your plans? I mean, have you simply come to London to work at anything or do you have something specific in mind?'

'I want to do the same as you,' she informed him.

'Really!'

'I'm a singer. Or at least let's say I can sing.'

'And you want to move into the halls?'

She nodded.

This was interesting. 'And how are you going about it?'

'I'm not yet. Finding this job was a start. I still haven't figured out what to do next. Any suggestions?'

He considered that. 'A lot of people try to join the halls. In the end it all boils down to talent and drive.'

At this point their conversation was interrupted by a sudden influx of noisy customers who milled round the bar clamouring to be served. It was the beginning of an extremely busy period during which Harry left without Roxanne seeing him go.

Roxanne blew out her candle, climbed into bed and drew the thin coverings up to her chin. The bed was hard and uncomfortable, not like the comfy one that she'd had at home.

She wondered how her family were, Linnet in particular. Had her sister found a new boyfriend yet? She missed them and the farm, but that was only natural. She certainly didn't miss them enough to want to return.

She thought about London and the sights she'd seen since she'd arrived. Her heart still raced with excitement when she walked along Upper Street, which she did as often as she could. She'd start at Islington Green and stroll all the way to Highbury Corner where she'd turn round and walk back again along the opposite side.

She never failed to be thrilled by the fancy carriages that rattled past, some of them containing women wearing breathtakingly gorgeous dresses. And such beautiful hats. How she envied them. Some day, she promised herself, some day.

The sound of raised voices came from next door. It was Bert, who owned the pub, a fearsome bear of a man, and his wife Rose. Roxanne sighed, those two were always quarrelling, night after night, often keeping her awake. And if they weren't fighting, they were in bed making love.

She'd been appalled when she'd first heard them. The bed had squeaked as Rose became more and more vocal, until with a last unmistakable cry, it was all over.

She thought of Harry Bright. He'd returned that evening to do his act, but they hadn't spoken further. He had caught her eye and winked though, which had pleased her.

Nice chap, Harry, if a real smooth talker. Perhaps he could help her in some way? That was always possible. Was he married? she wondered. She hadn't noticed a wedding ring, but that didn't mean anything. On reflection she doubted he was the sort to wear one. Not that it mattered to her whether he was married or not.

Her mind turned to the two other live-in barmaids, Judy and Babs, neither of whom had any aspirations towards the halls. They were friendly enough, and she got on well with both of them. Judy was a blowsy redhead while Babs was considerably older. Judy was walking out with a costermonger who ran a barrow in nearby Chapel Market.

She adored the wit and humour of the costermongers as they chatted with each other and their customers. She hadn't been to Chapel Market yet without getting at least one appreciative wolf whistle with the occasional ribald suggestion thrown in.

She winced as she heard the crack of a heavy slap from next door; Rose would have felt that. Then, almost immediately, the bed began to squeak. She wondered why Rose put up with it, for they didn't have any children. But even at her tender age she was wise enough to know that a married relationship could be far from simple. Maybe, despite everything, Rose loved Bert. Maybe he even loved her.

Whatever, she could have done without the squeaking. And Rose's moaning which started shortly afterwards.

'Give us a kiss, luv?'

A middle-aged man with bleary, drink-sodden eyes and a red nose addressed Roxanne. He'd just downed his fourth large Booth's.

'You behave yourself now,' she replied with a smile. She glanced about, wishing Babs would reappear. She was alone behind the bar.

'You're a real smasher, doll, know that?' the man slurred.

'Ta very much.'

'I mean it. A smasher.'

Suddenly the man's hand darted forward to grab her arm. 'Now what about that kiss, eh?'

She struggled to free herself, but couldn't. Other customers were watching, but no-one made the slightest move to intervene. They seemed amused by the situation.

'Let me go,' she pleaded, a tremor in her voice.

'Only after I get a kiss. Otherwise—' The man's face contorted into an ugly leer as he squeezed her arm.

'Let me go,' she repeated in alarm. 'You're hurting me.'

'And you're hurting me. Want me to show you?'

For a moment she didn't realize what he meant by that. Then the penny dropped. She went scarlet. Surely he wouldn't expose himself in a public place!

He squeezed even harder while some of those present laughed at her predicament. The man pulled her until she was stretched halfway across the bar. She closed her eyes in disgust as horrible, wet lips homed in on her own. But the lips never arrived on target.

A brass-tipped cane flashed, smashing into the back of the man's head. With a roar the man released Roxanne and swung on his assailant.

'I wouldn't if I were you,' Harry Bright smiled lazily.

The man launched himself at Harry, who neatly sidestepped, and tripped up the man, who went sprawling. Harry's foot thudded into him, just below the man's ribcage.

'What's going on here?' Bert, the owner, demanded, elbowing his way through the crowd.

'Our friend on the floor was molesting Roxanne. I put a stop to it,' Harry informed Bert.

Bert glared at the man who was now struggling upright. 'I've had trouble with you, Sam, for the last time. You're barred. Show your nose in here again and I'll flatten it for you.'

Having said that the bearlike Bert twisted Sam's arm behind his back and frogmarched him to the door where he unceremoniously threw him out into the street.

'Thank you,' Roxanne said to Harry, much relieved.

'Don't mention it. Pleased to be able to help a fair damsel in distress.'

'You were the only one,' Roxanne declared, glancing accusingly at the others.

'Only a bit of sport, luv,' one mumbled.

'You wouldn't call it that if it had been you.'

They all laughed.

Bert returned. 'Thanks, Harry. He's a nasty piece of work, and no mistake. Especially when he's had one too many.'

'I'm just pleased I was here.'

Bert turned to Roxanne. 'You all right?'

'Shaken.'

'Sorry, but that sort of thing happens from time to time. It is a pub, after all. Take a break and have a cup of tea. Rose has a pot on the go.'

'Thanks again,' she smiled to Harry.

He touched his hat in salute. 'Any time, Princess. Any time.'

She was not only shaken but shaking, she discovered as she left the bar.

Reynold paused in the kitchen doorway to stare at Phoebe who was slumped over the kitchen table. Head on hands, she was quietly sobbing.

His face furrowed with concern. How many times now had he found her like this? More than he cared to remember.

Going over to her, he squatted and put his arms round her waist. 'Phoebe love, this has got to stop. Tain't doing no good.'

She raised a tear-stained face to gaze at him. 'I know,' she croaked. 'But I just can't help it. I'm all right one moment, and then the next—' She trailed off in despair.

'Is there anything I can do? Get you?'

'Only my baby back.'

Reynold sighed. 'That I can't do, Phoebe. She's gone to London, could be anywhere there. It's just too big a place to try and search. I wouldn't even know where to start.'

'I thought I would soon get over it. But I haven't. If anything it just gets worse and worse.'

Blast and damn Roxanne! he mentally swore. The anguish and torment she'd inflicted on her mother were tearing Phoebe apart. His anger deepened even further.

Phoebe ran a hand over her face. Get hold of yourself, she thought, pull yourself together. But still the tears continued to flow.

Reynold noted that Phoebe had lost even more weight; why, she'd become no more than a scrawny bag of bones, while her face had lined and sunk in on itself. Her hair was now streaked with grey where before it had been pure auburn, hair that had become limp and lacklustre.

It was then that everything he'd felt towards his younger

daughter turned inside out, love into hate. And it came to him what he could do as a small act of revenge. Pay a little back for what she'd done to his darling Phoebe.

'Sit down, Reynold,' said Peter Wonnacott, senior partner in the St Petroc law firm of Wonnacott, Brooks and Hodge. 'Now what can I do for you?'

Reynold eased himself into a red leather armchair. 'I want to change my will, Peter.'

'Oh?'

'I want to cut my daughter Roxanne right out of it. As you know, not having a son to take over the farm when I'm gone, I instructed you to have it sold after Phoebe's death if she survives me, and after mine should I survive her, the proceeds equally split tween Linnet and Roxanne. It seemed the fairest way to me of dividing things up.'

Peter Wonnacott nodded. 'That's how I recollect it, Reynold.'

'Well, I wants to change that. Linnet's to get everything. Lock, stock and chicken coop.'

Peter sat back and regarded Reynold thoughtfully. 'It's none of my business, but that seems a bit harsh.'

'That's right, Peter, tain't none of your business. I've no need to give you reasons for what I do,' Reynold replied coldly. 'Your job is simply to carry out my instructions.'

'Fair enough,' Peter replied with a strained smile. 'Then let's get down to it, shall we?'

'Right,' Reynold nodded with satisfaction.

Roxanne frantically searched through the drawer where she'd left her treasured bracelet, but it wasn't there. It was gone.

Stolen, she thought, feeling sick. There was no other explanation for it. Stolen, but by whom?

She checked the drawer again before going in search of Bert.

'Why so glum?' Harry asked.

'I've had a gold bracelet stolen from my room.'

'Real gold or gilt?'

'Real gold, eighteen carat,' she told him. 'A present a few years back from my Aunt Elvira.'

'Must have been worth a bob or two.'

'I don't know how much exactly, but a lot.' Roxanne shook her head. 'It wasn't only the value, I loved that bracelet. It was beautiful.'

'Have you told Bert?'

'He said I was stupid to leave such a thing in an unlocked room. Which I suppose is true now I come to think of it. But where else could I have left it?'

Harry felt sorry for Roxanne who he could see was dreadfully upset. It was a nasty thing to happen. 'Bert's safe for one,' he suggested drily.

Roxanne stared blankly at him. 'I never thought of that.'

'Or you could have worn it. Only taking it off when you were in your room.'

'It was too precious to wear behind the bar. It might have got knocked or scratched.'

But not stolen, Harry thought. The girl really was green. 'Has Bert questioned the rest of the staff?'

'He did, earlier. But they all denied knowing anything about the theft. I asked Bert to call in the police, but he refused. And told me I'd get the sack if I did.'

Harry glanced about, ensuring they weren't being overheard. 'Bert wouldn't want the police nosing around. Doesn't like the Peelers, does Bert.'

'But why?'

Harry shrugged. 'That's for him to know and us to wonder about. I can only say he looks distinctly nervous whenever Bobbies come in. So make of that what you will.'

'Bert said he thought it was a customer who'd nipped up to my room, and that there was no point calling in the police as the bracelet would have been sold on by now.'

'He's probably right. It's doubtful they'd recover a small article like that, especially round here. I'm afraid it's long gone and you'll just have to accept the fact.'

Roxanne dropped her head to stare at the floor. Suddenly she felt very alone, lost even. For two pins she'd have . . . No, she put that thought from her mind. She wouldn't admit defeat. Why she hadn't even begun yet.

'How are you getting on with your singing?'

'I'm not,' she confessed. 'I have asked Bert to listen to me, give me an audition. But I can never tie him down. I don't think he takes me seriously.'

'Lots more venues, if you have the right material.'

'That's what's putting me off. I've been round a few of the music shops trying to find a new song but so far haven't come up with anything suitable.'

Nor would she, Harry thought. A new song such as she was

104

looking for was like gold dust. And certainly wasn't to be found in a music shop. You needed contacts.

'Tell you what, would it cheer you up if I was to listen to you?'

A smile lit up her face. 'Would you, Harry?'

He pointed an elegant finger at her. 'As long as you realize I'll be totally honest. I'm not about to give anyone false hopes, it's far too hard a game for that.'

'That's good enough for me,' she declared, delighted. 'Where and when?'

He smiled at her enthusiasm. 'I'll ask Bert if we can use his stage. As to when, any time during the day. How about your dinner break?'

'Fine by me.'

'Tomorrow?'

'I'll be here, waiting.'

'I'll go and have a word with Bert to make sure that's all right, and report back to you.'

Roxanne watched Harry walk away, now nervous at the prospect of singing for him. She'd sing the number she'd sung at the concert, the song she'd intended singing for Bert.

'Totally honest,' Harry had said. She was sure he would be and prayed it was in her favour.

Raw, Harry thought, with no sense of presentation whatever. But the voice was good, no denying that. And, perhaps most important of all, she had charisma.

When Roxanne had finished she came to the front of the stage and stared at Harry. 'At least you didn't fall asleep,' she joked.

He laughed. 'No, I didn't. Now come on down, I want to talk to you.'

Before she'd started, she'd been extremely nervous, a feeling which had completely disappeared the moment she'd opened her mouth. Now it came rushing back.

He gestured to the seat beside him. 'You have potential,' he announced.

That was what she'd wanted, craved, to hear.

'But there's a lot you need to learn.'

'Will you teach me?'

'I could do,' he demurred.

'Harry!'

How fresh and innocent she was, he thought, so unlike the women he was used to. He found it extremely attractive.

He wondered what she'd be like stripped off, and how she'd be in bed. A virgin? Probably. But there again—

He was certainly very attracted to her, not simply because she was pretty, but for herself. He thoroughly enjoyed being with her.

'Let me think about it,' he said.

Her face fell. 'Is that a polite way of saying no?'

'It's a polite way of saying I want to think about it. Now can we leave it there?'

'I suppose so,' she replied, rising.

He took out his pocket watch and glanced at it. 'I have to be off. I'm afraid I have another engagement.'

'When will I hear from you?'

He rose also and surprised her by kissing the tip of her nose. 'When I've decided what's what. All right?'

She could hardly argue. 'All right. And Harry, whatever, thanks for listening.'

'My pleasure,' he smiled.

She hoped it had been, she fervently hoped so.

Harry sipped his glass of claret and went back to staring into the fire Mrs Murphy had set earlier. Mrs Murphy owned the house in Duncan Terrace where he rented rooms. He was thinking about Roxanne.

What was it he'd said to her? She had potential. Well, she definitely had that, no doubt about it. On reflection her voice had been more than good, it had been damn good, like a bloody canary.

Oh, he could teach her all right, if she could learn. And he thought she could. But that wasn't what he was finding disturbing. It was her. She'd been in his thoughts more and more of late. And now this opportunity had presented itself.

So what was he to do? He pondered that. And while he thought he considered his own position. He was doing well, earning quite a bit. But no matter how hard he tried, he couldn't break out of the lower echelons of the music hall. The big venues and bills eluded him.

Why? he asked himself, not for the first time. Lack of talent? He didn't believe that for a moment. His material? He'd changed that a number of times without achieving the breakthrough. So why?

He just didn't have an answer. Or if he did, it was simply to keep banging away in the hope that one day the doors would open, doors that until then had remained firmly shut.

106

He could change his act yet again. But in what way? In which direction?

Comedy was his stronger suit, he knew that. There were nights when he was singing when he felt himself losing his audience in the middle of a number. Not losing them entirely, that had never happened, but not keeping them gripped like a top-class performer. Drop the singing and go all comedy? He could do that. It was a possibility. Or he could introduce something else in the place of singing, a new counterpoint. A comedy dance routine perhaps? An Irish or Scotch jig? They were always popular. Or what about a musical instrument? He could play the trumpet, though not very well.

Or – he sipped his claret – take on a partner. Someone to brighten up the act, add depth and colour. A female who could also be a stooge to his gags. That would mean splitting the money, of course, but he would take the lion's share. And it could be the key to opening those doors he'd been banging against.

He smiled; Roxanne. She was just the ticket with those looks of hers. The men in the audience would lap her up. And her voice, which was much better than his, would bring a finer balance to the act.

He nodded to himself. It also meant he'd get to see a great deal of her. He liked the thought of that.

He'd give it a go, he decided, wondering what she'd make of the suggestion.

Roxanne knew the Old Parr's Head in Upper Street, but had never been inside. Old Parr was a Shropshire man called Robert who'd died in 1757 at the age of 124.

Harry, who'd arranged to meet her there, rose when she appeared. 'What can I get you?' he asked when she reached his table.

'Lemonade would be fine.'

'Nothing stronger?'

She shook her head.

'You sit down then. I won't be a tick.'

She glanced round as he went to the bar. The pub had a far better tone than the Angel Inn with lots of prints and brasses on the walls. The clientele appeared more respectable than those who used the Angel.

'There you are,' said Harry, placing her drink on the table.

She was hoping he'd made this rendezvous to tell her that he would teach her. If not, she'd argued with herself, surely he'd simply have told her across the bar at the Angel.

'Before we start I have something for you,' Harry declared. From his jacket pocket he produced a red velvet box which he laid in front of her.

'For me?' she queried in astonishment.

'Go on, open it.' He sat back and watched her, looking amused.

Her mouth dropped when she saw what was inside the box. It was a gold bracelet.

'Eighteen carat, same as the one you had stolen,' Harry informed her.

'But . . . but—' She trailed off, momentarily lost for words.

'Like it?'

'It's gorgeous.'

'I thought so too. Now go on, put it on.'

Her fingers were trembling as she took the bracelet and fastened it round her wrist.

'They had fancy, engraved ones at the jeweller's, but I decided plain would suit you best.'

'The other was plain, too. But Harry, I can't possibly accept this. I – Well, I hardly know you. It wouldn't be right or proper.'

'Let me judge what's right and proper. Anyway, as for not knowing me well enough, that's something we're about to change. Providing you agree to what I have in mind, that is.'

He was going to ask her to walk out with him, she thought wrongly. What came next was a bombshell.

'A double act?'

'Bright and Breeze. Get it? The name came to me in my bath this morning.'

'Bright and Breeze,' she repeated.

'You're the Breeze, of course.'

'You want me to change my name, then?'

'Why not? People in the business do it all the time. I did so myself. My real name's Potts.' He pulled a face. 'Not very glamorous or memorable that, eh? Harry Potts?'

She giggled. Nothing could have been more ordinary or less theatrical than Harry Potts.

'Bright and Breeze,' he smiled. 'It has something. A certain zing!'

'Will I still be Roxanne?'

'I thought we should change that as well. How about Annie? Shortened version of Roxanne you see.'

Annie Breeze? How strange to think of herself being called that. It was so completely different to Roxanne Hawkins.

'I think it a good name for the halls,' Harry went on. 'Will look just dandy on a bill.'

All this had quite taken Roxanne's breath away. The bracelet, the proposed double act, the change of name – her mind was whirling.

'So you'll keep the bracelet, won't you? Look on it as a gift to celebrate the start of our professional relationship. If you're in favour of that relationship, that is?'

'Of course I am, Harry. How could I possibly refuse?'

'Now,' he declared, rubbing his hands briskly together. 'Let's get down to details. We're going to need lots of time together during the day, which means you'll have to give up barmaiding.'

'I can't do that, Harry,' she protested. 'I couldn't keep myself otherwise.'

'You don't have to worry about that. I'll pay all your bills until such time as you're earning.'

'Can you afford to do that?' she frowned, not at all certain it was a good idea.

'I don't think you understand just how much money can be made in the halls. And I play three venues every night, the Gluepot and the Highbury Barn as well as the Angel Inn, which ensures I'm well in pocket at the end of the week.'

'The Gluepot?'

'A nickname for Deacon's Music Hall. It's a dump, but popular.'

'But where would I stay, Harry?'

He reached across and patted her hand. 'I've already spoken to Mrs Murphy who owns the house where I have digs. She has a vacant room which she'll be only too happy to rent to you. You'll like Mrs Murphy, she's quite a character and fusses over her girls like an old mother hen.'

'There are other girls living there, then?'

'Three.'

'And men?'

'Only yours truly, I'm afraid. I have two of the best rooms in the house, up on the top floor. Your room is on the landing below.'

'And you'll pay for that, too?'

'Until you're up and running.'

'What about Bert?' she queried. 'He isn't going to be pleased.'

'You leave Bert to me. I'll handle him.'

She gazed at her lemonade, which remained untouched. It was all so much to take in at one go. Within the space of a few minutes her entire life had been transformed. This was a dream come true.

'When do we start?' she asked.

'Just as soon as possible. I'll go back to the Angel Inn with you and explain the situation to Bert. You might even be able to move into Duncan Terrace today if he's agreeable. Though I suspect that might be pushing it a little.'

He indicated her bracelet. 'And for the rest of your stay there I'd recommend you don't take that off. Not unless you want it to go bye-bye like the other.'

She moved into Duncan Terrace the following weekend; luckily Bert had found a replacement in the meantime.

'Deliver the song, don't sodding comment on it,' Harry called to Roxanne from out front. 'Get feeling into the words and, above all, meaning. The audience won't understand what you're singing if you don't.'

He came to the bottom of the stage and glared up at her. 'Another thing, you've got a cracking figure, flaunt it. Thrust out that bosom. Men love a fine pair of tits.'

Roxanne blushed.

'And there's no need to go all coy on me. There's a lot of earthy talk backstage, including from the so-called ladies. They'll f and blind with the best of them.'

'I'm not sure I understand what you mean by comment,' Roxanne queried.

He pulled himself up on stage. They were rehearsing in the Angel Inn as Bert had kindly allowed them to use his facilities. 'Comment means exactly that: spoken without conviction or understanding. Why, you might be reading out a shopping list. Deliver the lines, Roxanne, what you're doing is throwing them away.

'As for the singing, you've a powerful voice, use it. Belt out the number. When we get to proper theatres you'll have to hit the back of the gallery. The public have paid their money to hear you and that's what you must give them. Now you're quite capable of that, it's simply a matter of energy, oomph and commitment.'

'I'll try.'

'That's my girl.' He touched her cheek. 'Don't get too downhearted, you're coming on fine. Rome wasn't built in a day, you know.'

'I just feel so . . . inadequate.'

'Then don't. You've got the talent and equipment, it's just learning how to project them across the footlights.'

'Shall I start again at the beginning?' she queried.

He considered that. 'No, you've done enough for one morning. Let's get a bite to eat. And I could certainly use a pint.'

He stared at her as she gathered up her music. The clothes she was wearing, a shapeless black skirt and faded print blouse, were just too provincial, highly unsuitable for a music-hall artist. He'd have to do something about that.

And then there was her costume. He hadn't decided on that yet. Nor if he would change what he normally wore on stage. He had been considering pierrot outfits, but had gone off the idea. Another thought had been to present them both as tramps, but that was wrong as well.

It would come to him in time. All he had to do was keep on thinking. In the meantime he'd have to invest a few quid in her wardrobe. Nothing too extravagant, but reasonable enough for her to be presentable. Clothes maketh the man after all and, more importantly, the woman.

'What are you doing tonight?' he asked.

'I don't have any plans.'

'Then get yourself to Collins Music Hall on the Green. Marie Lloyd is making a guest appearance in aid of some charity or other. Watch and learn, you won't find a more talented or professional artist on the halls than her. There's someone who can belt out a number. And no-one works their audience better. She's brilliant.'

'I'll be there,' Roxanne promised.

'I'll arrange for a ticket to be waiting for you at the door. Might not get in otherwise. It's rare for there to be an empty seat in the house when the great Marie Lloyd sings.'

He took a deep breath. 'There's someone I want you to meet shortly.'

'An artist?'

'No, a friend. Her name's Celeste.'

Now who was Celeste? Roxanne wondered. When she asked Harry he told her she'd find out soon enough.

Harry and Roxanne were ushered into a small, but splendidly decorated, drawing room by a young maid. The seated woman awaiting them had lustrous brown hair piled on top of her head, a delicate fine-boned face and a body to match. She admitted to being twenty-five but was in fact thirty-three.

'Harry darling!' she exclaimed in delight.

Harry went straight to her, lifted her hand to his mouth and kissed it. 'How are you, dear Celeste?'

'Never better. And yourself?'

'Can't complain.'

Extricating her hand she waggled a ringed finger at him. 'You're a naughty boy, Harry, I haven't seen you for ages.'

'Only several weeks actually,' he replied drily. 'I've been busy.'

Deep brown eyes swung onto Roxanne. 'Ah yes, with your partner whom you told me about in your note. Miss Annie Breeze.'

Uncertain, Roxanne came forward, slightly overawed to be in the presence of such a lady. How on earth did Harry come to know this grand and ravishing creature?

She took in Celeste's dress which was a pale coffee colour, trimmed with masses of matching lace. The dress was tightly waisted, its skirt adorned with crossover folds. The sleeves stopped at the elbow with the addition of further lace that fell halfway down the lower arm.

'How do you do?' Roxanne mumbled, not sure whether to shake Celeste's hand or not.

Celeste solved the problem by rising and taking Roxanne's hand in her own. 'I'm delighted to meet you, Annie.'

'And I you.'

'Now, how about a glass of sherry. Harry, will you do the honours?'

While Harry was at the decanter Celeste invited Roxanne to sit down, as she returned to the chair she'd occupied on their arrival.

'Harry and I are old chums, aren't we, dear,' Celeste explained, correctly guessing what was going through Roxanne's mind.

Roxanne smiled. 'Really.'

'Oh, we go back a long time.'

'Celeste comes from Hackney same as me,' Harry said, pouring sherry into exquisite crystal glasses.

Roxanne was incredulous. Hackney!

Celeste gave a low, amused laugh. 'Things aren't always what they appear. I learned that early on.'

Her accent was flawless, Roxanne thought, without a trace of her origins. She sounded like she'd been born and brought up in Mayfair.

'Celeste was a proper actress who's appeared at Drury Lane. Haven't you, darling?'

'The zenith of my career.'

'She was very good too. I can vouch for that.'

'Not that you ever saw me much.'

'Well, most of the time you were out of town!' he protested.

Celeste sighed. 'I'm afraid all my good roles were out of town. I never really cracked it with the London managements.'

'But you just said you'd appeared at Drury Lane?' Roxanne frowned.

'Bit parts, darling. A line here, a couple there. Nothing really to get one's teeth into.'

Roxanne gazed round the drawing room. So how could Celeste afford all this? Unless she'd married well, that could be the explanation. She'd ask Harry later.

She sipped the sherry Harry had given her. It was a bit dry for her taste, she'd have preferred it sweeter, but it was delicious nonetheless. As for the glass itself, that was a joy to look at and hold.

'Now to the purpose of our visit which Annie knows nothing about,' Harry smiled. 'Celeste is taking you into the West End to buy you some clothes. I would have done it myself but she has far better taste in that department.'

The West End to buy clothes! Roxanne's excitement clearly showed on her face.

'We'll have a wonderful time. You'll see,' Celeste said to Roxanne.

Roxanne was certain they would.

Harry crossed over and laid a buff envelope on the mantelpiece. 'That should be sufficient for her needs,' he declared. 'And now I'll get on and leave you two to it.'

Celeste summoned the maid to see Harry out, at the same time instructing her carriage to be brought to the door.

Roxanne glanced excitedly about her. The West End! If only Linnet could see her now, her sister would spit with jealousy. While her Ma, well Phoebe simply wouldn't believe her eyes.

'You're a Devonian, aren't you?' Celeste queried.

Roxanne nodded.

'I thought so. Played Exeter once, charming city.'

'I'm from further south, close to the Cornish border. Just outside a place called St Petroc.'

'Sounds quaint.'

The pair of them chatted while they rattled down Bond Street.

Roxanne was now quite at ease in the older woman's company. Her eyes were continually flicking from side to side, not wanting to miss anything. This was a memory to treasure.

Roxanne flew to her door when she heard the knock. Harry was standing in the corridor, smiling.

'How did it go?' he asked.

'Wonderful. Simply wonderful!'

She slowly turned round. 'What do you think?'

He eyed the blue cotton dress with long lapels, fastened in the middle by a pale pink and blue bow. The generously cut sleeves had a shawl effect when she extended her arms.

'Very becoming,' he replied approvingly.

'The other two are being made for me, as is the coat. Why Harry, it must have cost a fortune.'

'Hardly that, though expensive enough,' he answered drily.

'I'll pay you back, every penny. I promise.'

The change in her appearance was quite startling, he thought. She looked quite the young lady. If anything, he was even more attracted to her.

'What about footwear?'

She lifted the hem of her dress to reveal pretty little black lace-up boots.

'Very elegant,' he murmured, gazing at her neat ankles and wondering what her legs were like. He had no doubt they were good ones though.

'I've arranged an appointment with a theatrical dress designer for tomorrow afternoon. I'll send Celeste a note asking if she can come with us. I'd appreciate her advice.'

'I liked her a lot,' Roxanne declared.

'She liked you, too. I could tell.'

Roxanne gazed up and down the corridor to ensure there were no listening ears. 'Is she married?'

Harry's expression became one of wry amusement. 'No.'

'Then . . . I mean how—?'

'Can she afford to live as she does?'

Roxanne nodded.

'She has an extremely wealthy patron, for want of a better word, who pays all her bills.'

'You mean—' Roxanne trailed off in consternation.

'That's right, Celeste is someone's mistress. He met her while she was at Drury Lane and one thing led to another. She's extremely fond of him and he simply idolizes her.'

'I take it he's married?'

'Oh yes.'

Roxanne was intrigued. 'Can I ask who he is?'

'Celeste will have to tell you that herself, should she ever choose to. I know, of course, but won't break a confidence.'

'I understand,' Roxanne murmured.

'And what I've confided in you is strictly between the pair of us. Understand?'

'I won't breathe a word,' Roxanne promised.

'I'm glad you like the dress. It suits you.'

'Harry.'

'What?'

She kissed him on the cheek. 'Thank you for everything.'

'My pleasure,' he smiled.

She really had come on amazingly, Harry reflected in the middle of a rehearsal. She just got better and better – no longer the shy, unsure girl he'd started working on. She'd come right out of her shell and now when she sang she put the number across like an old trouper.

She was ready, he decided. There was no doubt about it. He'd speak to Bert before leaving, the Angel Inn was as good a place as any for her to make her début.

Roxanne squealed with delight when he told her.

'How do you feel?' Harry asked Roxanne, they were standing in the wings waiting to go on. This was their first appearance as a double act.

'How do you think?'

'I'll give you a tip. If you're nervous stand on your tiptoes. I don't know why but it helps dispel the butterflies.'

She did as he'd advised.

'We're on,' he said a few moments later.

Heart hammering, she ran out to centre stage while Harry nonchalantly followed her.

Roxanne knew they'd gone down well from the applause they received. They took another bow, then, together, ran off stage into the wings where she collapsed into Harry's arms.

'Well done,' he enthused.

'It went by so quickly.'

'But did you enjoy it?'

'I adored it, Harry. I wanted to stay on for ever.'

He nodded his approval. Spoken like a true theatrical. 'You'll do,' he declared.

Eyes shining, she stared at him. 'Are you sure?'

'Never more so. You were born for this, Annie, born for it. And I know, because I'm the same.'

Born for it! The words thrilled her for she knew they were true. She only wished . . . her family could have been out front. Da, Ma and Linnet.

Harry clasped her hand and led her away. 'Just a few things I want to go over, tighten up, before I get off to the Gluepot.'

Roxanne couldn't wait for her next performance and turn in the spotlight.

'Now what will you have?' Harry asked. To celebrate the end of their first week at the Angel Inn he'd brought her to Gerry's Club, a favourite night spot for music-hall artists.

Roxanne gazed at the menu, unable to decipher it far less make up her mind. What on earth were petit pois?

'I'll have whatever you're having,' she declared, snapping the menu shut.'

'Right then.'

Their champagne, which had been ordered earlier, arrived and Harry insisted on opening himself. He expertly popped the cork and filled her glass with frothing wine.

'Hallo squire, how's life?' The speaker was a balding middle-aged man with a gap-toothed smile.

'Just dandy. How about yourself, Joe?'

'Packing them in, boy. Packing them in. I believe you've got yourself a partner?'

'Annie, this is Joe Jugg. Annie Breeze, my partner.'

Joe Jugg bowed low. 'Pleased to meet you, my dear. Heard about you, of course, news travels fast in this business. My Lord, it does.'

He ensnared Roxanne's hand and extravagantly kissed it. '*Enchanté*,' he murmured.

'Enough of the old soap, Joe. What do you hear?'

'That she's good and the pair of you work well together.' He gazed at Roxanne in admiration. 'Lucky lad. But then he always was lucky and successful with the ladies, our Harry.'

Harry frowned. 'I think you should be on your way, Joe. Annie and I have a lot to discuss if you don't mind.'

The point wasn't lost on Roxanne. So Harry was a ladies' man,

116

she'd guessed as much. He was too much of a charmer and smooth talker not to be.

'Lovely meeting you, Annie,' Joe smiled, and moved off.

'Now where were we?' Harry said. 'Ah!' He topped up Roxanne's glass, then filled his own.

Roxanne gazed round her at the red plush and flock wallpaper, the air filled with laughter and hum of conversation. She couldn't have felt more at home. These were her sort of people, this her natural habitat.

'What kind of act does Joe have?' she inquired.

'He's best as the dame in pantomine, only Harry Randall's better. The rest of the year he does a comedy monologue about his wife and mother-in-law.'

'Who's that he's talking to now?'

'Daisy Busnell. She's been in the halls over thirty years, was quite a name for a while till she took to drink. Now it's said she's never sober, poor cow.'

'And the woman with the outrageous feather boa?'

'That's—'

A dozen times during their stay at Gerry's people came over to say hallo and be introduced to Roxanne. Without exception they said they'd heard the new act was a success.

'Sshhh!' whispered Harry, putting a finger over his lips. 'We don't want to wake Mrs Murphy.'

He lit a candle that had been left on the hall table and, with him leading, they began creeping upstairs. It was just past three o'clock in the morning.

They halted outside Roxanne's door. 'Thank you for a marvellous evening, Harry,' she whispered.

'Can I come in?'

'What for?'

'Want to say something.'

'Can't you say it here?'

'Better inside. Don't have to whisper so much.'

She closed the door quietly behind them, as he placed the candle stick on a mahogany chest of drawers.

'Is it about the act, Harry?' she queried.

'No, us.' He swept her into his arms and held her close. 'You must have realized how I've come to feel about you. Surely it's been obvious?' And with that he kissed her.

The suddenness both of his declaration and of his kiss surprised Roxanne, and for a few moments she allowed the kiss to continue.

117

Then she recalled Joe Jugg's remark about Harry being a ladies' man.

She pulled her mouth from his and pushed herself free. 'I'm sorry, Harry, but that's not on.'

'But Annie—'

She turned to stare at him, his sallow face palely reflected in the candlelight. She did like him, she couldn't deny it, and in other circumstances—

'We're a partnership, Harry, and I don't want anything to come between that,' she stated. 'It would only complicate matters if we became romantically involved.'

Disconcerted, he replied, 'Nothing need get complicated—'

'But it would, Harry,' she interjected firmly. 'Especially if we were to break up at a later date. What then?'

'We could cross that bridge should we come to it.'

She shook her head. 'It's best, for both of us, if things remain as they are. A strictly business and professional relationship. That's the way I want it to be.'

He tried to take her in his arms again, but she avoided his grasp. 'I mean it, Harry. Why spoil a good thing?'

'I think I may be falling in love with you, Annie.'

'Then don't. I'm certainly not in love with you.'

'You enjoy my company.'

'That's a different thing entirely.'

He took a deep breath. This wasn't what he'd planned at all. He hadn't expected a pushover, but not downright refusal. 'Please reconsider, Annie? Sleep on it.'

'I don't have to. You and I have become good friends, Harry, and, as Joe Jugg said, we work well together. That's how I wish it to remain.'

He realized pressing his suit would be pointless. She was adamant, he could hear it in her voice. Well, he wouldn't give up, he wasn't beaten yet. He'd bring her round somehow.

'You are attracted to me, I know that,' he declared.

'How?'

'I just do. And I'm certainly attracted to you. I think of you all the time. You're never out of my thoughts.'

She dropped her gaze. 'You'd better go, Harry.'

'Are you angry with me?'

'Of course not. If anything, I'm flattered.'

'You are attracted to me, I know that,' he repeated.

He left abruptly, the door snicking shut behind him.

Had she done the right thing? Roxanne wondered. Of course

she had, common sense told her that. Getting involved would only jeopardize their partnership, which was the last thing she wanted. It would be just plain stupid to take the risk.

No, she'd done the right thing, she reassured herself.

For the first time since moving in to Mrs Murphy's she locked her door.

Chapter Six

'Glory be, tis bitter,' Phoebe complained, shivering.

Reynold glanced up at a cloud-filled sky. 'There's snow on the way, take my word for it. We should never have gone to your Thomas's in the first place.'

'We had to, Reynold. It was their anniversary, after all, and we hadn't seen them in Lord knows how long. We could hardly refuse.'

'I would have done,' Reynold grumbled.

Phoebe pulled the rug draped across their legs more tightly about her. 'If anything we should have left earlier.'

'I didn't realize the weather had turned as bad as this or I would have done.'

'You weren't noticing much except the cider you were guzzling,' she reproved him.

'Be fair, Phoebe, twas a party after all.' The other guests had all been Venns and near neighbours. Elvira and Ern had also been invited but declined.

A few minutes later the first flakes of snow fell, swirling and gusting in the biting wind, and quickly intensified.

'So far to their house,' Reynold commented. 'Tis a long drive home and that's a fact. And in the middle of February, too.'

Phoebe banged her hands together, thankful for the woollen mitts she was wearing.

'I hope Linnet's done all her chores properly. She can be lazy at times, that maid.'

'Now don't you go fretting. I'm sure she's done everything just as she should.'

Reynold snorted. 'She'd better have.'

'I thought Margaret had aged. Didn't you?'

'She's lost a lot of weight. Got a face on her like a prune now.'

Phoebe smiled. She'd thought that as well.

They continued chatting about the party as they trundled down the narrow track leading from the hills where Thomas's farm was situated.

'This is unbelievable, I've never known snow like it,' Reynold declared a short while later. The snow was falling so thickly he could hardly make out Barton's drooping head. They, the cart and Barton were covered in it.

Phoebe gazed about her, everything had turned into a white nightmare. And, if anything, it was even colder than it had been. If they'd known they were going to run into this they'd never have left Thomas's and Margaret's.

Linnet gnawed a fingernail as she gazed out at the raging blizzard. She was worried about Phoebe and Reynold and wondering how they were going to get back in that lot. Perhaps they'd remained at her aunt's and uncle's, she thought. That would have been the sensible thing to do. If this had blown up after they'd left they might have taken refuge somewhere along the way.

She glanced at the kitchen clock. They were well overdue, so that was probably it. They'd stayed on at her aunt's and uncle's or knocked on a door, asking to be taken in.

She'd stay up a while longer though, just in case they were battling through. And she'd keep the kettle boiling ready to give them some tea if they did arrive, for that would be the first thing they'd want.

She was glad she wasn't out in that blizzard but safe, and warm, at home.

The snow had settled so deeply that Barton was having to struggle to make any headway. He heaved and strained as he plodded on.

Reynold wasn't even sure they were still on the track; they could easily have strayed from it to be crossing open country for all he knew, possibly going in quite the wrong direction. If only they could come across a house or barn, but they had seen neither light nor building. Mind you, he told himself, with visibility almost nil they could easily have passed someplace without noticing it.

'I'm getting worried, Reynold,' Phoebe said through frozen lips.

'We'll be all right, my lover. No need to be concerned.'

'How much longer do you think?'

He didn't reply because he didn't have an answer. How could he when he didn't even know where they were? He cursed under his breath. What a ridiculous pickle to be in. Of all nights to travel they'd had to pick this one.

A few yards further on Barton suddenly stumbled, then keeled over, taking the cart with him. Phoebe yelled in alarm as both she and Reynold were pitched out into the snow.

'Phoebe dear,' Reynold croaked, crawling to her and taking her into his arms as she sat up.

'What happened?' she queried.

'Barton, I don't know. He just went down.'

For the first time real fear blossomed in Phoebe. 'You'd better see to him then.'

Reynold helped Phoebe to her feet, then made his way to where Barton lay struggling. A quick examination revealed the worst.

'Broke his leg,' he said to Phoebe who'd now joined him. 'Must have stepped into a rabbit hole or something.'

Phoebe gazed at Reynold in horror. 'So what do we do now?'

Again Reynold didn't have an answer.

The blizzard was still raging when Linnet woke the next morning. Shrugging into her dressing gown she went into her parents' bedroom to discover they hadn't yet returned.

Her anxiety had disappeared the previous evening as she'd convinced herself they were safe and sound somewhere.

She hurriedly threw on her clothes, had a bite to eat and then set about the morning chores.

Drift snow was piled high outside the front door so she had to dig her way out. When she eventually reached the chicken coop she found the hens cowering in their boxes. After the fowls all the other animals needed to be fed. By the time she'd finished that it was almost mid-day.

And all the while the blizzard blew unabated.

It was getting on towards teatime when she noticed the blizzard wasn't as fierce as it had been. After that it began to die away, though it was still snowing steadily when she went to bed.

The following morning dawned crisp, bright and calm. As far as the eye could see was a sparkling white polarscape. Linnet gasped in wonder when, on rising, she gazed out at it from her encrusted bedroom window. She thought it was quite beautiful, a view lifted straight from a Christmas card.

She checked her parents' bedroom again, not at all surprised to find it empty.

Lord knows how long it would be before they managed to get back, she thought as she dressed.

The snow lay thick on the ground before a thaw set in. It was a gradual thaw, however, the snow and drifts dwindling by small amounts every day.

A full week had now passed since the end of the blizzard, but still Linnet remained relatively unconcerned. Her parents would show up when they could get through, in the meantime she just had to get on with things.

It was on the ninth day after the blizzard that her Uncle Thomas unexpectedly appeared. 'How do, Linnet,' he smiled when she opened the door.

'How do, Uncle Thomas. Come in. Are Ma and Da with you?'

He frowned. 'No girl. It's they I called about. I'm on my way to St Petroc and thought I'd make sure they got home all right. They left before that blizzard started you see, and naturally me and Margaret were worried.'

Linnet shook her head. 'They haven't returned yet, Uncle Thomas. I assumed they'd either stayed on with you or else taken refuge in some farm along the way.'

Thomas's frown deepened. 'I managed down without too much trouble, though there were a few tricky spots, I admit. And if I can do it your Da certainly will.'

Linnet shrugged. 'They'll no doubt turn up later today. Knowing Da he won't stay away a minute longer than he has to.'

'Tell you what,' said Thomas, 'why don't I call in again on my way back from St Petroc? I can have a word with them then and hear how they fared.'

'Right, we'll be expecting you. Now what about a nice cup of tea? You must be frozen.'

'Tea would be marvellous. Just the ticket,' he enthused. 'It certainly is cold out there.'

He took off his boots before following Linnet into the kitchen, where he told her about the party and what a marvellous time they'd all had.

'Still no sign of them,' Linnet informed Thomas when he stopped by that afternoon.

'This is just not like Reynold. As you said, he wouldn't stay away from the farm a minute more than he needs to.'

Doubt assailed Linnet. 'You don't think . . . there's been an accident or anything?'

'Twas a terrible blizzard right enough. Tis rare for us to have such weather in Devon.'

Thomas scratched his bristly chin, wondering if he should stay the night, but then Margaret would get worried that something had happened to him.

'I'm sure they're fine, Linnet, and there's an explanation for this, but if I were you and they haven't appeared by tomorrow morning I'd inform the police.'

Grim-faced, Linnet stared at her uncle. 'You really think I should?'

He nodded.

'Da will be furious if I do and there's no need.'

'You tell your Da it was on my advice. Put the blame on to me.' Then, drily added, 'I don't have to live with him, after all.'

'Then that's what I'll do.'

She gnawed a fingernail as she watched her uncle drive away. She hadn't been alarmed before but was now very much so. Where were her Ma and Da!

Next morning, Reynold and Phoebe had still not returned, so after attending to the animals, she hitched Fern to a wagon and took herself off into St Petroc.

Billy Christmas and Kevern Stoneman found them. A large search party had been organized by Sargeant Bratton, and there had been no shortage of volunteers. The locals had turned out in force.

Thomas had been informed and he'd organized another, smaller party to make its way down the hills from his end.

Billy stared at the upturned cart and the two figures huddled inside. Wrapped in a rug, they were embracing.

'Christ!' Billy swore softly.

Kevern swallowed hard. 'They shouldn't have been anywhere near here,' he commented.

'Must have got lost.'

'Must have,' Kevern agreed.

'Cuddling to try and keep warm,' Billy said.

But there had been more to the cuddle than that. It had also been a last physical gesture of love and companionship.

*   *   *

Linnet stood with head bowed as the vicar intoned over the open graves, as Phoebe and Reynold were buried side by side. It was a huge turnout; nearly everyone who'd known them came to pay their last respects.

Linnet repeatedly asked herself why Roxanne wasn't present. It was Elvira who'd provided her with a plausible answer – Roxanne had got itchy feet and emigrated to Canada.

Elvira had known nothing of Roxanne's running away, and had been shocked when Linnet told her once she had arrived for the funeral. She'd agreed to support the story about Roxanne supposedly helping her through an illness, elaborating the story further that after she had recovered, Roxanne had decided to go abroad.

Ern, who for once had accompanied Elvira, glanced sympathetically at Linnet who, he thought, was bearing up extraordinarily well under the circumstances. His feet were like solid blocks of ice and if it hadn't been for the solemnity of the occasion he'd have stamped them.

Many of the women were crying, Marjery Tregale and Vi Privett among them, but not Linnet. Her emotions were numb and, strangely, it was as though she wasn't there. She still couldn't believe what had happened and half-expected to wake up in bed to find it had all been a bad dream.

The vicar stopped speaking and nodded, at which point the coffins were simultaneously lowered into their graves. Then he approached Linnet and, in a low, reverential voice, asked if she'd care to throw a handful of earth on top of each.

Then it was all over. People who hadn't already spoken to Linnet muttered their condolences, as she thanked them for their attendance. She waited until the gathering had more or less dispersed before allowing herself to be led away by Elvira and Ern. They would now return to the house where a meal had been prepared earlier for them by Elvira. Only a small group had been invited, which included Thomas, Margaret and their family.

'I'll stay with you as long as necessary, Linnet,' Elvira stated as they drove off.

'Thanks, aunt.'

Elvira squeezed Linnet's arm and received a wan, strained smile in return. It was then that Linnet broke down in a way that she hadn't since learning of her Ma and Da's death. She shook and howled while tears flowed copiously. Elvira, too, began to cry.

*　　*　　*

Elvira was outraged, Linnet stunned. Ern wasn't with them, as he'd gone back to his pickle factory the day after the funeral.

'Everything!' Elvira exclaimed.

'Everything,' Peter Wonnacott confirmed.

'Nothing at all for Roxanne?'

'Reynold came in some time ago and those were his instructions. Roxanne was to be completely cut out of his will. I must say I thought it rather harsh of him.'

'I should say it's harsh,' Elvira declared through pursed lips. 'The girl's lost her inheritance.'

'Do you know why he did such a thing?'

Spite for having run off no doubt, Elvira thought. But how grossly unfair! As there had been no male heir the two girls should have been left the estate jointly. Surely Phoebe hadn't known about this! She couldn't believe her sister had any idea. No, Reynold must have done this in secret and kept it from his wife.

'I don't know what to say,' Linnet muttered.

'Roxanne could contest—' Elvira began, then stopped speaking when the solicitor shook his head.

'It's all legal and above board, Mrs Pennington. If Roxanne contested she'd lose. I assure you she would.'

Elvira sat back in the red leather armchair and glared at Peter Wonnacott as though all this was his fault. Her darling Roxanne, who'd always reminded her of her dear sister, robbed, as she saw it, of her rightful due. This was simply awful and so unjust.

'So there we are,' Peter said.

There were a few minutes' further discussion between them, then Elvira and Linnet took their leave.

'But if I sold out where would I go?' Linnet said. 'The land is all I know.'

Elvira was busy cooking at the range; the pair of them had arrived home from the solicitor's shortly before. 'Can you manage on your own?'

Linnet considered that. 'I think I could cope to the extent of feeding myself and perhaps having a little left over to sell. There would only be one to provide for now, after all, and not three as there were previously.'

Or four when Roxanne was there, Elvira thought grimly. She really was incensed about Reynold's will.

'A lot of the land will have to lie dormant,' Linnet went on.

'Unless you rented it out. There's always that option.'

'Hmmh!' Linnet mused. 'Hadn't thought of that.'

'Well, you should. Would give you more income.'

Linnet liked the sound of that.

Elvira had rather hoped that during the drive back Linnet would announce that she'd have half the estate made over to Roxanne, which she was perfectly entitled to do. But Linnet had made no such suggestion. Perhaps if she were to prompt her niece a little, put the idea into her mind.

'And what do you think about the fairness, or lack of it I should say, of Roxanne being cut out of your parents' will?'

'She caused Ma and Da, Ma especially, a lot of grief by running away as she did, not even leaving a letter to explain what she'd done. Nor has she been in touch since. I suppose Da thought she'd forfeited any right she had to her part of the farm.'

'But what do you think, Linnet?' Elvira persisted.

'I doubt we'll ever see her again. It's my belief she's gone for good.'

'But what if she returns? What then?'

Pricked at last by conscience, Linnet shifted uneasily in her chair. 'It was Da's place to dispose of the farm, which was his, after all, as he saw right and fit. If he chose to exclude Roxanne then that's her fault. I won't go against Da's wishes.'

'And what about your Ma? I simply can't believe she knew anything about the changed will. She'd never have allowed it.'

'How do you know that? You never saw how hurt she was when Roxanne went.'

'I did know Phoebe. She would have been completely against such a thing, no matter how hurt she was.'

Linnet shrugged. 'What's done is done, aunt. For right or wrong, the farm's mine and I'm going to stay here and work it as best I can. Entirely through her own actions, Roxanne has lost out, and that's that.'

Elvira felt contempt for Linnet then. She was her father's daughter all right, possessed the same hard, opportunistic streak that Reynold had had. She had no doubt that if the boot had been on the other foot Roxanne would have reversed matters, or at least made some reasonable arrangement.

'That's your final word on the subject I take it?' Elvira queried.

Linnet nodded.

Elvira concentrated again on her cooking. Father's daughter all right, she repeated to herself.

*　　*　　*

127

Linnet gazed at the house, yard and fields beyond, which were all now hers. It was going to be difficult getting by on her own, and lonely too. The loneliness, she suspected, would be by far the worst to contend with.

She thought of her Aunt Elvira who'd gone back to Bridport earlier that day. She was well aware of her aunt's disapproval for Elvira had made it patently clear. It was too bad. The farm was now hers and that's how it would remain. Just how her Da had wanted it.

'Hallo.'

She turned to find Kevern Stoneman standing awkwardly behind her. 'I didn't hear you come up,' she smiled.

'I hope I didn't startle you?'

'Not at all.'

He twisted his cap in his hands. 'I thought I'd drop by and see how you were?'

'I'm fine, thank you.'

'Is there anything I can do to help while I'm here?'

'That's kind. But no, there's nothing.'

'Are you sure?'

'Certain,' she replied.

He glanced about. ''Tis a big farm for a woman on her own.'

'I'll get by.'

'I'm sure you will, Linnet. You're very capable, my Da said that t'other day.'

Ben, the dog, appeared round a corner of the yard. He ran over and stood panting beside Linnet. 'Hallo boy, what you been up to?' she said.

He looked up at her and wagged his tail.

'Rabbiting I shouldn't wonder,' Kevern speculated.

'Could be. He's a great rabbiter. There's some lurcher in him, you know.'

'No, I didn't,' Kevern answered, shaking his head.

'Lurcher and spaniel. It's quite a mixture.'

Kevern laughed. 'I should say!'

Linnet bent down and patted Ben who wagged his tail furiously. He was going to be her sole companion from there on in, she reflected sadly.

'Tell you what,' she declared, straightening up. 'I was just about to put the kettle on. Would you like a cup?'

He hesitated. 'I don't want to impose—'

'Nonsense,' she said briskly, cutting him short. 'I'll enjoy the company. And I have some apple turnovers I made. They've always been a great favourite of mine.'

'Me too,' he said.

'Then come on.'

Kevern relaxed and they began chatting freely as they went inside.

Chapter Seven

Annie and Harry came offstage at the Gluepot to discover a man had been standing in the wings watching them. Annie recognized him immediately as Max Levitt, owner of the Hollo- way Empire, a large and prestigious venue.

'Well done,' Levitt nodded affably.

'Thank you,' Harry replied.

'Let's move out into the corridor, shall we?' Levitt suggested.

Harry shot Annie a quizzical look as they followed Levitt from the wings. What did this mean?

Out in the corridor Levitt produced a leather cigar case and offered Harry a Havana, which Harry accepted. Both men then lit up.

'You have style, the pair of you,' Levitt announced through a cloud of smoke.

'Good of you to say so,' Harry replied, delighted.

'I don't believe we've met, Miss Breeze.'

'Oh, excuse me. Annie, this is Max Levitt. Max, Annie Breeze.'

'I know you by sight and reputation,' Annie declared, shaking hands with Levitt.

'You're acquiring something of a reputation yourself, Miss Breeze. Which is why I wanted to come and see you for myself. I enjoyed your act very much, very much indeed.'

'I think we're improving all the time.'

'Hmmh,' he murmured, studying Annie through the smoke.

'How are things at the Empire, Mr Levitt?' Harry inquired politely.

'Not bad. Could be better.'

'Oh?'

'Listen, I have a table booked at Gerry's Club this evening. Why don't you join me there later after your last curtain down?'

'We'd be honoured, Mr Levitt,' Harry answered quickly.

'Good, that's settled. I shall be expecting you.'

'We'll be there,' Harry assured him.

Max Levitt had no doubt they would. 'Till then,' he said, and gave Annie a small, courteous bow.

'Till then,' she repeated with a smile.

'This could be it, the breakthrough I've been after all these years,' Harry enthused to Annie when Levitt had left.

The Holloway Empire, Annie thought, that would be a big step up.

Max Levitt, smoking another cigar, rose as Harry and Annie approached his table. He was drinking champagne. 'How good of you to come,' he declared, taking Annie's hand and kissing it.

'It's kind of you to ask us,' Harry responded. 'And I'm sorry if we're late but Annie insisted on going home and getting changed.'

Levitt took in Annie's dress which was oyster grey with a frill round the neck and another down the front. The sleeves finished at the elbows where further frills of off-white lace dangled.

'Charming, absolutely charming,' he murmured. 'Any wait I might have had was well worth it. You're a confection, Miss Breeze, a pure confection.'

Annie flushed slightly.

'Now shall we sit?'

Levitt beckoned a waiter to pour out the champagne, as they studied the menu. Annie settled for veal while Harry announced he'd have the fillet steak.

'Now then,' smiled Levitt when their order had been taken. 'You're no doubt wondering why I've asked you here tonight.'

Harry's anticipation and excitement showed clearly on his face. He nodded.

'How would you feel about appearing at the Empire?'

Annie glanced at Harry, and smiled. 'We'd be delighted to,' she said to Levitt.

'Providing the money and billing are right,' Harry added.

'Ah yes. Of course!'

Levitt studied the tip of his cigar for a few moments. 'I can offer you fourth billing, how does that sound?'

'It depends who the other three are,' Harry replied.

'Dan Leno will be top.'

Harry swallowed hard. 'Agreed.'

'Gertie Gitana is second.'

'Agreed,' Harry said again. These were two very big names indeed.

'And Zakaree Kramov is to be third.' Zakaree Kramov was a Russian who juggled with large military weapons as well as simple things like bayonets. He was extremely popular with audiences.

Harry didn't think he could contest that either. 'Agreed,' he repeated.

'Then that's the billing sorted out. Now money.' He named a sum which made Annie's eyebrows rise.

Harry glanced sideways at Annie, he'd much rather have negotiated this without her, but there was no way round that. He fell to haggling with Levitt and managed to up the sum by another twenty per cent.

'You're being very quiet,' Harry said to Annie, on the way home in a hansom cab. Reaching across he grasped her hand and squeezed it.

'I take it we're going to split the money equally,' she answered coolly.

He laughed. 'Hardly that, Annie. I'm the senior partner in the act, after all, and as such should get more.'

She removed her hand from his. 'Is that how you've been dividing up the money in our present engagements?'

'Hey, let's not let things get out of perspective. I took you on and trained you, don't forget. You wouldn't be on the halls if it wasn't for me.'

'True,' she conceded. 'And I'm very grateful, and always will be. But now the people come to see me just as much as you.'

He laughed again. 'They certainly like you. I can't deny that.'

She turned and fixed him with a steely gaze. 'Let me point out that, on your own admission, you tried for years to break into the big dates and failed. Now you have – because of me.'

'I wouldn't say that!' he protested.

'Do you think Levitt would have booked you if you'd been on your own? He's had plenty of opportunity to do so in the past and never has. So it's us he wants, the pair of us. Bright *and* Breeze.'

Harry fell silent. Damn! he thought, for he knew she was right. 'How about sixty-forty?' he proposed.

'Fifty-fifty, straight down the line. That's the way it's going to

132

be for this booking and every other one from here on in. And I insist on being there when any future negotiations take place. Try and cheat me, Harry, and that's an end to the act. I swear it.'

He was appalled. 'You wouldn't do that, Annie, surely?'

'I would, Harry. You'd better believe me.'

He did; her voice told him this was no idle threat. 'Well, you've come a long way in a short time,' he answered lightly. 'Where's the green girl who used to work behind the bar at the Angel Inn?'

'Green no longer. So is it a deal?'

She had him over a barrel. 'It's a deal,' he agreed.

She extended her gloved hand. 'Then shake on it.'

They shook.

'You're harder than I thought,' he said.

'Let's just say I'm a better businesswoman than you thought, Harry.'

'I'm beginning to appreciate that.'

On a sudden impulse she kissed his cheek. 'I can't wait to tread the boards at the Empire. I hear it's a beautiful theatre.'

'I can't wait either. And on the same bill as Dan Leno! Now that is something.'

He touched the spot she'd kissed. 'I wouldn't mind more of that,' he said.

'More of what?' she teased, pretending not to understand.

'The kiss.'

She studied him in the darkness. She really was fond of him, they got on so well together. He was such fun to be with; there was never a dull moment with Harry.

She was still studying him when they drew up outside Duncan Terrace.

'Come in!' Annie called out when there was a knock on the door, thinking it was Mrs Murphy. But Harry popped his head round.

'How are you, my darling?' he asked.

'Fine.'

'I've brought you a present.'

'A present!'

A large bunch of flowers appeared from behind his back. 'I thought you'd like these.'

'Harry, they're gorgeous!' she exclaimed.

'Am I allowed to enter the inner sanctum? The Holy of Holies?'

She laughed. 'As long as you leave the door open.'

He raised an eyebrow. 'Don't you trust me?'

'Not an inch.'

'Very wise of you, young lady,' he smiled.

She went and took the flowers, burying her nose in the blooms. 'They smell wonderful.'

'Not just one present, but *two*. There's an envelope tucked into the paper.'

She found and extricated the envelope. 'What can this be?' she mused.

'There's only one way to find out, and that's to open it.'

She laid the flowers on her table, then carefully ripped open the envelope. 'A song!' she exclaimed.

'A *brand-new* song, for you to sing at the Empire. I knew the moment I heard it that audiences would love it.'

' "When I Take My Morning Promenade",' Annie said, reading the title. 'And it's by Rexford and Danks! Why, they wrote and composed "Silver Threads Among The Gold".'

'Top men in their field. All their numbers are a big success.'

'Oh Harry!' she beamed. 'This is fabulous.'

It warmed him to see how pleased she was. 'Let's go and find a musician to play it through for you,' he said.

Clutching the song to her bosom she flew to the wardrobe for her coat which Harry helped her put on. Her eyes were shining as she paused to stare into his face. 'You're a poppet,' she declared.

He wanted so badly to kiss her, but felt if he did, and she objected, it would spoil the moment.

They were laughing as they went downstairs where Annie told Mrs Murphy about the flowers, who said she'd put them in a vase.

'That's enough for now, let's get some lunch,' Harry declared. They were rehearsing some new 'business' that Harry intended incorporating into the act.

Annie hesitated. 'Would you be cross if I made a suggestion?'

'Of course not.'

'I think you should consider changing your character.'

Harry frowned. 'Change it, how?'

'To that of a happy drunk – not too drunk, but fairly tipsy. It seems to me if you did, you'd be far more effective.'

'A drunk?' Harry mused.

'In full evening dress, an upper-class toff, if you can do the voice, that is.'

'Oh, I can do the voice, all right. That's not a problem,' Harry replied. 'What you're talking about is a sort of Champagne Charlie, *à la* George Leybourne.'

'And what if I was to wear something formal as well?'

'A matching pair?' he smiled.

'Exactly.'

'But can you do that type of voice?'

'I can try, I have a good ear, after all. And you can help me.'

The more Harry thought about the idea the more he liked it. Leybourne had been exceptionally popular in his day, and there was nothing similar currently on the London halls. It would be quite a departure from what Harry normally did, but he was not against change if it was for the best. What would Max Levitt say, though? They'd have to speak to him, ensure he agreed.

'Harry?'

'Let's trot off to the nearest bar so I can get myself in the mood for this new character,' he joked.

A week later they performed the new act for Max Levitt who gave them the go-ahead to use it when they opened at the Empire.

'I had Harry round yesterday,' Celeste informed Annie. The pair of them were en route to the West End where Annie was having a final fitting for her new stage costume. Although basically formal in appearance it had a low cut, rather risqué, décolletage to show off her ample bosom. It was made from cream silk with matching lace trimming the waist and cuffs. The skirt was cut so that it trailed behind her when she walked.

'Oh?'

'I thought he was going to cry into his sherry, poor darling.'

Annie glanced at Celeste. 'Is there something wrong with him?'

'Only you.'

Annie was immediately alarmed. Was Harry unhappy about the new act? If so he hadn't said. 'Me?'

'He's in love with you, Annie, head over heels. You're all he ever talks about nowadays.'

Annie looked swiftly away.

'Have you any boyfriends?'

'No,' Annie answered quietly. 'Not for the lack of opportunity, mind, I get plenty of offers. I simply don't have the time.'

There was a pregnant pause, then Annie asked in the same quiet tone, 'What about Harry?'

'You mean, has he any boyfriends?' Celeste teased.

Annie laughed. 'Girlfriends, silly.'

'Not for a long time. He's remaining faithful to you.'

'Well, he shouldn't,' Annie replied, feeling angry for some reason.

'It's quite a compliment, believe me. Since meeting you he just doesn't want to know about other women. He's totally besotted.'

'Hardly that.'

'He is, I assure you,' Celeste said.

Besotted? Was Harry really in love with her? Despite the summer heat, Annie shivered.

'How do you feel about him?'

'If the circumstances were different—' Annie trailed off.

'You mean, because he's your partner? He told me your views about that.'

'If anything went wrong it would spoil things, Celeste. I simply don't want to take that risk.'

'Do you love him?'

'I, eh—' Annie was now confused. It was a question which disturbed her deeply, one she had trouble answering.

'Well?' Celeste pressed.

'I certainly like him an awful lot. We've become extremely close.'

'And if he wasn't your partner?'

Annie ignored that question.

'I think you're making a mistake, Annie. If I were you I'd reconsider my position.'

'Did Harry ask you to speak to me?'

Celeste shook her head. 'It was entirely my idea.'

'And he said he loved me?'

'Swore he did.'

Annie became even more confused. She was going to have to do a lot of thinking, but not now, not with their opening at the Empire only days away. She changed the subject and, wisely, Celeste let it be.

Annie took up a position centre stage and a spotlight focused on her; the rest of the stage was blacked out. She was about to sing her new number for the first time. Harry faded into the background. A hush fell as she delivered the opening lyrics:

'My Ma they tell me, wore a crinoline.

Then came the bustle, what a tussle,

women were tied up and bundled up in a dress.

Now fashion plates decide we must wear less—'

As she sang part of her mind was judging the audience's reaction. They were hanging on her every note, not a whisper or rustle could be heard. Every ear in the theatre was straining, every eye rivetted.

Then she came to the chorus which completely altered the tone of the piece, introducing a naughty flavour:

'For when I take my morning promenade
What a fashion card, on the boulevard.
Oh I don't mind nice boys staring hard
if it satisfies their desire.
Do you think my dress is a little bit?
Just a little bit?
Much! Not too much of it—'

During this line she placed her hands beneath her bosom.

'If it shows my shape just a little bit . . .'

Here, and with her hands still beneath her bosom, she turned sideways to the audience and thrust out her bottom.

'It's the bit the boys admire!'

The audience erupted in response to which she waggled her bottom repeating:

'It's the bit the boys admire.'

The audience were cheering wildly, clapping and stamping, when she finally finished.

Harry rolled drunkenly forward, took her hand and, together, they bowed.

'Listen to that,' he murmured. 'They're mad about us.'

They bowed again and again, the audience not wanting to let them go.

Max Levitt, standing in the wings, called out, 'Repeat the chorus Annie! Repeat the chorus.'

She did, and this time an ecstatic audience sang along with her:

'If it shows my shape just a little bit
It's the bit the boys admire!'

'Congratulations, well done.' Levitt beamed at them when they finally joined him in the wings. He warmly shook hands with Annie, then did the same with Harry.

'What if I took you to Gerry's Club afterwards to celebrate?' he proposed.

'That would be lovely,' Annie answered.

'It's the bit the boys admire,' Levitt chuckled. 'Oh yes, you two are going to do very nicely here, very nicely indeed.'

★   ★   ★

'Marry you?' Linnet said to Kevern.

He blushed. 'We have been seeing a lot of one another since . . . since your Ma and Da died. I thought . . . well, I rather thought you liked me, Linnet. That was the impression you gave anyway.'

It had crossed her mind several times during the past months that her relationship with Kevern might be leading to an eventual proposal. However, it was the abruptness of it, coming completely out of the blue, which had surprised her, quite taken her breath away.

'Of course I like you,' she replied.

'I feel an awful lot more than that for you, Linnet,' he croaked.

'Do you?'

'I, eh . . . I love you.' And having uttered these words, his face went bright red.

She didn't love him, but perhaps it might happen in time. And no other lads had come courting of late; why hadn't she been as popular with boys as Roxanne had been? It was a mystery to her. It wasn't as if she was ugly, quite the contrary. She simply wasn't popular with the opposite sex. However, she had to consider her position on the farm. It sorely needed a man about the place. Admittedly, she was getting by, as she'd told Aunt Elvira she would, but it was proving more difficult than she'd anticipated. And the loneliness was dreadful. Why only the previous week she'd been alarmed to find she was talking to herself, holding an actual conversation.

'We've never even kissed,' she stated coyly, now enjoying the situation.

'That's easy to fix.'

He put an arm awkwardly round her waist and drew her to him. He lowered his face towards hers, and their lips met. It was a pleasant experience, she decided, and quite exciting. How lovely it was to be held in such a strong, manly embrace.

'You smell wondrous,' he declared when the kiss was over. 'Like new cut grass.'

'Do I really?'

'So what do you say?'

'Kiss me again.'

He did, and this kiss lasted longer than the previous one. He ran his hands up and down her back which caused her to turn to jelly inside.

'When would the wedding be?' she asked when their lips eventually parted.

He was filled with elation. 'Does that mean you accept?'

She nodded.

He let out a loud whoop and slapped his thigh. 'You don't know how happy this makes me, my lover! I be happy as a pig in—'

She laughed when he broke off in consternation. 'I think I know what you were going to say.'

'Well, I be happy as that anyway. How about you?'

She realized she was happy, very happy indeed. Somehow, it was as though a great weight had been lifted from her shoulders. 'Me too,' she told him.

'We'll have to see the vicar and make arrangements,' Kevern enthused.

'You still haven't said when you plan this wedding?'

'Whenever suits you, but I'd like it as soon as possible. Early autumn, how about then?'

'Then that's when we'll have it.'

'We'll go into St Petroc on Saturday and I'll buy you an engagement ring. A real diamond one. No matter the cost.'

'Can you afford that, Kevern?'

'I can't, but my Da can. I'll make him cough up, the old guzzle guts.'

Linnet looked out over the hollyhocks, valerian and pink campion that were growing nearby. Mrs Kevern Stoneman, she thought to herself. She liked the sound of that.

And once she became Mrs Kevern Stoneman, there would be no more loneliness.

'Did you ask her?' Tom Stoneman demanded when Kevern appeared in the barn where Tom was forking hay.

Kevern nodded.

'And?'

'She said yes.'

A huge smile split Tom's face. 'Why, that's terrific, boy. Just think, her farm combined with ours.' He threw down his pitchfork and rubbed his hands in glee. 'Together we'll be one of the biggest farms in the area and all that means.'

Kevern thought wistfully of Roxanne whom, of the two sisters, he'd much preferred. But she had gone to Canada, so he believed, probably never to return. Anyway, he doubted she'd ever have accepted a proposal from him. Whereas Linnet had, Linnet whom he didn't love. He'd lied about that, but there was no doubt she'd make a fair wife. Oh yes, he'd see to that. Who could ask for more than that and the farm she was bringing with her?

Tom put an arm round Kevern's shoulders. 'Tis a grand day's work you've done. One you'll never regret, I promise you.'

Kevern banished all thoughts of Roxanne. She was in the past, history, best forget all about her.

'Tell you what, this calls for a firkin. More even!' Tom laughed.

It turned out to be a lot more.

'Come in, I want to talk to you,' Annie said to Harry. It was late on Saturday night at the end of their first week's engagement at the Empire.

'To your room?' he queried in surprise.

Once inside she crossed to the gas mantles and lit them. 'Close the door,' she instructed.

'Something bothering you?' he asked.

She was nervous, unsure of how to proceed. She had to get straight to the point, she decided. 'Celeste tells me you're in love with me,' she said.

He glanced at the floor, then up again to stare directly into her eyes. 'I am.'

'Oh Harry!' she exclaimed softly.

'These things happen. I'll get over it, I suppose.' He sounded most unconvincing.

'We have to sort this out. It can't go on as it is.'

'I don't see why not,' he murmured. 'It doesn't affect the act, after all. I won't allow that.'

Her emotions were in turmoil. Part of her wanted to let herself go, surrender to what she was feeling. Another part was fiercely resisting.

'You were great tonight,' he declared. 'The best yet.'

'Shut up!' she snapped.

'I'd better go, Annie. This isn't getting us anywhere.'

'No, stay, please.'

'For what? To torture myself. That's what happens when I'm alone with you. Not in rehearsal or "on the green". But like this.'

'On the green' meant onstage.

'You should see other women, Harry. Not cut yourself off like you have.'

'Who told you that? Celeste?'

She nodded.

'Just exactly what did she say to you?'

'Lots. It was quite a chat.'

'She should have kept her bloody mouth shut, interfering woman,' Harry replied sharply.

'Don't be foul, she's your friend. She has your best interests at heart.'

Harry pulled out his gold cigarette case, contemplated it, then returned it to his pocket. What he wanted more than anything was the whisky he had upstairs.

How sad he looked, Annie thought, rather like a little boy. He didn't appear at all the self-assured sophisticate she'd thought him when they'd first met at the Angel Inn.

'Shall I see you tomorrow?' she asked.

He shook his head. 'I intend sleeping late then going out for the rest of the day.'

'Where?'

'Richmond,' he lied. It was the first place that popped into his head. In fact he hadn't intended going out for the day at all; he'd made that up.

'Sounds nice.'

'By the river. I shall enjoy it.'

'On your own?'

'Maybe. Maybe not. I haven't decided.'

She moved towards him. 'Harry?'

'What?'

She didn't know. What she did know was that suddenly being so close to him was intoxicating, that he was the man for her, that she desperately wished him to hold her, to—

'I love you, too,' she whispered. 'I've been denying it for a long time, but it's true. I do.'

The tension that had existed between them disappeared as they melted into one another's arms.

This was so right, Annie thought, so very, very right. 'Oh, my darling,' she further whispered.

Then they were kissing, tongues entwined, as they hugged each other passionately.

Elvira laid down the letter she'd just received and sighed. The enquiry agents she'd contacted in London had been unable to find Roxanne. They'd scoured the music halls, they assured her, but no-one knew of any Roxanne Hawkins. They expressed their regret that they'd been unable to help.

So where was the girl? Elvira wondered. She'd wanted to contact her, inform her about her mother and father, and Reynold's shameful will, but it seemed impossible.

141

Perhaps Roxanne hadn't gone to London at all, but had settled in Bristol, Birmingham, Manchester, anywhere. All the large cities had their music halls. Maybe she hadn't even gone into music hall at all. Perhaps she'd tried and failed and was now doing something else.

Well, she'd done her best, Elvira consoled herself. She couldn't do more.

Picking up a chocolate from an opened box she popped it into her mouth. God bless and take care of you wherever you are, Roxanne, she thought.

She refolded the letter and placed it at the back of her bureau.

Chapter Eight

Annie came lazily awake, to gaze out of the window at the bright late spring sunshine. Beside her Harry lay fast asleep, a lock of hair dangling over his forehead.

She twisted round to stare at him, smiling at the memory of their previous night's lovemaking. What a revelation it had been going to bed with Harry, she totally inexperienced, he the complete opposite. Some of the things he'd taught her had been a real eye-opener. The heights of passion he was able to take her to amazed her, after which there was that glorious feeling of absolute satisfaction.

She thought of their Georgian house which they'd rented in Chantry Street, Islington where they lived as Mr and Mrs Bright. They'd moved out of Mrs Murphy's shortly after becoming lovers as the moral Mrs Murphy would never have condoned them sharing a room. It was Harry who'd found the charming, furnished house which had a tiny, but delightful garden at the rear.

Harry stirred, and grunted. 'Are you awake?' she murmured.

He blinked open his eyes. 'I am now.'

'Good morning.'

'Good morning to you.'

Leaning across she kissed him lightly on the lips, sighing with pleasure when a hand moved on to her naked buttocks. It was their custom to sleep nude. She jerked slightly when his hand slid down and under, and a finger went into her.

She stroked his penis to find it already hardening. 'There's no reason for us to get up yet, is there?' she queried with a catlike smile.

'None at all.'

'Good. I was hoping you'd say that.'

'Annie?'

'What, my darling?'

'I love you so much. You're everything to me, Annie. The sun, moon and stars all rolled into one.'

'Flattery will get you everywhere, Harry Bright.'

He gathered her in his arms. 'You're the best thing that's ever happened to me, Annie. Life was dull and grey before you, now it's a riot of colour.'

Still in his embrace she twisted round to place a finger tenderly over his lips. 'What an old smoothie you are, Harry.'

'But it's true,' he mumbled in protest.

She removed her finger and kissed his bristly chin. 'When are we going to get married? I can't wait to be really Mrs Harry Bright.'

'I've told you, not until I can take you away on the sort of honeymoon I plan – Italy, Venice perhaps. And to do that properly means considerable time off work which would be stupid at the moment. We're doing so well, Annie, let's just keep things going on as they are.'

She sighed. 'A honeymoon like that isn't really necessary. I wouldn't mind if we didn't go anywhere.'

'But I would. I want the best for you, Annie, and that's what you're going to have – a honeymoon fit for a princess.'

She stroked his face. A honeymoon fit for a princess, what a romantic thought. 'I have to admit, I would like to travel abroad,' she said.

'See, I'm right! And that's what we'll do, travel in style and luxury, when the time is right. Now, what about breakfast? I'm suddenly ravenous.'

'In bed or downstairs?'

'You're insatiable,' he smiled.

'I am where you're concerned.'

'In bed then.'

Harry got up, put on a Paisley silk dressing gown that had been a present from Annie, and pulled the bell rope that would summon their maid.

'Have I ever told you how beautiful you are,' he said, waiting for the maid to arrive.

'Often. But you can do so again.'

'You're beautiful.'

Annie pulled the bedclothes into place and, lying back, briefly closed her eyes in contentment.

Life with Harry was sheer, utter bliss.

'Sit down, good of you to come,' Max Levitt beamed, ushering Annie to an ornate gilt and velvet chair. When she and Harry were both seated he settled himself behind his desk.

'Nothing wrong I hope,' Harry queried, sounding slightly anxious. During their extended run at the Empire this was the first time they'd been summoned to Levitt's office.

'No, no, no,' Levitt replied. 'Nothing's wrong, quite the contrary. Things couldn't be better. Business is magnificent, I'm delighted to say.'

He paused for a moment, then went on. 'I've decided to reshape my show and want to offer you third billing. What do you think about that?'

Harry shot Annie a triumphant glance. This was wonderful. 'Will it mean more money?' he asked.

'Of course. I can't deny how successful you've been, and success with Max Levitt has its just rewards. But first, there are a few matters I wish to discuss.'

Levitt opened a drawer and pulled out several pieces of paper which he placed before them. 'I think your act, excellent as it is, could be improved with a re-emphasis, which is why I want Annie to sing two numbers in future.'

'Two?' Annie queried.

'I've therefore taken the liberty of commissioning this for you.'

Turning to Annie he handed her a new song. 'Will You Be My Hollyhock' she read.

'A real tear-jerker if ever there was one,' Levitt declared, returning to his place behind the desk.

Harry was frowning. 'If Annie sings two songs that cuts down on my performance.'

'I'm afraid so, Harry. But this new balance will benefit the act, I assure you.'

'The act could simply take longer,' Harry proposed.

Levitt shook his head. 'Not on, Harry. Balance again, balance.'

Harry was outraged. If Annie sang two numbers he'd be reduced to supporting her instead of the other way round. 'I don't know,' he muttered.

'I think you'll find the increased money an inducement to your agreeing,' Levitt replied smoothly.

'Harry?' Annie queried, glancing over at him.

He was in a quandary. He didn't want to deny Annie this opportunity, but felt it shouldn't be at his own expense.

'Hollyhock will bowl them over, there won't be a dry eye in the house,' Levitt murmured.

'We could go elsewhere,' Harry stated, tight-lipped.

'True.' Levitt was gambling on the fact that this wouldn't happen, and explained why he was prepared to be so generous when it came to renegotiating their fee.

'What do you say, Annie?' Harry asked. The look in her eyes was answer enough. He felt his resistance melting away.

'Let's talk cash then,' he said.

Annie smiled her gratitude.

'You're not upset, are you?' Annie queried when they were outside Levitt's office, the door shut firmly behind them.

'Not at all,' Harry lied.

'You're a real sweetie, thank you,' she declared, and kissed him on the forehead.

Harry felt sick.

Kevern wolfed down the rabbit stew Linnet had cooked for their supper, thinking what an improvement her meals were on those he and his Da had made before his marriage. Linnet was certainly a dab hand with the pots and pans. He reached for a thick slice of bread which he used to mop up his gravy.

'Not hungry?' he asked Linnet who he now noticed was merely toying with her food.

She shook her head.

'Taint like you, my lover. Not poorly, I hope?'

She'd been waiting for him to finish before breaking her news, but now changed her mind and decided to do so there and then.

'I've something to tell you, Kevern.'

'And what's that?'

'I didn't want to say until I was absolutely certain, it would have been a disappointment to you if I was wrong. Now I know it to be so.'

She took a deep breath. 'I'm expecting.'

'Exp . . . !' He threw down his knife and fork. 'Why, that's marvellous. Proper job! I couldn't be more pleased.'

'I'm three months gone and by my figuring the little one should arrive somewhere round the middle of October.'

He banged a fist into the palm of his other hand. 'It'll be a boy of course, a son and heir.'

'Don't you go counting your chickens,' she warned him. 'It could just as easily be a maid.'

146

'Twon't be, I just knows it.'

'Well, there's nothing I can do about that. We can only let nature take its course and wait to see what arrives.'

'Expecting,' he repeated, face ablaze with delight. 'That's grand. I can't wait to tell my Da. In fact I'll go straight over there after I finish this.'

'He'll be pleased too. I know how much he wants a grandchild.'

'Grand*children*,' Kevern corrected her. 'For there'll be more than one, you can be sure of that. At least if I has anything to do with it, there will.'

Linnet had no doubt he was right, the good Lord willing that was. Kevern was regular as clockwork in his attentions.

'What name do you fancy?' Kevern asked, frowning in speculative thought.

'I've no idea. Haven't considered any yet.'

'I know!' he exclaimed. 'We'll call him Edward after the new king.' Queen Victoria had passed away earlier that year and her son, Edward VII, had succeeded her.

'Splendid,' Linnet enthused. 'And what if it's a maid?'

Kevern wasn't interested in that. He shrugged. 'You can come up with a name for her if it is. But I tell you, it's going to be a boy. I can feel it in my water.'

Linnet hoped he wasn't going to be disappointed.

Tom Stoneman's face was flushed bright red from the copious amount of alcohol he'd consumed. Having been told the news he'd insisted they hitch up a wagon and go into St Petroc to celebrate. He and Kevern were propping up the bar of the Hart Inn where they'd been drinking for nearly two hours.

Tom saw off the dregs of his pint and banged the pot on the counter. 'Drink up, lad, we'll have another.'

Kevern shook his head. 'Not for me, Da, I'll fall down if I has any more.'

Tom roared with laughter. 'And why shouldn't you fall down? Tisn't every day a man learns he's to be a father for the first time. Or a grandfather for the first time, come to that.'

'Still, enough is enough, Da. I don't want to throw up.'

'Aahh you youngster,' Tom replied, pulling a face. 'No stamina, that's your problem. When I was your age I could have drunk twice as much as you have, and often did I can tell you.'

Kevern smiled thinly thinking that was undoubtedly true. His father's drinking prowess was legendary. His own capacity was certainly nowhere near as much.

'Another pint for myself, Tina, and two more large brandies,' Tom instructed the barmaid. He turned again to Kevern and leered. 'Now surely you can manage that?'

Kevern groaned. 'I really can't, Da.'

'Then I'll do it for you.'

When the order arrived he threw one of the large brandies down his throat, had a long pull of his cider, then swallowed the second brandy.

Tom ran a hand over his sweating brow. 'Mother's milk,' he declared.

Kevern desperately wanted to go home, but couldn't until his father was ready to do so. He wondered how long that would be.

'Paul!' Tom boomed at someone who'd just entered the pub. Paul was a local trawlerman and long-time drinking companion of his.

Kevern groaned again; this would add another half hour, at least, to the proceedings.

Paul slapped Kevern on the back when told about the baby, and offered to buy him a drink. Kevern hastily explained that he simply couldn't take another drop on board.

'No stamina,' Tom repeated in disapproval. Then he bellowed, 'Tina! Over here my girl.'

Kevern watched six more large brandies, plus various pints of cider, disappear inside Tom, thinking his Da really was incredible. By now Tom's face was almost scarlet.

Paul was in the middle of a yarn when Tom, who'd been swaying slightly, suddenly stiffened, his expression one of surprise.

Paul stopped speaking. 'You all right, mate?'

Tom opened his mouth, closed it again, then croaked, 'Well, bugger me!' And with that he collapsed to the floor, where he landed in an untidy sprawl.

'Pissed as a fart,' Paul grinned.

Kevern could hardly wonder at that. 'Will you help me get him out to the wagon?' he asked Paul, for his Da was a heavy man.

'Will do,' Paul agreed, laying his drink aside.

The moment Kevern turned Tom on to his back he knew something was wrong, for Tom's eyes were open and staring with a peculiar, vacant look.

'It's more than being pissed,' Kevern mumbled, undoing his Da's shirt and feeling for a heartbeat. There was none. He then felt Tom's wrist, and failed to find a pulse.

'Christ,' he muttered, glancing in horror at Paul, then at the others crowding round.

Tom was as dead as mutton.

Lying in bed, where sleep eluded him, Kevern was jubilant. He was sorry to lose his Da of course, but with Tom gone everything that his father had owned now became his.

The two farms could be legally amalgamated into one of the largest farms in the area, with him as overall owner. What was his wife's was his, after all. Oh, what a sweet and wonderful thought that was. He began to laugh silently.

It was less than five hours since his father had died.

As Levitt had predicted when Annie came to the end of 'Will You Be My Hollyhock' on the opening night of the new bill, there wasn't a dry eye in the house.

She'd been sensational, Harry thought. There was no other word for it. She was right up there with the best.

The audience, regaining its composure, went berserk. The applause rose and rose in volume, becoming a tidal wave of sound battering against the stage.

Harry rolled drunkenly forward to take his place beside Annie and, together, they bowed.

'Annie! Annie! We want Annie!' a number of voices were heard to shout.

Annie, not the pair of them, Harry thought in dismay, his heart sinking.

'Annie! Annie!' More voices were taking up the call now, the demand coming from all sections of the auditorium.

The pair of them took a further bow, and still the calls went on – all for Annie. His name never mentioned.

Harry was too old a trouper not to give the audience what it wanted or, in this instance, demanded.

'Take single bows from here on in,' he whispered, releasing Annie's hand.

Breaking out of character Harry stepped backwards, he, too, applauding her.

Annie bowed again and again and again.

She found Harry in the parlour morosely drinking Scotch. 'Do you know what time it is?' she said.

He shrugged.

'How long have you been up?'

'Don't know.'

She glanced at the decanter by his side. 'Is this because of tonight?'

'Whose little protégée brought the house down?' he replied sarcastically.

'It was the song Harry, not me.'

'Oh fuck off, that's nonsense.'

'It's not!' she protested.

He took a sip from the Edinburgh crystal glass he was holding, thinking how sensual she looked in the peach-coloured silk wrap she was wearing. A sudden flame of desire raced through him which, he decided, he had no intention of giving into.

'Come back to bed, Harry?'

He shook his head.

'But it's cold down here.'

'Not with enough Scotch inside you it isn't.'

She went and knelt beside him. 'Don't be angry. Please?'

He didn't answer. Instead his eyes bored into hers.

'I'm sorry.'

'For what? Stealing the limelight.' What he didn't add was, *from me*.

'I didn't mean to. Honestly.'

He believed that, which somehow made matters even worse. 'But you did, princess. You did.'

'I'll speak to Levitt, we'll change the act back to the way it was.'

Harry barked out a laugh. 'After tonight! He'd never agree in a thousand years.'

'Then we'll go elsewhere when we're finished here.'

'Don't be stupid, Annie. There's not a management in town who'd take the old act now. They'll all want it the way it is.'

She sighed. 'So how often do you want me to say I'm sorry? I never meant this to happen.'

He ran a hand through her loose-flowing hair. 'Maybe not, but it did. Quite eclipsed out there tonight I was, quite eclipsed.'

'No, you weren't. I swear.'

'If you believe that then you're deluding yourself. I've been in this business a lot longer than you have. I know what's what. If I say I was eclipsed then I sodding well was. A flickering candle to your incandescent spotlight.'

She winced. 'You're being ridiculous.'

His pent-up emotions exploded causing him to twist a handful

150

of her hair viciously which made Annie gasp in pain. 'Don't tell me I'm ridiculous. Never do that,' he hissed.

'Harry, you're hurting me!'

'Good. Now you know what it feels like.'

'I love you, Harry,' she choked.

'And I love you too. But right at this moment I could slap you from one end of the room to the other.'

'Don't say things like that, Harry.'

He released her and, with a sob, she fell away from him. 'Come back to bed,' she pleaded again.

'When I feel like it and not before.'

She started to cry, small tears running down her cheeks. 'Don't let this come between us, Harry. I couldn't bear it.'

He regarded her coldly.

She rose, attempting to wipe away her tears. 'Come back to bed,' she repeated yet again. 'Let's make love.' She ached for the closeness.

'I'm not in the mood, princess, simply not in the mood.'

'Oh Harry,' she breathed, distraught.

'Now you toddle off and leave me alone.' He gestured at her with his glass. 'This is the only companion I want tonight.'

As she left the parlour she heard the chink of glass on glass.

Linnet screamed in agony. It was as if her body was being ripped apart by unseen giant hands that had thrust themselves inside her and were pulling in opposite directions.

When her screaming had subsided a cool cloth was placed on her forehead while the midwife murmured soothing, comforting words in her ear. All was going well. There was no need to worry.

Linnet panted, dimly aware she was covered in hot, sticky sweat, her hair plastered to her head and cheeks. How could she live through this? It seemed impossible. Then she was screaming again, a scream that turned into a high-pitched shriek.

Finally it was over, the baby delivered. She mumbled feverish thanks to God that she was still alive.

Somehow she found the energy to pull herself on to an elbow. 'Is it a boy or girl?' she queried.

'A beautiful girl, me dear,' the midwife beamed back. 'You should be proud.'

A girl. But Kevern had so wanted a boy. She'd warned him, but he hadn't listened. He'd been insistent that she'd bear him a son and heir.

How disappointed he was going to be, how terribly disappointed.

Those were Linnet's last thoughts as she drifted off into an
exhausted sleep.

Annie was taking tea in their parlour, while Harry was reading
the *Illustrated Mail*, when Ruby the maid appeared to announce
they had a caller. She then handed Harry a card, and he flinched
when he saw the name engraved on it.

'Show him straight in,' he instructed Ruby.

'Who is it, Harry?'

'Only Samuel Dearing, owner of Collins,' Harry replied excitedly.

Annie gulped: Collins' Music Hall, a by-word in their pro-
fession. She'd gone there to watch Marie Lloyd and knew that
all the greats had appeared there at some time or another.

'This is an unexpected pleasure, Mr Dearing,' Harry declared,
advancing upon the tubby figure as he was shown in.

The two men shook hands.

'May I introduce my partner, Annie Breeze,' Harry said,
indicating Annie.

Dearing gently shook her by the hand. 'How do you do?' he
smiled.

'I'm well, thank you.'

'Please sit down. Can I get you something? A drink perhaps?'
Harry queried solicitously.

'A cup of tea would be most pleasant.'

Harry hurried to the bell pull with the intention of ordering
Ruby to bring another cup and saucer.

'You have come a long way in a relatively short time,' Dearing
complimented Annie after he'd sat down.

'Why, thank you.'

'I watched your act the other night. It was most impressive,
most impressive indeed. In fact I couldn't get you out of my mind
afterwards.'

Annie acknowledged this further compliment with an in-
clination of her head.

'A wonderful voice. When you sang the Hollyhock song you
even reduced me to tears. And believe me, that takes some doing.'

Having spoken to Ruby, Harry returned to hover beside Annie.

'And how is my old friend Max Levitt?' Dearing inquired
politely.

'Never better,' Harry answered.

'You've been a huge success for him,' Dearing stated, addressing Annie.

'He's made pots out of us,' Harry preened.

'Indeed!' Dearing declared softly.

He had hard eyes, Annie thought, hard, though not unkind. This wasn't a man to trifle with. There again, neither was Max Levitt. They were cast from the same mould.

'Do you mind if I smoke?'

'No, please do,' Annie consented.

Instantly Harry had his gold cigarette case out and open. 'I've no cigars I'm afraid,' he apologized.

'Cigarettes are my preference,' Dearing admitted, after a slight hesitation. He accepted one of Harry's cigarettes, and a light. Harry lit up as well.

'Tell me something about yourself, Annie. Is that a West Country accent I detect?'

The way Annie spoke had changed considerably since her arrival in London. Although she'd dropped all local dialect and phraseology her voice still maintained a slight Devon burr.

Annie talked for a few minutes about her background, during which Dearing's cup and saucer arrived. Annie insisted on pouring out his tea herself.

'How interesting,' he murmured when she came to the end of her tale.

'Unlike me, I'm a born and bred Londoner,' Harry declared jocularly, knowing Dearing had had a similar upbringing.

Dearing glanced at him, smiled thinly, then returned his attention to Annie. 'Which brings me to the purpose of my visit. I want you to head the next bill at Collins.'

Annie drew in a sharp intake of breath, while Harry swallowed hard.

'Top of the bill,' Annie breathed. 'At Collins!'

Dearing gave her an amused smile, and nodded.

'We accept of course,' Annie said quickly.

'Providing the money—' Harry stopped short when Dearing held up a hand.

'I think you've both slightly misunderstood. The offer is for you alone, Annie, not the act as it is.' He fixed Harry with a sympathetic look. 'I'm sorry, Mr Bright.'

Harry sagged where he stood. 'I see,' he managed to respond at last.

'Me alone?' Annie whispered, pale faced.

Dearing nodded.

'That's out of the question, I'm afraid.'

Harry knew what it must have cost Annie to say that, just as it was going to cost him to say what he had to. 'No, Annie, it isn't.'

She stared at him. 'You don't mean that, Harry.'

'Oh, but I do. You can't turn down Collins. That would be sheer folly.'

'But we're a double act?'

'Are we?' He gave a short, bitter laugh. 'Mr Dearing is right, you know. You're the class performer, not me. I realized that when you initially sang Hollyhock. I suppose I knew then it was only a matter of time, though I've been trying to pretend otherwise to myself.'

Dearing nodded his approval. 'Bravely said, Mr Bright. You have my respect, sir. It takes a wise man to appreciate his own level.'

'I'll be all right,' Harry said to Annie. 'Believe me. And now, if you'll both excuse me, I'll leave you to discuss terms.'

Annie watched him walk towards the parlour door, her heart bleeding. She'd make this up to him, she vowed. Someway, somehow.

'Now Annie,' Dearing declared when they were alone. 'Here's what I propose.'

Annie forced herself to listen and concentrate.

On her opening night at Collins Annie captivated her audience just as she'd done at the Empire. Harry sat quietly listening to the rapturous applause, jealous beyond belief. He would have given anything, even signed a pact with the Devil himself, for that applause to be his.

And still on it went, the cheering, the clapping, the calling of her name.

'Excuse me,' Harry said, abruptly rising and pushing his way along the row, much to the annoyance of those he had to get past. 'Excuse me . . . excuse me . . .'

When Harry arrived at Annie's dressing room he found it already crowded with wellwishers and other artists. She stood in the centre, glass in hand, holding court.

'Harry!' she shouted above the din when she saw him. 'Over here.'

He elbowed his way through the throng, kissing her on the cheek when he reached her. 'You were out of this world,' he said.

'Thank you darling. Was your seat a good one?'

'Excellent.'

'I looked but didn't see you.'

He was relieved she didn't appear to have noticed his exit. He gazed about him. 'Quite a party.'

'Isn't it just!'

'You were quite superb, darling. You must be thrilled.' The speaker was a middle-aged man whom Harry didn't recognize.

'Harry, I'd like you to meet Viscount Huntley. Viscount, this is Harry Bright, my ex-partner.'

Ex, the word was like a knife plunged into him. He muttered something to the viscount who clearly wasn't interested, only having eyes for Annie. He wished he'd never come backstage, but knew he had had no option.

Suddenly Dearing was standing beside them. 'Mr Bright, how lovely to see you.'

Harry forced a smile on to his face. 'You must be delighted with this evening, Mr Dearing.'

'I most certainly am.' Dearing put an arm round Annie's shoulders. 'Isn't she wonderful?'

'Wonderful,' Harry agreed.

'Now,' Dearing said to Harry. 'When this mêlée's dispersed a few of us are going on to the Savoy. I do hope you'll accompany us?'

Harry could think of nothing worse. Talk of the spectre at the feast! 'No, I don't think so. This is Annie's night, she doesn't need me there.'

'But I do,' Annie frowned.

'You enjoy yourself and tell me all about it later. I'll be agog to hear.'

Shrewdly, Dearing understood the situation perfectly; he'd known too many artists during his long career in the music hall not to grasp Harry's dilemma. 'I notice you haven't got a drink, Mr Bright. Let me take you over to our little temporary bar and get you one.'

A few minutes later Annie glimpsed Harry fall into conversation with a pretty young thing who'd come with one of Dearing's guests. When she next looked for him he'd disappeared.

Chapter Nine

Still half asleep, Annie reached out for Harry whom she vaguely remembered coming to bed sometime after her. Her groping fingers found only empty space on his side of the bed.

Snapping fully awake she sat up, her brow creased in puzzlement. Where was he? Had he gone to the bathroom? But a glance at his open wardrobe told her he couldn't be there as his dressing gown was still hanging up.

Her heart sank in dismay. He must have risen and gone out early, unless she'd only imagined him coming to bed. Then she spotted a small pile of discarded clothes which informed her she hadn't. He'd been and gone.

She sighed. Things were rapidly deteriorating between them. There had been the row several weeks ago when he'd stayed out all night. He claimed he'd got drunk and dossed down with a chum from the Gluepot where he was once again performing his original act. And now this.

But it wasn't merely these irritants; it was their personal relationship which, for his part, had become cold and distant. Gone was the spontaneous kissing and touching, the delight in one another's company, and all the other little intimacies that had existed between them. How long was it since they'd made love? A fortnight at least. She'd approached him night after night but there was always some excuse, tiredness, headache, not in the mood, princess, too much alcohol to do anything; the excuses went on and on.

She'd tried to be patient, knowing how much her success at Collins must have hurt his pride. But just how long was this nonsense to continue?

How she loved him, far more than she'd have believed she could love any man. He'd become like a drug, something she just had to have.

It was simply a bad patch, she assured herself, one they'd eventually get over when he came to terms with things. All she had to do was continue to be patient and let time, the great healer, take its course.

At least he was working again, earning his own money and not having to rely on her income. She'd thought he was going to have apoplexy the first time he'd asked her for cash, cash she'd been only too happy to give him. He'd made such an issue of it, though, reminding her how he'd funded her to begin with. She'd told him she'd never forgotten that, and would be eternally grateful. But still he'd stalked off, muttering under his breath, not saying where he was going.

That was another thing. He was becoming more and more secretive nowadays; half the time she had no idea where he was or what he was doing. Here and there, was one of his favourite replies; no-one you'd know, when she'd inquired whom he'd been with.

'Oh well,' she murmured, flipping back the bedclothes. Another morning without Harry, her only hope being that he'd appear for lunch, though she doubted it.

The discarded clothing lay where it had been dropped, which annoyed her. Why couldn't he put it in the basket? Still, she mused with wry amusement, that was Harry for you.

Naked, she crossed to the clothes and picked them up. Other women in her position would have left them for the maid, but that wasn't Annie's way. Not having been born to a life of luxury and servants, she retained many of the habits drummed into her when young.

She frowned when she noticed the smear of lipstick on Harry's shirt. Bringing the shirt to her nose she sniffed, detecting the unmistakable smell of powder and personal female scent.

Annie went cold all over. Was he seeing someone else? Lipstick and powder might be explained, but personal female scent. There was no doubt that was what it was.

She wrinkled her nose in disgust and anger. Who had he been with? And doing what?

Surely he hadn't . . .

She threw the shirt from her, then went and sat on the end of the bed.

She mustn't jump to conclusions, she told herself. There might

157

well be a rational explanation. However, the thought that Harry might be cheating on her caused her to burst into tears.

Harry didn't return for lunch. In fact he didn't appear again until the small hours of the following morning when he found Annie waiting for him in the parlour.

'Hallo, princess,' he smiled. 'Still up?'

'I want to talk to you.'

He strolled over to the Scotch decanter. 'Then talk away. I'm all ears, sweetheart.'

'And who else is that?'

'I beg your pardon?'

'I said, who else is that? Your sweetheart?'

His face became devoid of expression. 'Whatever are you on about?'

'Who are you seeing, Harry? Are you sleeping with her? And I want the truth mind. No lies, the truth.'

'Drink?'

His coolness irritated her. 'No, I don't want a damn drink. I want an answer.'

He slowly poured himself a large whisky to which he added a liberal splash of soda. 'Believe it or not, first today,' he said.

'Harry?'

He sat facing her, his face still expressionless. 'Now what on earth is this all about?'

'Your shirt.'

'What about my shirt?'

She produced it from behind her back and threw it at him. 'It's got lipstick on it and smells not only of powder but some female. It stinks of her.'

The shirt had hit Harry on the chest and dropped to his lap. He now picked it up and stared at it. 'Dear me,' he murmured.

'Well?' she demanded harshly.

His features creased into an amused smile. 'The lipstick must be Elaine's,' he mused.

'Elaine?'

'One of the dancers at the Gluepot. I did her a favour and last night she came rushing up, threw her arms round my neck and gave me a kiss of thanks. Clearly her lipstick somehow got on to my shirt.'

'But why should her smell get on to it?'

'Annie darling, she was sweating like a stuck pig at the time having just come "off".'

'Oh!' Annie whispered, feeling somewhat deflated. She'd told herself there might well be a rational explanation, and the one he'd given her made perfect sense. Dancers did sweat profusely, she knew that only too well. And many music hall artists, like their theatrical counterparts, were flamboyant in their behaviour. It was quite natural for a dancer Harry had helped to kiss him in such a manner.

'Were you jealous?' Harry teased, a twinkle in his eye.

'What was I supposed to think!' she retorted, a slight sulk in her voice for she was feeling foolish.

Harry crossed his heart then held up a hand. 'Totally innocent guv, I swear. Don't send me to Botany Bay.'

Annie sighed, and with the sigh all the anger and tension drained out of her. 'I'm sorry,' she mumbled.

'And so you should be!' he further teased. 'Imagine suspecting me of carrying on with someone else. I'm mortified.'

A niggle of doubt returned. 'You're not, are you, Harry? I couldn't bear it if you were.'

He laid his drink aside, and went over to her, going down on his knees. 'You have no worries in that respect Annie, believe me. I love you, with all my heart.'

'And I love you the same way Harry. I don't know what I'd ever do if I lost you. The very thought makes me cringe inside.'

He took her hand and kissed its palm. 'I think you and I should go upstairs, princess.'

A thrill ran through her, for there was nothing she wanted, craved, more than for them to make love.

He pulled her to her feet. 'You go and get ready, I'll sort out down here.'

'Kiss me.'

Her senses swam under the kiss which was like fire on her lips and in her mouth.

'Now go, I won't be a minute,' he said when the kiss was finally over.

She almost ran from the room.

'Oh Harry,' she crooned as he slid off her. 'That was just unbelievable. It's been too long. It mustn't be so long again.'

'No,' he agreed softly.

'I know you've been upset, and I can understand that. But it mustn't come between us, Harry.'

'It won't,' he assured her.

'Promise?'

'Promise.'

He curled an arm round her, while with his free hand he stroked her hair. 'How was the show tonight?' he asked.

'Fine. And yours?'

'All right.'

'Just all right?'

He hadn't been good, he thought. Somehow he'd lost part of his self-confidence and that was affecting his act, which worried him. Since splitting with Annie his timing simply wasn't what it had been. Why only the other night . . . He recalled the solitary boo with a shudder.

'What is it?' she demanded.

'Nothing.'

'Are you sure?'

He smiled in the darkness, thinking of Elaine. He'd never truly appreciated before just how supple dancers were; it was amazing what they could do with their bodies. The shirt had been a stupid mistake on his part, one he mustn't repeat. He would be more careful in future.

He was still reflecting on Elaine when, wrapped in his arms, Annie fell asleep.

For the next three months life went swimmingly as far as Annie was concerned. It seemed to her that she and Harry were as close as they'd ever been. Bed was fantastic, while the old intimacies were back in place. He bought her flowers, chocolates, made her laugh a great deal, took her out to meals. She couldn't have been happier, believing him to have come to terms with the fact she was topping the bill at Collins while he could only manage middle of the bill at the Gluepot, the Angel Inn and Highbury Barn.

Then slowly, almost imperceptibly to begin with, it all started to turn sour again. She'd catch him looking at her in a strange, antagonistic way, while the late-night suppers decreased in frequency, and the intimacies, the spontaneous touching and caressing diminished.

It finally came to a head one night when he arrived home blind drunk.

'You've had enough, Harry,' she stated as he unsteadily tried to pour Scotch from the decanter, getting more on the carpet than in his glass.

'Fuck you!' he snarled.

'You can hardly stand.'

160

He chucked the contents of the glass down his throat, hiccuped and, with one eye shut to aid concentration, began refilling his glass, spilling more Scotch on to the carpet in the process.

She laid a restraining hand on his arm. 'Enough Harry,' she pleaded.

He shrugged her off. 'Don't think because you're Miss High and Mighty you can give me orders. I won't stand for it, d'you hear?'

'I'm not giving you orders.'

'Oh yes you fucking well are. If I want a sodding drink I'll have one and that's that.' He stuck his chin out belligerently. 'Do you understand?'

'There's no need to swear,' she chided softly.

'I'll swear if I fucking well want to!'

He looked dreadful, she thought. Deep lines were etched under his eyes and down from his nose. His normally sallow skin was dead and lifeless – it might have belonged to a corpse.

He lurched across the room and dropped into a chair. He'd completely lost his audience that night for the first time ever. And he blamed Annie. The split-up of their act was causing all his problems. Something had been switched off inside him when that had happened. Now he was actually scared to go on, while his timing went from bad to worse. He knew if this continued he wouldn't be invited back to any of the venues he was currently playing.

'What's wrong?' she asked.

He glared at her, but didn't reply.

'Harry?'

He slopped whisky into his mouth, with some of it dribbling down his chin. 'Leave me alone,' he hissed.

'I can't stand seeing you like this.'

'Then sit down,' he riposted, and laughed, imagining he was being uproariously funny.

Annie found herself shaking, though she was quite calm inside. She stared at him, thinking for the millionth time how much she loved him. Well, her man was in trouble and she must somehow help.

'I think we both need a break,' she declared.

'A break! And how will we do that? I have to work to earn and you're the big star at Collins. So how can we take a bloody break?'

'We've money put by—'

'You mean you have!'

'All right,' she said patiently. 'So I have. We can use that and go somewhere for a while. How about that honeymoon you always promised me?'

'Honeymoon!' He barked out a laugh. 'Ooohh, lovely,' he added, voice filled with sarcasm.

'I can arrange matters with Dearing, stress how important it is. He can hardly refuse when I tell him we're getting married.'

Harry fixed her with a baleful, bleary, stare. 'I can't marry you, Annie. Never could.'

She gazed at him in astonishment. 'Why not?'

'Because, dear heart, I'm already married.'

'Already . . .' He was joking, had to be. There had never been any mention of this before. 'I don't believe it,' she replied thickly.

'I swear it's true.' His lips thinned into a malevolent smile. 'So what do you think of that?'

'You're lying?'

He slowly shook his head. 'Word of honour Miss Top Of The Bill. Her name's Brenda, another Eastender, who was also in the business, which is how I met her. We had a marvellous two years together and then the cow met someone else and left me. End of story.'

Annie needed to sit down, her mind was whirling. This explained Harry's reticence about setting a date, and all that nonsense about insisting on an exotic foreign honeymoon.

'Why didn't you tell me before?' she queried.

He shrugged. 'Don't know. I thought . . . maybe I'd lose you if I did. Maybe you'd never have agreed to live with me. Whatever, my reasons don't matter. I've told you now.'

'Are there . . . any children?'

Harry took another swallow of Scotch, then pulled himself to his feet and headed back to the decanter. 'No. At least none of mine.'

That was something at least, Annie thought. What a bombshell! Harry already married. She still hadn't taken it in.

In the middle of pouring, Harry paused in reflection. 'She was quite a girl, Brenda. Great fun. Rotten performer though, but pretty. Got by on her looks.'

Annie was instantly jealous. She wanted to know all about this Brenda, Harry's wife.

'And she ran off with someone else?'

'A sodding tightrope walker of all people. The Great Galloni, a greasy Iti.'

'Where are they now?'

162

Harry made a face. 'No idea, and don't care either. Hell mend the bitch for what she did.'

He stumbled returning to his chair, splashing more whisky onto the carpet. 'Christ I'm pissed,' he mumbled. 'My head's going round and round like a bleeding carousel.'

'Are you still in love with her?'

Harry leered at Annie. 'It was never love between us, but unbridled lust. Pure and simple.'

Annie thought it was awful. She folded her hands in her lap, and stared down at them, her mind curiously blank. When she glanced up at Harry his head was thrown back and he was fast asleep, his refilled whisky glass still clutched tightly in his hand.

She removed the glass then covered him with a rug. He could stay in the parlour that night as it would be impossible for her to get him upstairs by herself.

She turned out the gas mantles, then stood beside him, staring down at him in the darkness. He had now begun to gently snore.

'Brenda,' she said aloud. What a loathsome name.

Harry suddenly snorted as though in disagreement.

Harry was dreadfully hungover at breakfast, and looked it. There were purple patches under his eyes while his cheeks were concave.

'Do you remember anything about last night?' Annie asked quietly.

He nodded, which proved to be a mistake, and groaned, clutching his head.

Serves him right, Annie thought with grim satisfaction. Her own emotions were mixed; anger, betrayal, but above all, love. Which he hardly deserved, she told herself.

'Tell me more about her, this Brenda,' she said.

'Not much to tell.'

'What colour hair did she have?'

'Red. Well auburn really.'

'And figure?'

'Bit boyish. Quite different to yours.'

That pleased her. 'Age?'

Harry did a quick mental reckoning. 'She'll be twenty-five now. No, six.'

'And you weren't in love with her?'

Harry gazed down at his kipper in disgust. He couldn't possibly eat it. He pushed the plate away from him and reached for his coffee cup. 'At the time I thought I was.'

'But you weren't?'

'Afterwards, I decided I hadn't been. Now I know for certain.'

'How?'

'Because I know what real love feels like.'

'Don't smooth talk me, Harry Bright!' she flared.

'It's true though,' he mumbled contritely.

She softened towards him. 'I didn't sleep a wink last night,' she said. 'Hardly surprising, under the circumstances, I suppose.'

'I'm sorry.'

'You look awful.'

He touched his still unshaven face. 'I feel like something the cat dragged in.'

She laughed.

'Do you forgive me, just blurting it out as I did? It was a terrible way to tell you.'

'And a shock, coming as it did straight out the blue. I had no idea.'

'Why should you?'

'But it's over, finished? She's with another man?'

'Completely over, Annie. I swear.'

'And you wouldn't want her back?'

'Not for anything. In retrospect the marriage was a mistake, she did me a favour by running off with the Great Galloni. Even if he hadn't happened along we'd never have lasted.'

It pleased Annie to hear that. 'Why have you never divorced?'

'There was never any need to. Anyway, divorce costs a lot of money.'

'There's a need to now,' Annie stated softly.

He stared at her across the table. 'Are you talking about us?'

'Of course.'

'There's still the outlay,' he sighed. 'And although I'm working I have been spending a great deal recently.'

'I have an account,' Annie said. 'We'll use my money.'

He shifted uneasily in his chair. 'I don't really want to do that. It doesn't seem fair.'

'You'll do it nonetheless. These things take time, so the sooner you see a solicitor the better. I'll foot the bills.'

'I don't deserve you,' he smiled weakly.

'Probably not. But you've got me, come what may.'

'Yes,' he breathed.

Then his face fell when he recalled the previous evening's performance. To lose an audience! The humiliation and shame. And all because . . .

He picked up his coffee cup and had another sip. He felt

terrible. Besides the headache his nerves were strung out, and there was a gnawing, nauseous sensation in the pit of his stomach.

Annie gazed at Harry over the rim of her own coffee cup. The jealousy that had raged in her through the night was still there, though now somewhat muted. He might be married to Brenda, but he was now hers and would remain so. He loved her and had never loved Brenda. He'd be hers for ever, till death them did part.

It was hardly an ideal situation, but she could cope with it. Harry would get his divorce and marry her. The divorce was merely an unforseen obstacle that could relatively easily be overcome. They'd have that divorce yet, she promised herself. Just as one day *she'd* be Mrs Harry Bright and not Brenda.

'And you'll lay off the booze for a while. Getting drunk doesn't help anything.'

He gave her another weak smile. 'I promise.'

'Just make sure you keep it, that's all.'

'I'm going up to shave,' he announced, rising from his chair. He pecked her on the cheek before leaving the room.

Annie attacked the remains of her kipper, pretending it was Brenda's face she was cutting into with her knife.

'Well, you used to be a lot better than that,' Celeste said to Harry who was in the process of lighting a cigarette.

'Sorry, gel. I'm just not myself of late.'

'I'll say. You were in and out faster than a jack rabbit.'

He grinned at her. 'What the hell do you know about jack rabbits coming from Hackney?'

'Only by reputation, darling. If you take my meaning.'

He reached across and ran a hand over her smooth flank. 'When does Rafe return to London?' Rafe was her friend and patron.

'Not for another four days.'

'So while the cat's away—'

Celeste smiled lazily at him. 'I was always fond of you, Harry, you know that.'

'And I of you. I had high hopes for us once.'

'We're good friends, Harry, but it could never be more than that. The occasional dalliance between the sheets is fine, fun for both of us. But we'd never get on in the long term.'

'Perhaps it would be different if I was rich,' he replied cynically.

That amused her. 'Perhaps, perhaps not. We're not likely to find out though, are we?'

His good humour vanished abruptly. 'No,' he agreed harshly.

'Poor Harry,' she murmured, returning his caress.

'I honestly believed I had what it takes, Celeste, that I would someday get to the top. And then . . .' He almost spat the words out. 'Annie came along.'

'Who *has* got to the top.'

'Bitch!' he hissed.

'Oh come on Harry, it's hardly her fault she's made it and you haven't.'

'The galling thing is I taught her everything she knows. If it wasn't for me she'd still be pulling pints at the Angel Inn.'

'Her success really rankles, doesn't it?'

'She was a nothing, a nobody until she met me. And now look at her, a sodding star at Collins while I'm back where I started. And . . .' He trailed off, then said vehemently, 'not even doing *that* well.'

'How do you mean?'

He explained to her how his timing had gone off and that he was losing his audiences. 'I've gone to pieces since splitting with her,' he complained.

'It'll all come back, you'll see.'

His expression darkened to become thunderous. 'I wish we'd never met.'

'You don't really mean that, Harry,' Celeste said softly.

'But I do!'

Celeste contemplated him thoughtfully. It never crossed her mind that she was wronging Annie by sleeping with Harry. She was an ex-actress after all, a breed whose morals and ethics are far more elastic than those of so-called conventional society.

'Maybe you should leave London,' she declared.

'What?'

'At the moment you're a little fish in a big pond. Why not try the provinces where you'd be a big fish in a little pond? It's certainly worth thinking about.'

'The provinces?' Harry mused.

'Why not? A break from town might do you the world of good, rebuild your confidence which, from what I can see, is at a very low ebb.'

'It would mean leaving Annie,' he stated.

Celeste shrugged. 'So? From what you've told me things aren't going very well between you anyway. A separation might help that as well.'

It was an idea, Harry thought, although he felt unwilling to leave London, where he'd been born and brought up. The capital was food and drink to him.

As for Annie, well . . . There was always another woman round the corner, always had been where he was concerned. He certainly didn't love her any more, though she believed he did. He encouraged that belief because it suited his purposes.

Love her? How could he when she had what he wanted most and he was eaten up by jealousy because of it. His jealousy had turned poisonous within him, permeating his whole being, body and soul. He hated her, more like. Why there were times when he had an almost overwhelming desire to punch her in the face, to wipe off that smug, self-satisfied look she wore so often nowadays, to revenge himself a little for his humiliation. It was bad enough knowing he'd never get to the top, but to come so close and then be dropped while she went on to acclaim and glory. That was almost beyond enduring.

'Harry?'

'What?' he snapped.

'I said, a separation might also help matters between the pair of you.'

He grunted, and drew heavily on his cigarette. The longer the separation the better as far as he was concerned. In fact, if he was totally honest with himself, it wouldn't bother him in the least if he never clapped eyes on the bitch again. Then perhaps the wound might begin to heal.

But Celeste was right; as long as he stayed in London she'd be around as a constant reminder. The provinces could well be the answer to his problem and dilemma. He would make enquiries, put out a few feelers for he had no contacts outside London.

He ground out his cigarette, feeling somewhat better. 'You're a real pal,' he said to Celeste, who laughed throatily.

He put Annie from his mind as he gazed at Celeste's naked form.

'Again?' she smiled as he moved purposefully towards her.

'Again,' he confirmed.

This time there was no mention of jack rabbits.

Linnet stared at herself in the mirror, dismayed by the reflection gazing back. She was in her twenty-third year and looked forty. She ran a calloused hand through her hair which was like straw. As for her face! How tired she appeared, tired and worn out before her time.

It was the baby of course, Morwenna. Looking after the child and doing a full day's work round the house and farm had exhausted her beyond belief. Kevern made no allowances for the added burden of a child; he expected her to do everything she'd done before, and without complaint. On the one occasion she'd mentioned it he looked at her in astonishment, replying she was no different to any other woman in her position. Everyone else managed, so why couldn't she?

If only she hadn't had such a terrible birth; that had really taken it out of her. Nor had Kevern been sympathetic when it came to subsequent lovemaking. She'd told him it was painful for her, but that didn't seem to bother him. He was there whenever the mood took him and all she could do was put up with it, hoping he'd be quick and it would soon be over.

She dreaded the thought of falling pregnant again, and the subsequent birth. Hopefully, when it did happen, she'd have the boy Kevern so desperately wanted. Maybe then she could persuade him somehow to be less demanding. Not that he was over demanding, but he was certainly consistent.

She let out a long, weary sigh. There was butter to make, and then the pigs needed feeding, and after them the hens. After that the supper followed by the clearing-up and . . .

She could have screamed, she thought, or gone running from the house.

'Oohhh!' she groaned when Morwenna began to wail in the next-door room. Would it never end!

She threw one last glance at herself in the mirror. A hag, that's what she'd become, a hag!

'Coming darling,' she muttered, dragging herself from her chair. 'Coming!'

She groaned again when she found that Morwenna's nappy had worked itself loose and the cot clothes were soiled as a result.

Cold, clammy, yellow fog swirled and eddied round the hansom cab as it clattered through the night. Inside Annie sat reflecting on the supper she'd just had with Samuel Dearing and A.E. Mathews, currently appearing at the Grand, whom she'd liked enormously and who'd been an ideal supper companion.

'Cab!'

The voice that cut through the fog was unmistakably Harry's. 'Cab!' he called again, and laughed.

Annie was about to instruct the cabbie to halt when she saw the two figures entwined round one another – a male and a female.

'Cab!' Harry shouted yet again.

Annie shrank back in her seat, disappearing into the shadows. Harry and a woman!

'Don't worry, Elaine, there'll be another along in a moment,' Annie heard distinctly as the cab went by. Elaine! The name of the dancer who'd supposedly kissed him because he'd done her a favour. She could well imagine just what that favour had been. Bastard, she thought. Bastard! He was cheating on her, after all. She was certain of it. Entwined together like a couple of copulating snakes, out on the street too. No, there was nothing platonic about that friendship. They were lovers.

'Bastard,' she repeated as the cab continued on its way, rattling over the cobblestones.

Harry didn't return that night, and the following morning Annie, still furious, decided to visit Celeste and air her grievances.

Celeste listened sombrely to Annie's tirade, every so often making a sympathetic face and nodding.

'My poor dear,' Celeste murmured when Annie eventually paused for breath.

Annie twisted her hands in her lap. 'How could he, Celeste? How could he? He knows how much I love him, just as I know he loves me.'

'Men,' Celeste smiled thinly, and shook her head.

'I could kill him. I really could.'

'Try and calm down, Annie, you'll have apoplexy if you carry on like this.'

'I'm sorry, I shouldn't burden you with my problems.'

'You're my friend, Annie, and that's what friends are for. Now why don't you have a drink or I'll send for some tea.'

'Tea please,' Annie answered.

'And have a slice of lovely Madeira cake.'

'No cake, Celeste, I couldn't eat a thing.'

'I've been wondering all night what she looks like, I couldn't see her properly in the fog,' Annie went on, resuming the subject. 'Just a figure, draped round him.'

'You might have got this wrong, you know. The pair of them may simply have been drunk . . .'

'Then why didn't he come home?' Annie interrupted.

'Perhaps he passed out somewhere.'

'That's an excuse he's used before,' Annie responded hotly. 'No, Harry just isn't the type to have a platonic relationship. And certainly not with a dancer. He's sleeping with her, you can bet on that.'

'What are you going to do?'

'Have it out with him, what else?'

'Do you think that wise?'

'Of course it's wise!' Annie exploded. 'You don't think I'm going to sit back quietly and let him carry on, do you? What do you take me for?'

'And what if you lose him?'

'I won't,' Annie replied emphatically. 'He loves me too much for that.' She paused, then said, 'Everything was fine until I got top billing at Collins. I thought he'd got over that upset but apparently not. It's only a matter of time before he accepts the situation, you'll see. In the meantime, no matter how frustrated he is, I won't have him sleeping with any little tart that takes his fancy. That'll stop right now.'

Celeste felt sorry for Annie whom she liked enormously. The girl really was distraught. Could Harry talk himself out of this pickle? It would be interesting to see if he could. Rising, she crossed to the bell pull and tugged.

'Can I use your lavatory?' Annie asked.

'Of course. Help yourself. You know where it is. And before you go, are you sure about that cake? It's quite delicious.'

'I'd be ill if I ate anything Celeste, and that's the truth.'

'Oh dear,' Celeste murmured when Annie had left the room, and wondered how far Harry had progressed with his plans for the provinces. He hadn't been in touch for the past few weeks. Now she knew why – a dancer called Elaine.

Annie used the toilet then washed her hands in the sink. She was drying them off when she noticed a faint gold sparkle in the corner of the room. She re-hung the towel, then crossed to the sparkle, curious to know what it was. It proved to be a gold cufflink that was partially hidden by a loose section of linoleum.

She recognized it immediately. It was Harry's, one of a pair she'd given him. He must have dropped it during a visit, she thought.

Then it struck her that things didn't quite make sense. If Harry had dropped it while using the sink he'd have searched until he found it. The room wasn't that large, after all. And he could hardly have failed to have noticed that it had fallen out as he would have had a flapping cuff.

This was a mystery. Unless of course he'd searched and been unable to find it. But that didn't really make sense either. He would have known it was somewhere and would surely have gone on looking until he had found it.

Then her own words, spoken earlier, came thundering back into her brain. '*Harry just isn't the type to have a platonic relationship*' – which was precisely what she'd thought he had with Celeste, what she'd *presumed* he'd had with her.

That would explain it. If they'd been up to high jinks together then he might not have known where he'd dropped the cuff link, nor where to look for it.

Harry and Celeste! Had that been an affair, as well? And there she'd been, pouring out her heart to a woman who'd also been sleeping with the man she loved.

She was imagining things, she told herself, jumping to conclusions. Harry and Celeste were old friends. And yet, the fact remained that Harry wasn't the type to have a platonic relationship, not with someone as gorgeous as Celeste.

Of course it could be that Harry had tried in the past and been rebuffed by Celeste, who simply didn't fancy him. But there again, it was highly unlikely that Harry would maintain such a friendship without there being a sexual element to it.

What a fool she'd been, she berated herself. Why had she never twigged before!

She stared at the cuff link cradled in the palm of her hand, remembering Harry's delight when she'd given him the pair.

Was she wrong? Doing Celeste an injustice? There was one way to find out.

Annie was composed when she returned to find Celeste waiting for her. She positioned herself opposite Celeste, and smiled.

'How long have you been fucking Harry?' she asked.

A momentary guilty look flashed across Celeste's face, enough to tell Annie she was right. The denials that followed were meaningless.

Celeste was still spouting those denials when Annie took her leave.

Harry slapped Annie so hard she flew backwards a good six feet before becoming entangled with a small table and crashing to the floor.

'I've wanted to do that for so long,' he breathed heavily.

'How could you, Harry? You love me,' she sobbed. She had just confronted him about both Celeste and Elaine.

'Love you? I did, but not any more, Miss Top Of The Bill.'

171

She started to get to her feet but stopped when he advanced to stand towering over her, his face contorted and inflamed.

'You don't mean that, Harry.'

'Mean it? I've never meant anything more in my life,' he spat in reply.

Fear rose in her, not of physical abuse, but of the fact that he might actually be telling the truth. Grabbing his leg she desperately clung to it.

'Harry,' she wailed.

He stared at her in contempt. 'Let go,' he commanded, trying to shake her off.

'You're not thinking straight, Harry. You're confused. I can see now you're even more upset than I thought. But we'll sort it out,' she babbled hysterically.

He hit her again, the palm of his hand cracking against the side of her face. Despite the blow she still didn't release him, but tightened her grip.

'I'm going out,' he stated.

'No, Harry. We have to talk.'

'We have talked. There's nothing further to say.'

She raised a tear-stained face to him. 'Don't leave me now. Not like this. Please?' she pleaded.

'I'm meeting Elaine.'

That was a blow of another kind. 'You can't.'

'Why not?' he sneered.

'You just can't. You love *me*.'

'I told you, not any more. Just accept it.'

'I won't. I won't,' she further babbled.

He attempted to prise her hands from his leg. Pity her? He didn't in the least. She had top billing at Collins for consolation, whereas he . . .

'I'll do anything you want Harry, anything. Just say and I'll do it. Here, in bed, it doesn't matter.'

He finally succeeded in releasing his leg. When he pushed her, she cried out as she tumbled over on to her side.

'I won't be in tonight either,' he said, backing off a little.

'Don't do that. I need you here.'

'Sod you,' he snarled, and turned away.

'Harry! Harry!'

She began crawling after him with the intention of grabbing his leg again, but stopped short when the door was banged shut in her face.

'Harry,' she moaned. The pain of what he'd said and his hasty departure threatened to destroy her.

'*Harry!*' she yelled at the top of her voice. But there was no response.

Bowing her head, she continued to weep.

When Annie got back from a West End hairdressers, she knew the moment she saw Ruby's expression that something was terribly wrong. 'What is it?' she demanded.

'It's the master, madam. He's gone.'

'Gone?' Annie repeated in a croak.

'Came back while you were out, packed his things and left.'

Annie staggered to a chair. This had been her worst nightmare. During the two previous sleepless nights she'd convinced herself that her differences with Harry would soon blow over, that he'd see his affairs with Elaine and Celeste as nothing compared to their relationship.

Annie ran past Ruby and raced upstairs to their bedroom. She stopped abruptly, hand flying to her mouth, when she saw his empty wardrobe, the doors wide open.

She started to tremble all over. Harry gone! She just couldn't believe it.

Then she noticed her jewellery box was open as well. He'd taken everything, all the jewellery she'd bought herself and that he'd given her, including the gold bracelet.

Her cash box was missing from the drawer where it had been kept. She couldn't think offhand how much had been inside, but it had been a fairly substantial sum as she hadn't been to the bank for weeks.

She sat on the edge of the bed and gazed at it, remembering the many times they'd made glorious love between its sheets. Pictures flashed through her mind, memories of that lovemaking.

Ruby appeared in the doorway. 'Is there anything I can do, madam?'

Annie shook her head.

'A cup of coffee maybe?'

'No,' Annie whispered, stunned and shocked to the very core of her being.

'Is there a letter or note?' she asked Ruby.

'I'm sorry,' Ruby answered.

No letter nor note, not even that. For the first time she truly appreciated what it must have been like for her mother and father when she'd disappeared.

173

'Did he say where he went?' she queried.

'No, madam. Only that he was leaving and wouldn't be back.'

'He will be. He will be, I'm sure of it,' Annie answered quickly.

Ruby doubted that very much, but kept her opinion to herself. Annie clasped her hands in her lap and stared into space. When Ruby returned to the bedroom several hours later she found Annie in the same position, not having moved. She might have been carved from stone.

Chapter Ten

Roxanne stared out of the train window at the lush Devon countryside rolling past, thinking how good it felt to be going home. It was a beautiful summer's day with the crops ripening in the fields; that year it promised to be a bumper harvest.

It was now four months since Harry had decamped and during those months she'd suffered something of a breakdown. She'd never sung again since that fateful day and her spot at Collins had been filled by the popular Kate Carney. With Harry's departure she'd simply gone to pieces. Distraught in the extreme, she'd found herself unable to set foot in Collins, far less sing and entertain.

Samuel Dearing had proved a brick. He'd come round that first evening when she hadn't appeared, listened to her tale of woe, and been most sympathetic. He believed wrongly that she'd soon get over it, or at least be able to go back on stage before too long. But instead of getting better her mental condition had worsened. Soon she'd refused to leave the house, and then she'd taken to her bed.

Her tears had been endless, day upon day, night upon night, and all the while she firmly believed that Harry would reappear begging her forgiveness and reaffirming his love.

But Harry hadn't; he'd simply vanished without trace. She'd had enquiries made but neither Bert at the Angel Inn nor anyone else knew of his whereabouts. She'd even steeled herself, despite the humiliation, and contacted Celeste who'd written back saying she'd no idea either.

She might have remained in bed for ever, waiting, hoping, except that her financial situation had forced her to make a decision. She'd been earning good money for the past couple of years, but a lot of it had been spent there and then, as she and Harry had indulged themselves living an extravagant life.

The sensible thing would have been for her to return to the stage, but she'd simply been unable to do so. Why that should be the case she didn't know – perhaps because the stage, in her mind, was inexorably tied up with Harry.

Anyway, she doubted she'd have been much good if she had made a come-back. She'd lost all heart and as a consequence would have been dull, which would have been no use to anyone, least of all her. And so she'd decided to give it all up, turn her back on music hall, and return to her family and her roots.

Dearing had been appalled when she'd told him, arguing that all she needed was more rest, perhaps a holiday. But she'd been adamant, her stage career was over, for the time being anyway. She needed a complete break from music hall, Islington, London. She'd left Dearing with the hope that she'd return one day, but in her heart of hearts she didn't believe she would. A part of her life had ended, horribly so. Now it was time for a new beginning, a fresh start, but a fresh start from a place she knew, where she would be at ease, loved and welcome.

She smiled thinking how marvellous it would be to see her family again, and what a surprise it would be for them when she turned up on the doorstep. Return of the prodigal!

'Cooeee!'

Linnet paused to wipe her hands on her apron. Now who was that? 'In the kitchen!' she called out in reply.

At first she didn't recognize the glamorous figure that appeared in the doorway, then her jaw dropped. Unconsciously she smoothed back her hair which badly needed washing.

'Hallo,' Roxanne smiled.

'You!'

'In person.'

Roxanne rushed to Linnet and threw her arms round her. 'I'm home,' she declared.

Linnet was momentarily lost for words. 'Roxanne,' she managed at last.

How lovely to hear her real name again, Roxanne thought with delight. Annie Breeze was no more. She was Roxanne Hawkins again, a girl from St Petroc and a farmer's daughter.

Linnet was furious. If only she'd had some warning she'd have tidied herself up a bit. She must look such a mess, particularly compared to this elegant creature who was embracing her. Damn Roxanne, she might have written.

Roxanne held Linnet at arms' length and stared at her. 'You look tired,' she commented.

Of course she was tired! She always was nowadays. 'And you look . . . well, fantastic.'

Roxanne ignored the compliment in her excitement. 'Where's Ma? And I suppose Da's out in the fields?'

Oh heavens, Linnet thought, of course, Roxanne didn't know. 'I think you'd better sit down and I'll put the kettle on.'

'But I want to see Ma.'

'You can't,' Linnet stated heavily.

'Why not?'

'I said, you'd better sit down. A lot has happened round here since you went away. There's a deal for you to catch up on.'

Roxanne settled in one of the chairs in front of the range and gazed at her sister, looking puzzled.

Linnet began with the tragedy in the snow.

After a while Roxanne made Morwenna's acquaintance, then changed into something simpler and more appropriate for the farm. She insisted on visiting her parents' graves alone where she grieved for over an hour.

The last thing she'd expected was this. It had simply never occurred to her that her Ma and Da wouldn't be there on her return. And why should it have done? They'd both been relatively young and full of life, after all. Now they were dead and she'd never see them again.

She wouldn't have believed that she had any tears left in her after Harry, but she had. Filled with deep regret, bitter remorse and shame, she wept over the two graves, begging their forgiveness for what she'd done.

If only she'd left a letter, and how that act had rebounded on her, written to tell them where she was or at least that she was safe and doing well, something to relieve the pain and agony they must have experienced by her disappearance.

How thoughtless she'd been, how callous. But, if she had any defence at all, it had been a callousness born of youth and inexperience. No wonder her Da had reacted in the way he had, by cutting her out of his will. She didn't blame him in the least, she understood. Not that she'd ever given any thought to her inheritance, that had always been something in the far and distant future.

177

If there was one consolation it was that they'd died together with one another for comfort. It was a small consolation perhaps, but one nonetheless.

And now Linnet was married to Kevern Stoneman and they had a little girl.

Her world had turned upside down when Harry left. Now, only a few months later, it had turned upside down again. What she'd expected to be a joyous homecoming, knowing there would be recriminations of course, had been transformed into another profound loss and hammerblow.

It was still a beautiful summer's day, but as she walked slowly back to the farm it might have been deep midwinter.

Kevern, in stockinged feet, came into the kitchen, saw Roxanne and went white. He thought her a vision of loveliness.

'Hallo, Kevern,' she smiled.

'Well, bugger me,' he declared.

She kissed him on the cheek. 'I only found out when I arrived in earlier that you're now my brother-in-law. That and a few other surprises.'

He shot Linnet a perplexed glance. Did this mean trouble? 'I'd hardly have recognized you,' he said to Roxanne.

She smoothed down her plain skirt. 'I've lost weight recently, but that's another story. How are you?'

'Never better.'

'You're certainly looking fit.'

'As a flea, Roxanne, as a flea.'

Linnet set a cup of strong tea for him on the table which she did every evening when he returned from work.

'You'll have learned about your Ma and Da then,' he stated.

She nodded, her expression grim.

'And that Linnet inherited everything because of you running off like you did.' He waited anxiously for her reply.

'Yes.'

'So what's your reaction to that?'

Roxanne shrugged. 'I suppose I got what I asked for. I don't blame Da for what he did. It was understandable in the circumstances, I suppose, Da being Da and all.'

Kevern relaxed. She'd accepted the situation, which was a great relief. Not that she could have done anything about it, but at least there wasn't going to be any friction.

He went and picked up his cup, taking a large swallow from it. 'I'm worried about Henrietta,' he said to Linnet. 'She's down

178

on her milk which tain't like her.' Henrietta was one of their cows.

'What's the matter do you think?'

'Don't know. But whatever, I hopes it don't last or get worse. Good beast that.'

Morwenna toddled into the room and ran to her father.

'Hallo, my lover,' he declared, scooping her up into his arms.

'Da, Da!' Morwenna burbled in reply, obviously delighted.

'What's for supper?' Kevern asked Linnet.

'Stargazy pie.'

Roxanne was thrilled; she had fond memories of the dish, recalling that it had been one of Aunt Elvira's favourites.

'Roxanne's home to stay,' Linnet informed Kevern.

'Oh?'

'Naturally she didn't expect to find things as they are. I said she could have her old room back, if that's all right with you?'

Kevern glanced at Roxanne, who was even more beautiful than he remembered. It would be a treat having her round the house.

'I'll be helping of course, earning my keep,' Roxanne said.

'Then I don't see why there should be any problem.'

'And I can certainly use the extra pair of hands,' Linnet went on. 'They'll come in right handy.'

'That's settled then,' Kevern declared, returning Morwenna to the floor.

Over supper Roxanne told them about her life in London, intentionally failing to mention she'd lived with Harry, describing him briefly and simply as an ex-partner, while they informed her of the lie that had been put about that she'd gone to Canada to account for the non-appearance at her parents' funeral.

'Hurry up, it's sore,' Linnet complained to Kevern later that night in bed.

'But I've hardly started!' he retorted.

'I knows that, Kevern, but it be sore all the same. There's nothing I can do about it, I'm sorry.'

His lips thinned in the darkness. To be told that was enough to put any man off his stroke. Their lovemaking, to his chagrin, had never been the same since Morwenna.

'I'll be as quick as I can,' he grunted in annoyance.

Linnet closed her eyes. She hated herself for complaining, but it was only right he knew of her discomfort. She hoped that it would soon be over.

'They be real ladies' clothes and no mistake,' Linnet said to Roxanne who was ferreting through her wardrobe. 'You don't see many like they round St Petroc,' she added wistfully.

Roxanne thought of all the gowns and dresses she'd got rid of before leaving Chantry Street because many of them had held such painful memories. Besides, she'd reasoned, she'd hardly need such a large ensemble in St Petroc.

She picked out a blue and white checked dress that had a high collar, puffed sleeves and white belt. 'This would suit you,' she said, holding it against Linnet.

Linnet gazed down at it. 'Tis a beauty, that's a fact.'

'Then have it.'

'Me!' Linnet exclaimed.

'Go on, it's yours. And there are a few more here you can have as well.'

'Oh I couldn't,' Linnet protested, sounding flustered.

'Of course you can. Try it on.'

Linnet ran her calloused hands over the dress, marvelling at the quality of the material. 'This must have cost a fortune,' she commented.

'I can't remember how much. But it must have been quite a bit.'

Linnet gazed enviously at the dress. 'Tis too big for me anyway,' she murmured.

'Then we'll take it in.'

'No point,' Linnet sighed. 'Kevern and me never goes anywhere I could wear it. We're proper stay at homes.'

'Who knows what might come up,' Roxanne argued, reaching for a dark green day dress which she also thought would suit her sister.

Linnet clasped the blue and white dress to her, thinking how grand she'd look in it – a proper Duchess. 'I've never owned anything near as pretty,' she said.

'Well you do now. And how about some decent underthings. I've plenty of them.'

Linnet finally accepted three dresses and a small pile of underlinen, thrilled to pieces by these gifts.

Several times during the rest of the day Linnet returned to her room to gaze at the dresses in amazement that they were now hers. She was grateful to Roxanne, but resentful too, knowing she would never look as good in them as Roxanne would have done.

*　　*　　*

'It was just like old times,' Roxanne thought one Saturday morning as she helped sort out the produce and goods in the rear of the cart that had brought them to market in St Petroc. And again like old times, as her father would have done, Kevern had gone off to try and strike a few deals after which he'd call in at the pub.

'Roxanne! Roxanne!'

She stopped what she was doing when she heard her name. She turned round and saw Billy Christmas rushing towards her, clearly excited.

'Billy,' she smiled when he reached the cart.

'How do Roxanne, I heard you was back. You know how word gets round.'

'Oh I do that,' she laughed in reply.

'Are you home to stay?'

'I think so. That's my plan anyway.'

He gazed admiringly at her. 'And how was Canada?'

She and Linnet had already talked this through and agreed there was nothing else for it but to perpetuate the lie.

'What did you do there?'

'I worked for a family in a big house,' she lied.

'Proper job! So what brings you back?'

'Homesickness. I enjoyed Canada but couldn't really settle. I missed Devon and St Petroc too much.' She tweaked his cheek. 'And the likes of you, Billy.'

He blushed bright scarlet. 'I'm married now you know.'

'I didn't.'

'I be indeed,' he beamed. 'To Annie Littlejohns. Remember her?'

'Of course.'

'And we have a babe. Three months old, a boy.'

'Congratulations,' she said warmly.

'I was right lucky with Annie. Never thought she'd look at me. But there we are.'

'I'm pleased you're happy, Billy. I really am. You deserve it.'

'And what about you?'

She pulled a face. 'Still single I'm afraid. I haven't yet met my Mister Right.' The words almost choked her.

'Well, there's plenty time yet, Roxanne, especially for such a good-looking maid as yourself.'

Maid! That made her want to laugh – if only he knew. Then she spotted a face that brought back more memories.

Billy followed her gaze to see who she was staring at. 'Cory Vranch,' he murmured.

'Is he married?'

'He be indeed, to Sally Tutching that was. Happened not long after you went off to visit your aunt.'

Roxanne recalled seeing Cory and Sally together on the day of the Autumn Fair when she'd left St Petroc. So that had been the outcome. Knowing Sally, she might have guessed as much.

Billy's face suddenly darkened. ''Twas a great sadness about your Ma and Da. I'm sorry.'

'Thank you,' Roxanne muttered in reply.

He reached out and touched her arm in sympathy, his plain face filled with compassion. 'It must have been awful for you to miss the funeral.'

She nodded.

''Twas a grand turnout. But no doubt you know that. It was very moving.' He sighed, then smiled. 'I best be getting on, lots to do today. Annie and I are going to the pub later. Why not join us for a drink?'

'I'd like that.'

'The King's Arms then, that's where we'll be. We'll look out for you.'

Impulse prompted Roxanne to kiss Billy on the cheek. 'You were always a good and true friend, Billy. And I always appreciated it.'

He coloured again. 'As you were to me, Roxanne.'

'Hopefully see you later.'

'Did you ever have any regrets about Cory Vranch?' Linnet asked when Billy had gone.

'None,' she answered truthfully.

'He's still as handsome as ever. Sally did well for herself.'

'As did you.'

Had she? Linnet sometimes had her doubts about that. But she would never have admitted to them, and certainly not to Roxanne. 'I did indeed,' she enthused, then turned away to serve a customer.

It was a marvellous day for Roxanne who encountered many old friends and acquaintances, all of whom had heard she was home again. And she even managed to have that drink with Billy and Annie, and admired the baby whom Annie had brought along, strapped to her front in a shawl.

When she finally went to bed that night she had the best, and most contented sleep, she'd had in a long time.

Kevern paused in his haymaking to gaze at Roxanne. How attractive she was, he thought. Even sweating like a pig under the hot sun she knocked spots off any other female he knew.

Working in the music halls, he reflected. Well, everyone knew what women who did that sort of thing were like. Linnet had told him that her mother had referred to them all as tarts. Had she been with men? He imagined so. Went without saying, didn't it? How many? he wondered. Plenty no doubt. Dozens maybe. Proper gentlemen too perhaps, he'd heard they frequented music halls. What were they called again? Stage door Johnnies, that was it. Only after one thing of course, and getting it too more often than not.

Oh no, she was no innocent. Might possibly have been on leaving St Petroc, but not on her return. Used goods, that was Roxanne. Well used too, he'd imagine. Stood to reason, she being so pretty and all.

What would she be like in bed? he mused, trying to picture her stripped off, in the raw. The image he conjured up so excited him that he had to shift his stance. And to think she was only through the wall from him at nights, almost within touching distance.

Roxanne was milking when Kevern appeared in the doorway to stare at her.

'I thought you were in the fields,' she said, glancing up.

'I'm looking for a tool I think I might have left in here.'

She concentrated again on the cow, her hands dextrously squeezing its udders. She enjoyed this job finding it both soothing and relaxing.

Kevern pretended to look for the non-existent tool knowing Linnet was safely busy in the house, and would be for some while.

'You seem to have settled in all right,' he commented after a few minutes.

'I have. In fact there are moments when it seems I've never been away.'

'Oh, but you were, there's no getting away from that.'

His tone, and what he'd said, surprised her. 'No,' she agreed.

'You're different, changed to what you were. But I suppose that's to be expected.'

'I'm also older,' she declared somewhat drily.

'Tain't only that. Tis you. I suppose it's all that experience on stage that's done it.' He paused, then added significantly. 'And other things.'

He was being rather strange, she thought as she moved on to the next cow. 'What other things?'

He grinned knowingly. '*Just things.*'

'Like what?'

'All they fancy dancy stage door Johnnies you met. They must have given you a fair old time I shouldn't wonder.'

What on earth was he driving at? 'I can't say they did,' she answered truthfully.

'Get on!' he leered.

'I met many, yes, but was never involved with any.'

'I bet you were!'

'I said not, Kevern. And I don't lie.'

'There must have been others, then. Buzzing round you like bees at a honey pot.'

He really was being most unpleasant and insinuating. 'I did have a chap for a while,' she confessed. 'But only one, no more.'

'Did he do you often?'

The crudity and bluntness of the question shocked her. 'Do?'

Kevern made a pumping motion with his arm and fist. 'Do, as in fucking.'

She couldn't believe what she was hearing. It was outrageous. 'No he didn't,' she snapped in reply. Keep your temper, she counselled herself. But for two peas she'd have chucked the pail of milk over him. What did he take her for?

'Do you like it then, Roxanne? A big lusty female such as yourself. Flat on your back with a man ramming it home?'

'Get out,' she hissed.

'Don't tell me to get out of my own property. You're the guest here,' he countered.

'And what if I told Linnet about this conversation?'

'You won't though, will you? Twould make her very unhappy if you did. Anyway, I'd swear no such conversation took place and that you'd made it all up to cause trouble.'

'Why should I do that?'

'Simply to be nasty. Linnet says there's a nasty streak in you. That as a young'un you could be real mean and spiteful.'

'We both could,' Roxanne stated.

He stared at her bosom bulging beneath her blouse. 'Let's feel they tits,' he said, advancing on her.

Roxanne shot off her stool and snatched up a pitchfork. 'Lay

184

one filthy hand on me, Kevern Stoneman, and I'll stick you for your troubles. I swear I will.'

He halted, nose dilated, breathing heavily. 'You're some sight when you've got your dander up, Roxanne. Yes indeed, some sight.'

'Get out of here,' she repeated.

Was she bluffing? He wasn't certain. He took a step forward, then hastily retreated when she jabbed the fork at him.

'Now go,' she commanded, white with fury.

Kevern laughed. 'I can waits my time. But I wants you, Roxanne Hawkins, and one day I'll have you. I promise you that. And not only will I have you, but you'll enjoy it into the bargain and beg for more.'

'You're disgusting,' she spat.

'Fine tits though,' he said, strolling away.

When he'd left she threw the fork from her and shook all over. Her own brother-in-law! Linnet would be appalled if she ever found out.

'Oh Harry,' she suddenly mumbled. 'Oh Harry!'

It was a good ten minutes before she had sufficient control to resume milking.

There was a dreadful atmosphere at the breakfast table emanating from Kevern who was like a bear with a sore head. He whacked the top off his boiled egg sending yolk spraying everywhere.

'Careful,' Linnet smiled, but was rewarded with a glare. She immediately turned to Morwenna and busied herself there.

Kevern wolfed down his egg and toast, then belched loudly, staring at Linnet and Roxanne as though daring them to comment. He scraped his chair back, stood up and stalked from the kitchen, banging the door shut behind him.

'What's wrong with Kevern this morning?' Roxanne inquired.

'Don't know,' Linnet lied, knowing only too well. They'd had a bad-tempered row in bed the previous night about her soreness. When she'd gone to the doctor about it he'd informed her there was nothing he could do, discomfort during intercourse was a result of having Morwenna and she was simply going to have to live with it.

Linnet rubbed her forehead. She was so tired! Even with Roxanne helping her the pressure never seemed to let up. She was on the go from early morning till night. What she would have given for a day off – a whole glorious day with nothing to do except eat, sleep and take her ease. But there was no chance of

185

that with Morwenna to look after and the interminable chores.

'You all right?' Roxanne asked.

'Fine.'

'You appear rather peaky and drawn.' Even more so than usual she might have added.

'Well that's hardly surprising!' Linnet snapped back.

Linnet wiped egg from Morwenna's face. The child was a dear, but so demanding. There again, she supposed all children were. And now Kevern was in a filthy mood which would continue all day. He was simply paying her back for the night before. Why couldn't he just understand and accept the situation? She'd explained it often enough. It was not as though she wanted things to be as they were.

'I'll clear up,' Roxanne said.

Linnet gave her a grateful smile.

'He doesn't mistreat you, does he?' Roxanne asked softly. It was something that had been worrying her of late and she'd been waiting for the right opportunity to query.

'Who?'

'Kevern of course.'

'He's the perfect husband,' Linnet said. 'He'd never mistreat me in a thousand years.'

Roxanne was pleased to hear that and wondered yet again about her recent encounter with Kevern and hoped there would never be a recurrence. If only he'd stop staring at her the way he had been whenever Linnet was either not present or not watching. It was a sly look with sexual overtones.

'Well, I'm sorry Kevern's upset,' Roxanne declared, not meaning a word of it.

'He'll get over whatever's bothering him,' Linnet replied, wishing that she didn't get so sore.

Linnet chose to tell Kevern when they were alone in the fields together, while Morwenna played a little way off. 'I'm pregnant again,' she announced.

Kevern paused to stare at her. 'You sure?'

She nodded. 'It's definite all right.'

His face lit up; this was what he'd wanted to hear. 'It'll be a boy this time,' he enthused. 'No doubt about it, a *boy*.'

Linnet sincerely hoped so.

He rubbed his hands in glee. 'A son and heir at last, I couldn't be more pleased, my lover.' And with that he threw his arms round her, swept her off her feet, and whirled her round.

When he set her down again he eagerly demanded to know when the baby was due.

Roxanne and Linnet had had a great deal of difficulty in persuading Kevern to attend the Christmas dance in St Petroc, as he kept saying that he couldn't be bothered with such nonsense any more. But Roxanne, who'd known Linnet would love getting out for once, had, with Linnet's assistance, worked on him till finally he'd relented.

Linnet looked a treat, Roxanne thought, watching her sister and Kevern dancing a slow waltz. She'd washed Linnet's hair and then done the best she could to restore it to something of its former glory, which hadn't been easy as it had been neglected for so long. When she'd finished, she'd set about her face, plucking and shaping her eyebrows, after which she'd applied powder and lipstick using tips she'd picked up while on the music halls. The result had bemused Kevern who'd gallantly stated his wife was a picture.

The dress Roxanne had eventually chosen for Linnet was pale yellow with frills round the shoulders and a large embroidered black flower on the full skirt. They'd worried that Linnet's pregnancy might have meant alterations which would have spoiled the line, but thankfully Linnet wasn't yet showing and the dress had fitted with only a small bulge at the tummy which Roxanne had declared, truthfully, was hardly noticeable.

'How do, Roxanne.'

She turned to find Cory Vranch and Sally beside her, Cory with an arm round Sally's shoulders.

'How are you both? And I believe congratulations are in order.' This was the first occasion Roxanne had spoken to them since her return.

'We're fine, and thank you,' Sally smiled.

She chatted with them for a bit, then they moved off. They'd no sooner gone than Dickie Webber appeared asking if she'd care to dance.

She found talking to Dickie excruciatingly boring. All he could speak about was farming and problems connected with it. She couldn't wait to excuse herself, much to his obvious disappointment, once that particular number was over.

She rejoined Linnet and Kevern, hoping that Kevern wouldn't ask her up, although if he did she could hardly refuse, certainly not in front of Linnet.

Roxanne gazed about, wondering what Harry would have made

of this. He'd probably have thought it laughable, for there was no denying it was a very rural affair with absolutely no sophistication about it whatsoever.

Roxanne noted that she and Linnet stood out as the best dressed women there. All the other women's apparel was downright dowdy and unfashionable by comparison. She was delighted, for Linnet's sake, it was just the sort of boost she needed, to be that little bit special.

'Like a drink?' Kevern asked Linnet.

She shook her head. 'Not for me thanks.'

He focused on Roxanne, eyes mocking. 'And you?'

'Me neither.'

'Then I won't be long.'

Roxanne was about to launch into a conversation with her sister when Billy Christmas tapped her on the shoulder. 'I've been given permission by the missus to ask you up. What do you say?' he beamed.

'I'd be delighted, Billy.'

'I'm not much good mind, rather a clodhopper, I'm afraid. I only hope I don't trample all over your feet.'

'You'll be terrific, Billy. Now come on.'

A little later she was approached by a handsome chap she didn't recognize who asked if she'd consider him for a turn round the floor. She thought that a delightful way of putting it, and readily agreed.

'My name's James Booth,' he said shyly as he tentatively took her into his arms.

'And I'm Roxanne Hawkins.'

'I know. I've made inquiries about you.'

'Did you now!'

He moved gracefully, if a little unsure of himself. 'So how was Canada?'

She immediately became cagey as she always did when that subject was broached. 'Different and interesting.'

'I would imagine so. Did you see any bears?'

She was surprised by that question. 'Not one. I was in the city all the time.'

'And which city was that?'

'Toronto. Have you been overseas yourself?'

He laughed. 'Not me. Never been outside Devon meself.'

She discovered that he came from the far side of St Petroc, the opposite direction to their farm, and that he was the eldest of seven children. His story was ordinary enough for thereabouts and they both expressed amazement that they'd never met one another in the past. She found his company relaxing; he was amusing in a quiet way and most polite. When that dance came to an end she was happy to stay up for a follow-on.

Kevern studied Roxanne and James, jealous of the latter, wishing he was in Roxanne's embrace. She was gorgeous, particularly all dolled up as she was that evening. She was quite the belle of the ball and had attracted a lot of comment among all the males.

He cursed again the fact that he was married to Linnet and not Roxanne. What was galling was that she was under the same roof as him, always present, tantalizing him. And Linnet's continuing soreness didn't help matters either.

'Penny for them?' Linnet asked, wondering why he was so deep in thought.

Kevern roused himself from his reverie. 'Eh?'

'You were quite far away.'

'Was I?' he replied evasively. He shrugged his shoulders. 'Tweren't thinking about anything, Linnet. Nothing much anyway.'

'Shall we have another dance? I'd like that.'

'Don't want you overdoing things, mind,' he prevaricated.

She thought that was funny considering the amount of heavy work she did round the house and farm. Compared to that, a little dancing would hardly hurt her.

'Don't worry about me,' she replied, grasping his arm. 'I think I'll survive.'

'Can I get you something from the bar?' James asked Roxanne after their fourth dance together.

'No thank you. But get yourself a drink if you wish.'

'I'd rather stay up,' he answered hastily.

He was keen, she thought, wondering whether to leave the floor. Four dances were a lot with one partner, particularly as they'd been in succession.

'Please?' he pleaded, pulling an imploring face.

That touched her. 'All right,' she conceded.

He couldn't wait to get his arms round her when the band started up again.

Damn the bloody man, Kevern inwardly raged, as he watched them glide across the floor. Was he never going to let Roxanne go! At this rate he'd never get a dance.

'How do. Enjoying yourselves?' said Dick Metherill, joining Kevern and Linnet.

189

'I'm having a wonderful time,' Linnet responded with a large smile.

'That's the stuff,' Dick smiled back. He then engaged Kevern reluctantly in conversation.

Time whizzed past for Roxanne, who was taken by surprise when the last waltz was called. How many dances had she had now with James? She couldn't remember; one had seemed to merge into another until she'd simply lost count.

The waltz was almost finished when James asked, 'Can I take you home? I have a buggy outside.'

Roxanne was jolted by the question, but then immediately admonished herself for not having predicted this. Of course he'd ask to take her home, how stupid of her.

She dropped her head to gaze at the floor.

'Did you hear me, Roxanne?'

'It's been very pleasant, James, but . . . no,' she said eventually.

His expectant expression disappeared.

'I'm sorry,' she mumbled.

'But I thought . . . We were getting on so well together.'

'I like you, James, tremendously. I just don't want to get involved, that's all.' It hurt her to see how disappointed he was.

'Is there someone else?'

'In a manner of speaking,' she answered. 'Not locally, but . . . yes there is a man.' After a few, silent, leaden moments she added, 'I wouldn't want to lead you on, you're far too nice for that. The fault's entirely mine, I should never have danced all this while with you. It must have given you the wrong impression. I'm sorry.'

'That's all right,' he replied quietly.

They didn't speak again until, with a final flourish, the band stopped playing.

'It's been a pleasure meeting you,' he said stiffly as everyone around clapped.

She felt dreadful. 'And meeting you, James. Again, I'm sorry.'

He escorted her from the floor, muttered a stilted 'goodbye', then walked dejectedly away.

'What happened?' Linnet queried. 'I thought you'd found yourself a beau there.'

Roxanne gave her sister a strained smile while Kevern, jubilantly, looked on. 'A silly mistake on my part, that's all.'

'Oh!'

Roxanne glanced over to where James was talking to some chums. It was only then that she was struck by a vague facial

190

resemblance between him and Harry. *Harry*, with whom she was still desperately, heartachingly, in love.

During the journey home she came to the conclusion she'd never marry. How could she, when she'd always be in love with Harry.

Linnet gasped in pain, clutched her middle, and bent over. Instantly Roxanne hurried across the room to her side.

'What is it?' Roxanne demanded with a frown. There were still six weeks to go until the baby was due.

Linnet took a deep breath, and straightened. 'It's over now. A sudden stab in the tum.'

'Here, you'd better sit down.'

'Too much to do,' Linnet protested.

'Blow that. You shouldn't be doing so much as it is, not with the baby so close.'

Linnet wiped a wisp of hair from her forehead as Roxanne helped her to the nearest chair.

'I'll make you a cup of tea,' Roxanne said, concerned.

Linnet sucked in several more deep breaths. 'That's better,' she stated.

'Is there anything else I can get you?' Roxanne queried from the range.

'I don't think so,' Linnet replied dispiritedly.

'I meant what I said, you really should take things easier.'

'I can't, Kevern would be cross if I tried. He says I'm not expected to do more than any other woman in my position. And I suppose he's right. Though how they manage I don't know.'

That made Roxanne angry. How unsympathetic of Kevern, who might have shown a bit more understanding. Yet it was typical of him. The more she knew about Kevern Stoneman the less she respected him.

'It might help if he didn't keep going on about having a son,' Linnet continued. 'He's obsessed with the idea of a son and heir to inherit the combined farms.'

She paused as a sudden thought struck her. 'Just as I inherited this one,' she declared quietly.

'I've told you, I know how Da was. What he did didn't really surprise me in the least. The nature of the beast I suppose.'

'Still,' Linnet mumbled, feeling guilty, yet at the same time unrepentant.

'I think you should go to bed for an hour or two,' Roxanne suggested.

'I couldn't!'

'Oh yes you could. It's simply a matter of doing so.'

'Kevern—'

'Sod Kevern!' Roxanne interjected angrily. 'He wouldn't thank you if you lost the baby.'

'Oh don't say that,' Linnet whispered.

'Not that there's any chance,' Roxanne assured her. 'But he's not to know it, is he? At the moment you've got the whip hand my girl, use it.'

A couple of hours in bed during the middle of the day. What a glorious prospect! 'But what about me jobs? He'll expect them done.'

'Leave everything to me. Including him. I'll set him right, you take my word for it.'

Linnet rubbed her stomach. What a weight! And the birth not that far off.

'You need rest to keep your strength up and that's an end of it,' Roxanne stated. 'So off you go and I'll bring your tea through.'

'I don't know . . .'

'Well I do. Now go!'

When Kevern later returned Roxanne spun him a yarn about abdominal pains and the possibility of a premature delivery, which put the wind up him.

From there on in Roxanne insisted that Linnet had a long afternoon nap every day, for which Linnet was profoundly grateful.

Linnet's eyes widened as another contraction gripped her. Seconds later she was shrieking in agony, threatening to crush Roxanne's hand which she was holding.

'That's it Linnet, don't hold back,' Doctor Weeks urged. He hadn't been present at Morwenna's birth, but fearing complications on this occasion, he was.

It was taking so long, Roxanne thought anxiously. Linnet had gone into labour over twelve hours ago.

'There,' she murmured soothingly when the pain subsided.

'Oh God! Oh God!' Linnet whimpered. 'Please let it be over soon. Please.'

'Not long to go, me dear,' the midwife told her as she peered yet again at Linnet's crotch.

The doctor was more worried than he was letting on, something the midwife was aware of though it hadn't been articulated between them. She'd delivered too many babies not to know what was what.

192

'Would you like some water?' Roxanne asked.

Linnet managed a small nod.

Roxanne released her hand, which was surely going to be black and blue the following day, and hurried over to where a jug and tumbler stood atop an oak chest of drawers. She'd just lifted the jug when Linnet began screaming again.

Kevern was pacing to and fro in the kitchen when the doctor appeared. Morwenna had been taken to a neighbour's for the duration.

'Well?' Kevern queried.

'Mother and baby are fine, though Linnet's really been through the mill with this one,' Weeks replied.

'It's a boy, isn't it?'

'A little girl, Kevern. A fine, healthy, bouncing baby girl.'

Kevern stared at him, aghast. 'But it was to be a boy. I thought . . . was certain . . . *absolutely* certain . . .' He trailed off and bit his lip in disappointment.

Weeks frowned, knowing nothing of Kevern's obsession.

'Next time. It'll be a boy next time,' Kevern muttered.

'Ah!' Weeks breathed heavily. 'I have to speak to you about that.' He paused for a brief moment to collect his weary thoughts, then went on. 'First of all, Linnet is completely exhausted and must stay in bed for quite some time – a month, perhaps longer. Do you understand?'

Kevern nodded.

'The second thing is there were complications which might mean she'll have trouble conceiving again. In fact I would say it's very unlikely.'

'Very un . . .' Kevern put a hand to his forehead, unable to take in what the doctor had just said. It had to be a mistake, surely. 'But she might?' he managed at last.

'She might, but I certainly wouldn't count on it.'

Kevern swore as tears welled up in his eyes. Another girl, now this. 'I need a drink,' he croaked.

He fetched the bottle of whisky he'd laid in for the birth of his son and opened it. 'You?' he queried of the doctor.

'A small one wouldn't go amiss.'

Kevern vaguely noted his hand was shaking as he slopped whisky into two glasses. There was still hope though, he told himself. Still hope. He had to cling on to that.

Weeks accepted his drink, which he felt was well earned. 'I'll be calling back again tomorrow to see how they both are,' he stated.

Kevern nodded numbly. The news had shattered him. When he glanced at his glass he was astonished to find it empty.

'There's one more thing,' Weeks said quietly.

'What's that?'

'I recommend you refrain from sexual intercourse for a considerable while. That would be highly desirable.'

'Considerable while?' Kevern repeated.

'Six months, perhaps longer. She was . . .' He thought of how to put this delicately. 'Rather badly damaged I'm afraid.'

Kevern returned to the whisky bottle, knowing he was going to get drunk before the day was out.

'Would you like to see Linnet and the child now?' Weeks asked.

Kevern shook his head. 'Not yet.'

Weeks frowned again. 'Don't you think you should?'

'Shortly,' Kevern husked. 'Shortly.' He couldn't face Linnet for the time being and had no desire whatever to see the baby. A bloody maid when he'd so craved a boy.

When Weeks had taken his leave Kevern poured out some more whisky and slumped into a chair. 'Still hope,' he mumbled, desperately trying to reassure himself.

Why had he married a woman who could only produce maids and had now got herself into this predicament? Why? Black despair overwhelmed him and the glass flew from his hand to smash against the range.

Chapter Eleven

The only noises disturbing the quiet of the room were the steady tick tock of the clock on the mantelpiece and Tamsin greedily sucking at her mother's breast. Morwenna had gone to bed a short while previously.

Usually Linnet enjoyed breast feeding; it gave her a wonderful sense of contentment and general peace with the world, but not that evening. She was agitated. Kevern was sitting in his chair before the range pretending to be asleep but in reality he was watching Roxanne through slitted eyes as she turned the collar of one of his shirts.

After two months of inactivity, Linnet's figure was slack, loose and remained heavy with fat in places. She couldn't bear to look at herself naked and refused point blank to allow Kevern to see her without something on. The thick varicose veins that had appeared on both legs were also causing her acute distress. They were horrible and ugly and it seemed that, unlike the fatty deposits, they were with her for life.

She glanced at Roxanne, hating her sister for being so beautiful and desirable, a fact obviously not lost on Kevern. Whenever possible the dirty bugger never took his eyes off her, staring at her as though he was a starving man gazing at a sumptuous feast. Which in a way he was, she conceded. They had not had sex since Tamsin's birth, and she knew only too well how that must be affecting him.

'The range needs seeing to,' she suddenly snapped.

Kevern pretended to rouse himself. 'Right, my lover. I'll do that straight away.'

Linnet shifted Tamsin from one breast to the other.

195

Roxanne glanced over and smiled. 'All right?'

'Fine,' Linnet replied with a thin smile. Although Roxanne had been a great help since her arrival, she wished her sister had never reappeared. She was like a cuckoo in the nest, an interloper. She may be family, but wasn't part of *their* family.

Roxanne used her teeth to sever the thread she'd been sewing with and laid the shirt aside. She then picked up another and began the same process all over again.

Varicose veins, Linnet thought in disgust. Her Ma had never been plagued by those; Phoebe's legs had been clear and shapely right up until the day of her death, just as Roxanne's were. They were the sort of legs she now passionately envied.

It wasn't that she wanted Kevern making love to her again, far from it. And thank God there had been a six month ban. It was simply that she wanted to feel attractive, instead of the wreck she'd become.

Roxanne could feel the atmosphere in the room, but was ignoring it. Just as she'd been conscious, and ignored the fact, that Kevern had been watching her. She could well understand the sexual pressure he must be under, but had little sympathy for him, and dreaded a repeat of the milking incident. It seemed to her the time was rapidly approaching when she'd have to leave the household and to take lodgings elsewhere, although she wouldn't do that until Linnet was properly back on her feet again.

Poor Linnet, she'd been through such a lot with both babes. She really did feel sorry for her.

Kevern finished at the range and returned to his chair, where he opened a farming magazine he'd been reading off and on for the past week.

'Wouldn't mind a cup of tea,' he said to no-one in particular.

'I'll make a pot,' Roxanne volunteered, as Linnet was busy.

When Linnet saw Kevern stare hungrily at Roxanne's bottom as she went by she could have spat.

'Come on now, my beauty, come on,' Roxanne muttered to the ewe she was attending, something she'd often done in the past when assisting her Da.

'How's it going?'

She started, not having heard Kevern approach. 'No problems so far.'

Kevern squatted beside her to take in the current state of

196

proceedings. 'You shouldn't have trouble with her. Just slips them out, year after year, she does.' He suddenly grinned. 'Children and lambs, eh? Nature's wonderful process.'

'Not quite,' Roxanne replied drily. 'It's ewes who have lambs, women who have babes.'

He considered that distinction amusing. 'But as I said, tis all the same thing.'

Roxanne regarded him coldly, thinking he was an unfeeling brute. 'Ewes are beasts whereas women are human beings. Or perhaps you disagree with that?'

He shrugged. 'No.'

'And women have minds which animals haven't. They can *think*.'

'My, my,' he smiled scornfully. 'You did learn some fancy things while away in London.'

'Nothing to do with London,' she declared. 'It's common sense.'

'Hey, you're not one of they suffragettes I've been reading about I hope?'

'No, I'm not.'

'Glad to hear it. Never heard such nonsense in all me life. That Mrs Parkhurst, or whatever her name, should be taken out and shot.'

'Something you'd do yourself if you had the chance I suppose,' Roxanne jibed.

'I'd be tempted, I can tell you. A woman's place is where it's always been . . .'

'Either on her back or grafting till she drops,' Roxanne interjected sarcastically.

He nodded, which incensed her even further. 'Tis so Roxanne, tis so. That's a woman's lot. As for giving them the vote . . .' He broke off and laughed raucously for which Roxanne could easily have slapped him.

'Some day men like you are going to get the shock of their blinkered lives,' she stated.

'Are we indeed!'

'Oh yes,' she said softly. 'I'm certain of it.'

'You'll be lucky!' he sneered.

The ewe suddenly convulsed, claiming Roxanne's attention. Instantly Kevern was aiding her, offering advice as she coaxed the lamb from its mother. He was transformed during this, becoming tender and caring, full of concern for ewe and lamb. When the first lamb was born he took it aside and dealt with it while she prepared for the second, as the ewe had a history of bearing doubles.

Despite herself Roxanne was impressed by his knowledge, skill and, above all, love. Yes, that wasn't too strong a word for it, he showed the animals love. When it was all finally over she commented on the fact.

He blinked at her uncomprehendingly, as though she'd just stated the obvious. 'But of course I'm that way with the beasts,' he declared. 'They're valuable, after all. Worth a lot of money.'

This time her impulse to slap him was almost overwhelming.

'You been out there with her half the night. Look at the time!' Linnet accused when Kevern eventually got home. She was sitting up in bed with the shawl Elvira had given her mother draped round her shoulders.

'We were lambing, my lover. You know what that's like.'

'There were only two ewes due,' she further accused.

He shrugged. 'These things can take time. After what you've been through recently you should appreciate that.'

It was a pertinent point, but she remained unconvinced. Jealousy raged hot within her.

Kevern regarded her as he began undressing. 'Tweren't nothing going on if that's what's worrying you.'

'I should hope not!'

'Twas all business, nothing more.' Worst luck! he added to himself.

'I've seen the way you look at her.'

'What way?' he queried, pretending innocence.

'Don't get smart or lie to me,' she snapped in reply. 'You know exactly what I'm talking about.'

He threw his shirt over a chair and scratched his belly. 'You're imagining things, my darling. Tis having the babes that's upset you so.'

'In a pig's eye! I'm imagining nothing. I knows what I see, and I sees clearly enough I can assure you. Lay one hand on her Kevern Stoneman and God help the consequences.'

'Leave me, would you?' he replied, tongue in cheek, knowing it was rare, no matter what the provocation, for women of their class to leave their husbands. It was almost unheard of.

'I'll do worse than that.'

'Oh?'

'I'll . . . I'll . . . stick you with the carving knife. On my life I will.'

That momentarily alarmed him. Then he dismissed it as an idle threat, thinking that Linnet didn't have it in her to commit such an act. She simply wasn't the type.

'You'd best snuggle down to sleep,' he said. 'Remember what the doctor told us, you still need lots of rest.'

She thought of her body in its present state with loathing. If only she wasn't so down all the time. What had Doctor Weeks called it? Some long word she couldn't remember.

'You keep away from Roxanne,' she warned him.

'Hard to do when we're all living under the same roof,' he answered drily, sliding into bed beside her.

'You understand me well enough.'

He leaned across and pecked her on the forehead. 'Now turn out your lamp so we can both get some shut eye.'

She lay fuming in the darkness, and continued to fume after Kevern started to snore.

'Hallo.'

Roxanne glanced up from the box of cauliflowers she'd been wrestling with to find James Booth, her partner from the Christmas dance, smiling at her.

'Why hallo,' she replied.

'Wondered when I'd run into you. Knew I'd be bound to sooner or later. How are you?'

'Couldn't be better. And yourself?'

'Work work work, the usual.'

She nodded in sympathy, thinking again that he did indeed bear a vague facial resemblance to Harry. 'Enjoying market day?'

'Always do when I manages in. Tis a break after all, and they're always welcome.'

'Always,' she agreed.

'Fine-looking caulis those,' he remarked, his interest purely professional.

'Thank you.'

'We had trouble with ours this year. Lost half the crop.'

'Sorry to hear that,' she commiserated.

'Did well with our tats and onions though. Better than for ages.'

'Good for you.'

He became nervous, shifting from one foot to the other. 'I thought I might drop by the pub for a drink. I don't suppose you'd care to join me?' When she hesitated he quickly added, 'Just a friendly glass, that's all. Nothing else in mind. No harm in that, is there?'

'I'm not sure if I can,' she replied truthfully. 'It all depends on my brother-in-law whom I've come in with. If I did manage it would have to be later on in the afternoon.'

'I'll wait and see if you turns up. If you do, grand. If not, I'll understand.'

'Which pub then?'

'I use the Hart normally, but it can be any one you like.'

'The Hart it is, providing I can get along. But as I say it all depends on my brother-in-law and his plans.'

'Fair enough. Ta-ra then.'

'Ta-ra.'

Sweet man, she thought as he walked away. She decided there and then she wouldn't go to the pub. He'd promised it was only a friendly glass, and no doubt meant it, but he fancied her and might be secretly hoping that a friendly glass would lead to another rendezvous and so on. No, best leave things as they were, that way there was no possibility of raising his hopes or of him getting hurt. The dance had been a mistake on her part, a mistake she wouldn't compound.

She thought of Harry, which she'd done so often since that fateful day when he'd left her, and all the old questions came crowding back. Where was he? What was he doing? Was he with someone? Elaine the dancer? Or had he moved on to another? Knowing Harry there was bound to be a woman involved somewhere.

Harry, whom she could see as clearly as if he were standing in front of her. Despite everything, all the pain and anguish he'd caused her, she'd have given anything for him to be there in the flesh rather than in her mind's eye, her very soul to be in bed with him.

She shivered as she remembered their physical relationship, and a deep longing stirred inside her. How she ached for what had once been. The touching, caressing, the abandoned passion he'd introduced her to.

Despite herself, she smiled. If she'd suggested even half of those things to James Booth he'd probably have run a mile. For the Jameses of this world were straightlaced when it came to sex; her experience with Harry was way outside their imagination.

When she and Kevern left St Petroc later they passed the Hart, where she briefly glimpsed James inside.

She was doing him a favour, she told herself as the cart trundled on.

*　*　*

Kevern came to the end of a furrow and paused in his ploughing to wipe his streaming forehead. Where was his damned dinner. He was starving! The two women were probably gabbing or simpering over the babe, and had forgotten all about him.

Then he spotted Roxanne, silhouetted with the sun behind her. A lump rose in his throat. What a sight, what a beautiful, gut-wrenching sight!

'You took your time,' he snarled when she reached him.

'Sorry, but one of the cows was acting up at milking. That's what got me behind.'

'Which one?' he demanded.

'Marigold.'

'Don't usually have no trouble with her. Good as gold that beast.' Roxanne had brought him a tied napkin containing his dinner along with a bottle of cider which he now took. 'Your clumsiness no doubt.'

Roxanne bit back a caustic reply, not wanting to cause a row. Her clumsiness indeed! There hadn't been any question of that. If anything she was a better milker than Linnet or Kevern himself.

Kevern threw himself on to the ground where he took a swig of cider, then proceeded to undo the napkin.

Without uttering another word, Roxanne swung on her heel and strode away.

As Kevern gazed after her he was suddenly filled with an intense fury, thinking he could have knocked the silly bitch from here to eternity.

But he knew that wasn't what he wanted to do at all.

Roxanne exclaimed as the hand brushed over her bottom. Whirling round she confronted Kevern, who was smiling at her.

'Sorry,' he muttered insincerely.

'Don't you ever do that again!' she hissed.

'Go on, you enjoyed it.'

'I did nothing of the sort. You keep your paws to yourself.'

'I don't mean no harm, Roxanne. I can't help the way I feel.'

'Bugger how you feel. I want none of you, can't you get that into your thick skull.'

He decided to chance it. Grabbing her he pulled her into his arms and attempted to kiss her. She struggled for all she was worth.

When his mouth succeeded in fastening on to hers she brought her knee up sharply, taking him full in the groin.

Kevern broke off with a howl to go hopping away.

'Serves you right,' she stated angrily.

'You're driving me crazy woman, I swear.'

She knew then what she had to do, despite the fact that Linnet wasn't fully recovered. The situation had simply become untenable.

He was still hopping from foot to foot, and clutching himself, as she left.

'I've decided to leave St Petroc,' Roxanne stated quietly the next morning over breakfast.

Linnet's immediate reaction was one of elation, while Kevern stared blankly at his sister-in-law.

'But why?' Linnet queried, knowing full well what the reason was, and dreading Roxanne's answer, just as Kevern was. He was suddenly terrified he'd misjudged Roxanne and she'd come out with the truth.

'I'm finding farm life too quiet for me after the hurly burly of the big city,' Roxanne lied, to the relief of the others. 'I thought I'd fit in again, but that's just not the case. I need the excitement a city has to offer.'

'So it's back to the music halls I suppose?' Linnet said.

Roxanne shook her head. She'd considered that and quickly come to the conclusion it was the last thing she wanted. Music halls would always be associated in her mind with Harry. Life without Harry was bad enough, but to return to that environment would only make things ten times worse. 'I've done with them,' she replied.

'But you will go to London?' Linnet went on.

She wouldn't go to London for the same reasons, too many painful memories. 'Plymouth or Exeter I think.'

'Plymouth is the nearest, not that far away at all,' Kevern declared, finding his voice at last. Roxanne promptly chose Exeter, though she didn't say so.

'When will you leave?' Linnet asked.

'Soon as possible. No use hanging about.'

'I see,' Linnet murmured. This really was good news, something she'd been secretly hoping might happen.

'How soon is that?' Kevern enquired.

'It's Friday now, Monday morning.'

'We'll miss you of course,' Linnet lied. Kevern might, but she certainly wouldn't; apart from the help that was. 'And you will write? You must let us know how you're getting on.'

'I'm not much of a letter writer,' Roxanne prevaricated, wondering if keeping in touch was a good idea.

'We'll worry otherwise. Won't we, Kevern?'

Kevern nodded, feeling wretched and doing his best not to show it.

'Besides, you owe us that having gone off once already and worrying us all half to death,' Linnet burbled on, feeling better than she had done in a long time.

'I'll write then,' Roxanne promised, still not sure whether she would or not.

'Auntie Roxanne is going away. Isn't that a shame,' Linnet smiled at a wide-eyed Morwenna. Her response was to burst into tears, for she and Roxanne had become extremely close during Roxanne's stay.

That night, although six months wasn't fully up, Linnet allowed Kevern to make love to her and it still hurt.

Roxanne gazed about her as the cart neared St Petroc. How she loved this place – she was really going to miss it. The surrounding countryside was so dear to her; the fields, the grazing animals, the multitude of different smells.

She didn't want to go but in the circumstances thought it best to get right out the area altogether. But it was going to be a terrible wrench.

She'd been so happy to be back on the farm, with the exception of Kevern that was, and was going to miss the day to day routine, hard though it had been.

Then there was Morwenna and Tamsin, she'd probably miss them more than anything, particularly Morwenna whom she'd come to think of almost as her own.

Damn Kevern, she thought angrily, glancing sideways at him, as he was driving the cart. Here she was paying the penalty for him not being able to keep his feelings and emotions under control. So he fancied her! He was a grown, married man who should have been able to cope better than he had.

A seagull cried overhead, wheeling first one way, then another. And in the distance, a buzzard flew high in the sky. She recalled watching buzzards as a child, thinking them wonderful birds.

'Slaughtering a pig this afternoon,' Kevern said.

Roxanne knew what that entailed and was pleased she wouldn't be around to witness it. The poor animal was hauled, by its hind legs, up on a rope to dangle above a zinc tub. In that position it had its throat cut.

She shuddered in memory of previous slaughterings she'd seen. That was something she certainly wouldn't miss.

'I said . . .'

'I heard you,' she snapped.

Kevern shrugged. 'Only trying to make conversation, that's all.'

'You take care of Linnet now,' she declared. 'She still isn't fit and must continue to take things easy.'

'I don't need you to tell me what's what,' he replied coldly.

'She is my sister after all.'

'And *my* wife.'

'All the more reason to see to her well-being.'

Kevern couldn't think of a reply to that. Instead he pursed his lips and flicked the reins.

A short while later he brought the cart to a halt in front of the station. Her case was in the cart but Kevern made no attempt to jump down and get it for her.

'There's still time to change your mind,' he said gruffly.

'Not for all the tea in China,' she informed him, which caused him to colour.

She fetched her own case, which was lighter than when she'd arrived as she'd given so many of her clothes to Linnet.

'Goodbye,' she said.

Kevern's reply was to crack his whip and the cart jolted off. He didn't look back as he drove away.

Good riddance to bad rubbish, Roxanne thought. At least that was over and done with, there would be no further worrying about her brother-in-law and what he might say or do next.

She pitied Linnet for being married to him; Linnet deserved better.

'Why hallo Roxanne,' Mr Boal, the stationmaster, smiled when she presented herself at the ticket office. 'Off on your travels again?'

She nodded.

'London is it?'

'No, Exeter.'

'Fine city that. Lovely cathedral.'

'So I believe.'

'Just visiting, are you?'

Typical of country folk, she thought. They always wanted all the details. 'No, I'll be staying there.'

'Ah!' he exclaimed in surprise, eyebrows rising. 'So it's a single then.'

'Please.'

He busied himself at his counter. 'Beautiful day for travelling.'

'Yes,' she agreed, wishing he'd hurry up. The last thing she either wanted or needed was to stand there idly chatting.

The truth was she was more than apprehensive about going to Exeter, another step into the unknown. Well, she'd managed all right in London, she told herself, she'd do the same in Exeter. It shouldn't take her long to get established.

Out on the platform she recalled the last time she'd left St Petroc. Her Ma and Da had been alive then, and she was yet to meet Harry.

She was still thinking about Harry when eventually her train came clanking and hissing alongside.

Chapter Twelve

The scream that rang out was so horrific it might have curdled the blood. Roxanne immediately ceased work to gaze at Mary who was facing her across the machine they shared. They both worked for McSween's cigarette factory turning out cigarette cards.

'Jesus!' Mary swore softly.

The scream halted abruptly, followed by an eerie silence. There were ten of them in that section of the factory, and now, as one, they hurried to the door leading out on to the main floor. There they found bedlam.

'What's happened?' Roxanne queried, grabbing hold of a passing girl.

'It's Lily Roach. A belt on her machine broke and smacked her across the face. She's in a terrible state apparently.'

Roxanne knew Lily; she was a pretty maid of about seventeen who lived not far from her. They sometimes accompanied one another to and from work.

Lily was lying face down in a pool of blood, the offending leather belt dangling from the now immobilized machine. Mr Horrell, Lily's supervisor, was squatting perplexedly beside her.

'I don't think she should be moved,' he stated in a cracked voice, clearly deeply shaken by what had happened.

'She's unconscious,' a girl informed Roxanne who was peering between heads and over shoulders.

'An ambulance has been sent for,' Horrell told those crowding round.

'Make way. Make way for Mr McSween,' a voice yelled.

McSween, the owner, was a bluff, older man with huge protruding whiskers of which he was extremely proud. He elbowed his way through the throng till he reached Lily and Horrell.

'Belt broke,' Horrell informed him.

'Is she bad?'

'It caught her in the face.'

'Stupid girl,' McSween muttered.

'Wasn't her fault the belt broke,' Mary whispered to Roxanne. 'Damned machines are old as Methusalah.'

Roxanne knew that was true, the ancient machines were forever malfunctioning in some way. They should all have been replaced ages ago, but that would have meant capital expenditure which McSween was determined not to lay out. His only interest was maximum profit.

Lily moaned as she came to, then she twisted onto her side, letting those opposite see her face.

'Oh my God,' Roxanne breathed. Lily's face, covered in blood, was completely smashed, her nose broken and squashed to the side. One eye had come out of its socket and was hanging on her cheek.

'I'm blind,' Lily further moaned piteously. 'I'm completely blind.'

A girl standing close to Roxanne suddenly bent over and threw up.

Roxanne strode through the chill January night at the completion of her eleven-hour shift. She was bone weary as usual, and still distressed by the day's events. Twenty minutes after the accident, an ambulance had arrived to take Lily to hospital, while the rest of them had been instructed by McSween to resume work. An hour after Lily's departure the broken leather belt had been repaired and another girl delegated to take her place.

Frog Street, where Roxanne had lodgings, was narrow and cobbled, the centuries-old houses leaning inwards at the top. To the casual observer it might have appeared picturesque, in reality it was an infested slum.

Roxanne had initially stayed at a boarding house on her arrival in Exeter, but as time passed and her money dwindled she'd been forced to look for something cheaper which was how she'd come to end up with Madeleine Rowe and Madeleine's three children. Madeleine was a widow whose husband had been killed in an industrial accident eighteen months earlier. The two women had

taken an instant shine to one another and soon become the best
of friends.

'How are you tonight?' Madeleine inquired as Roxanne let herself into the small kitchen where Madeleine was busy at the range.

'Dead beat. It's been a long day.'

Madeleine nodded her sympathy.

'How was yours?' Madeleine worked part-time in a laundry.

'Uneventful.'

'Which is more than can be said for mine.'

'Oh?'

Tim, aged six, came squealing into the kitchen, hotly pursued
by his brother John, who seemed intent on doing him a mischief.
John was eight.

'Stop it you two!' Madeleine declared firmly, waving a wooden
spoon at them. 'Or you'll get this across your backsides.'

'He kicked me, Ma,' John complained.

'Did not.'

'Yes you did.'

'Liar!'

'Liar yourself.'

Madeleine sighed. 'Whatever the rights and wrongs of it the
pair of you be quiet. Supper won't be long.'

'I'm starved,' Tim replied.

'So what's new. You're always hungry.'

By now Roxanne had hung up her coat and begun to lay the
table. 'What's to eat?' she asked, for she too was famished.

'Stew. Mainly vegetables I'm sorry to say, but that's the best
we can do till pay day.'

Roxanne remembered then she'd brought the boys back a
present. Returning to her coat she delved into one of its pockets.

'There you are, share them equally,' she said to Tim, handing
him the dozen cigarette cards she'd pinched from the factory.

'General Sir Redvery Buller,' John breathed in delight, staring
at the top card. Buller was a local hero of the Boer War.

'And Lieutenant General R.S.S. Baden Powell!' Tim exclaimed
at the second card.

'Play in the corner with them,' Madeleine instructed, flashing
Roxanne a grateful smile. These new cards, added to their
existing collection, would keep the boys engrossed for ages.

Jane, Madeleine's twelve year old, breezed into the kitchen.
The boys took after Madeleine, but Jane was the spitting image
of her dad whose photograph stood in a wooden frame on the
mantelpiece.

'Help Roxanne with the table,' Madeleine told her.

'What's for supper?'

'Stew.'

Jane screwed up her face. 'I hate stew.'

'Then go without. That's all there is, and lucky we are to have it, times being what they are.'

Despite professing not to like stew Jane proceeded to polish off every scrap on her plate.

'So tell me about this accident at the factory,' Madeleine said later to Roxanne as they settled in front of the range. The children had gone to bed. The Rowe family slept in the same bed, Madeleine and Jane at the top facing down, the boys at the bottom facing up. It was an arrangement born of necessity, as Madeleine needed the money from the room she rented to keep the family going.

Roxanne went on to explain about the broken belt and what it had done to Lily's face.

Madeleine shook her head. 'Poor girl. That's tragic.'

'It was the eye that really got to me, hanging out on her cheek.'

'Let's just hope and pray the other one's all right,' Madeleine replied.

'But her face,' Roxanne said quietly, with a shudder. 'God knows how that'll end up. She was such a pretty thing too.'

'Something should be done about people like McSween,' Madeleine declared. 'They're a national disgrace.'

'Perhaps he'll give Lily some compensation. That would only be fair and right.'

'What have fair and right got to do with it!' Madeleine laughed scornfully. 'Not a sodding thing. When did McSween ever pay out compensation, or most of the other bosses come to that? I didn't get any when my Joe died, and that was his firm's fault as well. Not so much as a brass farthing came my way, and me with three young'uns to bring up. I tell you, Roxanne, there's many a night I lie in bed worrying myself sick about how to make ends meet.'

'Look on the bright side though, you've got by so far.'

'So far, but that doesn't mean I always will. Who knows what else may lie just round the corner. All it would take is for me to lose my position at the laundry and I'd be sunk.'

Roxanne thought of how long it had taken her to find employment, endlessly tramping the streets until finally she'd been lucky with McSween's. If you could call grafting in that hellhole luck! When she'd come to Exeter she'd had no idea how hard work was to find. Jobs were like gold dust, and those fortunate enough to have one clung onto it for dear life, no matter how appalling the working conditions or how low the pay. Quite simply, the bosses had the whip hand in every instance.

Madeleine glanced at the picture of her Joe on the mantelpiece. He'd been a good man whom she sorely missed and wouldn't replace in a hurry, even if she did meet someone who would take on three children.

'Thanks for bringing those cards home, the boys adore them,' Madeleine stated, knowing the risk Roxanne had taken. If the theft had been discovered she'd have been sacked on the spot.

'They're little enough, and give so much enjoyment.'

'Considering how well you get on with children you should have some of your own,' Madeleine continued.

Roxanne thought of Harry, whom Madeleine knew nothing about, then of her sojourn in the halls. Although she and Madeleine had become extremely close those were secrets she'd kept to herself. 'Perhaps some day,' she replied, thinking that day would never arrive.

'You should find yourself a chap.'

Roxanne laughed. 'Chance would be a fine thing! There's no-one at McSween's, and where else would I find one?'

Roxanne then changed the subject.

'Have you heard anything about Lily?' Roxanne asked Mary the next morning when she arrived at the factory.

'They're saying she'll live, but is going to be awfully disfigured. I got that from Liza Collins on the way in.'

'And where did Liza get it from?'

Mary shrugged.

'Sodding machines,' Roxanne muttered, staring at the one she and Mary operated. At least it didn't possess any leather belts that might suddenly snap, though it did have an unguarded guillotine blade of which she was extremely wary. A finger in the wrong place at the wrong time and . . . She swallowed hard.

A hooter blew, announcing it was time to start. With a roar the factory burst into life.

Another night sitting before the range, only this time Roxanne was alone as Madeleine had already taken herself off to bed, complaining that she thought she had a cold coming on.

What was to become of her? Roxanne reflected. Was this going to be it for years to come, or perhaps even the rest of her life?

The ironic thing was she was happy; she had Madeleine and her children to be thankful for that. She found great solace and contentment in the little house in Frog Street which had become like a home to her. It was as though she'd found a niche where she belonged, and was needed.

She wondered about Linnet and Kevern; how were they getting on? Better than previously she hoped. And what of Morwenna and Tamsin? She decided to write as she'd promised, and made a mental note to do so soon.

And what of Harry, *always* Harry. How was he? Did he ever think about her, recall their time together? Surely he must do.

She sang softly to herself:

'My ma they tell me, wore a crinoline.

Then came the bustle, what a tussle,

women tied up and bundled up in a dress.

Now fashion plates decide we must wear less . . .'

Roxanne broke off with a choke, unable to go on. Did she regret meeting Harry? she asked herself. The answer was no. She wouldn't have missed him for the world. Not the world. Even if it hadn't worked out, though how she wished, with all her heart, it had.

'And so, regretfully, all wages will have to be cut by a quarter,' McSween announced to the entire factory workforce which he'd ordered assembled.

Roxanne gasped, as did many others present. A whole quarter! And their wages already incredibly low.

Mutterings of anger and disbelief ran through the workforce. This unexpected news had stunned and shocked them all.

McSween held up his hands for silence. 'I really am sorry, but it's either that or to lay a number of you off. I thought this the better and more humane option.'

'Lying swine,' Mary whispered to Roxanne. 'It's only a way of increasing his profits. We're selling all the cigarettes, cigars, tobacco and snuff we produce. Everyone knows that.'

'Thank you for your attention,' McSween declared, and swept away to his office.

'Back to work now. Back to work!' several of the supervisors called out.

Roxanne's mind was whirling with the implications this was going to have in Frog Street as she returned to her machine.

211

'There's nothing we can do, nothing at all,' Liza Collins said at dinnertime, a small group of workers having gathered together.

'He's got us exactly where he wants us,' Betty Stamp added, and swore vehemently.

'Lay off a number my arse. That's the last thing he wants,' Mary declared.

'Slave labour, that's all this is. We're no better off than those darkies in America,' Liza went on.

'Damn the man!' Beryl Percival hissed.

'It's all right for him in his big mansion and swanky car. He doesn't have to scrimp and scrape as we do,' Betty stated, face tight with fury.

'If only there were more jobs available, but there aren't. Which he's only too well aware of. He has us over the proverbial bloody barrel,' Mary spat.

'My husband's going to go daft when he learns,' Beryl said, sagging where she sat.

Roxanne gazed from one irate female to the other. Pitying them, pitying herself.

'Perhaps if we got together, all of us, the whole factory, and spoke to him. Pleaded with him,' Roxanne suggested softly.

Liza laughed. 'He'd only tell us to bugger off. That McSween has a swinging brick for a heart. He only cares about himself, the rest of us can go to hell as far as he's concerned. He can replace each and every one of us at any time, don't forget.'

'Any time,' Mary repeated.

'I hope my Ralph never meets him up a dark alley one night. He'd murder him,' Betty declared.

Further conversation was halted by the hooter ending their break.

Roxanne pulled her collar up around her ears. It was freezing out. Under normal circumstances she might have been tempted to catch the electric tram to Frog Street, a treat she occasionally allowed herself after work, but now she couldn't afford that luxury.

She was walking along the pavement when she heard the distinctive sound of an approaching motor car. She turned to glance at it, cars were still something of a rarity after all, and there was McSween lying back in its rear puffing a fat cigar.

Rotten bastard, she thought, as a fresh wave of anger swept through her. Off to his big mansion no doubt where he'd sit down to Lord knows what for supper. Certainly not stew made mainly from vegetables.

How smug and self-satisfied he looked, probably delighted with himself for further exploiting workers who couldn't retaliate, and adding up the extra profits that further exploitation would bring him.

A brick for a heart Liza had said. Well if she'd had one in her hand she'd have chucked it through the windscreen. That would have wiped the smug smile off his face.

She couldn't resist shaking a fist as the car disappeared round a corner.

Madeleine stared, aghast, at Roxanne. 'He did what!'

'Everyone by a quarter,' Roxanne repeated. 'That means I'm down to seven and six a week.'

'Seven and . . .' Madeleine broke off, and shook her head. This was awful.

'Ma can I . . .'

'Be quiet,' she snapped at John.

'I only . . .'

'I said be quiet!' she shouted.

John pouted in frustration and annoyance. 'Come on, we'll play upstairs,' he said to Tim, and the pair of them left the room.

Madeleine stared after them in consternation. 'I shouldn't have done that,' she declared, turning back to Roxanne.

'Understandable. All the way home I felt like shouting myself, which wouldn't have done any good at all.'

'How are you going to manage on seven and six?'

'That's what I've been wondering. I may have to find somewhere else to live. Somewhere cheaper.'

'Oh no you won't,' Madeleine declared stoutly. 'You're staying put. No question about it. You're one of us now, family.'

A warm surge of emotion tingled through Roxanne to hear that. 'Oh Madeleine, what a mess,' she whispered.

Madeleine stirred the pot of lentil soup she was making. 'We'll get by somehow, you'll see. It isn't the end of the world after all.'

'What's so irritating is there's no reason for the cut other than his own greed for profit. The factory's booming.'

'Everyone smokes Silver Firs and Lid Lals,' Madeleine said, referring to the brand names of McSween's cigarettes. Another popular brand name was Tipsy Loo.

'Where's Jane?' Roxanne asked.

'At the shop. I ran out of salt. She'll be back in a minute.'

'Seven and six a week, slave labour one of the girls at work called it.'

'And she was right.'

Roxanne thought of what she'd earned at Collins, which brought a wry smile to her face. How her fortunes had changed in a relatively short time.

'We'll just have to tighten our belts, as if they weren't tight enough already,' Madeleine stated.

'Perhaps I could find something else?'

'Fat chance, and you know it,' Madeleine answered. 'But on the off-chance I'll keep my ears open in case I hear of anything.'

'He passed me after work going home in his car. You never saw anyone look so smug and self-satisfied. I shook my fist at him.'

'Did he see you?' Madeleine queried in alarm.

'I don't think so.'

'Lucky for you he didn't or it would be the sack for you when you got in tomorrow. McSween wouldn't tolerate fist shaking.'

'I was just so furious,' Roxanne explained lamely, thinking that to have lost her job would have been a total disaster.

They were still discussing McSween and the cut in wages when Jane arrived in with the salt.

'I'm cold,' Tim whined.

'Well I'm sorry about that, there's just no more coal for the fire,' Madeleine said.

'And it's only Tuesday,' Jane mumbled. Friday was pay day for both her mother and Roxanne.

'Best thing you can do is get off to bed. You'll be warm in there,' Madeleine suggested to her youngest.

'But it isn't bed time yet, Ma!'

'Then stay up and be cold.'

'I wish it was summer,' grumbled John.

'Don't we all,' Jane breathed wistfully.

Roxanne shivered, having half a mind to take herself off to bed. She shouldn't feel guilty, she thought, it wasn't her fault her wages had been cut.

'And I'm still hungry,' Tim further complained.

'There's nothing I can do about that either,' Madeleine informed him, sounding wretched.

'Let's go to bed,' John said to his brother. 'Ma's right, it'll be better than staying up here.'

214

'And I'm coming with you,' Jane declared, rising from her chair. She too was perished.

'I hate bosses,' Madeleine said when the children were gone.

'Yours is all right.'

'Maybe, but he's an exception.'

Roxanne stamped her feet on the floor, trying to put a little warmth into them.

'Tell me some more about your St Petroc,' Madeleine asked. 'I enjoy hearing about farming and the like. It's so different to anything I've ever known.'

Roxanne was an excellent story-teller and always managed to thrill Madeleine with her tales.

The story she liked best, and found fascinating, was the one about the wreck which Roxanne and Billy Christmas had helped loot.

Jane's face was white and tears weren't very far from her eyes. She'd landed herself a job in service and was departing Frog Street that Sunday morning to take up her post.

'Nervous?' Roxanne asked.

Jane nodded.

'I'm sure there's no need to be. You'll soon settle in.'

'I hope so. It's just . . . leaving home I suppose.'

'Ten pounds a year and all found. You'll be far better off there than you would be here with things as they are,' Madeleine declared, trying to sound cheerful and jolly. Inside she was eating her heart out.

Jane gazed around her, then at her two brothers standing nearby. 'Goodbye you pair,' she husked.

Tim flew into her arms to hug her and be hugged in turn. 'I'll miss you, Jane,' he croaked.

'And I'll miss you.'

She reached over and ruffled John's hair. 'And you, a lot.'

'She will be coming back one Sunday afternoon a month so it's not as if we won't be seeing her,' Madeleine said.

'They're a nice family according to your Ma,' Roxanne smiled, the smile forced.

'Very successful too. He's a prominent banker,' Madeleine added.

'The butler terrifies me,' Jane confessed.

Madeleine laughed. 'All butlers are like that, it's their job to terrify the staff and keep them in line. You'll probably find that underneath he's a real sweetie.'

215

Jane doubted that.

Madeleine glanced at the clock. 'It's time to go, love.'

Jane's lower lip trembled; this was the moment she'd been dreading ever since she'd received the letter confirming her acceptance.

'It's a long trek,' Madeleine reminded her.

Jane picked up the small bag containing her personal items, all she'd need while there. Everything else would be provided.

'Do I get a hug?' Roxanne asked.

Jane squeezed her tight. 'Ta ra, Roxanne.'

'Ta ra. Just do your best, no-one can ask, or expect, more.'

'I will.'

'And never answer back. That's always a mistake. No matter what the provocation.'

'I won't. I promise.'

Roxanne had mentioned that specifically, for Jane had a habit of being 'lippy', as Madeleine called it.

'Right then,' said Madeleine briskly.

Tim started crying, followed immediately by John.

Roxanne felt dreadful as the door snicked shut behind Jane and Madeleine.

'I can't help but think it's all my fault,' Roxanne declared later to Madeleine when the boys had gone off to bed.

'You mustn't. It was time for Jane to go to work anyway. She's old enough now to pull her weight. And look at it this way, it's one less mouth to feed which will make it easier for the rest of us.'

'I just wish she could have got something that didn't entail living in.'

Madeleine shrugged. 'You know what the employment situation is like. She was fortunate to land what she did.'

'If only my wages hadn't been cut,' Roxanne said bitterly.

'That didn't help matters, I admit. But there we are, there's no use crying over spilt milk. And as I say, it was time for her to get a job anyway.'

'I hope she'll be all right.'

So did Madeleine who was worried sick about her daughter. Her only comfort was that she believed she was going into a decent household. Still, you never knew, appearances could be deceptive. All she could do now was wait to hear from Jane on Jane's first Sunday afternoon off.

'She'll be eating better than us, that's one thing to be thankful for,' Madeleine stated.

'She looked so young and . . . scared this morning. I could easily have wept myself.'

'I did, on the way home. But at least not in front of her. I managed to avoid that.'

Roxanne held her hands out to the range, and rubbed them. Thank God, as it was Sunday, they had some coal.

'You're losing weight,' Madeleine observed.

'So are you.'

As were the boys, Madeleine thought despondently. The two of them were thin as rakes.

'It's a bloody hard life,' Madeleine commented.

Roxanne couldn't have agreed more.

Later, in bed, Roxanne heard Madeleine sobbing through the wall that separated their rooms.

The Paris Street Music Hall was run down and shabby in appearance, but from inside came the sound of laughter and merriment.

All she had to do was go in and present herself to the management, Roxanne thought, and all their problems would be over. Having topped the bill at Collins they'd grab her with both hands, she had no doubt about that. Any provincial music hall would have done the same.

She forced herself to walk into the foyer where she studied the photographs, drawings, cartoons and old bills that decorated the walls. Her thoughts drifted to Madeleine and the boys, Jane in service and the privations they were undergoing. An engagement here would end all that. There would be more than enough coal for the range, heaps of food for the table, and new shoes for Tim who desperately needed them.

Go on, she urged herself. Just take that first step, ask for the management. Tell them who you are and your history. But even as she was thinking these things she knew she simply couldn't do it. And all because of Harry.

He'd be everywhere backstage, in the dressing room, the wings, 'on the green'. It would be like opening an old wound. Memories haunted her now of course, but not as keenly as they'd first done. She was gradually coming to terms with her loss, but going back would be a nightmare that could even threaten her sanity.

How she'd loved that man, still did. Beyond belief. She stuffed a hand into her mouth, and bit it. The emotion within her a violent, raging storm.

'Something wrong, miss?' a uniformed employee asked her.

217

She didn't reply. Instead she turned and ran out into the night.

And there she saw nothing of her surroundings, only Harry, a sardonic, mocking Harry.

She ran and ran, and was almost back at Frog Street before she finally stopped.

'I can't,' she wailed, leaning against a wall. 'I just can't!'

Chapter Thirteen

Beryl Percival hit the floor with a jarring thump, causing her workmates to look up in surprise and consternation. Roxanne, who was closest, was the first to her side.

'She's fainted,' Roxanne declared, having quickly checked that there hadn't been an accident. Beryl's face was grey and gaunt, and there were dark, almost purple, patches under her eyes.

'I'll fetch some water,' Liza Collins said, and rushed off.

Roxanne, with Mary's assistance, heaved Beryl into a sitting position. 'She looks dreadful,' Mary murmured.

Mr Smith, their new supervisor, appeared. 'What's going on?' he demanded nervously.

'It's Beryl, sir, she's fainted,' Roxanne replied.

Smith frowned. 'Fainted? Dear me.'

Beryl's eyes fluttered open, though remained unfocused. A long, weary exhalation hissed from her mouth.

'She just keeled over,' Betty Stamp explained to Smith, as she was Beryl's companion at their machine. 'One moment she was fine, then this.'

Roxanne realized how emaciated Beryl was, something she hadn't noticed before. When she felt Beryl's ribcage she discovered the bones were sticking out. She remembered then that Beryl had six children.

Beryl came to with a groan and another weary exhalation.

'You fainted,' Roxanne informed her.

'Sorry,' Beryl mumbled. 'I don't know what came over me.'

'When was the last time you ate?' Roxanne queried.

Beryl gave her a strained smile. 'My husband's been on short time for the past month.'

'And you've been feeding the children and not yourself?'

Liza returned with a cup of water. 'Here my darling, drink some of this,' Liza instructed, squatting beside Beryl.

Beryl drank the water greedily. 'That's better.'

'I think you should have a sit down for a spell. Give you a chance to recover,' Roxanne suggested.

'No,' Smith snapped. 'She won't do any such thing. She must get back to work. You all must.'

Roxanne fixed him with a withering look. 'Can't you see the state she's in?'

'I don't care, that's hardly my fault. She must get right back to work. I can't have any sitting about.'

He waved an arm at the girls. 'Come on, you heard what I said. Any more time wastage and there'll be a stoppage in your pay.'

Out of the same mould as McSween himself, Roxanne thought contemptuously. There wasn't an ounce of sympathy or charity in the man, no wonder McSween had taken him on as a supervisor.

'I'm all right now,' Beryl declared, struggling, with Roxanne's and Mary's help, to her feet where she dusted herself down.

'That's the ticket,' Smith approved.

'Thanks,' Beryl said to Roxanne and Mary. Then, apologetically to Smith, 'It won't happen again, sir, I promise.'

'It had better not,' he muttered.

Pig, Roxanne thought. 'Are you sure now?' she queried of Beryl.

Beryl nodded, and staggered back to her machine where she resumed work.

All the girls in the section kept an eye on her for the rest of the day but luckily she didn't faint again.

Roxanne had only just got home that night when there was a knock on the door. Madeleine went to answer it.

'It's for you,' Madeleine said to Roxanne. Adding, with a wink, 'A chap.'

A chap! Who on earth? Roxanne wondered, wiping her hands on the pinny she'd donned.

'Come in,' Madeleine invited their caller.

Roxanne was flabbergasted when Smith, her supervisor stepped into the kitchen, clutching a bowler hat.

'You!' she heard herself exclaim.

'I apologize for this intrusion but was hoping for a few words with you. That's if it's not inconvenient,' he stammered.

Madeleine glanced over at Tim and John, staring quizzically from a corner where they'd been playing battles with some old lead soldiers. 'You two upstairs,' she commanded.

'Oh Ma . . .' John started to complain.

'Upstairs!'

Madeleine turned to Smith, whom she found a rather attractive young man. 'Would you care for a cup of tea, Mr . . . ?'

'Smith,' he informed her.

'A cup of tea, Mr Smith?'

'No, thank you. I wouldn't want to put you to any bother.'

'It's none at all. And I insist.'

'Well then, if you put it that way.'

He smiled tentatively at a bewildered Roxanne. 'I have to pass close by here on my way home and took the opportunity of dropping in. I hope you don't think it presumptuous of me?'

'That depends what you've dropped in about,' Roxanne replied coldly.

'It's concerning today, the incident with Mrs Percival. It's been preying on my conscience ever since.'

'I should think it might.'

'That's why I wanted to explain. And as I was passing anyway . . .' He trailed off.

Roxanne felt some of the tension drain out of her. At least it wasn't the sack. Thank God!

'Take a seat, Mr Smith,' Madeleine said, spooning tea into the pot. 'I'm afraid we can't offer you a biscuit. We don't run to those nowadays.'

'I fully understand,' he answered gravely.

Roxanne realized she hadn't introduced Madeleine, which she now did. 'You were saying?' she prompted Smith when that was over.

He twisted his hands together. 'There was nothing else I could do, Miss Hawkins. Mr McSween would have had a blue fit if he'd found out I'd let an employee take time off, no matter what the reason. It could even have meant my job which is very important to me.'

Roxanne began to soften towards him. 'I suppose it might have put you in a difficult position,' she conceded.

'Very. If it had been up to me I'd gladly have let Mrs Percival take a breather, she looked positively awful. But I'm directly accountable to Mr McSween, and you know what he's like.'

She'd make herself scarce as soon as she'd poured the tea, Madeleine thought, leave the pair of them alone.

'I'm young to be a supervisor, you see,' Smith went on. 'The job is a big opportunity for me. And frankly, the money, which is considerably more than I was earning before, most welcome.'

How old was he? Roxanne wondered. Mid-twenties she judged. He was right, he was young to be a supervisor.

'I'm sorry there's no sugar, but we do have milk,' Madeleine stated.

He dismissed that with a gesture. 'Milk's fine. It doesn't bother me to do without sugar.'

Madeleine handed Smith a cup, then placed another within Roxanne's reach. 'Now if you'll excuse me I'll just pop upstairs and see what those two scallywags of mine are about.'

Roxanne frowned at Madeleine, wishing that Madeleine would stay. But Madeleine had other ideas.

'It's kind of you to explain yourself to me,' Roxanne said to Smith when Madeleine had gone.

'I didn't want you to think me an ogre.'

'Why me in particular?'

Smith coloured. 'Yours happened to be the house I was passing, that's all.'

'And can I tell the other girls?'

He nodded. 'But I don't want it referred to in the factory. And you may point out that I'll have to carry on as Mr McSween expects.'

Smith remained for a further few minutes. Then he left, courteously taking his farewells at the door.

'He was a bit of all right,' Madeleine declared on her return.

Roxanne snorted. 'Now don't you go getting any silly notions. He was merely telling me what was what.'

Madeleine couldn't help but wonder if there hadn't been more to it than that. She hoped there was, she'd liked Mr Smith. And Roxanne was free, after all.

'Miss Hawkins!'

Roxanne turned to find Smith hurrying after her. It was the week after his visit to the house.

'Hallo,' she smiled when he reached her.

He was clearly embarrassed and flustered. 'Can I walk with you for part of the way?'

'Of course.'

'I, eh . . . was looking out for you,' he confessed.

'Oh?'

222

'I'm thinking of going to the music hall this Saturday and wondered if you'd care to accompany me?'

Roxanne blanched. *The music hall.* Of all places! 'I'm sorry, I don't like music halls,' she lied.

'I see.'

His wretched expression told her he believed she'd turned him down flat, which wasn't true. Or was it? She wasn't sure.

'I'm sorry to have bothered you,' he apologized. 'We'll just forget the whole thing if you don't mind.'

'I was literally telling the truth, Mr Smith, I just don't like music halls,' she further lied, taking pity on him.

'Does that mean you might consider going elsewhere?'

'An evening out would be most enjoyable. I haven't had one for a long time.'

His face lit up. 'Then you choose. Anywhere will suit me.'

They arranged that he would pick her up from Frog Street.

'I knew he fancied you!' Madeleine exclaimed in delight.

Doubts assailed Roxanne. She wasn't interested in a romance, that was right out of the question. Perhaps she'd made a mistake in accepting Smith's invitation. She didn't want him to get the wrong idea.

'I simply thought it would be nice to go out for a change,' she explained.

'And why not! Pretty women like you shouldn't be stuck in night after night. It's high time you got yourself a bloke.'

Roxanne didn't want a bloke, as such. But it would be pleasant to have some male company. She'd missed that.

'Now what are you going to wear?' Madeleine inquired eagerly.

'Haven't thought about it yet.'

They fell to discussing the matter.

Smith had been surprised when Roxanne had suggested a pub. He wasn't overly keen on pubs himself, not being much of a drinker, but if that's what Roxanne wished then he was only too happy to accommodate her.

'What'll it be?' he asked, when she'd settled into a booth. The pub, The White Hart, was part of an hotel he knew, by reputation, to be an acceptable place to take a young lady.

'A port I think, Mr Smith.'

'Dennis, please. I can't have you calling me Mr Smith, now can I?'

She smiled at him. 'And I'm Roxanne.'

223

'It's so . . . unfair,' Mrs Roach choked.

'I've got to accept it, Ma, and so have you.'

'I know but . . . it's so hard, my darling. So hard.'

'Bloody machine,' Lily said angrily. 'I've never stopped cursing it since this happened.'

Damn McSween, Roxanne thought, wondering what his reaction would have been if he'd been there to see Lily. He'd probably callously shrug it off, say it was bad luck, or somehow make out it was Lily's fault.

'How's the food?' Roxanne queried. It was all she could think of to say at that moment.

'Wholesome enough. I can't complain.'

'Do they let you up to go to the . . . toilet?'

'No. That's one of the worst things. Having to use a bedpan. I hate it.'

Roxanne could well understand it. She would have found that humiliating as well.

'How long before the bandages come off?'

'They don't know. It all depends on how quickly I heal.' The one eye focused on Roxanne. 'They won't let me see myself when they change them. I keep asking but they always refuse.'

Roxanne didn't know how to reply to that.

Lily reached up and tentatively touched her bandages, her single eye suddenly glistening with moisture.

'Is there much pain?' Roxanne asked.

'Quite a bit. When it gets too much they give me a draught that makes me sleep.'

'And how are you sleeping?'

'It varies, Roxanne. There are nights when I'm all right, others when I just lie staring at the ceiling, wondering what the rest of my life is going to be like. I'll never get married now, that's right out of the question, for what man's going to look at me? None. And that means there won't be any children, which I really wanted. I'm going to be a . . . monster.'

The screens moved and a man entered. 'Sorry, I didn't know there was someone else here,' he apologized.

'My Da,' Lily explained.

Roxanne was profoundly grateful for Mr Roach's appearance as it meant she could escape.

'All the girls send their love,' she smiled to Lily.

'Tell them I was asking after them, and miss them. Though not the factory, not bloody McSween's.'

Roxanne took Lily's hand and squeezed it. 'I'll come again.'

226

'I'd like that.'

Outside the hospital Roxanne gulped in several deep lungfuls of air. That had been simply horrendous.

She found herself walking away from the hospital as fast as she could without actually breaking into a run.

That night she dreamed of Lily. Only it wasn't Lily in the bed, but herself, *her* face swathed.

Then a doctor was there unravelling the bandages which fell away in long white streams.

'I want to see myself,' she said.

The doctor held up a mirror that she stared into, and from which a monster gazed back.

She woke screaming, lathered in sweat and shaking from head to toe. Thank God it had only been a nightmare.

Madeleine, roused by the scream, rushed into her bedroom demanding to know what was wrong. Roxanne's friend couldn't have been more sympathetic, cuddling her when she explained, and stayed with her till she was relatively calm again.

There was a rapid drum of footsteps and then Dennis was by her side. 'How are you? I thought you looked pale today,' he enquired anxiously.

She gave him a wan smile. 'I went and saw Lily Roach at the hospital yesterday.'

'Oh! I heard what happened to her.' The accident had occurred before he'd joined McSween's.

'It was terrible. She's in an awful mess.'

'I'm sorry.'

'In fact I had a nightmare about it last night. She's lost an eye and . . .' Roxanne broke off and shuddered.

'If there's anything I can do you only have to say.'

That was kind of him. 'No, not really Dennis.'

'I've been meaning to ask if you'd care to go out again? I've just been waiting for an opportunity.'

He glanced at her, his expression still anxious. 'Perhaps this is the wrong time?'

She turned up the collar of her coat as it had started to rain. There was also a sharp, swirling wind which was causing the loose strands of her pinned-up hair to flutter.

When she failed to reply he went on. 'It may be just what you need. A sort of tonic?'

He was good company, she thought. And she had enjoyed their evening at the pub together. 'What did you have in mind?'

'Not the music hall,' he joked, which made her smile. 'How about the dancing?'

'When?'

'Saturday night?'

'Same arrangement as before?'

'I'll be there.'

He hesitated, then reached out and took her arm. 'Now tell me about Lily Roach, I'd like to hear.'

They spoke about Lily all the way back to Frog Street.

'How am I doing?' he asked.

'The honest truth?'

He nodded.

'You're awful. Two left feet.'

'At least I haven't stood on yours yet.'

'*Yet*,' she emphasized, teasing him.

'We can sit down if you wish?'

'No, I'd rather dance.'

'Then I can't be that bad.'

She raised an eyebrow.

'I'm better at the polka. I'm quite good at that.'

'Are you indeed!' she further teased.

He pulled her fractionally closer. 'How about fish and chips on the way home? I adore them.'

She thought of London and the posh meals she'd had there. 'Fish and chips sounds marvellous.'

'Then that's what we'll have. With pickled onions.'

She laughed.

'What's so funny?'

'Pickled onions. I can't think of anything less romantic.'

'We'll go without them then.'

Suddenly he looked at her closely and said, 'You're the most beautiful girl on the floor, by far.'

'Hardly.'

'You most certainly are.'

She felt flattered, and pleased, her spirits quite lifted. Later, when they got to the fish and chip shop, they had pickled onions after all. She insisted that he bought them.

'Did he kiss you?'

Roxanne shook her head.

228

'It was only your second time out, mind, he wouldn't want to rush things.'

Roxanne put the kettle on, dying for a cup of tea after the fish and chips. 'He tried, but I wouldn't let him.'

Madeleine regarded her grimly. 'Why not?'

Roxanne shrugged. She'd been about to, and then an image of Harry had flashed before her. 'I don't think I'll see him again,' she said.

'But he seemed such a nice chap!' Madeleine protested.

'Oh he is, extremely nice. It's just . . .' She trailed off.

'I simply don't understand you,' Madeleine stated, shaking her head in exasperation.

Roxanne decided to confide in her friend, at least partially. She needed to talk about this. 'There was somebody else you see,' she confessed. 'Somebody I've never got over and know I never will.'

'What do you mean, never will?' Madeleine retorted angrily. 'That's ridiculous.' Then, in a softer tone, 'You were very much in love?'

'Totally and utterly.'

'What happened?'

'He chucked me over.'

Madeleine swore. 'When was this?'

'A couple of years ago.' Roxanne leaned against the range and stared at the kettle. 'He was in love with me, then stopped. When he walked out it broke my heart.'

Madeleine went to Roxanne and put her arms round her shoulders. 'Someone else will come along, in time. You take my word for it.'

'No,' Roxanne whispered. 'There will never be another for me. Harry was it, the one and only.'

'Was there another woman involved?'

'Several actually, that I know of. He'd been cheating on me a while before the end.'

'Sounds like a bastard to me.'

'He was, but that didn't stop me loving him. Love's a funny thing you know, there's no rhyme or reason to it. Certainly not the sort of love I felt for him.'

Madeleine thought of her Joe, whom she missed desperately. 'It still doesn't mean you've got to throw your life away, a life that's all ahead of you. I can imagine how difficult it must be, but all you can do is mark it up to experience.'

Experience, Roxanne thought bitterly. It had certainly been that, one that would haunt her till her dying day.

229

'Why don't you give Dennis a further chance?' Madeleine suggested.

Roxanne made up her mind. 'No,' she stated flatly. 'It wouldn't be right. Not for him, nor me.'

'I think you're making a mistake,' Madeleine said, sighing.

Roxanne remained convinced she wasn't.

'Fuck!' Mary exclaimed.

Roxanne glanced across in surprise. For although many of the girls in the factory swore like troopers it was rare for Mary to do so.

Mary held up a hand and stared at it. 'My thumb,' she croaked. 'The guillotine.'

Roxanne noted with horror that Mary's thumb was missing, sliced clean off.

Mary's eyes rolled upwards and were closing as she slumped to the floor.

Chapter Fourteen

'It could so easily have been me, it was my machine after all,' an appalled Roxanne said to Madeleine.

'Ma, I'm hungry,' Tim piped up.

'Supper won't be long.'

'What's the soup, Ma?' John queried.

'Barley, rice and a good bone to give it body,' Madeleine replied. She'd managed to wheedle the bone from the butcher for next to nothing.

'Something must be done,' Roxanne went on.

'What? McSween would just laugh in your face. Or sack you more like, if you suggested it to him. You know his reputation, it stinks.'

'But things just can't go on as they are. Everyone's fearful they'll be next.'

'And someone will be, you can count on it. It's always been the same at McSween's. It has a name for accidents.'

'Which could be avoided. The guillotines should have guards on them for example. That would hardly cost a fortune.'

'With cost being the operative word. Anything that costs is out as far as McSween is concerned, the tight fisted old bugger. Not that he's tight fisted with his own, his wife walks around dripping furs and diamonds I'm told.'

'What's she like?' Roxanne queried, wondering if Mrs McSween might be the answer. Was she aware of conditions in her husband's factory?

As if reading Roxanne's mind Madeleine replied. 'It's said she's as hard hearted as him. The servants in their house supposedly have a terrible time of it. She's a real slave driver.'

'How long will the soup be, Ma?' Tim asked, eyeing the pot bubbling away on the range.

'Soon. Now stop pestering me. Can't you see Roxanne and I are talking?'

'I want to be an engine driver when I grow up,' Tim announced. The previous week it had been a ship's captain. He then started chuffing round the kitchen pretending to be a train.

Madeleine paused to stare at him. He was such a loveable little boy, as was John. How she loved them both. She thought momentarily of Jane, now well settled into her job and enjoying it. She smiled as she remembered something Jane had told her during her daughter's first Sunday visit. Apparently it was one of Jane's tasks to stitch the folds of the morning newspaper together with cotton, so that it didn't fall apart when read, then iron the newspaper, after which she had to douse it with scent for the mistress. That story had amused her no end. How ludicrous and pretentious could people be! Still, the Ferriers, whom Jane had gone to, were kind to her which was all that mattered.

Later that night, long after her usual bedtime, Roxanne sat up thinking about the factory, and McSween.

'A deputation!' Liza Collins exclaimed. 'You must be joking.'

Roxanne had decided to broach the subject with her immediate workmates during the next day's dinner break, wanting to sound out their reactions.

'McSween would show any deputation the door,' Beryl Percival declared.

'Do we know that for certain? Has anyone ever approached him?'

Betty Stamp laughed. 'No-one has, to my knowledge. And no-one would dare. Except an out and out lunatic that is.'

'Perhaps if we went about it in the right way?' Roxanne argued.

'And how would that be?' Liza asked.

'I'm not sure yet.'

'There is no right way,' Beryl said. 'Take my word for it.'

'You're mad even to think about it,' Liza stated.

'Marilyn?' Roxanne queried. Marilyn Wilcox had replaced Mary, having been transferred from another part of the factory. She was a fat, jolly girl of eighteen.

'I agree with the others. You can count me out of any deputation, I want to keep my job. I'm saving up to get married don't forget.'

'It's hopeless Roxanne, you have to accept that,' Beryl said.

232

'McSween is a law unto himself, who'd never listen to any of us. Not in a million years.'

'And what happens if you have an accident like Mary and Lily. Will *you* accept that?'

Beryl's lips thinned with fear and anxiety. 'I have no other choice but to take my chances along with the rest of us. There's no other work available just now and we need the money.'

'Have you been to see Lily?'

Beryl shook her head. 'With my children, and husband, I just haven't had the time.'

'Well I have. When the bandages come off she says she's going to be a gargoyle, a monster. And not a penny piece of compensation either.'

'I'm sorry for her, of course I am,' Beryl replied in a whisper. 'But she knew the dangers same as we all do. She was simply unlucky, that's all.'

'So none of you would back me?'

Each, in turn, shook her head.

Well that answered that, Roxanne thought. She had no support whatever, not amongst this lot anyway. Although she fully understood their reasons it still filled her with dismay, and anger at McSween.

'These toilets are disgusting,' declared Eileen Salmon. 'An animal would be ashamed to use them.' Eileen was a Scot who'd recently moved to Exeter, having met and married a labourer who was working temporarily north of the border. She was a fiery, no-nonsense, redhead known for her quick temper.

Roxanne, who'd only previously nodded at Eileen, regarded her with interest. 'Why don't you complain?'

'I have on several occasions, each time to my supervisor who says the matter's in hand. Always in bloody hand! But nothing's ever done.'

'Then why not go directly to the top, speak to McSween himself?' Roxanne suggested softly, and held her breath.

Eileen's green eyes blazed. 'By God and I will. They're all terrified of the bugger, but not *this* lassie. I'll ask for an appointment.'

Roxanne, feeling a twinge of guilt at having made the suggestion, though it had been Eileen's decision to act on it, couldn't wait for the outcome of that appointment.

*　　*　　*

'Roxanne?'

She turned, and her heart sank to see Dennis hurrying towards her. She thought she'd made it clear she didn't want to go out with him again.

'Hallo,' he smiled tentatively.

'Hallo. How are you?'

He fell into step beside her. 'Fine. And yourself?'

'Tired. But that's nothing unusual.'

They walked a short way in silence, which was finally broken when he said, 'Are you sure you won't change your mind about us?'

'No Dennis, I'm sorry.'

His shoulders sagged underneath his heavy woollen coat. 'Did I do something wrong? Is that it?'

'You didn't do anything wrong, Dennis.'

'Because if I did I apologize.'

'There's no need for an apology. None at all,' she assured him.

'So it's just me,' he said wistfully.

He was making her feel awful, but she had no intention of changing her mind. 'If it's any consolation I wouldn't get involved with any man right now.'

'Why?'

'I have my reasons, let's leave it at that.'

'I like you tremendously, Roxanne. You must have guessed.'

'And I like you too, Dennis. But that doesn't alter matters. I'm simply not in the market for romance.'

She stopped and grasped his arm. 'We can remain friends though. I'd hate us to be otherwise.'

'Friends it is then,' he smiled thinly.

'And that's *all*.'

'I'll leave you here, I'm not going straight home tonight,' he said, lying.

That was a relief she thought. 'I hope I haven't hurt you, Dennis. I certainly never meant to.'

'See you tomorrow, Roxanne.' And with that he hurried off across the street.

Roxanne stared after him in sorrow. She'd done the right thing in breaking it off when she had, she told herself. He'd already become too fond of her, but she couldn't allow that fondness to develop into anything else, not when it was impossible for her to respond in kind.

*   *   *

'Eileen's gone up,' Brenda, one of the packers, whispered to Roxanne. 'Everyone's agog.'

Eileen still hadn't returned to the factory floor at dinner break. Nor when the hooter sounded ending the day's work.

Roxanne later learned that McSween had dismissed Eileen on the spot and ordered her to leave the premises immediately. She'd had to wait on the street while her coat and hat were fetched.

'You should get a doctor,' Roxanne murmured to Madeleine, sitting on the edge of her bed sponging Tim's fevered brow.

'You know I can't afford one,' Madeleine replied, trying not to show how desperately worried she was. 'This will pass off given time. In the meanwhile all I can do is keep him well tucked up.'

'But it's been three days now! And, if anything, the fever's worse,' Roxanne argued.

Madeleine chewed a nail that was already bitten to the quick. 'The doctor won't come unless he's paid, which I simply cannot do. If I could I'd be round to him like a shot.'

If only she had something to pawn, Roxanne thought. But she hadn't. Anything that could be popped had already found its way to 'uncle's'. All that remained was her coat, and to pop that, in the current weather, would be downright stupid as it would only lead to her falling ill herself.

'What about moneylenders?' Roxanne queried.

'There is one nearby, but his charges are exorbitant. Once you get into his clutches you never get out again. Poor Mr Bainbridge, who lived along the street, hung himself because of that.'

'I'm thirsty, Ma,' Tim mumbled.

'Here we are,' she smiled, reaching for a cup of water by the bedside which she held to his lips, supporting him behind the neck while he drank.

'I wish you didn't have to go to work, Ma,' he said weakly.

'So do I my lamb. So do I. But I must, they'd dock me if I didn't turn up and we need every farthing we can get.' She paused, then added to no-one in particular, 'There's no coal again and Lord knows what I'll manage for supper.'

Madeleine bowed her head, and closed her eyes.

'I'll be home as quickly as I can,' Roxanne said, as it was time to leave for the factory.

Madeleine returned the cup to its place and rose unsteadily to her feet, having hardly slept a wink since Tim had taken ill.

'It's at moments like this I miss my Joe the most,' she husked to Roxanne.

235

Roxanne hugged her friend, then kissed Tim on the cheek before departing for McSween's.

That night the fever intensified even further and Tim lapsed into deliriousness during which he cried out again and again.

When morning came Madeleine knew what she had to do; it was the only recourse left to her.

Roxanne returned from work to discover the range radiating heat and the kitchen filled with the succulent smell of roasting meat. She went directly upstairs to Madeleine's bedroom where she was attending to Tim. A large bottle of medicine stood by his bedside.

'The doctor's been and gone,' Madeleine explained.

Roxanne frowned. 'But how . . . ?'

'Tim's going to be all right. The doctor gave him some tablets and me a prescription to get from the chemist's. I've to send for him again if Tim doesn't show signs of improvement within the next twenty-four hours. But he feels better already, don't you pet?'

Tim nodded. 'Not so hot anymore.'

'His temperature's right down,' Madeleine beamed.

'Where did the money come from?'

Madeleine's face clouded. 'I'll tell you later. But now I must see to the supper. It's pork tonight.'

'I smelt it when I came in,' Roxanne replied, mystified.

Madeleine turned to John who was hovering nearby. 'You keep your brother company and I'll shout when supper's ready.'

'All right, Ma.'

Madeleine went over to John and ruffled his hair. 'Let's just hope and pray you don't catch it as well.'

'There's always the chance of that when we're all living cooped up together like this,' Madeleine murmured to Roxanne as they left the bedroom.

When they reached the kitchen Roxanne closed the door behind them. 'Well?' she demanded.

Madeleine put on an apron. 'Will you keep an eye on the boys for me this evening? I have to go out again straight after supper.'

That was unusual to say the least. Madeleine never went out in the evening.

'What's going on? Have you found another job or something?'

'Sort of.'

'And what exactly does that mean?'

Madeleine's good humour vanished and her face crumpled in on itself. She leant against the table for support. 'I'm thoroughly ashamed of myself. But it was the only way. The end justifies the means.'

Roxanne put her arms round her friend's shoulders. 'What have you done, Madeleine?'

'You'll think me dreadful.'

'No I won't. Whatever you did was for Tim. I understand that.'

Madeleine sobbed. 'Oh, Roxanne. I feel so . . . dirty. It was horrible.'

'What have you done Madeleine?' Roxanne asked a second time.

'You won't believe this, Roxanne. I don't believe it myself. The first was the worst, the rest only a little easier.'

'What are you talking about?'

Madeleine gulped in air, then ran a hand over her face. 'There are girls use the laundry whom I've come to know quite well. They're very pleasant girls, always good for a laugh. And kind, marvellously kind. They agreed to help me as soon as I explained the situation.'

'Doing *what*?' Roxanne questioned, still mystified.

'They're . . . prostitutes.'

Roxanne stared at Madeleine in horror. 'You . . .' She trailed off, aghast.

Madeleine nodded. 'I was lucky, I chose an extremely busy day. A big warship had just docked and the sailors were virtually queuing up. They let me use one of their rooms. There were two of us in it, with a blanket down the middle.'

'Christ!' Roxanne breathed.

'I made more money in a few hours than I do in a fortnight at the laundry.'

'But . . . how could you sell yourself?'

'For Tim, Roxanne. For him. You said you understood.'

Roxanne, with tears in her eyes, pulled Madeleine to her and hugged her tight. 'Oh my poor darling,' she whispered.

'I pretended it wasn't me lying there. That it was someone else. I thought of the cash, and Tim.'

'You're not going back, are you?'

'I said I would. Just for tonight, and then that's it.'

'How . . . how many?'

'Don't ask me that Roxanne, please.'

'I'm sorry. I shouldn't have.'

Roxanne swallowed back the bile that rose in her throat,

throbbing inside with pity and compassion for Madeleine who'd been forced to sink so low because of her ailing child.

It was then she noticed that Joe's picture had been lain face down on the mantelpiece.

'I thought you might be interested in this,' Clementina Carter said to Roxanne, handing her a small sheet of paper. They were in the toilets which were in an even worse state than when Eileen Salmon had complained about them. One of the lavatories had been blocked for the past three days and the stench from it was revolting.

Roxanne glanced at the sheet of paper to find it was a cheaply printed flyer advertising a forthcoming union meeting. The speaker was a Mr James Read.

'What makes you think I would be?' Roxanne queried.

Clementina shrugged. 'People talk. I heard of the little chat you had with your section.'

Roxanne hoped McSween never learned about it. 'Are you going?'

'I am. My boyfriend's mad keen on the unions. He says they'll be the saviour of the working classes in this country. He belongs to one.'

'I'll think about it,' Roxanne murmured, folding the flyer and slipping it into her pocket.

Later, at home, she took it out and studied it properly.

Roxanne judged there were several hundred, mainly men, who'd turned up to hear James Read speak. She sat enthralled by his words, as he was a most eloquent, and passionate, orator. At the end of his speech she, and everyone else present, leapt to their feet to give him thunderous and tumultuous applause.

Afterwards, Read was thronged with well-wishers and admirers to such an extent that Roxanne, who'd stayed behind hoping to talk with him, felt hers was a lost cause. But fortune was on her side when she caught his eye, and smiled. He crooked a finger, beckoning her to his side.

'You were wonderful, Mr Read,' she told him.

'Why thank you.'

'Everything you said was just so true. The workers need to unite in defence against the injustices that take place. My own factory is a case in point. McSween's, have you heard of it?'

'I'm sorry Miss . . . ?'

'Hawkins. Roxanne Hawkins.'

'I'm afraid I haven't. I come from London you see, I'm only down here as a guest.'

'Yes I know that. It was explained on the flyer and again when you were introduced. I simply wondered if you had.'

'Is there any form of union at all at this McSween's?' Read asked.

'No, but there should be. I'd certainly join if there was.'

'Then you must try to organize one.'

'I wouldn't know where to start,' she confessed. 'And if I did, I'd soon be out on my ear. McSween would be totally against a union.'

Read reached into an inside pocket to produce a notebook and pencil. 'Tell you what, Miss Hawkins, why don't you go and see this man and explain your problems to him. He should have been here tonight but is, unfortunately, caught up in union business. Perhaps he can help.'

Read hurriedly wrote on the first page of the notepad, then tore off the page and gave it to Roxanne. 'Good luck.'

'Thank you,' she beamed.

Read turned his attention elsewhere.

Jamie McBride was a Scot, the same as Eileen Salmon. He had thinning, swept-back, mousey hair and a pug nose. His eyes were bright and intense, those of a fanatic or zealot.

'Please sit down Miss Hawkins,' he said, indicating a badly chipped and scarred wooden chair. He gestured about him; the room they were in was small, smelling slightly of damp. 'Not the most salubrious of surroundings I'm afraid, but the best we can afford for now.'

When Roxanne was seated McBride perched himself on the edge of a rickety desk on which papers were scattered. 'Thank you for your letter. And you say James Read himself suggested you contacted me?'

'That's correct.'

'Great man, great speaker,' McBride enthused. 'He's a pillar of the movement and someone I hugely admire.'

'He certainly spoke well. I was extremely impressed.'

McBride rubbed his short, stubby hands together, for it was cold in the room, as there was no heating. 'Let me explain a little about myself to begin with; that way you'll know who and what you're dealing with. I'm a union official newly appointed to the post. I must also confess that I'm still learning about Exeter and the manufacturing industries down here. I come from Scotland you see.'

'I can tell from the accent.'

'That noticeable?' he smiled wryly.

'Only a little bit,' she joked in reply.

He laughed. 'My accent's thick as porage, and so it should be hailing from Clydeside. I take it you understand me all right?'

'Perfectly, Mr McBride.'

'Jamie, if you don't mind. I don't believe in standing on ceremony.'

'And I'm Roxanne.'

'I'll happily continue calling you Miss Hawkins if you prefer. You may consider the use of your Christian name over-familiar.'

'Roxanne's fine,' she assured him.

'Right. So what can I do for you, Roxanne? You mentioned McSween's in your letter. A terrible man by all accounts.'

'He's a swine of the first degree,' Roxanne stated.

'There are plenty of bosses like him around, oh aye indeed! They need to be brought under control, which is one of the primary aims of the trade union movement.'

'He's heartless, completely heartless.' Roxanne then went on to explain about conditions at McSween's; the pay cut which had been simply to further line McSween's pockets; the accidents to Lily Roach, Mary, and others that had occurred; and what had happened to Eileen Salmon when she'd spoken to McSween regarding the condition of the toilets.

Jamie shook his head in sympathy when she reached the end of her sorry tale.

'Mr Read suggested I try and form a union within the factory. I told him I wouldn't know where to start, and should I attempt to I'd soon get the sack.'

'Which is what often happens in these cases,' Jamie replied. 'The bosses see it as picking off the so-called troublemakers, which puts the fear of God into the others.'

'So what hope is there?'

Jamie smiled. 'That's where I would come in, initially anyway. Any local union that could be formed could associate itself with the Women's Trade Union League, which would give it a far stronger hand when dealing with management. But first things first. What response do you think there would be at McSween's towards forming a union?'

Roxanne pulled a face. 'I've had a word here and there, and I have to say the response wasn't good. It's not that they don't want to better their conditions and pay; it's simply that many of them are scared of losing jobs which they desperately need.'

'The same old story,' Jamie sighed. 'But there again, it has to be said that women tend not to look upon the unions the same way as men do. Single women, for example, tend to view their work as merely a temporary necessity, so why rock the boat? Married women, on the other hand, find that home duties fill in such leisure time as they have when the day's work in the factory or workshop is over. Their estimate of their own position is a low one and they seem to think that any display of independence on their part would oust them from the labour market entirely.'

'I see,' Roxanne murmured.

'As for pay differentials between the sexes, there are an enormous amount of men who wish it to remain that way, trade union members included, because they believe it their duty to earn enough to keep their wives at home without the women having to go out to work at all. But that's another argument I won't elaborate on here and now.'

'Is it one you personally hold to?' Roxanne asked softly.

Jamie's face broke into a wide, appealing grin. 'As it happens, I don't. There are certain women who have to work, and if they do why should they be paid less than a man performing exactly the same task? I can't think of anything more unfair than that.'

Roxanne thoroughly agreed with him.

'But back to McSween's. Why don't we test the water?'

'How do you mean?'

'Let's have a meeting which I'll address. Do you think you could put the word about informing the workforce of the time and place?'

Roxanne nodded. 'That shouldn't be hard.'

They fell to discussing the details.

It was a disappointing turnout with less than half the girls from McSween's putting in an appearance in a nearby hall that Jamie had rented for the occasion.

When Roxanne judged that all who were coming had arrived she walked on to the platform and introduced Jamie.

He was nowhere as good an orator as James Read, but his belief in, and commitment to, the trade union cause shone out from him like a beacon.

'It's up to you,' he declared, nearing the end of his speech. 'All of you here and those who aren't. If you want a union formed to fight on your behalf then it can be done. But if the will isn't there

241

then I'd be wasting my time and yours, which I will not do. Now, let's have a show of hands. All those in favour of us taking the matter forward?'

A few hands struggled aloft, then a few more.

'Come on girls, what are you waiting for!' a voice Roxanne didn't recognize rang out. 'Remember Lily Roach. Do you want to end up like that poor bitch!'

Suddenly dozens of hands shot into the air, filling Roxanne with delight and bringing a slow smile to Jamie's face.

When the meeting was over Jamie declared it to have been a success. The next step was the drawing up of rules and regulations and recruiting members.

Roxanne had been seeing quite a lot of Jamie McBride in the evenings, the two of them developing a strong bond of friendship and mutual respect. They sometimes met in McBride's office, on other occasions in a nearby pub where it was a lot warmer. When they did the latter they only ever had one drink each, usually a half pint, which Jamie insisted on paying for out of his own pocket.

One evening, Jamie sat back and scratched his chin. 'We're coming on, but the membership isn't high enough yet for us to make a move. We must get over fifty per cent to do that.'

'It hasn't been that long, after all,' Roxanne argued. 'They need time.'

McBride regarded her thoughtfully. 'I hope you're right, otherwise this is a dead duck. We can only operate from a position of strength.'

'Even if we had the entire workforce behind us we'd hardly be doing that.'

'You know what I mean!' he chided.

Roxanne enjoyed her meetings with Jamie, admiring his quick and intelligent mind. She was learning a lot from him, not only about the trade union movement but all manner of things. Like Dennis, he was basically a self-educated man.

'Do you miss Scotland?' she suddenly asked.

'Scotland?' he queried in surprise.

'The Clydeside.'

'Oh aye, that's where my roots are. For me it'll always be special.'

'Tell me about it.'

He sighed. 'The people are hard, but soft as well. Practical, but also sentimental. And loyal, they're loyal above all else. To themselves, their city and their country. They're also extremely proud.'

'You've never mentioned your family, Jamie. Are you married?'

He laughed. 'Good Lord no, I haven't had time for that. Besides . . .' He hesitated, then added, a slight blush coming into his cheeks, 'I havnae met the right lassie yet.'

So he wasn't married, she'd been curious about that as she knew next to nothing about his personal life. 'What does your father do?'

'Works in the shipyard, same as his father before him. That's where I started and first got involved with the unions. There was a chap I had dealings with who put me forward as a full-time official.'

'And now here you are. Far from home in Devon.'

'Far from home, true enough,' he mused wistfully.

'How long will you stay down here?'

'I've no idea,' he replied. 'I could be shifted in a few years, or I could remain in Exeter until I retire. It all depends.'

'On what?'

'The powers that be. Or maybe how successful I am in the job.'

'Where are you staying?'

'In a lodging house run by a Mrs Parfitt. Kindly body who treats me as a son. I fell on my feet with her.'

'And where is this boarding house?'

'Heavitree.'

She'd heard of Heavitree, but had never been there. It was in a different direction to Frog Street.

'But enough about me,' he declared. 'As we're getting personal how about you?'

She didn't mention London, the music hall or Harry, but told him that the main reason for leaving St Petroc had been that there hadn't been enough room for her in the house after the arrival of Tamsin.

'Are you mad getting involved in such nonsense?' Dennis Smith demanded, having waylaid Roxanne in a corner of the factory.

'What nonsense?'

'This union business.'

Alarm flared through her. 'Who said I was involved? And what union business?'

'Don't play the innocent with me, Roxanne Hawkins. I'm not

daft you know, I hear things. You and others are trying to set up a union. McSween will hit the roof if he finds out.'

'I don't know what you're talking about,' she lied.

He gripped her arm hard. 'Take a word of well meant advice, drop the whole thing. You'll only bring disaster on yourself if you don't. Yourself and others, but it's you I'm worried about.'

'Thank you for your concern, Dennis, but it's quite unnecessary. If anything is nonsense it's what you've heard.'

Doubt flashed across his face. 'Do you swear that?'

'Dennis!' she exclaimed, feigning anger.

'I'd just hate you to do anything foolish, Roxanne,' he said softly.

'I have to get back to work or I'll be for the high jump. See you around.' And with that Roxanne hurried away.

She must tell the others to make sure they kept their mouths well and truly shut, she thought. If Dennis had heard something then so might the other supervisors, any one of whom could go straight to McSween. And they weren't ready for that yet.

Denial, she told herself. For the time being any other accusations must be met with strict denial.

But it had been nice of Dennis to be worried about her. He was a good chap and would make someone a smashing husband someday. But it would never be her.

'You're the obvious choice for shop steward,' Jamie stated.

'Me!'

'Of course, Roxanne. You're the one who came to me in the first place. Who else?'

'That means really sticking my neck out.'

'Then swear everyone to secrecy. No-one will know, for now anyway, except actual union members. So what do you say?'

'But what exactly would it entail?'

She listened intently as he outlined the duties and responsibilities of a shop steward.

Reluctantly, she agreed.

Tamsin had a cold, Roxanne read, while Morwenna was growing at an amazing rate.

Roxanne had arrived in from work to find a letter waiting from Linnet; it was the first she'd received for ages. Although the two of them corresponded it wasn't on a regular basis.

Linnet had written a full page about the girls, the changes in them, what they'd been up to, the fact that Morwenna was still

244

missing Roxanne whom she often talked about. Roxanne felt sad when she read that bit, for she particularly missed Morwenna.

The rest of the letter was about the farm; the crops, the animals, the weather, neighbours – with a special mention of Billy Christmas, dear old Billy! – whom Linnet had bumped into the previous market day and who'd inquired after Roxanne.

When she came to the end of the letter Roxanne realized there hadn't been a single mention of Kevern. Intentional no doubt, she thought, nor would she have been very interested.

Roxanne laid the letter aside and stared at the range. She was alone, as Madeleine was upstairs with Tim and John, putting them to bed. Her mind filled with memories of St Petroc, her early childhood, growing up, her Ma and Da. Mainly happy times, now gone for ever. Slowly her head began to droop.

Roxanne blinked her eyes open with the realization she must have dozed off. Madeleine, large tears rolling down her cheeks, sat weeping opposite her.

'Madeleine!' she exclaimed, coming to her feet. 'What is it?'

Madeleine glanced at Roxanne, her expression one of anguish. 'Don't bother about me. I'm just being silly, that's all.'

'It can't be that silly to make you cry,' she said, squatting beside her friend.

'It's just . . . just . . .' Madeleine broke off, and sobbed.

'Has something happened?'

Madeleine shook her head.

'Then what?'

'Every so often I get to thinking about what I did that day . . . for Tim when he was ill, and it simply overwhelms me.' Madeleine stared into space. 'I feel so ashamed. Those men . . . that room . . . the bed. Me lying there, them coming and going. Me taking their money.'

'Hush!' Roxanne crooned, curling an arm round Madeleine's shoulders.

'You've no idea what it was like. The humiliation. I was no more than a piece of meat. A piece of meat to . . . satisfy their needs.' Madeleine gulped. 'I'll never forget that till my dying day. It'll always haunt me.'

She gulped again, then croaked. 'I'd die if the boys ever found out.'

'There's no reason they will,' Roxanne pointed out.

'And Joe . . . he must be spinning in his grave.'

'You made a tremendous sacrifice for your children. If he was a reasonable and understanding man, which from all you've told me he was, he could only have been proud.'

'Proud!'

'Tim might have died if you hadn't done as you did. Your actions have to be balanced against that.'

'I wonder,' Madeleine murmured, eyes straying to the mantelpiece where Joe's picture remained face-down.

'Now what if I make a cup of tea to buck you up? I only wish we had some biscuits in, or cake.'

'Sponge cake, with lashings of cream. I adore that,' Madeleine further murmured.

'Tell you what, we'll pretend we have and go through the motions of eating it.'

Which was precisely what they did, a bit of a pantomime which had the desired effect of partially dispelling Madeleine's wretchedness.

'Mary!' Roxanne shouted, having spotted her workmate in the crowds thronging the street. 'Mary!' This was the first time she'd seen her since the day of the accident.

Mary turned, spied Roxanne and frantically waved. When they reached one another the two women warmly embraced.

'How are you?' Roxanne demanded anxiously.

Mary held up her injured hand which was still lightly bandaged. 'Almost better. Though I must say it's funny being without a thumb. Takes some getting used to.'

'So when are you coming back?'

Mary's face fell. 'I'm not.'

'But why?'

'McSween won't have me. Told me I wasn't up to the job anymore. That I'd be a liability.'

'He did what!' Roxanne exclaimed, outraged.

'He said I wasn't capable of handling my machine, or any other machine in the factory now. The sod never even apologized for what happened.'

'But surely you are capable?'

'I would have thought so. I might be a little clumsy to begin with, but I would soon get over that. However McSween was adamant. I'm finished there.'

'Did he offer you any compensation?'

Mary barked out a bitter laugh. 'Don't be ridiculous. When did he ever do that for anyone? All I received was what was owed me for the week leading up to the time of the accident, not a penny more. He actually gave the impression he thought me damned lucky to get that.'

'I am sorry, Mary,' Roxanne breathed sympathetically. This was awful and, like many of the things McSween did, hideously unfair.

'I'm looking for other work, of course, but have drawn a blank so far. It's very worrying.'

She would speak to Jamie about Mary's plight, Roxanne thought. He should know about it. 'What's your address by the way?' she asked. 'I don't have it.'

Roxanne memorized the address Mary gave her.

'Now tell me all about the factory, how is everyone?' Mary queried.

Roxanne looked thoughtful as eventually she continued on her way to Frog Street.

'You're right, it is diabolical,' Jamie responded when Roxanne had finished recounting her conversation with Mary.

'Is there anything we can do?'

Jamie took a deep breath, carefully weighing up the situation. Membership at McSween's was now just under sixty per cent, with the hope that others would be joining before long.

'All right,' he declared finally, 'we'll take up her case. I'll personally go and see McSween. But first Mary has to join the union, she must be a member before I can make a move.'

This was precisely what Roxanne had wanted to hear.

'Don't get your hopes up though,' Jamie warned her. 'McSween is going to be a tough nut to crack.'

'But cracked he must be.'

They both raised their glasses and drank to that.

Chapter Fifteen

The hooter sounded unexpectedly. At the same time the power was cut, bringing the factory to a standstill. Roxanne, and the rest of the girls, knew what it must be all about. Jamie's appointment with McSween had been scheduled for fifteen minutes earlier.

Dennis went hurrying away, congregating in the centre of the factory with the other supervisors. Then the cry rang out that everyone was to foregather to be addressed by McSween.

'Here we go,' Liza Collins murmured to Roxanne.

'Well, we'll soon find out what happened,' Roxanne replied.

Apoplectic, McSween appeared to glower at them, his huge protruding whiskers quivering with rage. When he spoke he ranted and raved, almost seeming to jump up and down on the spot.

'. . . I will never allow a union in my factory . . . I'll fire the lot of you if I have to . . .'

Dennis turned slightly and glanced at Roxanne, his face impassive. She knew precisely what he was thinking, hurt at her denial that a union existed, and considering her an absolute fool.

McSween's finger stabbed the air. 'You've been warned, heed it. This is my factory and I'll do with it and my employees as I please. Anyone who doesn't like that can leave right now.'

There was a few seconds' hiatus during which no-one moved.

'Now get back to work!' McSween snarled, and stalked off.

'He was excited, wasn't he?' Roxanne whispered to Liza as they returned to their machines. Liza put a hand across her

248

mouth to stop herself laughing. Excited was the understatement of the year.

'What do we do now?' Roxanne asked Jamie. They were in their usual pub with five other girls from the factory.

'There's no point in going to see him again. I think you'd all agree with that?'

When there was no reply he went on. 'Therefore the next logical step is to strike. It's either that, or forget the whole business.'

'There's no other way?' Ellen Douse queried.

Jamie shook his head.

Ellen gave a long, drawn-out sigh. 'Bugger,' she muttered.

'The man is simply not open to reason,' Jamie added.

'A strike means no wages,' Fran Banks stated.

'That's right.'

'We all knew it would come to this, surely?' Clementina Carter declared vehemently.

They had, but had hoped that sense and justice would somehow prevail.

'What about those people who don't belong to the union? What do we do about them?' Helen Hirons asked.

They began discussing the details, during which Jamie appointed the six girls as the strike committee, with Roxanne, as shop steward, their leader.

'A strike!' Madeleine exclaimed softly.

Roxanne nodded.

'Starting when?'

'We have to get organized first, so it'll begin on Monday morning.'

'A strike means no pay for you.'

'I know.'

Madeleine digested that fact. 'How long do you think it'll go on for?'

'To be honest, I've no idea. As long as it takes I suppose.'

'And how are we to get by?'

'Again, I've no idea.'

'Shit,' Madeleine murmured, white-faced.

'We won't be the only ones experiencing hardship. Everyone out on strike will.'

'That doesn't make it any easier,' Madeleine retorted sharply.

'I know. I'm sorry.'

There was a strained silence between them, then Roxanne said, 'Do you think I'm wrong to do this?'

'That's just it, I don't. I wholeheartedly agree. Something has to be done about bosses like McSween. It's only that, well, it's one thing talking and voicing opinions, another to face the harsh reality of taking action.'

'There's no other way. If there was we'd take it,' Roxanne stated.

'What if you lose your job altogether?'

'That's a possibility that has to be faced. If it happens then . . .' Roxanne broke off, and shrugged.

Roxanne had a sudden, appalling thought which she told herself she should have had before. She gripped Madeleine's arm. 'But whatever transpires, there'll be no repetition of what you did for Tim. Promise me? I couldn't bear that.'

Madeleine shuddered. 'I promise,' she whispered.

Roxanne released her friend. 'Good. Now what's for supper?'

For the rest of that evening a heavy, foreboding atmosphere reigned throughout the house.

'I want to go in,' a woman Roxanne didn't know by name stated.

'This is an official picket line which you can't cross,' Roxanne replied. Like many of those massed in front of the main factory door she was carrying a placard proclaiming their grievances.

'But I have to. I'm not a member of your sodding union,' the woman argued.

'Member or not, you can't go in.'

Several others crowded round. 'You mustn't strike break, Peggy,' Betty Stamp said to the woman, who now appeared frightened and confused.

'We need the money,' Peggy answered.

'We all do.'

'But we *really* need it.'

'We must all stick together. That's the only way to make McSween agree to our demands,' Roxanne said.

'Surely you want better, safer conditions and your pay packet restored to what it was?' Clementina Carter declared.

'Of course I do. But the pay packet as it stands is better than none at all.'

'You're being exploited. We all are,' Roxanne went on.

'And remember Mary who lost her thumb, she hasn't got a pay packet now. As you know McSween won't have her back. What if it was you who'd lost your thumb. What then?'

Roxanne spotted Dennis Smith pushing his way through the throng. His face was set, his expression determined. She left Peggy to the others and went over to him.

'Dennis?'

'I won't listen to you, Roxanne. I'm going in.'

'You can't.'

'Don't tell me what I can or can't do. I won't have that. Not under any circumstances.'

'Some of the other supervisors have agreed to stay out.'

'Who?'

She named several.

'Well more fool them.' His expression suddenly softened. 'You won't win you know. McSween will never give in. Doing that is totally against his nature.'

'We can try though, can't we?'

'You certainly can, except you'll fail. Mark my words. This won't get you anywhere. Not in a month of Sundays.'

They both hesitated as chanting broke out all around them, and as the girls chanted a litany of their grievances and demands those with placards jabbed them up and down in the air.

'Idiots,' Dennis muttered.

'But brave ones.'

Dennis opened his mouth to say something further, changed his mind and brushed past Roxanne, battling his way to the main door amidst howls of protest and condemnation.

Roxanne watched as he disappeared inside. She hadn't really expected him to do otherwise, but it still saddened her nonetheless that he'd chosen not to support them. She would have thought so much more of him if he had. But Dennis just wasn't a man to put his own position in jeopardy.

'Look!' Liza Collins said to Roxanne, nudging her and pointing up at the factory.

McSween stood framed in a window glaring down, his expression malevolent. It was the third day of the strike.

'Thank God the police are here. I dread to think what he might have done if they weren't.'

It had been Jamie's idea to involve the police for that very reason; to protect them from any repercussions – such as strike breakers – that McSween might have arranged. The police were there not only to keep order but also as a safeguard against possible violence.

'I feel like sticking my tongue out at him,' Liza declared.

'Well don't. If he saw you he'd remember.'

'Bastard!' Liza hissed.

McSween vanished abruptly from the window. And moments later it started to rain, rain that was soon pelting down.

'Talk about a drowned rat,' Liza moaned after a while, now thoroughly soaked. The rain showed no signs of abating.

McSween reappeared at the window, and this time he was laughing.

'I'm starving, Ma!' Tim said, lower lip trembling.

Madeleine stared at her younger son in dismay, her heart going out to him. He wasn't the only one who was suffering, they all were. The strike had now entered its fourth week.

For the umpteenth time she racked her brain, trying to think of some way to lay her hands on some cash. She thought of the promise she'd made Roxanne, but despite the revulsion of what it would entail, she was tempted to break that promise.

'I'm sorry, son, there's nothing in the house to give you.'

Roxanne, sitting by the unlit range, gnawed a finger. Like Madeleine and the boys she too had lost weight since the beginning of the strike. Her cheeks were gaunt, her eyes beginning to look sunken.

'Madeleine?'

Her friend turned to Roxanne.

'Maybe I should move out and let you get a paying lodger. This is all my doing and simply unfair on the rest of you. Why should you suffer because of me?'

'There'll be no moving out,' Madeleine retorted firmly. 'We're all in this together and that's how we'll stay.'

'But the children . . .' Roxanne trailed off, thinking about the music hall. All she had to do was present herself, make her identity and history known to end this misery. And how could she? She'd initiated the strike by approaching Jamie in the first place, she could hardly desert the other girls now. That would be an act of gross betrayal.

'I don't know how much longer the girls can hold out,' Roxanne stated miserably. 'They're already showing signs of cracking. And who can blame them! In the meanwhile McSween just sits tight and waits. The odds are all in his favour.'

'He's losing profits, that must hurt,' Madeleine replied.

'True enough. Except he isn't going hungry, neither him nor

his family. God alone knows how long he can afford to cock his nose at us. Years probably.'

'Why don't you go out and play lads?' Madeleine suggested to the boys, for it was late summer and the nights were light until well on.

'Don't want to,' John answered listlessly.

'It might do you some good. Perk you up a little.'

'I don't want to play either,' Tim chipped in, lower lip still trembling.

Madeleine was seized by the sudden urge to throw back her head and scream in sheer frustration, not simply with the boys but the general situation. Her stomach rumbled loudly.

'Think I'll go to bed,' John announced.

Perhaps that was for the best, Madeleine thought. You weren't hungry when asleep.

'Me too,' added Tim. And with that the two lads trooped disconsolately from the room.

'I feel awful, so guilty,' Roxanne declared quietly.

'You've started this and you must see it through,' Madeleine responded.

Her stomach rumbled again, this time even more loudly.

Roxanne gazed about her at the assembled strikers. Gone was the placard waving and chanting. Instead the girls were just standing there staring blankly, occasionally exchanging a few words with a neighbour.

'Oh Jamie, have we done the wrong thing?' Roxanne asked McBride who'd come to join them for the afternoon.

'Do you want to stop? Pack it all in?'

'I don't know.' She shrugged. 'I just don't know anymore. If only I could think clearly, but I can't.'

'That's lack of food,' he commented.

'I know.'

He took her hand and squeezed it. 'I've come to admire you a lot, Roxanne. You've got guts.'

She gave him a weak smile. 'All the girls have. I'm no exception.'

'You are to me,' he declared softly.

She saw in his eyes that he wanted their relationship to go further than it had. If he hadn't already fallen for her he was in the process of doing so. For some reason that depressed her immeasurably.

'I'll take you for a drink later,' he proposed.

253

She shook her head. 'No, I must get back to Madeleine and the children.'

'Just the one, as usual?'

'To discuss strike business?'

'Not necessarily.'

She removed her hand from his. 'Don't spoil things, Jamie. I wouldn't want that.'

'I thought . . . was beginning to think . . .'

'Then you've been wrong,' she interjected.

'Are you sure?'

'Absolutely positive.'

He stared hard at her, then looked away. 'My mistake, sorry.'

'Still pals though?' she queried, touching him lightly on the shoulder.

'Always that, Roxanne,' he replied. 'Always that.'

A few seconds later McSween's motor car appeared round the corner to sweep majestically past them all. McSween stared disdainfully ahead.

'I wonder what he's having for supper tonight?' Roxanne mused.

'Whatever, I hope he chokes on it.'

They both laughed, and with that laughter the tension between them evaporated.

Two days later a miracle happened. Roxanne was speaking to Clementina Carter, the pair of them discussing ending the strike, when Jamie, grinning from ear to ear, drove up in a horse and cart, the cart piled high with boxes and cartons.

'It's bloody Christmas!' he yelled to Roxanne, waving.

He stopped the car in the midst of the strikers, tied off the reins and jumped down. 'Sent by the Yorkshire miners,' he announced, indicating the cart's load.

Mystified, Roxanne stared at the boxes and cartons. 'What's in them?'

'Food, lassie. Oodles and oodles of it.'

Someone squealed, and immediately women were scrambling on to the cart. 'Equal shares!' Jamie called out. 'Everyone to get the same.'

'Oh Jamie,' Roxanne breathed when several of the cartons and boxes had been ripped open to reveal their contents.

'Isn't it wonderful?' Jamie beamed at her. 'All those bonny lads who've responded on hearing about your plight. That's solidarity for you.'

254

'And their wives and families,' Roxanne pointed out, hungrily eyeing the tins, jars and packages now being handed round.

'Oh aye, indeed.'

'Did you know about this?'

'I received a letter, but didn't want to say anything in case something happened and it never came off. Besides, I thought it better it was a surprise.'

She nearly hugged him then, but changed her mind, not wanting to give him the wrong impression or false hope.

'Three cheers for the Yorkshire miners!' Clementina Carter shouted. 'Hip hip . . .'

Three resounding, grateful cheers rang out.

'How do we cook a chicken with no fuel for the range?' Roxanne asked Madeleine.

'Leave it to me,' a ravenous Madeleine replied, advancing on one of the wooden kitchen chairs. 'John, get me the hatchet.'

John scuttled off to obey.

Madeleine attacked the chair with gusto, and soon there was a blaze in the range.

That night, for the first time in a long while, they all went to bed with full stomachs.

Roxanne knew when she saw the deputation coming towards her what they were going to say. The strike was over, the girls had had enough. McSween had beaten them. The various consignments of food that they had been sent had merely prolonged the strike.

The following morning they all, sheepishly in some instances, defiantly in others, went inside while Jamie spoke with McSween.

McSween kept the girls waiting for an hour before gracing them with his presence. He strode through the silent factory, his expression one of exultation. The girls listened, appalled, when he spoke.

Their wages were to be cut by a further shilling a week, with an extra hour added to the working day. The union was banned forthwith, and anyone found to be a member from now on would be shown the door immediately.

The bastard, Roxanne thought in despair, the rotten, lousy bastard.

McSween went on. 'I understand from Mr McBride, who's

given me his word of honour on the matter, you all acted in concert and that there were no ringleaders among you. If there had been an example would have been made of them.'

'Good old Jamie,' Roxanne muttered. He'd managed to save her bacon, and the rest of the strike committee.

'I could of course have replaced you all,' McSween continued, 'but I have decided to be magnanimous.'

Only so you can gloat, Roxanne thought. She had no doubt whatever that was his real reason.

Several minutes after McSween had stopped speaking the power was turned on and the factory roared into life once more.

A further shilling off their weekly pay, an extra hour on the working day. Roxanne felt like throwing up.

Towards the end of October McSween was visited by his daughter Christabel and his grandson Bobby, who was the apple of his eye. It was the first time Bobby had been to the factory and proudly McSween decided to show him round.

The irony that Lily Roach's old machine was involved wasn't lost on anyone, nor the fact that it was the same belt that had inflicted such awful damage to Lily's face which now broke again just as the boy was walking past it with his grand-father.

The belt snapped, slicing viciously sideways. There was a solitary moment of heart-stopping fear for young Bobby, before he was neatly decapitated.

'Miss Hawkins, ma'am,' the butler announced gravely.

Roxanne was nervous, yet determined, as she strode towards Christabel Speke whose son had been buried the previous week. As she would have expected the pain and anguish of that loss was deeply etched on Christabel's face.

Christabel rose from her chair with a frown. 'Miss Hawkins?'

'It's very kind of you to see me, Mrs Speke,' Roxanne stated, having already taken in the wealth of the surroundings.

'So how can I help you?'

'First of all let me offer you my condolences over the death of your son. It was a terrible tragedy.'

Christabel bowed her head slightly. 'Thank you,' she whispered.

Roxanne had known this was going to be difficult, but now

faced with the situation it was proving even more traumatic than she'd anticipated. Then she thought of the girls at the factory and steeled herself.

'I work for your father,' Roxanne explained. 'I'm the shop steward for the new union that's been formed.'

Mystified, Christabel frowned again, and waited for Roxanne to continue.

'Do you know much about your father's business?' Roxanne queried gently. 'I mean the working conditions and such like.'

Christabel shook her head, then said, 'I don't really think I should be—'

'Please hear me out,' Roxanne interrupted. 'For Bobby's sake.'

Christabel stared hard at Roxanne, liking what she saw. There was a basic honesty and resolve about this woman which impressed her. 'Sit down,' she declared, indicating a chair next to hers.

As Roxanne sat down she realized the butler had silently withdrawn, meaning they were alone. Somewhere in the house a clock chimed.

'There is something you might be able to do that would ensure Bobby didn't die in vain,' Roxanne stated.

Christabel arched an elegant eyebrow.

Roxanne knew the risk she was taking. If Christabel reported this conversation to McSween she'd be out on her ear. But, once the idea had been born in her mind, it was a risk that had to be taken.

Roxanne began to speak to a confused, then appalled and finally angry Christabel.

'The running of my factory has got absolutely nothing to do with you,' McSween snapped at Christabel, who had arrived to confront him in his office.

'How can you say that after what has happened?' she queried icily, her strength of character equalling that of McSween's. She wasn't her father's daughter for nothing.

'Who's been talking to you, telling you damned lies?' he demanded.

'They aren't lies. I've been making inquiries and know the allegations are true.'

McSween threw down the pen he'd been using, grunting in annoyance when ink spattered over some papers. Now he'd have to redo those.

'Balderdash!' he snarled.

Christabel regarded him coldly. 'Knowing what I do now I blame you entirely for Bobby's death.'

'That's preposterous,' he spluttered.

'Is it?'

'Of course. It was an accident. It . . .'

'An accident that should never have occurred,' she cut in. 'And Lord knows how many more deaths and maimings there'll be if you don't do something about those machines.'

McSween rose suddenly and stared out of the window, not wanting Christabel to see his expression.

'Replacing them would cost a fortune. Besides, they have years of life left in them,' he argued.

'Money, Father, how can you talk about that with your grandson, whom I know you loved, and who loved you, hardly cold.'

McSween blanched, and bit his lip.

'I'd give everything I have to bring Bobby back, everything. Every last brass farthing. Only nothing ever will. But what I can do is try to see what happened to him doesn't to anyone else. Then Bobby might not have died in vain,' Christabel said, echoing Roxanne.

McSween rubbed his chin. He still couldn't believe Bobby was gone. Why, he'd idolized the child. And to die in such a horrible fashion.

'Father?'

'It would cost a fortune,' McSween repeated doggedly.

'Is that all that really matters to you? Money? If so then I pity you beyond belief.'

McSween opened his mouth, about to swing round and exclaim, How dare you! But he didn't move, and his mouth slowly closed.

Was she right? Was that all that really mattered to him? He'd never seen it like that. A good and astute businessman was how he'd always considered himself. And making money, profit, was what business was all about. But . . . and for the first time ever doubt assailed him . . . had he been too hard, too unyielding?

'As a memorial to Bobby?' Christabel begged softly.

He didn't reply. Then, when he'd considered what he wanted to say, the door to his office snicked shut and Christabel was gone.

McSween stood staring down at Bobby's grave. In his mind he could visualize the belt of Lily Roach's machine snapping, slicing viciously sideways, decapitating Bobby whose head had . . .

McSween sagged, and sobbed. 'Bobby, lad. Oh Bobby!' he whispered, riven with grief and guilt.

He shuddered when the picture repeated itself. The belt of Lily Roach's machine snapping, slicing viciously sideways . . .

The hooter sounded as Jamie walked on to the factory floor flanked by two supervisors. The power was shut down, ending the roar and clatter of the many machines. Mr Pittkin, the most senior of the supervisors, ordered the entire workforce to assemble for an important announcement.

'I wonder what now?' Marilyn Wilcox said to Roxanne as they moved away from their machine.

There was a great deal of muttering and whispering, which died away when Jamie held up his hands for silence. When he had it he cleared his throat.

'I have just come from a meeting with Mr McSween who has informed me that changes are to be made.'

Someone groaned. Here it comes, many of them thought.

Jamie went on. 'First of all, wages. These are to be backdated to last week, which you are all to be paid for in full and they are to be re-instated to their original level. Which is to say before the quarter per cent and subsequent shilling cut.'

A long drawn-out sigh escaped Roxanne.

'Further, the added hour on the working day will be abolished, beginning from this evening.'

He had to hold up his hands again when excited chatter broke out.

'Further still, the union is to be allowed and from here on in there will be proper liaison between the union and Mr McSween who has promised to listen sympathetically to all just petitions and complaints.'

Roxanne felt herself go weak at the knees. This was simply wonderful. Christabel had come up trumps.

'Not only that,' Jamie continued. 'Every machine in the factory is to be scrapped and replaced by a new model. This can't be done all at once, unfortunately, but will take place over a period of time. In the meanwhile safety devices and measures will be installed where necessary until such replacement occurs.'

'Hallelujah!' Clementina Carter cried, which raised a general laugh and a few cheers.

Jamie held up his hands again. 'Mary Burston will get her job back . . .'

The cheer for that was huge.

'And compensation will be paid to Lily Roach . . .'

The response to that nearly raised the roof.

Even Jamie, who'd been in a sombre mood when he'd arrived on the floor, was grinning now.

'Last of all, the toilets are to be completely refurbished.'

Roxanne thought of Eileen Salmon, who'd been fortunate enough to find employment elsewhere. Eileen would undoubtedly be delighted for them when she heard about that.

The girls were laughing and joking as they returned to their machines, with the exception of Roxanne. They'd won, but at what a price. A young boy's life. She wished with all her heart it could have been otherwise.

The following week the first machine was replaced – the one that had been Lily's.

Roxanne pushed open the glass-panelled door which admitted her to Slocomb, Crosse and Wilson, solicitors, situated in Southernhay, one of the most imposing and grandest streets in Exeter. She was clutching a letter from Mr Slocomb asking her to call.

Roxanne explained about the letter to a pleasant faced young woman who asked her to wait. The young woman disappeared, returning a few minutes later to say that Mr Slocomb would see her straight away.

Roxanne judged Slocomb to be in his late fifties or early sixties. He was a slight, dapper man who rose the moment she entered his office.

'How good of you to come, Miss Hawkins,' he smiled, extending a hand which she shook. 'Now, will you take coffee, or a sherry perhaps?'

'Coffee would be lovely.'

Slocomb nodded to the hovering young woman who now left them. 'Please sit down,' he said to Roxanne, returning to his own chair as she did so.

'I haven't got long I'm afraid. I'm on my dinner break,' Roxanne informed him.

'Indeed. I understand you're now living and working in Exeter.'

Roxanne frowned.

'From correspondence with your sister who informed us of your whereabouts. Originally this matter was handled by our Plymouth office, who asked us to deal with it on learning that you now lived here.'

Roxanne's frown deepened. 'And what exactly is this matter you're referring to?' she queried.

Slocomb made a pyramid with his hands, and smiled again. 'I've got some rather good news for you, Miss Hawkins.'

Later, a stunned Roxanne arrived back in McSween's just in time to get to her machine before the hooter sounded.

Chapter Sixteen

'Hallo, Linnet. How are you?'

'Roxanne!'

The two women fell into one another's arms. 'Why didn't you warn us you were coming?' Linnet demanded breathlessly when the embrace was over, smoothing back her hair and thinking this was just like her sister. She would have tidied herself up a bit if she'd known about Roxanne's visit.

'It was a last-minute decision. I did intend to write but somehow never got round to it,' Roxanne lied. She hadn't written for various reasons, the main one being that she intended calling when the chances were Kevern would be out in the fields.

'Come away in, don't just stand there,' Linnet said, grasping Roxanne and pulling her inside.

Roxanne laughed. 'How are the maids?'

'Never better. But you can see for yourself.'

Morwenna and Tamsin were in the kitchen; Morwenna was dumbstruck with shyness and embarrassment when her aunt appeared.

'You were right, they've both grown a lot,' Roxanne stated, staring with fondness at the youngsters.

'Say hallo to your aunt,' Linnet urged Morwenna.

'Hallo, Auntie.'

Roxanne went over to her and hugged her tight. 'And how are you, my darling?'

'Fine, thank you.'

Roxanne kissed her on both cheeks, then crossed to Tamsin who of course didn't remember her. Tamsin was now eighteen months old while Morwenna was four.

Roxanne squatted beside Tamsin, who was sitting on the floor playing with a pair of wooden spoons. 'And how are you?'

When Tamsin didn't reply Roxanne gave her a hug.

'Well, this is a surprise,' Linnet declared. 'I'll make a cup of tea.'

Roxanne straightened up, and gazed about the well-remembered kitchen of her own childhood and youth.

'So how did you get from the station?' Linnet queried.

'I hired a pony and trap.'

'Hired! That's a waste of money when we could so easily have fetched you.'

Roxanne smiled. 'As I said, I never got round to writing.'

'And how long will you be staying?'

'I'm not sure yet. A week perhaps, maybe longer. It all depends.'

Linnet began laying out cups and saucers. 'When did you arrive in?'

'Yesterday.'

Linnet stopped what she was doing to stare at her sister. 'Yesterday?'

'I've taken a room at the King's Arms.'

'The King's . . .' Linnet broke off in confusion. 'But why?'

'I thought it best,' Roxanne stated quietly. 'I didn't want to put you out.'

Irritation and dismay flashed across Linnet's face. She was most displeased by this information. 'You wouldn't be putting us out. You're family after all. And what will people say! That'll cause a few chins to wag I can tell you.'

'I'll simply let it be known there wasn't really enough room here and that I'd be more comfortable at the pub.'

Linnet glanced away, realizing the real reason Roxanne had elected a pub rather than the house. 'As long as you appreciate you are more than welcome,' she said hollowly.

'I know that.'

Linnet crossed to a cupboard and took out a tin containing a seed cake she'd baked. 'You will stay to dinner, though?'

'I'm afraid not. I've got things to do, folk to see.'

'Oh?'

Roxanne didn't elaborate on that lie. She just didn't want to be at a meal with Kevern. 'But don't worry, there will be lots of opportunities for us to get together.'

Linnet was about to say that Kevern would be disappointed, then changed her mind. 'So how's the job going?'

'I've finished with that.'

'Oh?' Linnet said again.

'I handed in my notice after . . . Well, do you remember the correspondence you had with Slocomb, Crosse and Wilson?'

'I didn't do wrong in giving them your address, did I? I thought, they being solicitors and all, twould be important.'

'It was indeed,' Roxanne replied, sitting at the kitchen table. She reached down and lifted an unprotesting Tamsin on to her knee. 'They wanted to tell me I'd come into an inheritance.'

Linnet was quite taken aback. 'An inheritance!'

Roxanne nodded. 'When was the last time you heard from Aunt Elvira?'

Linnet considered that. 'Dunno. Ages I suppose. We sort of lost contact after Ma and Da died.'

'Then you don't know she's dead.'

'Dead!' Linnet exclaimed.

'As is Uncle Ern. Apparently he just dropped down one day and that was that.'

'Dear me,' Linnet muttered.

'The pickling factory hadn't been doing all that well and the anxiety and strain – he was getting on, don't forget – was just too much for him. Aunt Elvira was beside herself with grief, well you know how close they were.'

Morwenna, thumb in mouth, clutched at Linnet's apron.

'As for Aunt Elvira, she never really recovered from his death. Passed away in her sleep Mr Slocomb informed me.'

'And what's all this got to do with the inheritance you mentioned?'

'Before she died Aunt Elvira sold the factory, not for what it was once worth I'm afraid, but a reasonable sum nonetheless. What was left of that on her death, there had been a few unwise investments in the meantime I understand, she willed to me as sole beneficiary.'

Linnet coloured. 'Did she now.'

'Her reason for that was that she felt I missed out when Ma and Da died.'

Linnet's colour deepened. 'Which was entirely your own fault. You should never have run off as you did. Can't blame me for what happened. Won't have any of that.'

'I'm not blaming you,' Roxanne replied quietly. 'I'm merely trying to explain why I'm Aunt Elvira's sole beneficiary.'

'She always had a soft spot for you,' Linnet said, a touch of malice in her voice. 'You were her favourite.'

Roxanne couldn't deny that for she knew it was true. Not that anything had ever been said, but she'd known it anyway.

'So now you're a wealthy woman?'

Roxanne laughed. 'Hardly that! But it's enough to make me exceptionally grateful. Particularly considering the financial circumstances I was in in Exeter.'

Linnet, with Morwenna still clutching her apron, moved to the range where the kettle was now boiling. This was a turn up for the book, she thought jealously. 'And what are you planning to do with this money you've come into?'

'To be honest, I've no idea. Getting out of McSween's was my first thought, for I certainly had no love for that place, and a holiday in St Petroc as second. As for what happens next?' She shrugged.

'Well congratulations anyway,' Linnet said, though not as wholeheartedly as she might.

Roxanne detected the lack of enthusiasm, which prompted her to jibe, 'So now we've both come into inheritances, eh?'

Linnet gritted her teeth. 'That's right. We've both been lucky.' Then she snapped, 'Will you let go child, before you get yourself burnt!' at Morwenna, who immediately complied, and backed off.

'Damn children, they can be a real pain at times,' Linnet muttered.

'Do you want any help?'

'No, I'm quite capable, thank you,' Linnet retorted.

Roxanne left as soon as was reasonable after the tea and cake.

Roxanne stood staring out over the harbour, savouring the smell she'd always thought so wonderful, a combination of salt, fish and tar all mixed together.

There were seven boats in the harbour, with another, returning from fishing, about to enter. Overhead gulls were wheeling and crying round the stern of the boat approaching the harbour entrance.

Roxanne had gone to Topsham once, an old Roman port near Exeter, on the Exe estuary. But that hadn't been the same as this. There was a wild, natural splendour about the sea off St Petroc that had been missing.

She drew in a deep breath, and sighed with pleasure. She adored the sea: winter gales, summer tranquility, its ever changing moods and colours, blues, greens, greys and night-time black. As for the fishing boats, she still found them romantic.

What a contrast the quayside was to McSween's, she thought, or the music hall come to that. Here was where her heart lay, on this quay and the surrounding countryside. Nothing would ever change that.

The boat had entered the harbour now and was gliding towards the harbour wall. She stayed to watch it being tied off and the fishermen begin to unload their catch before turning away and climbing back onto her hired pony and trap.

Roxanne reined in when she spotted a familiar figure toiling in a nearby field. She smiled; here was someone she wanted to see and speak to, her dear friend Billy Christmas.

Billy was sowing by hand and was concentrating so hard on his task, that he wasn't aware of her until she was almost beside him. When he finally noticed her his homely face split into a broad grin.

'How do, my lover,' she smiled.

'How do, Roxanne.'

She shook his dirt-encrusted hand and then kissed him on a stubbly cheek.

'You look marvellous,' he declared, eyes shining.

'You don't look so bad yourself, Billy. Just as I remember you.'

'Older mind. But then, tain't we all?'

'We are indeed,' she agreed with a laugh. 'How's Annie and the babe?'

'Two babes now, Roxanne. And they're both fine as can be. We be thriving right enough.'

'I'm glad to hear it.'

'And you?'

'Pleased to be home, Billy. Even more pleased than I imagined.'

'So are you back for good?'

She shook her head. 'Only a holiday I'm afraid. And a short one at that.'

His face fell. 'More's the pity. We miss you girl, all of us. You're often talked about.'

'I can believe it,' she replied, a trace of sarcasm in her voice. Like most country people the folk thereabouts were great gossipers and idle speculators.

'Why don't you come over for supper one night? If you ain't too busy that is. We'd love to have you.'

'That would be lovely,' she enthused.

'And you can see the babes. Grand they are, absolutely grand.'

266

'I'll look forward to it.'

His expression became sad. 'I wish you were home to stay, Roxanne. Truly I do. Tain't the same without you around.'

Roxanne gazed about her, thinking how beautiful it all was. 'I wish I was too,' she murmured.

'Can't you do something about it?'

It was impossible for her to return to the farm, she thought. Not with Kevern there. Even if he had got over his feelings for her, it would always be a barrier between them, making life under the same roof uncomfortable and a strain.

She shook her head. 'It's out of the question I'm sorry to say.'

'Ah well!' he breathed in disappointment. 'As long as you gets back from time to time. We'd hate to lose you altogether.'

'We or you, Billy?' she teased.

He went pink underneath his weatherbeaten tan. 'You knows what I mean, Roxanne.'

She did, only too well. Billy had always been sweet on her. 'How are you and Annie getting on?'

'Couldn't be better, girl. Best thing I ever did in life was marry Annie. She be the cream on me pudding.'

Roxanne roared with laughter; that was an expression she'd never heard before. Cream on his pudding indeed! Although it was ridiculous, at the same time it was touching; especially when said with such sincerity.

They had a fine old chat and finally agreed on an evening when Roxanne would call by.

Kevern was doing his damnest not to show Linnet the turmoil he was suffering. Roxanne in St Petroc! The very thought made him all jittery and jumpy inside.

To think she'd been in this very room only that morning. Was it his imagination or could he actually smell her? He believed he could. He could recall her smell so well, its memory had often brought him out in a cold sweat.

He closed his eyes, visualizing her the day he'd taken her to the railway station. Had she changed much? he wondered, for he hadn't dared quiz Linnet about Roxanne. And if so, how? Was there a man in her life? Someone she'd met in Exeter?

He wanted to speak her name, shout it aloud. Roxanne! Roxanne!

She was a witch that woman, one who'd cast a spell over him, a spell he couldn't break and, in his heart of hearts, didn't want to.

If only . . . he thought bitterly. There would have been happiness and joy with Roxanne, instead of the little he had with Linnet.

Roxanne in his bed, Roxanne in his arms lying under him, Roxanne writhing and panting his name as he . . .

Kevern gulped, and opened his eyes to stare in disgust at Linnet. Once she'd been pretty, though never in Roxanne's class. Now she was a mess with her varicose veins, the loose flesh in places that so repulsed him, and the continual complaining about the pain she experienced whenever he had sex with her.

He felt himself become aroused, not because of his wife, but the images still flitting, oh so tantalizingly! through his mind.

Market day, and Roxanne had invited Linnet and the family to the King's Arms for dinner; this was a ploy to enjoy a meal with her sister without Kevern's presence as he had to remain with the cart and produce.

'How's your steak?' Roxanne asked Linnet.

'Proper job.'

'And you Morwenna, what about the sausages?'

'They be smashing, Aunt Roxanne. Real tasty.'

The dining room at the King's Arms was oak panelled and cosy, the tables set with white Irish linen, the cutlery good plate. It was busy, as was usually the case on a Saturday at that time.

Linnet paused to rearrange Tamsin, who was sitting on her lap. 'You all right my darling?' she queried, smoothing back the toddler's hair.

Overawed by the occasion, Tamsin nodded.

'You'll have some pudding soon, eh? There'll be treacle tart which you'll enjoy, or apple cake and custard.'

'She can have both if she wants,' Roxanne said.

Linnet gave a low laugh. 'I don't want her being sick. One pudding will be enough, Aunt Roxanne, thank you very much.'

'She be a smart little property and no mistake,' Roxanne heard a man at the next table declare. 'And I'll get her for a song before I'm finished. I'll beat them down so low it'll be a steal.'

'Kevern will be furious at missing out on this,' Linnet said. 'He loves a treat.'

'I've had me eye on Cobwebs for years,' the man at the next table went on. 'Just waiting for that old pair to die, knowing their son who farms Tiverton way would want to sell. Tain't no use to him, being down here, after all. And it'll suit me dandy, adjoining my land as she do.'

Cobwebs, Roxanne liked the sound of that. She thought it had charm. Glancing sideways she noticed a man she knew vaguely. She racked her brain to come up with his name, but failed.

'Twenty acres, not a lot of land, nor the best quality, I grant you, but she be ideal for sheep which is what I plan for her. And I've always envied that view out over the sea.'

That caught Roxanne's interest even further. A view over the sea! How wonderful.

She suddenly remembered her Da talking to the man years previously, and the name she'd been searching for popped into her mind. Buster. The man's surname was Buster.

She sneaked another surreptitious glance. Fiftyish, she reckoned. Small, thin, with mean piggy eyes. Not a man to trust or do business with in her opinion.

'What about the cottage itself?' Buster's companion inquired.

'He can stay as he is. No use to me. At present anyway. And I won't put a tenant in there because of where he's situated. Probably use him as a storehouse, or lambing shed, or both.'

What a waste of a cottage, Roxanne thought. Especially one with a sea view.

'I wonder what sort of tats these are?' Linnet mused, prodding those remaining on her plate. 'Can't place they by taste.'

'I want my pudding,' Morwenna announced, having gobbled down the last of her sausages.

'You'll just have to wait young maid until your elders are finished,' Linnet told her.

The child pursed her lips and frowned. She didn't want to wait, she wanted her pudding right away.

'You have to wait at home, it's no different just because you're in a posh restaurant,' Linnet explained.

Roxanne could have laughed. The dining room of the King's Arms a posh restaurant! But then it was to Linnet who'd never been away from St Petroc, she reminded herself.

'What have you knocked them down to?' Buster's companion asked.

Buster replied in a low voice, but not low enough for Roxanne not to hear. She considered the sum named to be daylight robbery.

She continued listening to the conversation at the next table throughout the remainder of her meal.

*   *   *

'Unusual for a property to come up for sale round here. Most of the land belongs to Squire Palfrey and is tenanted out,' Mr Acland, the agent, informed Roxanne as they bowled along in his pony and jingle.

'That's what I thought.'

'There is a potential buyer, but every time I think we've agreed a price he backs out only to return later with a lower offer. I'm beginning to think he wants the place for nothing at all.'

Roxanne laughed 'You're referring to Mr Buster, of course.'

'You know him?'

'Not personally. But my father did. Though how well I can't say.'

'His land is next to Cobwebs,' Acland stated. 'Whch makes it ideal for him.'

'And he's the only one interested?'

'So far. Six months now I've been negotiating with him. But he isn't in any hurry, which makes me wonder . . .' Acland trailed off.

'Wonder what?'

Acland gave her a shrewd glance. 'He's not a chap to cross, is Ted Buster. Maybe he's put the word about that no-one else is to come forward.'

Roxanne recalled those mean, piggy eyes and thought it entirely possible. 'How big is his farm?' she inquired.

'A hundred and ten acres, which is large for this area as I'm sure you appreciate. Half of it's arable, the rest pasture.'

They turned off the lane onto a track. 'This is Cobwebs land from here on in,' Acland said. 'This is your access to the lane, one of several access points.'

'What's the water situation?'

Acland smiled. 'Excellent. A deep well in the cottage, and a stream which comes out of the ground over there.' He pointed to his right. 'To empty into the sea. A stream that's never been known to run dry, not ever.'

Acland paused, then said, 'A stream like that would be a welcome addition to the Buster farm of course, which is another reason he wants Cobwebs.'

'Does the stream have a name?'

'The White.'

'Just The White, not The White Stream?' Roxanne queried.

'Just The White,' Acland confirmed.

They drove in silence for a while, Roxanne gazing interestedly

270

about her, till finally the cottage appeared. Even at that distance Roxanne could see its thatch was in urgent need of repair.

Closer to she could make out how run down the cottage had become. 'Are the walls cob?' she asked.

'That's right.'

There were two outbuildings, both small, situated to one side of the cottage. These were also cob and thatch.

'How old were the couple when they died?' she queried.

'To be honest I don't rightly know. But if I was to make a guess I'd put them in their eighties. She went first, then him not that long after.'

They pulled up in front of the cottage which had a sad, forlorn air about it that Roxanne put down to years of neglect. And yet . . . despite that there was something about it, something that appealed to her.

'I'll show you inside,' Acland said, getting down. He came round to help Roxanne but when he reached her she was already on the ground, her eyes flicking this way and that, taking everything in. Directly behind the cottage was a panoramic view of the sea.

The door creaked when opened, its wood cracked and split in places, the hinges red with rust.

'I can't deny there's a great deal of work required,' Acland declared.

The door led directly into the kitchen which was low ceilinged with traversing beams. An inglenook fireplace dominated one wall.

A short hallway contained a larder and led to a back door with privy beyond. They returned to the kitchen and from there proceeded to the parlour, the only other room downstairs.

'They did let it go quite a bit,' Acland sighed. 'But there again, that gives the buyer an opportunity to totally refurbish to personal taste.'

Despite its condition the parlour, like the kitchen, had a good feel about it, Roxanne thought. When she examined the nearest window she discovered its woodwork was rotten.

'That'll have to be replaced,' she said, poking the soft wood which depressed to her touch.

Acland didn't reply.

From there they went upstairs where there were two bedrooms, a main one and a smaller one. These were light and sunny, as opposed to the parlour which was cool and darkish. Here the windows were positioned at the rear staring out over the sea.

'It's a grand view,' Acland stated quietly.

Roxanne couldn't have agreed more, the view was magnificent, quite spectacular. There and then she fell in love with Cobwebs, knowing she desperately wanted it to be her home.

As they went downstairs again she thought of Kevern. Would he continue to be a problem if she returned to St Petroc? The possibility was certainly there. But now she'd be on the far side of St Petroc as opposed to under the same roof. Contact between them, which she'd keep at an absolute minimum, would be infrequent.

She toured the complete cottage a second time, noting things she'd originally missed, then went outside.

The outbuildings were in an even worse state of disrepair; though on the credit side, far more spacious than she would have guessed.

Behind the outbuildings Roxanne found an absolute delight, a large vegetable garden that wouldn't take much to be restored to its former glory.

'Mr Kenton, the previous owner, was very keen on his veggies,' Acland explained. 'With age, it was the only thing that retained his interest.'

From there they walked to the nearest field where Roxanne was able to confirm that Buster had been correct when he'd said the land wasn't of the best quality.

'This too has been let go. Hasn't been tilled or worked in a long time,' Acland said.

It would be hard, back breaking graft getting this back in order, Roxanne told herself. But rather than depressing her the thought of it had the opposite effect.

The field sloped down to cliffs, which in turn fell away to a strip of golden sand and the sea.

'This will need to be fenced in, of course, should you decide to keep beasts,' Acland stated.

They strolled along the clifftops for several hundred yards, Acland all the while keeping up a running commentary about the farm, pointing out an interesting feature here, another there.

'I know what Mr Buster's latest offer was,' Roxanne informed him when they eventually returned to the cottage.

Acland raised an eyebrow.

She mentioned the figure she'd overheard, and he nodded. 'That's right.'

'What was the original asking price?'

He told her.

'Then I'll pay you a sum slap in the middle, and if you agree I promise there will be no backing out or further haggling on my part. So what do you say?'

His face creased into a broad smile. 'You've got yourself a deal, Miss Hawkins.'

They shook on it.

'Ted Buster is going to be hopping mad when he finds out,' Acland laughed.

'Which he mustn't do till all the relevant papers are signed. If he did it might only cause trouble.'

'You have my word on that, Miss Hawkins. Mum's the word until the final signatures.'

She'd use an Exeter solicitor, Roxanne thought, as they headed back to St Petroc. That way she was assured there wouldn't be any leaks to Buster. A small town was a small town, after all, where even professional secrets weren't guaranteed.

Which was how she came to engage Mr Slocomb of Slocomb, Crosse and Wilson, as he seemed the obvious choice.

'You've bought a farm!' gasped Madeleine, dumbfounded.

Roxanne nodded. 'Isn't it exciting?'

'What sort of farm?'

'Any sort I wish to make it. And you should see the view over the sea, it would take your breath away.'

Madeleine's face dropped as the news began to sink in. 'That means you'll be leaving us and Frog Street.'

'I'm afraid so.'

'Don't want you to go,' Tim said, gazing at Roxanne in dismay. He, like his brother John, was clad in the new clothes with which Roxanne had kitted them out.

'Me neither,' John added.

Roxanne went to them, squatted down, and gathered them into her arms. 'I'll miss you both. But maybe you can come and visit me sometime, eh?'

Madeleine didn't want Roxanne to go either. The pair of them had become so close it would be like losing her right arm. Lonely evenings stretched ahead of her again, she thought, with no-one to talk to but the boys.

'When will you leave?' she asked, a lump in her throat.

'As soon as all the necessary paperwork has taken place. I'm not sure how long it will take.'

'I'm pleased for you, you know that,' Madeleine mumbled. 'It's just . . .' She broke off and swallowed hard.

Roxanne had an idea then, and wondered why she hadn't had it before. 'I'll tell you what. Once the cottage is done up you could all come and live with me. It's only two bedrooms same as here, but we'd manage. And it would be a far healthier life for the boys. I'm certain they'd enjoy the country.'

'Leave Exeter, you mean?'

'Well what is there for you here? Not a lot.'

'There's my job . . .'

'You'd be helping me, earning your keep that way,' Roxanne interjected.

'And Jane. She's the big drawback. What about her? I'd lose her altogether then. It's bad enough as it is, but at least I do see her when she gets time off.'

Roxanne could understand that. 'Well maybe not,' she conceded. 'It was only a thought.'

'But a kind one. Thank you.'

'No kinder than the kindness you've shown me.'

Madeleine crossed to the range and fiddled with a pot. 'Damn!' she muttered. 'Why does life always have to be so hard?'

Roxanne, suddenly thinking about Harry, had no answer to that. Why did it? 'Tell you what,' she said. 'Why don't I pop out and get some fish and chips?'

'Oh yes!' squealed Tim.

'With extra chips all round.'

John scuffed a foot on the floor. 'Still miss you all the same.'

Was she making a mistake? Roxanne wondered, although she knew that she wasn't. 'I'll get those fish and chips,' she declared gathering up her coat.

'Damn,' Madeleine repeated softly when Roxanne had gone.

Roxanne reined in the rented horse and cart before Cobwebs, and stared at it with pride. Her own house, her own land. *Hers.*

She was temporarily staying at the King's Arms until the cottage was fit for habitation. It should only be a week she reckoned, before she moved in. And that would just be the start, an enormous task lay ahead. There was so much to do, inside and out, and then she needed to tend the land itself.

But she wasn't daunted, not one little bit. She'd set to and enjoy what had to be done with relish.

'Cobwebs,' she said to herself. Her home from there on in.

Before doing a hand's turn she walked to the clifftops and stared out over the sea which was angry and crashing ashore on the sand below.

As far as she was concerned, it couldn't have been more perfect. Her only regret was Madeleine and the boys.

Chapter Seventeen

'There's certainly a lot to be done,' Billy Christmas declared, having just been shown round Cobwebs and over some of its land by Roxanne.

'You can say that again.'

'But it has promise. I'll give you that. What sort of farming are you going in for?'

Roxanne shrugged. 'Don't know yet, haven't decided. I plan to get myself self-sufficient first, or as much as I can, then go from there.'

'If there's anything I can do you only have to ask.'

She flashed him a grateful smile.

'And what about Kevern? Surely he'll help out.'

Her smile faded; that was the last thing she wanted. She'd be delighted if Kevern never even set foot in the place. 'He's got more than enough to do where he is,' she answered levelly, which brought a puzzled frown to Billy's face.

'Even so, he is your brother-in-law.'

'In time, I'm thinking about putting a toilet and bathroom inside. Though where I've no idea. I may have to build an extension at the rear,' Roxanne said, changing the subject.

'That would be wonderful,' Billy enthused. 'I wish we had the like at our house. Those outside privys are murder in winter.'

'Cold on the old bum, eh?'

They both laughed.

'You want to consider sheep. The land is ideal for they,' Billy said.

'That's what Buster intended doing.'

'Have you spoken with him yet?'

Roxanne shook her head.

'Nasty piece of work, be careful. He certainly won't be pleased at you buying Cobwebs out from under him.'

'Have you heard anything?'

'Not a dicky bird. Though I'm bound to say we don't exactly move in the same circles.'

'No doubt he'll call by at some point.'

'Perhaps it would be better if he didn't,' Billy mused. 'As I said, he's a nasty piece of work. One who doesn't appreciate not getting his own way.'

'Well he didn't in this case. Which is something he'll just have to come to terms with.'

They strolled to the vegetable garden where Roxanne had been busy before Billy arrived. 'You were lucky with this,' Billy declared, nodding his approval. 'They taters are ready for lifting.'

'I plan making a start on them later in the week.'

He examined a row of runner beans. 'These be a fine crop and no mistake. Better than mine.'

'I wish Mr Kenton had kept his interest in everything and not simply his veggies,' Roxanne sighed.

'Then you'd have had to pay more, look at it that way,' Billy pointed out.

He was right of course. 'Come on and I'll make you a cup of tea,' she offered.

'Now you're talking!'

She hooked an arm through his as they returned to the cottage where she plied him not only with tea but fresh bread she'd baked that morning.

After waving him off Roxanne fed the chickens she'd bought, thinking a hen house was another job she'd have to get round to in time. In the meanwhile she locked the chickens away at night in the smaller of the outhouses where they seemed happy enough.

She was utterly exhausted when she later fell into bed; she'd been on the go almost non-stop since shortly after dawn. Pigs, she thought wearily. That was what she'd get next. And a couple of milk cows so she could make her own butter and cream.

She was thinking about pigs and cows as she fell asleep.

'Done,' smiled Jack Gifford, and held out his hand. He and Roxanne solemnly shook on their deal, as she had bought four young pigs from him.

'And you'll deliver?' she said.

'If that's what you wants, Roxanne, then that's what you'll get. Later on today suit?'

'The afternoon will be fine.'

'Then you keeps an eye out for me and I'll be there.'

'Thanks, Jack.'

'How are you getting on anyway?' he inquired. 'Running a farm single handed is a big task for anyone, far less a maid.'

'I'll manage, it's simply a case of working all the hours God sends. Anyway, I haven't started farming properly yet. That'll come later in the year. For the present I'm focusing on the cottage, which is in a right old state I can tell you.'

'You be living there though? Leastways, that's what I was led to understand.'

Roxanne laughed. 'If you can call it living, camping out more like. I'm up to my eyes in paint and whatnot.'

'It'll come right in the end though, my lover. And I'm sure you'll make a proper job of it.'

'If I don't it won't be for lack of effort, that's a fact. Now I'd better get on Jack. I want to look at some milk cows.'

'Try the Pipe twins, Roxanne. I know they brought a few to market.'

'I'll do that, Jack. Thanks again, see you later.'

'You can count on it, Roxanne. Me and your porkers.'

Roxanne turned away from Jack Gifford to find Ted Buster glaring at her, his face contorted. A flutter of apprehension rippled through her.

Buster stalked slowly forward. 'You be Reynold Hawkins' girl I believe. The one who bought Cobwebs?'

He had bad breath which washed over her causing her nose to wrinkle. 'I am,' she replied civilly.

'I had my eye on that place. Wanted it for meself,' he spat.

'Really?' she answered, pretending innocence.

'Really,' he repeated sarcastically.

'Then I'm sorry. All I can say is that my offer must have been higher.'

'No doubt,' he snarled. Reaching out he grasped her hard by the arm, making her wince. 'Just let me tell you this Miss Hawkins, don't ever come to me for help. For you won't get it.'

'Take your hand off me.'

He squeezed even harder. 'Nor look to me to be a good neighbour. I won't be that either.'

'Take your hand off me right now,' Roxanne repeated.

278

Buster released her. 'Not that I thinks you'll make a go of it. A maid on her own!' He laughed nastily.

'I'll make a go of it. You can bank on that.'

'We'll see!' And with that he brushed past, bumping into her to send her reeling.

Jack Gifford, who'd been listening to the exchange, hurried over to steady Roxanne. 'You all right?' he asked anxiously.

Roxanne was fuming. 'What a horrible man!'

'He be that and no mistake.'

'Quite awful.'

'Try not to let him rile you,' Jack counselled. 'A cool head is what's needed when dealing with the likes of him.'

She stared at Buster's retreating back. Well at least she now knew what was what. There would be no friendship or assistance from that quarter.

The encounter left her shaken for hours afterwards.

Roxanne woke, wondering what the racket could be. For a few moments her still tired mind remained muzzy and muddled, then she snapped fully alert with the realization it was her chickens squawking and screeching.

She rose, and lit the lamp beside her bed. Then she slipped on a warm coat and, carrying the lamp, hurried downstairs.

She pulled on a pair of boots as quickly as she could, flipped the latch on the door, and went out into the night, heading for the smaller of the outhouses.

Halfway there the noise suddenly stopped, causing her to fear the worst. And the worst was what she found.

She'd thought the outhouse secure against predators, which evidently wasn't so. A fox had somehow got in to slaughter every last bird.

'Bugger!' she swore, glancing about her.

There was a swift, darting movement, the culprit escaping. She caught a glimpse of a bushy tail, then the fox was gone, swallowed up in inky darkness, as there were neither stars nor moon.

Roxanne stared in dismay at the remains of her chickens, most with their heads bitten off, the others ripped to shreds.

Typical of a fox, she thought. Instead of simply killing one it had done the lot. There were feathers and blood everywhere, a right old mess which she'd clean up in the morning. The chickens would have to be replaced, but not before she'd built that hen house. One that would defy any fox.

Her shoulders slumped; this was her first setback since arriving at Cobwebs. Nor would it be her last, she told herself, others were bound to happen.

'Foxes,' she muttered, no wonder farmers hated them. Destructive, evil vermin.

She returned to the cottage and bed where she lay staring at the ceiling, feeling very alone, and vulnerable.

Roxanne gazed up at Mr Bull, the thatcher she'd employed, busy on her roof. Most things she'd been able to tackle herself, but thatching was a specialist task beyond her.

The cost of a total rethatch had been prohibitive, so Bull's instructions were to repair and revamp where necessary and it seemed he was doing an excellent job so far.

'Would you like a cup of tea, Mr Bull?' she called up, knowing the answer. He was someone who never turned down tea. Bull gave her a cheery thumbs up, replying he'd be down for it shortly.

Roxanne glanced out over her fields. She'd almost made up her mind to buy a small flock of sheep, building up and bettering the flock as time went by. The market was good for sheep, she'd discovered. And sheep had the advantage of being relatively easy to look after. But she also wanted to grow crops, and had plans in that direction – broccoli as her Da had done, plus oats and barley.

She went back inside which she'd finally finished several days previously. Everythng was now to her satisfaction, the kitchen, painted white, gleaming like a new pin.

What she still required was furniture, however, mainly for the parlour and bedrooms. But that was something she didn't have to rush at. She'd pick up pieces as she went along, secondhand of course; far better value there.

She began humming as she filled the kettle while in the corner her dog, a mongrel pup named Bobby, watched her through large soulful eyes. Bobby had become her constant companion, following her everywhere, and even sleeping in her bedroom at night where he lay on his own special blanket at the foot of her bed.

Besides Bobby there were also two cats, essential on a farm – a ginger tom called Samson and a grey and white female called Delilah.

During her solitary evenings she found the company of Bobby and the cats most comforting and reassuring.

Roxanne excitedly tore open the envelope, always delighted to receive a letter from Madeleine and hear her news.

'Well, well, well,' she murmured in surprise halfway down the first page. Here was a turn-up for the book.

Dennis Smith, her supervisor at McSween's, who'd been sweet on her, had called in at Frog Street to inquire if Madeleine had heard how she was getting on. He and Madeleine had had a long chat during which she'd brought Dennis up to date on Roxanne's news. As he was leaving he'd asked if he could drop by again, which he'd promptly done several days later, staying for another long chat. The upshot of all this was Dennis had eventually asked Madeleine out, and now the two of them were courting.

Roxanne couldn't have been more pleased for her friend. How wonderful that Madeleine appeared to have found another man despite the liability of two small children.

Roxanne offered up a silent prayer, hoping that nothing went wrong to sour this new relationship. Madeleine so desperately needed a husband, lover, provider and protector.

No-one deserved a second chance more, Roxanne thought.

Madeleine and Dennis Smith. Who would have foreseen that one!

A bell tinkled as Roxanne entered the seed and grain shop where she intended buying oats for the field she'd ploughed the previous week. The plough was old but serviceable, pulled by Hercules, a splendid young Shire she'd bought one market day.

'How do Roxanne,' smiled Mr Havill the proprietor.

'How do,' she replied.

She placed her order which Mr Havill said he'd load on to her cart – another recent buy, as was Dingle the pony drawing it.

She was leaving the shop when a voice exclaimed, 'Why hallo, Roxanne!'

For a moment she didn't recognize the speaker, then she placed him. He was James Booth whom she'd met at the Christmas dance when staying with Linnet and Kevern.

'Hallo, James. How are you?'

'Right as rain. I heard you'd moved into the Kenton place. How's it going?'

'Fine. Hard work mind, but when was farming anything but?'

He laughed. 'I don't live in St Petroc anymore. Moved to Gunnislake where I'm working on a daffodil farm.' Gunnislake was just over the border in Cornwall.

'Daffodil farm,' Roxanne mused. She had heard of them, but never seen one.

'Things were a bit difficult at home and . . . well I fancied a change. So why not move right out the area I thought, expand my horizons a little. And that's what I did.'

'Good for you. There are too many people in the country who never leave the place they were born into.'

'I love it there, Roxanne. The people are so friendly, particularly the family I work for. You couldn't meet nicer folk. The Cornish have a reputation for being standoffish and closed, but that tain't how I've found them at all.'

He glanced down, suddenly looking embarrassed. 'Tother thing is I've met a maid there, daughter of the house. We plan to wed next year.'

'That's marvellous, James!' she enthused. 'What's her name?'

'Simone. Simone Tresillion. We fell for one another on sight. I looked at her, she at me and . . . that was that. We get on handsomely together.'

A tinge of regret and jealousy stabbed through Roxanne. First Madeleine and Dennis, now James and this Simone. Everyone else was falling in love, and finding happiness it seemed. She would never love again. For no-one would ever, could ever, replace Harry in her affections. Sadness filled her at the thought of what she'd lost, but might have had.

'Are you home on holiday?' she queried.

He shook his head. 'Me Ma died and I'm back for the funeral which is tomorrow.'

'Oh James, I am sorry.'

'Tis a hard loss, but there we are.'

'How's your Da taking it?'

'He's bearing up, trying to put a face on things. But it's gone deep, they were very close you see.'

Roxanne commiserated with him for a while longer, then took her leave. He said as they parted that he hoped they might bump into one another again as he was going to be around for about a week.

If they didn't, Roxanne replied, she wished him all the very best for his marriage when it happened.

Early that evening Roxanne strolled over to the clifftops where she sat, arms wrapped round her legs, gazing out to sea. She'd been thinking about James on and off since their meeting.

A daffodil farm, how fascinating she thought, recalling the clump of daffodils that had grown outside her Ma and Da's house. She'd adored those flowers, looking forward to their arrival every spring, finding great joy, and rejuvenation, in

282

their appearance. What a marvellous crop they must be to grow, considerably more exciting than broccoli and oats, not to mention mangolds!

No-one in the surrounding area grew daffodils commercially, though she didn't see why it wasn't possible. The local weather was similar to that of Gunnislake which only lay a little further south.

Then it struck her that cultivating daffodils would mean that she wouldn't be in direct competition with any of the other locals, a big point in its favour. Excitement began to mount within her as she considered the possibility. The fact it was such a venture appealed to her. It was different, and would be a tremendous challenge.

Not that she knew anything about daffodils, other than that they were yellow, lovely to look at, and appeared in the spring. But farming was farming after all, which she'd been brought up to. And a crop was a crop, whether it be root vegetable or flower.

'A daffodil farm,' she mused aloud. It certainly beat sheep any day. The more she pondered the idea the more it gripped her imagination.

'Why not?' she muttered to herself as she wandered back to the cottage with Bobby bounding along beside her. 'Why not?'

She decided to wait until after the funeral and then have a word with James.

Roxanne had timed her visit hoping Kevern would be out, but this time she was unlucky.

'Aunt Roxanne!' Morwenna exclaimed, running towards her.

'Hallo precious.'

Linnet wiped her hands on the apron she was wearing. 'Nice to see you, Roxanne. Tis been a while.'

'I've been up to my eyes in it. You know how it is?'

'Oh I do indeed. Always something to be done.'

Kevern turned his back on Roxanne so that neither she nor Linnet would note his expression. He'd wondered if she'd come by that day, which was why he'd found a succession of jobs to keep him in and around the house.

'Happy birthday, Linnet,' Roxanne declared, embracing her sister.

'Why thank you. Don't get no younger, do we?'

Roxanne laughed. 'That's a fact, though neither of us is hardly in her dotage yet.'

283

'Except one of you looks it,' Kevern muttered darkly to himself.

'What's that?' Linnet queried, glancing at him.

'Nothing,' he replied with a shake of his head.

'And here's a present,' Roxanne declared, handing Linnet the small parcel she'd been carrying. 'Couldn't let my sister's birthday pass without giving her a little something, could I?'

'What is it, Ma? What is it?' Morwenna clamoured.

'Well I won't know that till I opens it.'

Kevern turned round again to stare at Roxanne. 'So how's the farming going?' he sneered as Linnet opened her parcel.

She gazed levelly at him. 'Fine thank you.'

'I hear you're going to run sheep. That so?'

'I was considering it, but have changed my mind.'

'Why it's lovely!' Linnet exclaimed, shaking out the pale blue blouse Roxanne had bought her.

'Another blouse never goes amiss. And I've always thought that colour suited you.'

Morwenna immediately lost interest when she saw what the parcel contained. A blouse was boring.

Linnet pecked Roxanne on the cheek. 'Ta very much.'

'My pleasure. And what did Kevern give you?'

Linnet's lips thinned. 'Nothing I'm afraid.'

'Tain't exactly so!' Kevern protested angrily. 'I explained, didn't have time last market day to find anything. I will this Saturday, I promise.'

'You still had time to go to the pub,' Linnet reminded him.

'That were business, nothing more. Had to be done.'

'And how long were you there for?'

'Only a short while.'

'Not according to the way your breath stank afterwards. You must have downed pints of cider. And you was weaving. Could hardly stand upright.'

'You're exaggerating woman.'

'Gets more like his old man every day,' Linnet said to Roxanne. 'Becoming a proper boozer.'

Kevern bit back a stinging retort which he would have made if Roxanne hadn't been present.

Linnet laid the blouse on the table, smoothed out and folded the brown paper it had come in, and put that, along with the string which had tied it, away for future re-use. 'I'll stick the kettle on,' she declared.

'Not for me. I'm in a bit of a hurry.'

That alarmed Kevern who wanted Roxanne to stay as long as

possible. 'Well I could certainly use a cup,' he stated. 'Right parched I am.'

'Won't take long,' Linnet cajoled Roxanne. 'Anyway, you can't leave without seeing Tamsin. She's having a nap.'

'All right then,' Roxanne relented, not wishing to cause offence.

'We'll look in on her in a moment,' Linnet declared, further busying herself.

'So what are your plans for Cobwebs?' Kevern queried.

'I'm going to plant daffodils.'

Kevern stared at her in amused astonishment. 'But we don't grow they round here. Tain't traditional.'

'I've already spoken to a friend of mine who works on a daffodil farm in Gunnislake and he's all for it.'

'Daffodils,' Kevern mused, shaking his head. 'You knows nothing about they.'

'I can learn.'

'You're taking a big risk in my opinion.'

Frankly, Roxanne didn't give a damn about his opinion. 'Perhaps.'

'You should keep to what's always been grown locally. That's my advice.'

'Cake?' Linnet asked Roxanne with a smile.

'No, thank you.'

''Tis chocolate. I knows you like that.'

Roxanne's sweet tooth got the better of her. 'Just a small slice then. And I mean small.'

'You ain't worried about your weight, are you?' Kevern mocked, thinking that was the last thing she had to worry about. She looked perfect to him.

'No I'm not,' she replied irritably.

He chuckled. 'Daffs! Wait till I tell the lads at the pub. That'll get a few hoots of laughter.'

Her irritation increased. 'And why should it?'

'They'll think you've gone barmy, that's why.'

'There's nothing barmy about growing daffodils, it can be a very lucrative crop. They know that only too well in Cornwall and the Scillies.'

'But never done before in St Petroc. There must be a reason for that?'

'As you said, tradition,' she argued. 'That's all.'

'Hmmh!' he snorted, clearly unconvinced.

'I'm going to Gunnislake to have a chat with the owners,'

285

Roxanne informed Linnet. 'I should be able to pick up quite a few pointers from them. The do's and don'ts.'

'Never been to Cornwall,' Linnet replied, who'd never been anywhere outside St Petroc.

'Neither have I. So I'm looking forward to it.'

'And who is this friend of yours who works there?' Kevern queried.

'James Booth, the chap I met at the Christmas dance two years ago.'

Jealousy flared in Kevern.

'I remember him,' Linnet declared. 'Nice fellow I recall.'

'Hasn't his Ma died or something?' Kevern said, frowning.

'That's right. He's home for the funeral.'

'Is he married yet?'

'Engaged.'

Kevern's jealousy vanished, to be replaced with relief. Booth couldn't have designs on Roxanne if he was engaged. 'I still think the whole idea's daft,' he muttered.

'Well I disagree,' Roxanne snapped in reply.

'So do I,' stated Linnet, which earned her a glower from Kevern who thought she should have been supporting him.

'It's your time and money to waste as you sees fit,' he growled at Roxanne.

'That's right. They are.'

For the rest of her visit, which she kept as brief as possible, Roxanne did her best to ignore Kevern, rapidly terminating any conversation in which he tried to engage her.

Roxanne thought the fields of flowers stretching away from one side of the road a wondrous sight. She couldn't place the blooms which were small and white, some shot through with pink. She sat gazing at them for some minutes before geeing up Dingle and continuing her journey to Gunnislake which she could see in the distance.

Once there she selected a decent looking pub and booked herself in. James and the Tresillions were expecting her for supper that evening.

The Tresillions couldn't have been more welcoming or charming. Roxanne had been slightly surprised by Simone, who was a plumpish girl and hardly the beauty she'd somehow expected. But it was obvious Simone doted on James, and he on her.

Besides Mr and Mrs Tresillion there were six children over

and above Simone, three boys and four maids in all. The entire ensemble were a happy, laughing lot round the well-laden supper table. Roxanne had been given the place of honour next to Mr Tresillion.

'What kind of flowers were those I saw on the way in?' Roxanne inquired, doing her best to plough through the mountain of food that had been set before her. What a contrast to the starvation rations of Frog Street!

Mr Tresillion scratched his nose. 'You must be referring to anemones on that road. Were they white and pink?'

Roxanne nodded.

'Then that's what they were.'

'Anemones at this time of year?' she queried in amazement.

'Jessell be experimenting with a new hybrid that flowers in the summer,' Mr Tresillion explained. 'This is his second crop.'

'Nice. But give me daffs any day. You can keep your anemones,' Mrs Tresillion beamed.

They chatted congenially till the end of the meal at which point Mr Tresillion produced a pipe, leant back in his chair and lit up. 'Now what do you want to know about daffodil growing?' he asked Roxanne as Mrs Tresillion and the girls began clearing the table and washing up.

'Everything,' she answered quickly.

'Everything,' he chuckled. 'That'll take a fair bit.'

'I'll listen for as long as you'll talk.'

He regarded her keenly. 'Then we'll start with bulbs and varieties and go from there.'

It was late when Roxanne finally returned to her room at the pub where, despite her tiredness, she immediately got out the notebook she'd brought with her and jotted down all that Mr Tresillion and his sons had told her.

She stayed at Gunnislake for three days during which the Tresillions did their best to impart as much information to her as they could about the cultivation and marketing of daffodils. When she eventually departed she had sheaves of notes to study and refer to when she got home, while her mind was buzzing with all that she'd learned.

Chapter Eighteen

Mr Scorrier was the bulb supplier closest to St Petroc and had been mentioned to Roxanne by the Tresillions. He was a middle-aged man with a huge stomach and hearty, jovial manner. His eyes twinkled as he gazed at Roxanne.

'King Alfreds and Butter and Eggs,' he murmured. These were two varieties of daffodils which Roxanne had just asked if he had in stock. 'Can do, can do.'

'Good,' she smiled. 'At what price?'

'Three bob a bag. Won't do better anywhere.'

Roxanne knew that was fair. She pointed through his office window at the large wagon she'd hired, as her own wasn't big enough. 'And you'll load?'

'My men will be happy to do that, Miss Hawkins.'

'Then it's a deal.'

They shook on it.

'You're just starting up you say?'

'That's right,' she confirmed. 'This will be my first crop.'

'Excuse me for being inquisitive, but it's unusual for a lady to visit me on her own. I do get them of course, but always with their husbands.'

'I'm not married, which is why I'm a Miss,' she stated quietly.

His eyes twinkled even more intensely. 'Quite. But surely you're going to have some male help in this venture?'

'I was born and brought up on a farm. There's nothing a man can do, or very little anyway, that I can't.'

'Bravely spoken, Miss Hawkins, bravely spoken. You have my respect. Yes indeed.'

'Now can you see to my order. It's a long journey back to St Petroc.'

'Pretty place I should imagine. On the sea, isn't it?'

She nodded.

'And you'll be farming all by yourself. No other help?'

'I'll obviously need that at cutting and packing time, but only then.'

'Hmmh,' he breathed, thoughtfully stroking his chin.

'Is there something wrong?'

'Not at all. A lot of hard work for one person though.'

'One person meaning a woman,' she smiled cynically. 'Well, hard work is something I'm used to.'

'Naturally, being farm bred and all. I must say you've chosen two of my favourites, especially Butter and Eggs. Pretty daff that. Very pretty. Now if you'll just wait here I'll organize that order for you.'

Roxanne paid Scorrier as the wagon was being loaded, carefully placing his receipt in her bag.

Scorrier waved her goodbye, calling out 'good luck' as the wagon lumbered away.

Roxanne stared in dismay at the first bag of bulbs she'd emptied out among which was a copious amount of earth and small stones. They made up a good third of the bag's contents by her reckoning. A second bag proved the same, as did the next. As the bags were sold by weight, she'd clearly been diddled.

'Oh the sod,' she murmured angrily, meaning Scorrier. 'The rotten lousy sod.' As every bag she'd bought was similarly packed she'd been cheated out a third of her money.

It might be a long haul back to Scorrier's, but she'd make it, she decided. She was damned if she was going to let him get away with this.

'I want a refund or more bulbs,' Roxanne stated to Scorrier, his eyes still twinkling, hers blazing with fury.

'Do you now.'

'Yes I do! Don't think you can make a fool of me just because I'm a woman.'

Scorrier regarded the earth and stones piled on her cart, finding the situation extremely amusing. A woman trying to do business by herself was very funny. The earth and stones was an old trick which none of his regular customers would have fallen for; they'd

289

have made a random check of the bags before acceptance and handing over cash.

'How do I know you're not trying this on? You might be trying to cheat *me* for all I know.'

She stared at him, aghast. The cheek of the man! 'I can assure you that rubbish came out your bags.'

'I've only your word for it, Miss Hawkins,' he replied with a shrug.

'Well where I come from my word means something,' she snapped.

'So you say.'

She fought back an impulse to strike him. 'Don't play me for a mug, Mr Scorrier, I won't have it.'

'And don't try to dictate to me, Miss Hawkins. I won't have that,' he replied, his voice suddenly taking on a steely tone.

'A refund or more bulbs, Mr Scorrier, or else.'

'Or else what?'

'I'll report you to the police for malpractice.'

He laughed. 'Report away, if you think it'll do you any good. I'd just remind you, though, that I'm a local while you're not even Cornish. I'll call you a liar and troublemaker to your face and that'll be the end of your credibility. Believe me.'

He paused, and smiled. 'Besides, I'm related to most of the police round here. And good friends with those I'm not.'

Roxanne ground her teeth in frustration. There was only one card she had left to play. 'Then you could see me right out of common decency,' she declared.

'Grow up, Miss Hawkins,' he chided her. 'Common decency indeed!' Throwing back his head he roared, at the same time slapping his thigh.

'I'll never use you again,' she stated.

'Then don't. That's no great loss to me. Now be on your way before I set my dogs on you.'

As Roxanne drove off she spotted the chaps who'd loaded her wagon laughing, as Scorrier was doing again.

It was a lesson well learnt, she told herself grimly. When it came to business she'd never take anything, or anyone, on trust again.

The first field she'd chosen to sow was one facing out over the sea. She sowed as Mr Tresillion had instructed her, dropping bulbs into the furrow just as the furrow was about to collapse into itself.

Following her, screeching and wheeling, was a swarm of seagulls, which darted groundwards to snatch up the worms she was unearthing.

Every so often she stopped Hercules and refilled the hessian bag she had strapped to her waist, taking quiet satisfaction every time it became empty, as that meant more bulbs were safely underground.

After a while, happy at her task, she began to sing which pleased Hercules who snorted his approval.

Winter came and went, during which Roxanne busied herself with the animals and generally getting the farm into better order.

She built a pig house out of cob and recalled Mr Bull to thatch it for her, then restored the smaller of the outhouses into a dairy. The larger of the outhouses she turned into a proper shippon instead of the make-shift one it had been up until then.

'She should be wed at her age, not working the land on her own,' Dickie Webber declared, referring to Roxanne who was the topic of conversation between him and some friends. They were clustered round the bar of the King's Arms, all of them having been there for a considerable while and now well in their cups. 'Tain't natural,' Dickie went on. 'Tisn't as if she were a widow. That would be different.'

'Different,' Algy Vranch, Cory's cousin, nodded in agreement.

Kevern, who was part of the group, finished his pint and banged the glass on the counter, calling for a refill.

'And growing flowers. We don't do that in St Petroc,' Tom Douse grumbled.

'Flowers!' Algy Vranch snorted in contempt.

'Always had queer ideas that one, though. Going off to Canada like she once did. I suppose we wasn't good enough for her,' Jack Billings said.

'Not only queer but ideas above her station,' Algy added, and hiccuped.

'She's a fair piece, mind. She shouldn't be having trouble getting wed,' stated Edgar Boal, the stationmaster's son.

'What do you make of her? You're her brother-in-law after all,' Algy asked Kevern.

Kevern threw a coin onto the counter. This talk of Roxanne was disturbing him. Couldn't they just shut up about her? Couldn't a bloke even get pissed without being reminded of the bitch?

291

'She didn't go to no Canada,' he slurred.

'Of course she did,' Dickie Webber frowned. 'Everyone knows that. Looked after an ailing aunt and then went off on her tod.'

Kevern accepted his refill and took another deep draught; the combined hate and love he bore Roxanne rose up within him. 'She went off on her tod all right; not to Canada, but to London.'

'London!' Algy exclaimed, eyes wide. 'What did she do there?'

'Worked in the music halls, that's what. Ran away from home without saying nothing and went to London where she sang in they music halls. Her Ma and Da would have been right shamed if they'd known.'

'Well I'll be . . .' Tom Boyce trailed off, and whistled.

'She told her Ma once what she wanted to do and her Ma said women who went on the stage're all tarts.' Kevern sucked in a breath, then slowly exhaled. 'So that's what Miss High and Mighty be. A tart!'

'Bugger me,' Dickie swore. This was a revelation.

'She's no maid,' Kevern continued, enjoying himself now by sticking the knife into Roxanne. 'Not after all they stage door Johnnies that must have been chasing her. God knows how many she went with, but my bet would be plenty.'

'A music hall singer,' Jack Billings mused. Wait till he told the missus about that!

'Changed her name and all,' Kevern informed his rapt audience. 'Called herself Annie something or other.'

'Are you sure?' Dickie queried.

'Of course I am! Heard it from her own lips, I did. She told me and Linnet all about it when she came back and stayed with us that time. It's true all right.'

'And the stage door Johnnies?' Dickie further queried.

'Stands to reason, don't it? And don't tell me she only held hands with them!' Kevern laughed nastily. 'A maid, my arse.'

'No wonder she wanted to keep quiet about it,' Jack Billings said.

'Well now you all knows her secret. It be a secret no longer. Roxanne's well soiled goods, that's what.'

'She looks so sweet and innocent too,' Algy nodded.

'Innocent as any whore,' Kevern spat, and laughed nastily again.

When he woke next morning and recalled the previous night's conversation his feelings were mixed. Delight on the one hand, awful regret on the other.

Linnet put his unusual quietness during breakfast down to his obvious hangover.

'How could you!' Linnet screeched. 'Her reputation's ruined.'

'Tweren't me,' Kevern mumbled, chastened. It was a week since he'd revealed Roxanne's past in the pub.

'Don't lie. It had to be you. Who else could it have been? Only the three of us knew about Roxanne, and I've certainly never said anything, nor has she. Which leaves only you.'

He shrugged. 'Perhaps I did let a few things slip in the King's Arms. I can't remember.'

'It's all round St Petroc, everyone's talking about it. How Roxanne sang in the music halls and slept with dozens of men.'

'I never said anything about her sleeping with dozens of men,' he protested without conviction.

'How do you know if you sodding well can't remember?'

Kevern had no reply to that, and glanced away.

'Apart from the damage you've done Roxanne, didn't you think how this would reflect on us? I'm her sister don't forget, you're her brother-in-law. The shame and embarrassment rub off on us.'

He hadn't thought about that.

'Or on the memory of my Ma and Da?'

'Enough, Linnet,' he growled.

'I'll give you enough, you stupid bugger.' She snatched up and threw a saucepan which he just managed to avoid as it whizzed past his head.

'Here, hold on a minute!'

'Get out. Get out of the house right now before I do for you.' She glared at him, hands on hips. 'I mean it Kevern, get back to work and don't dare show your face round this house till suppertime.'

He picked up his jacket and slunk from the kitchen.

As the door closed behind him Linnet burst into tears.

'I can't tell you how sorry I am,' Linnet apologized to Roxanne, who'd already heard what was being said about her from Billy Christmas, who'd dropped by to commiserate and give her support.

'Drunk in the pub, eh?'

'And opened his big mouth. I can't think what possessed him.'

Roxanne had a fair idea: resentment no doubt.

Linnet regarded her sister intently. 'Tain't true, is it?' she asked in a quiet voice.

'About the music hall. You know it is.'

'I mean all they stage door Johnnies you're supposed to have . . . gone with?'

Roxanne shook her head. 'That is a downright lie, Linnet. I swear.'

'Were there any?'

'*None*,' Roxanne answered emphatically.

'Not that I believed there were,' Linnet fibbed. She may not have believed out of hand, but had wondered. It was a possibility after all.

'People always think the worst,' Roxanne said. 'That's their nature.'

'It's just that folk in St Petroc don't understand about London and what goes on up there. It's outwith their comprehension. They think the place is a great big den of iniquity. As for the stage!'

If Roxanne hadn't been so upset she might have laughed.

Ted Buster spotted Roxanne gazing in a shop window, and frowned. How she had the gall to come into town he didn't know. Bold as brass if you please. And her on everyone's lips for the past fortnight.

Two little boys came clattering along the street, each propelling an iron hoop with a stick. Buster saw they were the Clancy lads, whose Irish father he knew well.

'Hey, come here!' he called out to them, beckoning.

'How would you like to earn a penny each?' he asked when they'd joined him.

'A penny!' Sean, the elder, breathed.

'What we got to do for that?' Mick queried.

Buster bent and whispered to them.

Roxanne turned away from the shop, about to continue on her way, when suddenly she was confronted by the grinning Clancys.

'Tart! Tart!' they shouted in unison.

She stood transfixed, appalled.

'Tart! Tart!' They started dancing round her just out of arms' reach.

'Tart! Tart!'

'Shut up!' she hissed.

'Tart! Tart!'

Buster, almost doubled up with laughter, thought this a huge joke. It was a little of the revenge he'd sworn for her buying Cobwebs out from under him.

Roxanne didn't have to wonder who'd put the Clancys up to this, that was obvious. She was tempted to cross the road and slap Buster, but thought better of it. She walked on in as dignified manner as she could, while the Clancys danced and kept up the name-calling.

Passers-by glanced in shock and embarrassment, the Tregales and Smellings among them.

It was Jack Gifford who came to her rescue, telling the Clancys to bugger off or he'd give them what for.

'Thank you, Jack,' Roxanne said when the Clancys had gone.

His expression was sympathetic. 'It'll blow by Roxanne, these things always do.'

She grasped his arm. 'The bit about the men isn't true, Jack. I'd swear to that on a Bible in church.'

'But the music hall is?'

She nodded.

'But not the men?'

'That is an out and out lie. I never went out with a stage door Johnnie in my life.'

'Then I'll see that gets around. By golly and I will. Your Da was a good friend of mine, I won't have his daughter painted black by lies.'

She could have kissed him.

Roxanne stood staring at her mother's and father's graves, deep in thought. The question she was asking herself was, should she pack it all in and move away, or stay on at Cobwebs and endure the gossip?

Damn Kevern, she inwardly raged, to have put her in such a spot. It was so grossly unfair. There had been Harry, of course, but only him; and she'd been in love, believing they'd be married. This stuff and nonsense about dozens of lecherous admirers was simply a figment of Kevern's fevered imagination.

Stay or go? She didn't know. She was so enjoying being back in St Petroc and at Cobwebs and was so excited at the prospect of farming daffodils, making a go of the venture.

If she left they'd presume what Kevern had said about her was true. Whereas if she stayed there would be ongoing humiliation, sniggers and sly elbow digs among folk wherever she went.

A tart, the word rang in her head.

'Damn you, Kevern Stoneman,' she muttered angrily. 'Damn you to everlasting hell for what you've done to me.'

When she finally left the gravesides she still hadn't made up her mind about the future.

'I was wrong about they stage door Johnnies,' Kevern said to the same pals who'd again foregathered in the King's Arms.

'Wrong?' Dickie Webber queried.

Kevern, who'd been forced into this by Linnet, nodded. 'She was in the music hall as a singer, tis so, but as for the rest, well that was assumption on my part. And quite wrong.'

Algy Vranch stared at him in consternation. 'You mean she be a maid after all?'

'She be,' Kevern confirmed, unaware that was a lie. 'She says she'll go to church and swear on the Holy Bible if that's what it takes to convince folk.'

'You made it up?' Jack Billings accused grimly.

'It was the drink speaking. I just assumed, that's all.'

'She never said any such thing to you or your wife,' Edgar Boal probed.

'About the music hall, yes. She was a singer there. But twere me who . . . I put two and two together and came up with five.'

'The poor woman,' Tom Douse exclaimed. 'The whole town talking too.'

'My tongue just ran away with itself,' Kevern mumbled.

'Has ee spoken to her since?' Dickie asked.

Kevern shook his head.

'But she knows the story came from you?'

'Linnet told her.'

'If I was her I'd take a horse whip to you for what you've done,' Tom Douse said, voice dripping contempt.

'And maybe she still will. She's a feisty one, Roxanne,' Dickie declared.

Kevern's face was now ashen, his shoulders drooping in misery. 'Sodding drink, I could never hold it like me Da.'

'I heard about they Clancy lads in the street. That must have been terrible for her,' Edgar Boal stated, a remark which was greeted with a sympathetic murmur.

Kevern turned to the bar and ordered himself the stiff whisky which he badly needed. Maybe life at home would return to normal now, for it had been sheer hell since Linnet had found out about what he'd said.

296

Hell during the day, and a spitting cat at night if he so much as laid a finger on her.

Roxanne glanced up from her sewing when Bobby suddenly bounded to his feet and barked at the window. Seconds later she heard a soft whinny from outside that informed her she had a visitor. She wondered who it was as she lifted a lamp and made her way to the front door.

'Tis me,' Kevern stated when she opened it.

Her face hardened as she stared at him; he was the last person she wanted, or expected, to come visiting. 'What do you want?' she demanded harshly.

'To apologize. Make my peace with you. Linnet insisted.'

'All right, you've apologized. Now on your way.'

She tried to shut the door again but was stopped from doing so by a hastily placed foot.

'Can't I come in?' he pleaded.

'I've no wish to speak to you, Kevern. And I'd be obliged if you'd never come back here again.'

'Oh, Roxanne,' he said, voice quivering with emotion.

'Now remove your foot.'

'I only wants to talk with you. I won't do nothing else, I promise.'

'Well I don't want to talk to you.'

First of all, he resisted her attempt to close the door, then began forcing it open.

'Roxanne, please. Just a few words. I . . .'

He broke off and yelled when Bobby darted forward to nip him hard on the leg, staggering backwards and thereby removing the offending foot.

'In Bobby, in!' Roxanne commanded. The moment Bobby was back over the threshold she slammed the door shut and bolted it. Leaning against the door she closed her eyes in relief.

'Roxanne? Roxanne!' Kevern wailed in anguish.

Bending down, she picked up Bobby and cuddled him. 'Good boy, good boy,' she whispered.

'I only wanted to talk,' Kevern choked.

Roxanne didn't answer.

Then she heard the unmistakable sound of Kevern crying.

She only budged from the door a few minutes later, when he rode away.

Chapter Nineteen

Roxanne stopped hoeing to gaze about her with quiet satisfaction at the green daffodil shoots marching in regimented lines up and down the field. Everything was going splendidly; she couldn't have been more pleased.

She thought of the letter she'd received that morning, telling her that Madeleine and Dennis were shortly to be married and inviting her to the wedding. She'd loved to have gone but didn't feel she could leave her daffodils for the time that would take. She'd simply worry herself sick every single moment she was away, which was hardly the frame of mind to attend anything, far less a wedding. No, she'd write and explain and hope they both understood.

With a sigh she stooped again to her task.

There was a cold wind blowing in off the sea as Roxanne gazed in dismay out over the first field she'd planted with bulbs. Something was wrong, the shoots weren't coming on as they should, many of them appeared ill-formed, others definitely looked unhealthy.

She chewed a finger and wondered what to do.

'Tis eelworm,' James Booth declared. He'd been dispatched by the Tresillions once they'd received Roxanne's letter.

Roxanne's heart sank. 'Eelworm.'

'You'll have to dig this lot up and burn them.' He turned to her and smiled sympathetically. 'I'm sorry, but Scorrier seems to have taken you good and proper. He not only sold you short measure, but diseased bulbs.'

'There's nothing I can do to save any of them?'

James shook his head. 'Fraid not.'

'The whole crop's like this,' she muttered.

'Then it'll all have to be dug up and burnt. And as it's far too late to plant again for this season you'll have to wait till autumn to plant again for next.'

She ran a hand despairingly over her face, then walked the short distance to the clifftops where she stood staring out to sea. All her hard work, for nothing. Her hopes of a bountiful first crop, dashed. Her money wasted.

'Tain't the end of the world,' James commiserated, coming to stand beside her.

'Right now it feels like it.'

'Mr Tresillion is going to be real upset when he learns about this. Twas he suggested you go to Scorrier, after all.'

'Wasn't his fault.'

'Nonetheless, he'll feel responsible. I knows him. He's a good and honest man.'

Roxanne glanced back at her blighted crop, bitterness and anger hot within her. 'Would Scorrier have known the bulbs to be diseased?' she queried.

'I say that be certain. He was no doubt keeping them, hoping a mug would happen along that he could offload them onto.'

'And that was me,' Roxanne said tightly.

'Words will be passed, you can be sure of that. Mr Tresillion won't take kindly to a friend of his being duped.'

'I'm hardly a friend . . .'

'That's how he'll see it, though.'

James put a comforting arm round her shoulders. 'I'll stay to help you with the burning. Mr Tresillion would want that.'

'Thanks, James.'

'So the sooner we get started the better.'

A sudden thought struck him. 'You do have enough cash to buy bulbs for next season I take it?'

She had, but it was an outlay she hadn't foreseen and would make things difficult. Aunt Elvira hadn't left her that much. 'Yes,' she whispered.

'Then let's go get the plough hitched up. Time's a wasting.'

She stared into his face. 'Mr Tresillion isn't the only good man I know. Your Simone's a lucky woman.'

Once they got back to the cottage she insisted James had dinner before going back to the daffodil fields.

He ate heartily while she only picked at her meal.

'You should get out and about more. Find yourself a husband,' Linnet chided Roxanne, having called in at Cobwebs with the girls.

'Don't want one,' Roxanne replied.

'Why not? Tis a waste for someone as pretty as yourself not to wed.'

'I prefer being on my own.'

Linnet frowned in puzzlement. 'Surely you wants children?'

'I did once, that's for certain. But now that just won't happen.' Roxanne swung out the chimney jack from which the kettle dangled, then removed the steaming kettle to make tea.

'There wasn't . . .' Linnet took a deep breath. 'There wasn't any truth in what Kevern said? About all they men, I mean.'

Roxanne paused in what she was doing to stare levelly at her sister. 'I told you before, not a grain of it. So that isn't the reason I don't wish to wed.'

'There must *be* a reason though?' Linnet prompted.

Roxanne poured water into the teapot, swirled the contents with a spoon, clicked the lid into place and set the pot by the hearth.

'Do you remember I once mentioned Harry Bright who was my partner until I went solo?'

Linnet nodded.

'Well he was more than my partner. We courted for some while and I thought we were going to be married. Except it transpired he didn't feel the same about me as I did about him. He ran off with a dancer called Elaine.'

'Oh Roxanne, I am sorry. Did you love him very much?'

'With all my heart and being. There will never be another man for me, Harry was it.'

'You can't say that Roxanne,' Linnet protested. 'You'll meet someone else in time.'

'No,' Roxanne declared softly. 'I won't. It went too deep with me for that to happen.'

Roxanne's eyes glazed in memory, a host of pictures flashing through her mind. 'It was me going solo that did it, you see. That and my success. I suppose his jealousy just became too much for him to cope with. Anyway, whatever, he ran off and that was that.'

'Was he handsome?'

'I thought so. But it wasn't simply his looks. We had something together. Something special. We just sort of fitted if you know what I mean.'

'Do you know where he is now?'

Roxanne shook her head. 'No idea.'

'Was that why you really came back to St Petroc?'

Roxanne picked up the teapot and began to pour, noting as she did that her hands were trembling. Even after all this time to talk about Harry still had that effect on her. 'Yes. I couldn't bear to remain in music hall, or London, after him. Too many ghosts.'

'Tell me more about him, I'd like to know,' Linnet requested, intrigued.

Roxanne smiled thinly. 'He was a cockney, and proud of it. It was he who got me into music hall when I'd been working as a barmaid, teaching me everything he could . . .'

Roxanne spoke at length about Harry, but purposely refrained from mentioning they'd been lovers or lived together.

That information she kept strictly to herself, not even trusting her own sister with it. She considered it prudent on her part that it remain her personal secret.

Roxanne was thrilled as she read Mr Tresillion's crabbed and laboured handwriting, indicating he was a person who rarely put pen to paper. He was outraged at what had happened, and would personally supply Roxanne's bulbs for next season, something he'd been unable to do when she'd visited him as his entire crop had already been promised to regular customers. And not only would he supply them, ensuring she got the very best he produced, but he would also deliver them free of charge.

'Bless you,' Roxanne murmured when she came to the end of the letter. 'Bless you, Mr Tresillion.'

'Bloody hell!' Roxanne swore when she spotted the angora goats in amongst her broccoli. This was all she needed!

'Get out! Get out you buggers!' she shouted, waving her arms at them.

One old billy, mouth full of broccoli, raised his head and looked at her in blank indifference. She knew goats could turn nasty, but at that moment she didn't care about her safety. All she wanted was to get them out of her broccoli and back where they'd come from. She shouted and screamed, to no avail; some of them continued to stand their ground, others trotted off a little way to resume munching. In the end she resorted to a big stick with which she whacked them, several over the head, when they refused to budge. It took her ages, but finally she succeeded in

301

herding them over the section of fence that had fallen down. They bleated in protest every inch of the way.

When they were all once more on Buster's property she threw the stick aside and set about making a temporary repair.

Now why should these stakes have become uprooted? she wondered as she pushed them back into the ground. There was no plausible reason she could think of because the last occasion she'd examined this particular fence it had been fine, solid as could be.

Then the answer struck her: Buster of course. The fallen section was no accident or caused by natural events, but done deliberately by Buster so the goats could wreak havoc with her broccoli.

She'd come straight back and fix the fence properly, she thought as she strode away, the goats glaring balefully at her from the other side.

She'd do or say nothing for now. But if the fence came down again . . . Well, that was a bridge she'd cross when she came to it.

Bobby's barking woke Roxanne, who struggled up on to one elbow. 'What's wrong boy?' she asked. 'What is it?'

When Bobby continued to bark, jumping up and down in front of her window, she knew he'd either heard or smelt something. A fox perhaps, she thought, remembering the one who'd decimated her hens. Those she had now should be safe enough, but she decided to investigate just to be sure. You couldn't be too careful after all, foxes were the wiliest and most determined of creatures.

She lit her bedside lamp, donned a coat and went downstairs with Bobby at her heels. She pulled on her boots, then, carrying the lamp before her, went outside where the moon was full and thousands of stars twinkled in the sky.

What she saw a few moments later brought her heart into her mouth. The dairy door was wide open, revealing flickering flames. The dairy was on fire.

She ran to the door and gazed inside. The fire was still relatively contained but would swiftly spread if not immediately extinguished. Fortunately there was a water trough just beside the dairy and a bucket close by.

She threw bucketful after bucketful onto the blaze until it finally hissed and crackled into oblivion. She then raked the debris, stamping out the few glowing embers that remained.

God, she thought when it was all over. If Bobby hadn't roused her when he had, the entire dairy would have gone up. And if that had happened so too would the shippon. And with both those ablaze Cobwebs itself could easily have . . .

She broke off, stunned as she realized that she might have been burned alive in her bed. The thought made her break out in a cold sweat and her flesh creep.

But how had the fire started? She kept nothing flamable in the dairy; no paraffin, oil or anything like that. She stared at the debris littering the floor, which she'd swept clean that very afternoon. What had it been, and where had it come from?

Her face hardened as the truth dawned. Like the goats, this was another deliberate act. Someone had intentionally set the dairy alight, with what might have been fatal consequences.

'Buster,' she said, knowing he had to be the culprit. Well, this was going too far.

Returning to the cottage she tried to get back to sleep, but sleep evaded her for the rest of that night. She kept imagining waking up to find herself surrounded and trapped by flames.

'If what you say be so then there can be no doubt about it. Twas deliberately started,' declared Sergeant Bratton, gazing round the dairy.

'And it must have been Ted Buster. He's never forgiven me for buying Cobwebs when he wanted it.'

Bratton regarded Roxanne while scratching his chin. 'Can you prove that, Roxanne?'

'No. But it had to be him. Who else?'

''Tis a powerful accusation, and one I can't follow through without proof. You need that you see.'

'But I know it was him!' she exclaimed angrily.

'Knowing, or suspecting's one thing, proving's another.'

'Well if you won't do anything I'll go to him and . . .'

'I shouldn't do that,' Bratton interjected. 'Accuse him in front of witnesses, or anyone else, and he could go straight to a solicitor and sue you for libel. Which is exactly the sort of thing Ted Buster would do.'

Roxanne exhaled slowly in frustration. The sergeant was right, she should have thought of that herself. Accusing Buster without proof would just be giving him a stick to hit her with.

'If you do come up with anything I can use against him then I will. But until then . . .' Bratton broke off and shrugged.

'I could have fried in my bed if it hadn't been for Bobby here. Then you would have had a murder case to investigate.'

Bratton bent and stroked Bobby. 'Mercifully that didn't happen, Roxanne.'

'But it might have!'

He gazed up at her. 'All I can advise for now is you be more careful in future. Take precautions if you can.'

'Like what?'

'Maybe another dog. One that stays outside all night.'

She would certainly consider that she thought.

'In the meanwhile you knows where I am if you needs me.'

Roxanne came instantly awake the moment Bobby started to bark. Why wasn't Rex doing the same she wondered, as she swung herself out of bed. Rex was the alsation she'd acquired the previous week. Downstairs she picked up the shotgun she'd bought and hurried outside.

By moonlight she saw Rex prostrate, with figures lurking in the shadows behind him. 'Right,' she muttered through clenched teeth, and raised the shotgun to her shoulder.

The first shot knocked her backwards, but not over. The second she was more ready for. She snapped the shotgun open, tossed the spent cartridges aside, and reloaded. 'And you'll get this every time you come back!' she yelled before firing again.

The figures had vanished abruptly after the first shot, but she could hear them running and scrambling away in the distance. She hoped she'd scared the living daylights out of them.

Rex was out cold, with a large swelling already appearing on his forehead. She couldn't imagine how they'd managed to do that to him without him barking first to rouse her, but somehow they had. So much for an outside guard dog.

Concerned, Bobby anxiously licked Rex's face, as the two of them had already become great pals. Rex whimpered in response and opened his eyes. Groggily he struggled upright.

He'd be all right, Roxanne assumed, reasoning he wouldn't be back on his feet so soon if his skull had been fractured, although he was bound to have a terrible headache from the blow.

She fetched a lamp and examined the dairy and shippon, but the intruders had been scared off before they'd managed to do whatever they'd intended.

She patted the shotgun which she was still carrying crooked in her arm. That had been an inspiration. Buster and whoever had

304

been with him would think twice before returning, knowing they'd be blasted at.

Later, as her tension eased, Roxanne began to laugh imagining Buster's face when he'd suddenly found himself on the receiving end of a shotgun.

It must have been a picture.

Early that Saturday Roxanne loaded up with broccoli and headed for St Petroc intending to sell what she could in the market. She arrived after Kevern and Linnet and intentionally parked on the opposite side of the square.

She'd been there for about an hour when Jack Gifford and Joe Tregale stopped by. 'Be it true what I hears Roxanne?' Jack asked, grinning.

'Depends what that was.'

'That you took several pot shots at a certain neighbour of yours t'other night?'

'And how do you know it was my neighbour?' she queried.

Joe winked. 'Word gets round. Understand what I mean?'

'Someone set fire to my dairy recently, and I believe that same someone returned during the week. And yes I did take a few pot shots which, fortunately for them, missed.'

Joe Tregale chuckled. 'Good for you, Roxanne. Nobody will better you, eh?'

'Nobody,' she declared emphatically. 'Just because I'm a woman on my own doesn't mean I can be bullied or pushed around. I'll fight for what's mine as hard as any man.'

Playfully, Jack punched her on the shoulder. 'You've got guts Roxanne, I admire that, just as others are beginning to. That certain neighbour we was referring to is not the most popular person around.'

'Did you aim to hit him?' Joe queried.

'I did,' Roxanne lied, wanting that to be spread about and to reach Buster. 'Which I'll do again if any other bugger comes sneaking round Cobwebs at night.'

'A one woman army,' Jack commented, and laughed.

'I hope I never gets on the wrong side of you, Roxanne,' Joe said, and laughed also.

'A chip off the old block. Reynold would have been proud of you,' Jack beamed.

Roxanne stared after Jack and Joe Tregale as they walked away, pleased with the conversation and their reaction to what had happened. So, folks were beginning to admire her for her guts.

305

That could be no bad thing.

'Roxanne! Roxanne!'

She turned to find James Booth waving at her; he was driving a large wagon pulled by two Shires. She immediately set down the buckets she was carrying having been en route to feed the pigs.

'I've brought you they bulbs as promised,' he declared when she ran to the wagon which he'd stopped.

Her eyes shone as she gazed at the many bags piled high in the rear of the wagon. 'If I'd known you were coming today I'd have had the cash ready,' she stated.

'No rush for that,' he replied, jumping down.

'It's good to see you again, James,' she said, pecking him on the cheek.

'And you.'

'How was your journey?'

'Uneventful.'

'You'll have to wait till tomorrow for me to get to the bank I'm afraid.'

'That's all right. I'd planned to stay overnight anyway. I'll unhitch these horses and start unloading.'

'Unhitch the horses by all means, but you'll have a cup of tea and bite first before you do any unloading.'

He smiled broadly. ''Twas hoping you'd say that. I be right parched and a mite hungry too.'

'I'll go in and put the kettle on.'

She looked again at the wagon's contents. 'King Alfreds and Butter and Eggs?'

'Same as you bought from Scorrier, only of the highest quality. No disease in that lot.'

She couldn't wait to get planting, Roxanne thought, as she hurried towards the cottage. It would be the bank first thing in the morning, planting in the afternoon.

''Tis a fine sight,' declared Billy Christmas, staring out over the daffodil fields. 'You'll be cutting shortly.'

'Another few weeks by my reckoning,' Roxanne replied.

'Doing it all by yourself?'

She shook her head. 'I'll need help. I've already organized some casual labour to come in.'

'You'll have to provide good eatins and drinkins then. That's the custom as you well know.'

'This will be *paid* help, Billy, not friends and neighbours lending a hand. But don't worry, they'll get fed well enough, I'll see to that.'

'Talking of neighbours, I hears you got new ones. Rented a cottage off Squire Palfrey. Seems they're known to the squire in some way.'

'Really!' Roxanne exclaimed.

'He's an artist I believe, paints pictures. Never had one of they in St Petroc before.'

'An artist,' Roxanne mused. That was interesting. 'What's their name?'

'Carey was what I was told. Don't know their Christian handles though.'

'Is he famous?'

Billy shrugged. 'Search me. You can ask him though when you meet him, which you're bound to sooner or later.'

'And where is this cottage?' Roxanne asked.

Billy pointed to his right, the opposite direction to Buster's land. 'Over that way a bit.'

Maybe she'd call in at some point and introduce herself, Roxanne thought, wondering what the wife was like. 'What sort of age are they?'

'A little older than you and I. If that's correct. You know what gossip be?'

Roxanne knew exactly what Billy meant.

'Now I'd best get home to Annie and the young uns. Don't want to be late for my Sunday dinner.'

They began strolling towards his horse. 'Thanks for calling by, Billy. It's good to get a natter.'

'Don't you get lonely here by yourself?' he asked, concerned for her well-being.

Roxanne sighed. 'I have to admit, there are times when I do. Usually late at night just before I go to bed. But there's always Bobby to keep me company. I'd certainly be lost without him.'

Billy glanced at Bobby scampering ahead. 'You should get out and about a bit more, tain't healthy being on your own so much.'

'Now don't you start!' Roxanne chided. 'I get enough of that from Linnet.'

'She has a point though. You have to admit it.'

'I'm all right, Billy. Don't go worrying about me now. I get into St Petroc most Saturdays and that does me for the moment.' He stopped beside his horse. 'Annie asks if you'd like to come to supper one night?'

'That would be lovely,' Roxanne smiled. 'But it'll have to be soon, for once the harvesting begins I'll be too busy to go anywhere.'

They agreed an evening before Billy rode away.

The figure stood on the clifftops watching a steamer chugging its way along the coastline. He wore a wide-brimmed hat, long coat to below his knees and a woollen scarf wrapped round his neck.

It had to be Mr Carey the artist, Roxanne thought, staring curiously at him. He was tall and slim with a mysterious detached air about him. Unfortunately he was too far away for her to make out his face and see what he looked like.

He was still watching the steamer as Roxanne turned to gaze at the field of daffodils she was in. Everything was ready for the harvesting which would begin the following morning. A shiver of anticipation ran through her at the prospect.

Her first-ever daffodil harvest, the culmination of a great deal of hard work.

When she looked again to where Mr Carey had been standing he had gone.

Roxanne paused in her picking, straightened and rubbed her itchy hands together. Mr Tresillion had warned her about daffodil rash, the cause of the itch.

The rash was a result of direct contact with daffodil sap which is poisonous. The itch was quite dreadful, rendering the area round the nails extremely painful. It could also affect the face by making it puffy and causing the eyes to swell.

'Damn!' she muttered, scratching one hand, then the other.

''Tis a right nuisance, tain't it, Miss Hawkins,' Iris Morrish, one of the girls she'd hired, called out cheerfully.

'Nuisance isn't the word,' Roxanne responded.

'Well I only hopes I don't get it,' Iris said.

Roxanne had another good scratch, then bent wearily again, continuing to pick the stems.

It was late, but still Roxanne and her girls worked on by lamplight, bunching and boxing daffodils to be taken to the railway station the next morning where they would be transported to Plymouth and from there transferred to the perishable train bound for London.

Roxanne was wearing a pair of thin cotton gloves, as were the girls; they were her answer to the rash. She considered herself lucky to have found enough gloves in St Petroc to go round.

She thought of the letter she'd received earlier from her Covent Garden wholesaler, recommended by Mr Tresillion, informing her he was delighted with what he'd already received and that his local Cornish agent would be calling in shortly, to pay her what she was so far owed.

Roxanne glanced about the dairy which she'd temporarily converted to a bunching and boxing shed, thinking it had proved ideal for the purpose.

Mary Scrivens paused to take a deep breath. 'I'm buggered,' she announced.

'Not too much more then you can all get off home,' Roxanne told her.

'I'll be asleep the moment my head hits that pillow. Tis a long day and no mistake.'

'Think of the money you're making though. You'll have no complaints about that,' Ella Pridmore pointed out. The girls were all on piece work, paid by what they picked and boxed.

'True enough, no grumbles there,' Mary conceded.

It was the early hours before the last daffodil was boxed and loaded, ready to be taken into St Petroc.

Roxanne totted up the column of her daffodil income, the season now over, from which she then deducted her capital expenditure, higher than she'd anticipated thanks to the loss she'd taken over Scorrier's bulbs.

The final sum showed she'd made a small profit, which wasn't bad considering it had been her first harvest, and that she'd been diddled by Scorrier. The venture had been a success, she told herself with a smile.

'A *definite* success,' she repeated aloud.

Bobby, sensing his mistress's elated mood, came and laid his head on her lap, and was rewarded by her stroking his ears.

'We did it, Bobby, we did it,' she murmured.

He growled happily in reply.

Chapter Twenty

The woman who answered Roxanne's knock was small and dark, with liquid brown eyes and olive skin. Her hair was piled high on her head, kept in place by two tortoiseshell combs. Roxanne judged her to be in her late twenties.

'Hallo,' Mrs Carey smiled.

'I'm Roxanne Hawkins and I live in Cobwebs, which is over there,' Roxanne explained, indicating back the way she'd come. 'As you're new in the area, and we're neighbours, I thought I should come over and introduce myself.' She offered Mrs Carey the cake, wrapped in a teatowel, she'd brought. 'For you.'

'How kind!' Mrs Carey exclaimed, accepting the gift. 'Please come in.'

The Careys' kitchen was larger than her own. Two young children, a boy and girl, were playing on the floor in front of the hearth.

Mrs Carey carefully placed the cake on the table, then turned to Roxanne. 'I'm India by the way, and this is Polly and Jonathan. Come and say hallo to Mrs Hawkins, children,' India instructed.

Both children rose and walked shyly forward. 'How do you do, Mrs Hawkins,' Jonathan murmured.

'It's *Miss* Hawkins actually,' Roxanne replied. 'And why don't you call me Roxanne. That's much less formal.'

'Roxanne,' Polly said, and shook hands with her.

'If you don't mind that is?' Roxanne asked India.

'Not at all, Christian names it is. Now why don't I put the kettle on and we'll have a nice cup of tea.'

'How are you enjoying being in Devon?' Roxanne asked Jonathan as India busied herself with the kettle.

'Very much, thank you.'

'Someone mentioned you came from Surrey. Is that right?'

'Sussex,' Jonathan corrected her.

'You must find it very different here.'

'The people talk funny,' Polly commented.

'Polly! That's rude,' India admonished her.

Roxanne laughed. 'I'm sure we do sound funny to people from Sussex.'

'I can't always understand them,' Polly elaborated.

'You'll soon get used to us and our accent,' Roxanne said, thinking how well spoken the Careys were. Whatever their origins, it certainly wasn't working class.

'What's in that?' Jonathan queried, pointing at the teatowel.

'A cake,' Roxanne informed him.

'Oooh, lovely!'

'What sort?' Polly asked.

'A sponge with cream in the middle.'

'Yummy.'

Roxanne glanced about the kitchen, noting how untidy it was. Nor was it all that clean either. The floor, and table, could both have done with a good scrub.

'I take it you're a Devonian,' India said, opening a cupboard.

'Born and bred. Though not at Cobwebs. I come from the other side of St Petroc.'

'And do you live alone at Cobwebs?'

Roxanne nodded. 'With my dog Bobby who's my constant companion. We're great friends, he and I.'

'Is he with you today?' Jonathan asked eagerly.

'No, I left him at home as he isn't feeling too well. But normally he would have come with me.'

'I love dogs,' Jonathan went on. 'Our grandpa's got one. He's a labrador called Winks.'

'We don't have a dog,' Polly stated, glancing disapprovingly at her mother.

'All in good time,' India said.

'I believe your husband's an artist,' Roxanne smiled.

'He is indeed. I'll call him through from his studio when tea's ready. I know he'll want to meet you.'

'He has a studio in the house then?'

'Not quite. There's a building out at the back he uses for that. He says he gets splendid light there.'

'Light?' Roxanne frowned.

'Good light is very important for an artist,' India explained.

311

She unwrapped the cake. 'Oh I say, this does look scrumptious. Far better than anything I could ever produce. Cooking and baking aren't really my fortes I'm afraid. I only manage to muddle by in those departments.'

'I'm sure that isn't so.'

'Oh yes it is,' Jonathan declared. 'Daddy says some of her meals are quite horrid.'

How ungallant of him, Roxanne thought. Even if it was true he shouldn't have said that to his wife. She'd been looking forward to meeting Mr Carey, now she wasn't so certain.

'What sort of painting does your husband do?' she asked India.

'Landscapes mainly, though he will attempt the occasional portrait from time to time. But landscapes are his first love. He's extremely talented if I say so myself.'

India laid out an odd variety of unmatching cups and saucers. 'I also paint, but am nowhere as good as Miles. He's been hung in the Royal Academy you know.'

'Really!' Roxanne was impressed.

'Oh yes, on several occasions. A considerable feather in his cap.'

'Has he always been an artist?'

'Much to his father's disgust. He wanted Miles to follow in his footsteps and become a vicar.' India laughed brittly. 'But Miles would have none of that.'

'So why Devon if you don't mind me asking?'

A strange expression clouded India's face, and a tic twitched on one cheek. Then expression and tic were gone. 'Miles spent a holiday here when young, which he's never forgotten. He says it's a wonderful county to paint, far better than Sussex in his opinion.'

'And so here you are.'

'Here we are,' India smiled, lifting the cake and putting it on a plate. Fetching a knife she proceeded to cut the cake into generous slices.

'Is there anything I can do?' Roxanne inquired.

'I think you've done enough by bringing us this sponge. Tea shouldn't be long now.' She turned to Jonathan. 'Will you run and tell Daddy we have a visitor.'

Jonathan scampered off.

'Why India? I've never heard that as a name before. I thought it was just a country,' Roxanne asked.

'Pa's in the army and was stationed there for some while. He adored the place and decided to name me after it. Simple as that.'

'I want to go to the lavatory,' Polly announced.

'Then do so. You know where it is.'

'Want you to come with me, Mum.'

India sighed in exasperation. 'Polly!'

'Please, Mum?'

India looked at Roxanne. 'Will you excuse us?'

'Of course. I'll make the tea while you're gone.' The kettle was now boiling.

'Caddy's over there, and you can see the pot.' Then, in a sing-song voice, she added, 'We won't be long.'

Roxanne was setting the pot on the hearth when the door opened and Jonathan reappeared, followed by a tall, slim man wearing corduroy trousers, a collarless shirt undone at the neck and a pullover. His hair was fair and longish, his face finely boned, with a full, but neatly trimmed moustache under a slightly aquiline nose. His eyes were also brown, quizzical and penetrating. Roxanne found his eyes disturbing, for it was as though they could see inside her head and read what she was thinking.

'You must be the visitor,' he said without smiling.

She straightened. 'Roxanne Hawkins, a neighbour.'

'Pleased to meet you,' he declared, and extended an elegant hand with long, tapering fingers. 'I'm Miles Carey,' he added as they shook hands.

'Roxanne's brought a sponge with cream in the middle,' Jonathan told him.

'Has she indeed!'

'Just a little something to welcome you to St Petroc,' Roxanne explained, curiously feeling somewhat embarrassed.

He now smiled at her. 'You're the daffodil lady. I've seen you a few times in your fields.'

'That's right.'

'How long have you been growing daffodils?'

'This was my first season. So I'm really a beginner.'

'You appeared to do well then. At least that's how it seemed to me.'

'I did. My first harvest was quite successful.'

'I wish they'd bloomed though. I would have enjoyed painting that.'

'You can do so next year. I'll be growing some for bulbs then.'

'Jolly good,' he nodded. 'I'll look forward to that.'

Older than India, Roxanne thought. By two, maybe three years, certainly not more.

'You think I don't look like an artist,' he suddenly stated.

That startled her, for it had crossed her mind. 'How did you know?' she queried.

'Because nearly everyone says that. I believe they expect someone more Bohemian and exotic.'

India and Polly returned. 'Ah, you've met then,' India said.

'Roxanne is the daffodil lady I mentioned to you,' Miles informed her.

'Is she now? We hadn't got that far.'

Miles stuck his hands in his pockets, moved over to the table and stared down at the sponge. 'Splendid,' he declared.

They chatted over tea and cake: India and Roxanne did most of the talking, while Miles lapsed into long silences during which he watched whoever was speaking.

Then, abruptly, he rose to his feet causing Roxanne to break off in mid-sentence. 'Don't think me impolite, but I must get back to work. Delightful to have met you, Roxanne. Call in again.'

What an odd man, Roxanne thought as he left the room. She'd never before met anyone quite like him. The kitchen seemed empty now he was gone.

'More tea?' India asked.

Later, as she was walking back to Cobwebs, Roxanne found herself thinking about Miles Carey. She wasn't sure whether she liked him or not. Probably, she eventually decided, probably.

'So tell me about him,' Linnet urged, having just been told by Roxanne that she'd visited the Careys.

Roxanne shrugged. 'He's a bit strange.'

'In what way?'

'His manner I suppose. He wasn't at all what I expected.'

'Is he handsome?'

'I'd say so. And she's very pretty. She and I got on quite well.'

'Did you see any of his paintings?'

'No,' Roxanne confessed. 'I did find out he does mainly landscapes though, and loves Devon which is why they moved here. He's got beautiful hands,' Roxanne mused. 'I especially noticed those.'

Linnet thought of Kevern's work worn and calloused mitts. And her own come to that. 'Not the hands of a farmer, eh?'

'Definitely not.'

'The whole town's talking about him you know. Wondering, speculating, especially as he's so different and all. Not the sort we're used to in St Petroc.'

314

'He's certainly different,' Roxanne agreed.

'And her, tell me more about her.'

Linnet didn't leave until she'd squeezed out of Roxanne every last piece of information about the Careys that she could.

'What a charming room,' India said, glancing round Roxanne's kitchen. She, Miles and the children had been invited to Cobwebs for Sunday tea. It was a return gesture for the tea Roxanne had taken with them. 'And so much neater and tidier than mine.'

'Any kitchen is neater and tidier than ours,' Miles declared, though not censoriously. It was more a statement of fact.

'Why don't you take Bobby outside and give him a run?' Roxanne suggested to Jonathan and Polly who were stroking him.

'Can we?' Jonathan asked Miles excitedly.

'Of course.'

'Go with them, Bobby. Go with them,' Roxanne instructed the dog, who was only too happy to oblige. 'And don't worry about Rex my alsatian,' she added to the children. 'He looks ferocious but is really quite friendly, particularly with Bobby there. You don't have to worry.'

'Now why don't you two sit down while I put things out,' Roxanne said to India and Miles when the door had slammed shut behind the children.

While she was doing this she became aware of Miles studying her, his forehead creased in puzzlement. 'I can't help feeling I know you from somewhere,' he said eventually.

'Oh?'

'I mean away from St Petroc. Have you ever been to Sussex?'

'I'm afraid not. I did work in Exeter for a while, and London before that.'

'London,' he mused. 'Perhaps it was there. I studied in London and afterwards often went up at weekends from Sussex to stay with some great friends of ours in Islington.'

Roxanne knew then what the connection was. 'Did you ever go to Collins Music Hall?' she asked casually.

'Yes, on several occasions. I . . .' He suddenly clicked his fingers. 'Good God! You were a singer. But the name wasn't Roxanne Hawkins?'

'That was me,' she confessed. 'Annie Breeze was my stage name.'

'Of course! You were marvellous. Top of the bill.'

'How extraordinary,' India murmured, bemused.

'She really was good,' Miles enthused to India. 'A tremendous voice.'

'So what made you give it up?' India asked.

'I had my reasons,' Roxanne prevaricated. 'Let's just say London and the music hall weren't for me any more.'

'And you went from there to Exeter?' Miles queried.

'No, I came home first. Then moved to Exeter where I worked in a cigarette factory. An aunt died, leaving me some money while I was there, which is how I came to buy Cobwebs.'

'There was one song I particularly enjoyed,' Miles went on. 'Hollyhock something or other?'

' "Will You Be My Hollyhock",' Roxanne reminded him. 'It was extremely popular with the audiences.'

'That's right. "Will You Be My Hollyhock". I can visualize you singing it now.'

'Well well well,' India murmured again, fascinated by this revelation.

'I knew I'd seen you somewhere before. I just knew it,' Miles said. 'I've got an excellent memory for faces.'

For some reason Roxanne found herself pleased that he'd seen her at Collins, the only person in St Petroc to have done so.

As they both left, India and Miles declared that they had had a wonderful time, India adding that she knew they were going to be the best of friends as well as neighbours.

For the rest of the day Roxanne felt quite uplifted.

Deep in thought, Roxanne jumped a little when she was suddenly tapped on the shoulder. She turned round to find Miles smiling at her.

'Sorry, did I startle you?'

It was market day in St Petroc and Roxanne had just packed up her unsold produce, ready to return home. 'My fault, I was miles away.'

'I get like that when I'm painting, rapt in concentration. I'm glad I ran into you by the way. India and I were wondering if we could come to some sort of arrangement with you.'

'What kind of arrangement?'

'Butter, eggs, milk, cream, those things. We don't really want to keep animals ourselves which means we have to use the shops in St Petroc. It would be far easier to simply nip over to you for the necessities. We'll pay the going rate of course.'

Roxanne thought it was a splendid idea, it helped out everyone. 'Fine, that's agreed then.'

'One of us will call by tomorrow. What's the best time?'

He hesitated once that had been settled. 'I'd intended dropping by the pub. Would you care to accompany me, or would that be deemed improper?'

'I don't see why it should, we are neighbours after all.'

'Then the pub it is!'

They went to the King's Arms, as it was the nearest; Roxanne chose a table by the roaring log fire while Miles went up to the bar. Her heart sank when she spotted Kevern staring at her. Just her luck for him to be there! She hoped he wouldn't come over.

Who was she with? Kevern was wondering. He'd never seen him before. Good looking chap too, which made it worse. A boyfriend?

'Who's that with our Roxanne?' he asked Algy Vranch when Miles had rejoined her.

Algy glanced over. 'Dunno. Stranger to me.'

'Edgar, do you know?'

Edgar Boal shook his head.

Jealousy raged in Kevern as he continued staring at Roxanne; he'd have given anything to have been sitting beside her, with her paying him the same attention she was to the bloke who was certainly no farmer by the cut of his clothes.

'It's your turn to get them in,' he vaguely heard Algy say.

'Eh?'

'Your round, Kevern. And don't pretend tain't, for tis.'

Kevern saw off what remained of his pint and banged the glass on the counter, wishing it was the bloke's face he'd banged instead.

'So why didn't India come in with you today?' Roxanne asked Miles.

'She decided to stay at the cottage as she suspects she's getting a cold.'

'Oh, I'm sorry to hear that. Is there any way I can help?'

'I'll let you know if there is.'

He glanced round the pub, then brought his attention back to Roxanne. They continued to chat.

Kevern watched Roxanne and the bloke leave, the two of them going off down the street together. He felt physically sick, a sensation that had nothing whatever to do with the alcohol he'd consumed.

'Did I tell you about they pigs of ours?' Jack Billings said to the company.

Kevern forced himself to listen to Jack's story about his pigs.

*   *   *

Linnet, who had Morwenna and Tamsin with her, saw with dismay that Kevern was drunk, which could only mean trouble. It always did.

'I been waiting ages. Expected you out of here long ago,' she chided him when she reached his side.

He glared at her, a picture of Roxanne still vivid in his mind. 'Haven't finished me drinking yet,' he slurred.

'From the sound of you you've already had a bellyful.'

Jack Billings snickered, and turned away; that snicker infuriated Kevern.

'So come on,' Linnet urged.

'I'll come when I'm good and ready, and not before,' Kevern answered hotly.

'You tell her,' murmured Algy, who was also drunk.

'Think of the children. They're tired and hungry, and want to go home.'

Kevern swallowed a large mouthful of cider. 'You gets on then. I'll follow on me own.'

'You mean walk! Tis a fair piece.'

'I've done it often in the past, and can do it again. So there!' he retorted, determined to hold his ground. He was damned if he was going to be pulled out of the pub like some errant baby.

'No need to worry about that,' Edgar Boal intervened. 'I'll give Kevern a lift. Tain't far out my way.'

'There we are then, tis settled,' Kevern said.

Now it was Linnet's turn to glare at him. It wasn't only him getting drunk that annoyed her, but the amount of money he was spending. Recently he'd been chucking more and more away on alcohol.

'Why don't you have a snifter while you're here?' Algy suggested to her, trying to placate matters.

'No thank you,' she snapped in reply.

'See you later,' Kevern said, turning his back on her and the children.

Linnet felt like swearing, but didn't. Whirling in anger, she swept out of the pub.

Kevern hiccuped. 'Fucking women, they're all the same. A pain in the bloody arse.'

Another round was ordered.

*   *   *

Kevern gazed blearily around; where was Edgar? He was meant to be giving him that lift. He hadn't seen him for some time as he had joined some other friends who were now leaving.

He glanced at the wall clock, having to squint in order to focus. Heavens, was that the time? No wonder he was well and truly pissed.

He lurched to his feet and staggered towards the bar. Where the hell was Edgar? He couldn't see him anywhere.

A word behind the bar confirmed his worst suspicions. Edgar had gone without him. Not intentionally, he must simply have forgotten he'd promised to give him a lift.

'Stupid bugger!' Kevern grumbled. He'd never have got himself into this state if he'd known he was going to have to walk.

Maybe there was someone else he could cadge a lift from? But as luck would have it there was no-one present who lived in his direction. So Shank's pony would have to do.

Outside he shivered as the cold hit him. Turning his collar up he wove his way down the street, thinking the temperature had dropped considerably since he'd entered the pub.

He didn't realize it, but the cold soon made him even drunker, to the point where he was only dimly aware of his surroundings.

Kevern cursed as he lost his footing and pitched headlong into a ditch. St Petroc was behind him now, the long dark road home stretching ahead.

'Fucking Edgar, fucking Linnet,' he swore, climbing out the ditch on his hands and knees. Halfway up he halted, thinking he was going to vomit. He retched several times, then resumed his journey till he reached the top of the ditch where he came to his feet. He continued to weave along the road.

It would be a short cut to go over the fields, he thought. Yes, that's what he'd do. He'd cut quite a bit off his journey that way.

A little further on he came to a stile against which he leant heavily, summoning up the will to get over it. Finally, after several abortive efforts, he succeeded in reaching the other side.

Kevern was laughing, almost hysterically to himself. This really was very funny. Would he have something to say to Edgar when he saw him next. Oh yes! Edgar would get the edge of his tongue all right. But in the meantime he could only laugh.

He tripped and fell for the umpteenth time, finding himself

sprawled out across wood, metal and small stones, lots and lots of small stones.

He was trying to imagine what it could be as he started hauling himself upright again, the world whirling all around him. He stared up at the stars dancing in the night sky, the moon bellowing at him.

Now why would the moon make such a strange noise? Bellow, and whistle and . . .

There was an almighty thump and the next moment he was flying through the air.

Someone was screaming.

Himself, he realized just before unconsciousness claimed him.

Chapter Twenty-One

Roxanne entered the hospital waiting room to discover a white-faced Linnet sitting alone clutching a cold cup of tea. She hurried to her sister's side and sat down beside her.

'I came as soon as I was told,' she said.

'Who told you?' Linnet's voice was thin and strained.

'PC Moresby.'

'It was Sergeant Bratton who told me. He was very kind and comforting.'

'Where are the children?'

'At the Tregales. Marjery said not to worry, she'd take good care of them.'

Linnet glanced down at her tea, frowning when she realized it had gone cold, and laid it on the floor.

'How is Kevern?' Roxanne asked.

'They're operating now. He was badly injured by all accounts. In fact it was a miracle he wasn't killed.'

'Hit by a train, the constable said?'

Linnet nodded. 'Blind drunk at the time, making his way home. Edgar Boal was supposed to have given him a lift, but couldn't have done.'

'I saw him with his cronies in the pub when I was there.'

'I went in and tried to get him to leave, but he was having none of it. Insisted on staying longer for more drink. And this is what's happened.'

'How was he found?'

'The engine driver heard the impact apparently, and the terrible scream that followed. He stopped, thinking he'd hit a beast, and thought he'd put the poor animal out of its misery if it was still

321

alive. Then he found Kevern. If he hadn't stopped Kevern would have bled to death.'

'Oh Linnet!' Roxanne breathed. Taking her sister's hand in her own she squeezed it.

'Know how I feel Roxanne?'

'How.'

'Bloody angry. He's no-one but himself to blame for what happened. No-one. And now what?'

Her reaction surprised Roxanne. Perhaps things had been even worse between Linnet and Kevern than she'd realized. She'd put a lot of the tension that had existed between the pair when she'd stayed with them down to her presence.

'If he does die he's leaving two small children behind,' Linnet went on bitterly. 'And I'll never get another husband. Not that I'd want one anyway. One is quite enough for me.'

Linnet paused, then added, 'Drink and what's between my legs, I sometimes think that's all he's interested in. A pint of cider and getting it up me.'

Roxanne didn't know what to say.

'Fool!' Linnet suddenly hissed. 'That's all Kevern Stoneman be. A fool.'

'Would you like some fresh tea?' Roxanne asked.

Linnet shook her head.

It was about half an hour later that Doctor Weeks appeared in the waiting room looking tired. Both Linnet and Roxanne immediately rose to face him.

'It isn't good I'm afraid,' Weeks said. 'We've had to amputate his left leg but have so far managed to save the right, though it's entirely possible that too might have to go later.'

'Does that mean he'll live?' Linnet queried tremulously.

Weeks sighed. 'It's too early to say. A lot depends on him. And of course should complications set in . . .' He broke off and shrugged.

Linnet dropped her gaze to stare at the floor. Part of her mind was numb, another part churning. One leg gone, the other in danger of being amputated as well. And he still might die.

'He'll be unconscious for some time, and when he does come round he won't be in any fit state to see anyone. It's best you go home, Linnet, and try to rest.'

'I'll take her,' Roxanne volunteered.

'Thank you, doctor,' Linnet whispered.

'I only wish it was better news. But we are doing everything we can, you can be assured of that.'

Reaching out Weeks placed a hand gently on Linnet's shoulder. 'I'm sorry.'

'Not half as sorry as I am,' she replied bitterly.

They picked up the girls from the Tregales en route to the farm.

'What's wrong? You look dreadful,' Miles asked Roxanne, showing concern.

She ran a hand over her face, then dragged it down through her hair. She was dogged tired, having had little sleep the night before. She planned to return to Linnet as soon as she'd tended her animals.

She recounted what had happened to Kevern, and how it had come about.

'That's awful,' he said, visibly shocked. 'Your sister must be in a terrible state.'

'Angry, more than anything else. I never realized things were so bad between them. It all came pouring out last night after we'd put the children to bed. She just sat there and talked while I made endless pots of tea.'

'Is there anything India and I can do? You only have to say.'

She smiled gratefully at him. 'Not for the moment. But I'll let you know if there is. In the meantime I'd appreciate it if you kept what I've just told you to yourself. About her being angry and things bad between them, I mean.'

'My lips are sealed, even to India. This is strictly between you and me,' he assured her.

Roxanne couldn't think why she'd confided in Miles, she hardly knew him after all. But he was that sort of man you instinctively knew you could trust.

'It's Linnet I feel for,' Roxanne went on. 'Whether Kevern lives or dies, this is going to have a profound effect on her life. And the children of course. God alone knows how she's going to cope in either event.'

'Are you two very close?'

Roxanne considered that. 'In some ways, and not in others. We're certainly very different as people.'

'Is she strong? In her mind that is. I think she's going to have to be.'

'I'm not sure about that.'

'Whereas you most definitely are.'

'Am I?'

'Oh yes. I recognized that in you the first time we met. I could sense it.'

She found his eyes boring into hers, and glanced away in sudden confusion. 'I take it you've come for your milk,' she said. It was usually Miles who dropped in every morning, rather than India, because he claimed he enjoyed the stroll prior to starting work.

'Please. And eggs if you have them.'

She'd already done the milking but, because she'd started later than usual, she hadn't yet been to the hen house.

'I'm not in a hurry,' he replied softly when she explained. 'I'll come with you while you collect the eggs if I may.'

After he'd gone she reflected that although she hardly knew Miles, she felt as if she had done so all her life.

'How are you now?' Roxanne asked Linnet later on, once she'd arrived at the farm. Linnet was sitting staring disconsolately into space.

'Thinking, wondering, worried.'

'Do you want to go back to the hospital?'

Linnet shook her head. 'Tomorrow will be soon enough for that. Sergeant Bratton will get in touch meantime should anything happen. Like Kevern dying.'

'Have you eaten anything?'

'No.'

'The children?'

'No. They haven't either.'

'Then I'll see to that. Where are they by the way?'

'Tamsin's still sleeping and Morwenna's in her room.'

Roxanne busied herself making them a late breakfast while Linnet continued to brood.

'Dead or alive, I'll never forgive him for this. Never!' Linnet said after a while. 'And if he do come home he needn't look for sympathy from me, that's the last thing he'll get. Hell mend the drunken sot.'

After breakfast Roxanne did the chores, only returning to Cobwebs in time to tend her own animals. She went back to the farm later and stayed a second night.

Linnet brusquely halted the cart, tied off the reins and jumped down. Kevern, who'd been sitting beside her, bent and picked up his crutches. Not only his life, but his right leg had also been saved although it caused him constant pain as it was now shrunken and weak.

'Do you want a hand?' Linnet asked him.

'I'm all right. Don't need no hand,' he answered sharply.

'Suit yourself.'

She walked round to his side of the cart and watched his ungainly descent to the ground in contempt. She didn't move when he nearly tumbled over, but was surprised that somehow he managed to stay erect. He shot her a triumphant, sneering look.

'Fat lot of use you're going to be round here from now on,' she said, which wiped the look off his face and made him flinch.

He hopped forward, heading for the door. She again watched him contemptuously.

He opened the door and hopped inside, only he misjudged the wooden bar on the floor, which kept out draughts, stumbled over it and, with a cry, went sprawling.

For a moment or two he lay prostrate, then, slowly forming a fist, he began to beat impotently against the floor. As he did this, he started to weep silently, his eyes filling with tears which then ran down his cheeks.

Linnet gazed at this spectacle, feeling no pity for Kevern, none whatever.

He was still silently crying when she helped him upright.

Roxanne was making cream when Miles appeared in the dairy doorway to smile at her. Bobby, who'd been lying beside her, immediately bounded forward to snuffle at his legs.

'I've come with a request,' he announced.

'Oh?'

'I wonder if you'd mind me sketching you next time you're working in the fields.'

She paused as a flush of pleasure washed over her. 'Sketch me?'

'That's right.'

'But why? I thought you usually only did landscapes.'

'Landscapes can have people in them you know. I intend putting a female figure in the one I'm doing now and immediately thought of you. You'd be perfect for what I'm after.'

'Why not India?' she countered, thinking that he'd succeeded in confusing her again.

Miles took a long wooden spoon from a hook on the wall and pretended to examine it. 'She doesn't normally do that sort of work so it would seem an unnatural pose for her to adopt. Anyway, I don't want someone to pose but want to capture them going about their normal daily toil. Can you understand?'

325

She nodded. His explanation made sense.

'So what do you say?'

'As long as India won't object.'

He laughed. 'Why on earth should she? I've sketched thousands of people in my time and she never objected to any of them. Why should you be any different?'

That was a good point, Roxanne thought. 'All right,' she agreed.

He beamed at her. 'Splendid!'

'I plan to take up some potatoes tomorrow, if that's any good for you?'

'Couldn't be better,' he enthused, returning the spoon to its hook.

'I've never seen any of your paintings,' she stated.

'Then we'll remedy that next time you're at the cottage. I'll show you round the little studio I've fixed up.'

'India says you're extremely talented.'

'Ahh!' he breathed. 'That's not for me to comment on, but for others to judge. I do seem to be highly thought of in some quarters though.'

He moved abruptly back to the door. 'See you tomorrow then. And thank you,' he declared over his shoulder, as he disappeared.

'Well, what about that?' she said to Bobby. 'Miles wants to sketch me.'

Bobby woofed his approval.

Roxanne was only too conscious of Miles sitting on a collapsible stool studying her intently one moment, pencil flying over his pad the next. He'd instructed her to forget about his presence and just get on and do things as she would normally, an instruction she was finding impossible to obey.

She continued to dig potatoes which she then loaded into wicker baskets, transferring those to the cart. It was hot work, making her sweat profusely, something else she was horribly aware of, thinking she must look and smell awful.

She paused to wipe her streaming brow. 'How are you doing?' she called out.

'Pardon?' he blinked.

'How are you doing?'

'Oh fine! I think I'll pack it in shortly. I've more or less got what I want.'

'Can I peek?'

He hesitated. 'If you like,' he answered reluctantly.

She went and stared at the top page of his pad. She'd expected one sketch, but instead there were a number of her in different positions, all with her face blank.

'Aren't you going to use my face?' she asked, disappointed.

His lips curled into a smile. He flipped over a couple of pages till he came to one that was filled with her face viewed from various angles.

Roxanne gasped. It was her to the life. 'They're wonderful,' she declared.

'Only rough. I'll improve on them when I put you in the painting.'

'I can't wait to see *that*,' she said.

'Well it won't be finished for a while. But I'll arrange you do when it is.'

He flicked his pad shut and stood up. 'On second thoughts I'll head back now. I want to spend some time with India and the children before they go off.'

'Off?' Roxanne queried.

'A sudden decision on India's part. She's taking the children to Sussex for a few weeks to visit relatives.'

'Her parents?'

Miles shook his head. 'They're overseas just now, they often are. That's why India was mainly brought up by an aunt, her Aunt Catherine. It's that aunt and some cousins she intends visiting.'

'But you're not going?'

'No, I'm staying and getting on with my picture which I plan to use as part of an exhibition I'm putting on in London.'

'Whereabouts in London?'

'Bond Street. The Elgin Gallery. Four of us are exhibiting. Quite a *coup* for me if I may say so.'

Roxanne was delighted for him. 'How will you manage for food with India away?'

'I'm not totally useless with the pots and pans,' he smiled. 'I'll get by.'

She could imagine. Burnt this, and half raw that, with an awful lot of bread and cheese in between. 'You must come to me for supper then,' she said. 'It's the least I can do as a good neighbour.'

'That would be marvellous!' he enthused.

'When does India leave?'

'Early tomorrow morning.'

Roxanne thought about that. 'How about Saturday night? I'll make something special.'

'That's fine by me. I'll bring some wine.'

'Eightish?'

'Eightish it is.'

He folded up the stool and tucked it under his arm. 'Shall I dress for supper?' he joked, tongue firmly in cheek.

'Well, I hope you don't come *un*dressed,' she bantered in reply. 'That would be embarrassing.'

He laughed. 'For you and me both. Till Saturday then.'

'Till Saturday.'

Roxanne handed Miles the corkscrew she'd bought especially for the occasion, not having owned one before. 'You do the honours,' she said.

'I hope you like Medoc. It was the best St Petroc had to offer,' he smiled.

'It'll go well with the venison.'

'Ah! I wondered what it was I could smell.'

'There's newly caught trout to start with, and fruit for afters. I hope that's satisfactory.'

'Sounds delicious.'

His long elegant fingers fascinated her as they drove the corkscrew home. He then positioned the bottle between his legs and pulled. The cork came away with a loud plop.

Roxanne smoothed down her hair which she'd washed earlier. She'd been through her wardrobe again and again before finally settling on a navy blue skirt and a cream blouse with clinging sleeves ending in a short frill.

He poured a little of the wine into one of the glasses she'd set out, which she'd bought at the same time as the corkscrew, held the wine up and peered at it.

'Looks like red wine to me,' he declared solemnly.

The absurdity of it all made her laugh. 'Are you sure?'

He glanced at her, then back at the wine. 'I'm certain of it,' he nodded.

'What does it taste like?'

He put the glass to his mouth, and sipped. 'Hmmh!' he murmured.

'Well?'

He sipped again. 'Most definitely.'

'Most definitely what?'

'Most definitely . . . red wine. No doubt about it. You can't fool me.'

She laughed again, thinking his little charade a right hoot. 'I see you're an expert.'

328

'Oh yes. Years of training behind my expertise.'

He filled both glasses and handed her one. 'Does it meet with madam's approval?'

She too sipped, the wine's rich aroma assailing her nose. 'Very much so.'

'I'm pleased.'

She laid her glass aside. 'Now why don't you sit down while I get on.'

'Get on what?'

'With supper! Why are you being so daft tonight?'

He shrugged. 'Because I feel like it. Nothing wrong with being daft is there?'

'Nothing at all.'

He sat down, crossed his legs and stared at her. 'Did you catch the trout yourself?'

She wasn't sure whether he was being serious or was teasing her again. 'No, they're a present from a friend of mine.' The friend was Billy Christmas.

'Could never get on with fishing myself. Too slow for my taste.'

'You might enjoy fly fishing. That's different. Then you're the hunter stalking your prey.'

'How barbaric,' he mused.

'That doesn't appeal. Stalking your prey that is?'

His eye lit up with amusement. 'Depends on the prey.'

She giggled when he waggled his eyebrows. 'Have you heard from India?'

'A letter in today. She and the children are fine.'

'And when are they back?'

'She hasn't decided yet.'

'You must miss them.' Roxanne said that as a statement, not a question.

'Of course.' Then, almost in the same breath, 'Why have you never married? Or is it rude of me to ask?'

'It's rude of you to ask,' she replied.

'Sorry.'

She glanced sideways at him. 'I thought I was going to once, but it didn't work out. And that's all you'll get from me on the subject.'

'You sounded sad when you said that, as if you'd been deeply hurt.'

That startled her. 'Did I?'

'Sound sad? Yes.'

'Then you're wrong.'

His smile called her a liar.

He'd confused her again, she thought. And those eyes of his, still amused, boring into her as if, as she'd so often imagined, they could read her thoughts.

'How's the picture going?' she asked, changing the subject.

'All right.'

'Just all right?'

'I can't really tell until it's finished. And even then I don't always know.'

'What does India say about it?'

'She hasn't seen it yet. I'd growl and bark at her if she tried.'

'Growl and bark?'

'I have a true artistic temperament. I'm very prima donna-ish when it comes to my work.'

'You sound difficult to live with.'

'I am,' he confessed. 'A tranquil summer's calm one moment, the full sound and fury the next. India says she never knows where she is with me.'

'I can imagine.'

'I'd really like to paint you sometime,' he said, the humour vanishing from his eyes.

'I thought that's what you were doing?'

'No, a proper portrait. Perhaps even . . .' He trailed off, and drank more wine.

'Go on.'

He shook his head. 'I don't know you well enough yet. Maybe some day.'

She was intrigued by his evasiveness. There agan, she was intrigued by Miles himself.

'The trout's ready,' she announced.

He rose, crossed to the table and gazed at the platter she'd placed there. 'I can see you're a good cook. I should have known.'

'Isn't India?' She knew it was naughty of her to ask that.

'Terrible. Takes all her time to boil an egg.'

'Surely not?'

'India has many talents; unfortunately cooking isn't one of them.'

'Isn't it rather ungallant of you to say so?'

He smiled thinly. 'Ungallant or not, it's the truth. Besides . . .' He hesitated, then added. 'She's not exactly in my best books at the moment.'

'Oh?'

'We had a flaming row before she left.'

'I'm sorry to hear that,' Roxanne sympathized.

'It's a row we've had before. And explains why we moved down here, why we really left Sussex.'

Roxanne was intrigued.

'All in her imagination of course. I've sworn that to her a thousand times, but she simply won't believe me. I thought coming here would have exorcised it from her mind, but I was wrong.'

'Sounds fairly serious whatever it is,' Roxanne said quietly.

'Oh it is, if it was true. But it isn't. That's what's so damnable about it all.'

Anger tinged with despair creased his face. 'I do love her you know, but there are times when . . .' He broke off and shrugged. 'I've never known anyone who can go on and on the way she can. It's enough to drive a man demented.'

'Do you want to say what this thing is, or do you think it best you don't? I don't want to pry, but if you want to talk I'm here and listening.'

He gave her a smile of gratitude. 'You're a good friend, Roxanne. And what's more I trust you to keep anything I might say to yourself.'

'You can bank on that, Miles, I swear.'

'Let's sit down,' he declared and assisted her with her chair.

'She is totally and utterly convinced that I had an affair with a neighbour in Sussex,' he stated.

'And you didn't?'

'No, not at all. But India got it into her head that we did and no matter how hard I denied it India remains convinced that I was unfaithful to her.'

'Oh, Miles,' Roxanne breathed, filled with concern. 'I am sorry.'

'Hence the move to Devon. I hoped that would resolve matters, put pay once and for all to this obsession of hers. But not so, I'm afraid. She still harps on about it, using very unladylike language into the bargain. India waxing lyrical on the subject can swear like a trouper.'

He stared moodily at his food. 'Well, hasn't that put a dampener on the evening. Now it's my turn to say sorry.'

'I only wish I could help.'

He shook his head. 'You can't. But at least it's done me some good to talk about it.'

He then changed the subject and gradually his good humour returned. The evening wasn't spoilt after all.

331

When he'd gone Roxanne thought about what he'd confided to her. One thing was certain, India might not believe him but she did, his voice during that particular exchange had rung with sincerity.

Poor Miles, and poor India to be so mistaken. It must be torture for her to remain convinced that Miles had betrayed her.

'I don't want to be with Da. He's a grouch,' Morwenna wailed.

'Bloody hell!' Kevern swore.

Linnet gathered her daughter to her. 'There, there, my darling, Ma's with you now.'

Tamsin, who'd been watching wide eyed, also burst into tears.

'Now don't you bloody well start!' Kevern exclaimed, exasperated.

Tamsin ran to Linnet and buried her face in her skirt as her mother put an arm round her as well.

'Can't you even look after the children properly,' Linnet said, tight-lipped, to Kevern.

'I'm doing my best.'

'Which clearly isn't good enough.'

'Christ!'

'And will you stop swearing.'

'I'll swear in my own home if I fucking well wants to!' he retorted.

She glared at him. He, balanced on his crutches, glared back.

'We want to be with you, Ma,' Morwenna said.

'But it's raining outside. You don't want to get wet.'

'Don't care.'

'Take them with you, let them get soaked,' Kevern snarled.

'I'll do nothing of the sort. They're staying indoors today, and that's that.'

'It's boring looking after the children,' Kevern declared petulantly.

'That's all you're fit for any more,' Linnet taunted him.

Kevern went white. 'Bitch!'

'Don't bitch me, it's not my fault you're a cripple hopping about on one leg. The blame for that rests entirely on your shoulders. Yours and yours alone.'

'It was an accident—'

'Because you were stinking drunk to the point you didn't even know you were on a railway line.'

'A working man's entitled to a drink,' he protested.

'A drink yes, but not to get himself hit by a stupid train.'

'It was an accident,' he repeated lamely.

The contempt she felt for him showed plainly on her face. How she'd come to loathe him, loathe him for what he'd done to her and the children. Useless now, that's what he was, totally useless.

'I'm going to bed. The pain in my leg's killing me. That's the only place where it eases a little,' he said.

'Then go! I'll manage somehow.'

'You're heartless,' he hissed.

'And you're a fool. Now go. Get out of my sight.'

'I'm hungry, Ma,' Tamsin sobbed.

Kevern was about to say he was too, then thought better of it. He hopped off to bed, filled with self-pity.

'There's no other way. You'll have to hire a labourer,' Roxanne said.

'That's what I've been saying,' Linnet agreed.

'Can't do that. Can't afford one,' Kevern retorted from his chair.

Roxanne sighed. 'You'll have to, that's all. Linnet simply can't cope on her own.'

'You do at Cobwebs.'

'I don't have two small children and a husband to see to. That's the difference.'

Kevern defiantly folded his arms. 'Can't afford no labourer. Tis out of the question.'

Linnet put her hands on the table and slumped forward. Her entire body shook with a combination of anger and frustration.

'There's no use going on like that,' Kevern told her. 'Anyway, don't impress me none at all.'

Cripple or not, Roxanne was tempted to slap him hard. Couldn't he take on board that the farm was too much for Linnet who'd aged appallingly since his accident. She looked more like fifty than twenty-seven.

Kevern rubbed his leg. 'And if you tries to go behind my back I'll just sack whoever you does hire. I'm still the man and head of this family after all. Anyone from round here will acknowledge that.'

He was right, Roxanne thought. Anyone they did hire would. That was the awful thing.

'I've another idea,' she said. 'Why not take on a young maid to help Linnet. You could easily pay for her board and lodging plus a little something per week.'

'Hmmh,' Kevern murmured thoughtfully.

'A strong and willing maid would be almost as good as a labourer.'

'She could take and fetch Morwenna from school for a start,' Linnet said hopefully.

'Board and lodgings,' Kevern mused, fancying a young maid round the house.

'And a little something in her hand every week,' Roxanne added.

Kevern nodded his assent. 'We'll do that then.'

'Thank God,' breathed Linnet, relieved.

'Leave it to me. I'll arrange everything,' Roxanne stated.

Which she did. Cara Weale, plumpish and plain, much to Kevern's disappointment, took up residence with the Stonemans the following week.

Roxanne arrived back from St Petroc to find a note pushed under her door. It was from Miles saying he'd called, but she was out. His latest painting was finished at long last and if she stopped by the cottage he'd be delighted to show it to her. She resolved to go over straight away.

India was hanging washing on the line when she drove up. India's hair, normally piled high on her head, was hanging free and blowing in the wind.

'It's a grand day for drying clothes,' Roxanne commented as she got down.

'That's what I thought.'

'I had a note from Miles saying his painting's finished.'

'So he said. You'll find him in the studio which is round the back. I'll put the kettle on when I'm finished here.'

Polly and Jonathan appeared to welcome Roxanne and Bobby with whom they immediately started playing. Roxanne left Bobby with them as she made her way to the back of the cottage, curious, as she'd been since meeting Miles, to see his studio.

There were several outbuildings, but she had no difficulty in recognizing the one converted to a studio on account of the large window he'd installed.

'It's Roxanne,' she called out, knocking on the door.

'Come in.'

As she walked in, she glanced about, thinking that Miles was certainly not a messy worker. Somehow she'd had the idea that all artists were untidy in their studios.

Several long shelves lined one whitewashed wall and these were loaded with an assortment of pots, jars, brushes, tubes and small tins. An easel with a canvas on it stood in a prominent position before the window. The far wall had a number of paintings hanging on it while others were stacked against the same wall.

'Impressions?' he queried.

'Surprised,' she confessed.

'Oh?'

'You're very orderly.'

He frowned. 'Is that a condemnation or a criticism?'

'No, just surprises me that's all.'

She looked at the hanging paintings, varying in size, and studied them in turn. India was right, he was exceptionally talented. Each painting breathed life and vibrancy.

He came to stand beside her.

'What do you think?' he asked casually.

'I like them very much. Are all these going to be in your exhibition?'

He nodded.

'Plus the one you've just finished?'

'Plus the one I've just finished,' he confirmed. 'Do you want to see it?'

He went over to the easel and removed the cloth covering the canvas. 'There you are,' he smiled.

She was central to the painting, digging potatoes just as she'd been the day he'd sketched her. She was staring out of the painting as if someone had just spoken to her, or something had caught her attention.

'You ended up figuring more than I'd originally intended,' he said.

'Did I now?' she mused in reply.

'It happens that way occasionally.'

'It's certainly me,' she commented. 'No doubt about that at all.'

'Better than the sketches?'

'Much. I look so very . . . alive. Yes, that's it. Alive.'

He was delighted because that, of course, was what he'd been after. 'You're a good subject,' he said. 'I empathize with you.'

'Do you indeed,' she teased.

'That's why I'd like to do another study of you sometime. A full figure, not head and shoulders.'

She raised an eyebrow.

'I thought, perhaps in a music hall setting with you dressed as you used to be in your act.'

'I don't have any of those clothes left,' she informed him.

335

'We could find something suitable I'm sure. I'll look around when I'm in London.'

'Wouldn't that sort of thing be a departure for you?'

He shrugged. 'Yes, it would. But why not! There's no rule which says I have to concentrate on landscapes.'

'No rule at all,' she smiled.

He ran a hand through his hair. 'Do you agree then?'

'I don't see why I shouldn't. As long as it doesn't take up too much of my time. I do have a farm to run.'

'We could come to some arrangement.'

'Then fine.'

'Good,' he enthused.

Miles picked up the cloth and threw it back over the easel.

'When are you off to London?' Roxanne asked.

'Next week.'

'And how long will you be gone for?'

'That depends. I really don't know.'

'Well, good luck with the exhibition, I'm sure your paintings will be a big success.'

'I just hope they sell, that's all. We need the money.'

'Tight, is it?'

'We live mainly on what India contributes. She has a private income, though not a large one. But enough to keep us generally ticking over.'

'But you have sold in the past?'

'Oh yes! I've been lucky.'

'I'd say luck had nothing to do with it,' she declared softly. 'Talent more like.'

'That's kind of you.'

'Not kind, but a fact.'

How beautiful he was, she thought. A strange word perhaps to apply to a man, but he was. His fine-boned face and slightly aquiline nose reminded her of pictures she'd once seen in a magazine of ancient Greeks and Romans. A sensitive face belonging to a highly intelligent and emotional man. On someone else it might have been weak, but not with Miles. It hinted at inner reserves of great strength and determination.

'What's so special about Roxanne that you want to do a full figure study of her?' India inquired casually.

'As I told her, she's a marvellous subject. I empathize with her and you know how important that is.'

'Hmmh!' India murmured thoughtfully.

336

The tone of her voice made him glance at her. 'What does that mean?'

'Nothing,' she replied with a shake of her head. 'Nothing at all.'

'India?'

'Well . . .' She trailed off.

Miles's expression became one of irritation and annoyance. 'There's nothing going on between Roxanne and myself if that's what's worrying you.'

'I should hope not!'

'She's simply a good subject, that's all.'

India, whose hair was hanging down in preparation for bed, caught a strand of it and wound it round her finger. 'I wish I could trust you,' she murmured.

'You can.'

'Can I?'

'You damn well know you can!' he exploded. 'Now stop this nonsense. You're letting your imagination run away with you again.'

'Again?' she queried softly, a haunted look in her eyes.

'I never slept with Hilary Catchpole and certainly don't intend sleeping with Roxanne. I swear on all that's holy on both counts.'

India bit the finger with the hair still wound round it. She knew he'd slept with Hilary. She'd never been able to prove it but all her instincts told her he had.

Miles sighed. 'I won't paint Roxanne if it bothers you. I'll tell her I've changed my mind. She's going to be terribly disappointed though.'

'No, paint her. You've promised and I don't want you going back on your word on my account.'

'Are you certain?'

'I couldn't stand it if . . .'

'There is nothing going on between us, India. She's a friend, to the pair of us. Nothing more.'

India went over to Miles, knelt down and placed her head on his lap. 'Then I'm certain. I'm just being an old silly.'

He bent and tenderly kissed her head. 'That you are. And you'd better not mention such suspicions to Roxanne, she'd be appalled.'

'I love you so much, Miles.'

'And I love you sweetest. With all my heart.'

She adored it when he called her sweetest. It made her melt inside.

Miles raised her head and kissed her again, this time on the lips. His irritation and annoyance vanished as their tongues slowly, and sensuously, intertwined.

Buster's goats were back in the same field as before. Roxanne stared at them, incensed. When she examined the fence she discovered that they'd got in through the same section as before. Anger erupted in her. She'd thought the business with Ted Buster was over and done with.

'Damn the sodding man,' she muttered as she began the arduous task of rounding up the goats which had done considerable damage to her broccoli.

When she'd finally succeeded in returning them to Buster's land and temporarily fixed the fence, she returned to Cobwebs and hitched up Dingle the pony. She would have this out with Buster, face to face.

Mrs Buster answered her knock; it was the first time she'd been to the Buster household. She disliked the woman on sight.

'I want a word with your husband,' Roxanne declared.

Mrs Buster sniffed. 'Who are you?'

'You know damn well who I am. I'm Roxanne Hawkins who owns Cobwebs.'

Mrs Buster sniffed again. 'Come to cause trouble, have you?'

Roxanne ignored that. 'Where's your husband?'

'So happens he's indoors.'

'Then would you be so kind as to fetch him.'

She was kept waiting on the doorstep for so long that she began to think Buster wasn't going to put in an appearance. But eventually he did, wiping his hands on the sides of his trousers.

'What do you want? I'm having me dinner,' he demanded nastily.

'I'm here about the goats.'

He smirked. 'What about they?'

'They're back in my field.'

Buster shrugged. 'Tain't my fault. You should keep better fences.'

'The fence has been pulled down deliberately.'

He wagged a finger at her. 'You'd better be careful about making false accusations. I'll see my solicitor otherwise.'

'Bugger your solicitor,' she retorted. 'I've just one thing to say to you, Mr Buster. If those goats get back on my land again I'll shoot every last one of them stone dead. And you'd better believe

338

I mean that, because I do. Just as I'll shoot any prowlers who come sneaking round, I'll shoot those bloody goats.'

'They be expensive beasts,' he declared, aghast at her threat.

'Hard cheese.'

He still had bad breath, she thought, recoiling as a whiff assailed her nose.

'Get off my property before I takes a gun to *you*!' he exclaimed, wagging his finger again.

'I'll be delighted to.'

And with that she whirled and stalked away, as Buster's front door slammed shut behind her.

She would shoot the goats too, she told herself. She'd hate doing it, but would if that's what it took to stop Buster's harassment.

Roxanne paused to take a breather; she had been forking hay. With a shock she realized she hadn't thought about Harry in ages. It was as if, and this was an even greater shock, he'd been wiped clean from her heart and mind.

She didn't love Harry any more. Her love for him had died, something she'd imagined would never happen. Harry was in the past and, if not exactly forgotten, reduced to no more than a memory.

At long last she was free of Harry Bright. He was no longer important to her.

'Free,' she said, and smiled.

She returned to forking hay with renewed gusto.

'Free,' she repeated to herself several times during the rest of that day.

Chapter Twenty-Two

'What's wrong with you?' Linnet demanded, having just emerged from the shippon to find Kevern slumped against the building.

'It's me leg. The pain's awful,' he groaned in reply.

She stared at him, face devoid of sympathy. 'Can you manage on your own?'

'I think so.'

'Right then.' And with that she made to stride off.

'Linnet!'

She halted, and turned. 'What?'

'When I gets in will ee make a nice cup of tea?'

'I'm busy. No time for tea making at the moment,' she answered, her voice cold and hard.

'Then sod you!'

'Sod yourself,' she muttered, and walked away.

Kevern gazed balefully at her retreating back. The heartless bitch! And him in such agony too. It was the first occasion he'd ventured out in over a week, and it would be longer before he did so again.

Then he thought of Cara who should be inside. He would ask her, she was always obliging. Good girl that.

He hopped towards the house, cursing with each excruciating hop.

Miles stared out over a field of golden blooms. 'That's a wonderful sight,' he declared to Roxanne. 'A veritable sea of daffodils.'

'These are ones I'm growing for bulbs as I once explained to you. Some of them I'll be replanting, the remainder are bound for Covent Garden.'

'Was it a good crop this year?'

'Excellent. Even better than last.'

'You'll be pleased then.'

'Delighted.'

'A sea of daffodils,' he repeated, reaching into a pocket for his sketch book.

'Do you want me to leave you alone if you're going to sketch?' she asked.

'Yes . . . I mean no. I mean, I want to talk to you first.'

'Oh?'

'Would you be available soon to pose for me as you agreed some while ago?'

That took her by surprise. 'It's been so long I was beginning to think you'd forgotten all about it, or changed your mind.'

He shook his head. 'I've had other projects on the go, besides this is your busiest time of the year. But now all your cutting is done I thought I'd come over and ask.'

'What about a dress?'

'I bought one in London. Didn't I mention it?'

'No, you didn't.'

'Must have slipped my mind.'

She doubted that. 'Miles?'

'What?'

'Is something wrong?'

'Wrong?' he queried, momentarily startled. 'Do I give that impression?'

'Yes seem so . . . off me lately.'

That flustered him. 'I'm sorry, I certainly didn't mean to give that impression.'

'Have I offended you in some way? Is that why you've been avoiding me?'

A flush crept on to his cheeks, he felt quite discomfited. 'There's been no offence, I assure you.' The reason he'd been avoiding her, and dismissing their friendship, was because of India.

'That's all right then.'

He shifted from one foot to the other, refusing to meet her gaze. 'I should have made more of an effort to be neighbourly, it's just that I've been so tied up. Painting from morning to night, hardly leaving the studio. It gets a grip on me like that sometimes.'

341

'Are you sure you want to paint me?' she asked gently.

'Of course.' He hesitated, then added, 'I wouldn't have brought the subject up again if I wasn't.'

That quashed any of Roxanne's doubts. 'Then we'll go ahead whenever you wish.'

He took a deep breath. 'Tell you what. Why don't you come to lunch this Sunday? We can discuss it further then.'

'Fine.'

'And I can show you the dress; it's hanging in the studio. It's a deep blue colour which should suit you.'

'What does India think of the dress?'

'She hasn't seen it. I hung it up but haven't removed it from the paper it's wrapped in.'

'It'll probably need ironing.'

'I hadn't thought of that,' he frowned. 'I'll get India on the job.'

Roxanne would have preferred to iron it herself, but didn't say so. 'I'd better get on. I'll leave you to your sketching.'

'Till Sunday.'

'Till Sunday.'

When she was some distance away she glanced back to find that he hadn't started sketching but was staring out over the gently nodding blooms instead.

He really was quite beautiful, she reflected again. A Roman or Greek statue come to life.

India was a very lucky woman.

'It's the mister, he's running me ragged with his demands,' Cara complained to a grim-faced Linnet. 'Twenty times a day and more he's banging on the ceiling wanting something or other.'

As if to emphasize Cara's point there was a loud rapping from above.

'Leave it to me, I'll sort him out,' Linnet said.

'Thanks, missus. I don't like making a fuss you understand, but it's just too much.'

Linnet, who'd become fond of Cara, and heavily reliant on her, patted the girl on the shoulder. 'I'll speak to him now.'

'Why aren't you in they fields?' Kevern asked querulously when Linnet entered their bedroom.

'What's that to you as long as things get done.'

'Onions needs planted. You should be doing that.'

'I'll plant the onions when I get round to it. In the meantime will you stop annoying Cara.'

'Ain't annoying her!' he protested.

'Oh yes you are. You're forever banging that crutch wanting this, that or whatever.'

'I gets lonely,' he stated petulantly.

'Then get up and come downstairs.'

'The only relief for me leg is in bed when me leg's straight out.'

Linnet sighed with anger and exasperation. 'Be that as it may, the banging's going to stop or we'll lose Cara. And that I won't have! I need her too much.'

'I'll bang if I want to,' Kevern declared defiantly.

'Then bang away, no-one will answer you. That's what's going to happen if you keep on making a pest of yourself.'

There was something else she'd been meaning to say for some time, and decided to do so now. 'One more thing, I'm moving into another bedroom as from tonight. I can't get my proper rest with you tossing and turning all the time. I haven't had a decent night's sleep since you came home from the hospital.'

He was appalled. 'You can't do that, Linnet.'

'Oh but I can, and will.'

'But what about . . .'

'That's over between us, Kevern,' she interjected harshly. 'I don't know why I've allowed it to continue knowing the way I feel about you.'

'But I can't go without that!' he wailed.

'You'll just have to, that's all there is to it.'

'You don't mean it, Linnet. Tell me you don't?'

'I mean it all right. In fact I've never meant anything more in my life. And stop bloody well banging!' she repeated before slamming the bedroom door behind her.

She paused and took a deep breath, smiling thinly when she heard a muted, strangulated sob coming from her husband. A husband who from that point onwards would be hers in name only. On that score she was utterly determined.

'Well, what do you think?' Miles queried, having ripped the wrapping paper away to reveal the dress he'd brought from London.

The dress had a low scoop at the bodice with full, elbow-length sleeves. It was gathered at the waist to fall away in folds that would end a little below the knee.

He'd been right about the colour, Roxanne thought. It would

343

set off her ash-blonde hair perfectly, while at the same time accentuating the startling blueness of her eyes.

'That must have cost,' she commented.

He grinned. 'A fair amount. But what's money when it's for your art?'

Roxanne removed the dress from where it was hanging to hold it against herself smoothing down the front.

'Why don't you put it on? I'll wait outside until you're ready.'

When he was gone she stripped off her blouse and skirt, then slipped into the dress which was fractionally large for her. That would be easily remedied, she thought.

'Miles!' she called out.

He entered quickly, to stop short, his eyes shining. 'Stunning,' he breathed.

She twirled round.

'Absolutely stunning,' he repeated. 'I've got ideas for some props I want to use. A few bits and pieces I'll build on for the background.'

'Oh, I say!' exclaimed India whose appearance in the studio neither Roxanne nor Miles had heard. 'Don't you look gorgeous.'

'It'll do nicely. I'm pleased,' Miles nodded.

'Lunch is ready when you two are,' India smiled at them.

'I don't know about anyone else, but I'm starving,' Miles declared.

'We'll leave you to get changed again,' India said, taking Miles by the hand and squeezing it.

'You can begin to dish up, I won't be long,' Roxanne said.

Miles couldn't have made a better choice of dress, Roxanne thought as she rehung it. Wasn't he clever!

India gave a loud, almost raucous, laugh and clapped her hands with glee. 'Oh, that is funny Roxanne, quite priceless.'

'And true too, according to Billy Christmas.'

India wiped a tear from her eye. 'I've never heard anything so hilarious. I'll be laughing on and off for the rest of the day whenever I think of it.'

India had called in with the children and Roxanne had insisted they stay for tea and crumpets. The pair of them then proceeded to have a right old natter.

'More tea?' Roxanne offered. All the crumpets had been eaten, which was why Jonathan and Polly had scampered outside to play with Bobby.

'I shouldn't really . . .'

'Of course you'll have some,' Roxanne insisted. 'Waste not want not was how I was brought up.'

India beamed at Roxanne. 'I do adore these chats of ours. Life would be lonely without them.'

'You have Miles,' Roxanne replied in surprise.

'Of course. But you know what I mean, it's just not the same talking to a man.'

Roxanne understood perfectly. 'As I've said before, come any time you want. You're always welcome.'

'Except when you're up to your eyes in it.'

Roxanne grinned ruefully. 'There is that to consider.'

'And you work such long hours, and so hard.'

'It isn't that bad when you enjoy it, which I do.'

'That's what Miles always says. He doesn't view painting as work but a pleasure and privilege.'

India spooned sugar into her cup. 'Know something, I think he's contemplating doing a portrait of me after you.'

'Oh, that would be wonderful!' Roxanne enthused.

'Not that he's actually said anything. But he's dropped a few hints.'

'Why don't you broach the subject yourself?' Roxanne suggested. 'Let him know how keen you are.'

'I might. I just might,' India mused.

'I would if I was you.'

When she was leaving India touched Roxanne lightly on the arm. 'It was tremendous, as always. Thank you.' She then kissed Roxanne affectionately on the cheek.

'Take care.'

'And you.'

She definitely would broach the subject with Miles, India decided en route home. But not yet. She'd wait till he'd nearly finished Roxanne's. That would be the best time.

'Don't move!' Miles snapped.

Standing in front of a black drape in his studio, Roxanne sighed. 'I'm getting cramp,' she explained.

'Eh?'

'I said I'm getting cramp.'

That sunk in. 'Oh, I am sorry. Do you want to sit down for a bit?'

'Please.'

'Then help yourself.' He waved vaguely at a nearby stool, then concentrated again on the canvas before him.

345

'How's it coming on?' she asked when she'd stretched and perched. So far she hadn't been allowed even a glimpse of his work.

'All right,' he murmured.

She massaged herself. 'I really must go shortly. I have the animals to attend.'

He glanced across at her, his expression one of acute disappointment. 'Damn! Do you have to?'

'I'm afraid so.'

'Just a little longer?' he pleaded.

She smiled inwardly. How could she deny such an earnest and heartfelt request? He looked like a little boy under threat of having his favourite toy taken away from him.

'Only a short while then,' she conceded.

He flashed her a brilliant smile. 'Thanks, Roxanne.'

How she loved these sittings, she thought. He wasn't always as distracted as he was now. Sometimes they had marvellous conversations from which they'd learned a great deal about each other and their pasts. Although she said nothing regarding Harry; that episode remained her secret.

He laid his brush aside and wiped his hands on a rag. 'A few more visits should see it done,' he declared.

That pleased her, but also filled her with sadness. For once he'd finished his painting, it would mean the end of her sittings. But every good thing has to come to an end and it had been great fun while it lasted.

'When you're ready,' he said, picking up his brush again.

She resumed her standing position and a few seconds later he set to once more.

'What hints have I been dropping? I haven't dropped any that I'm aware of,' Miles asked India, mystified.

She regarded him coldly, eyes glinting with anger. 'Oh yes you have. Don't try and deny it.'

'But I haven't. Honestly!' he protested.

'You did. You did!' she insisted.

Fury was mounting in India, increasing with every passing second. She'd been so convinced that he intended painting her portrait. She'd been absolutely certain of it.

'And what's wrong with me?' she demanded. 'What's Roxanne got that I haven't?'

Miles was stumped. 'There's nothing wrong with you. I just felt the . . . wish to paint Roxanne, that's all.'

India snorted.

'I'm sorry if you're upset—'

'Upset! I'm fucking furious.'

'Don't use that sort of language, please. It's so unladylike,' he chided.

'I'll use any language I fucking well want!' she retorted, tugging at her hair and dislodging the tortoiseshell comb holding it up. Her hair tumbled down.

God! Miles thought. He knew how this was going to develop. 'What did I say that gave you that idea?' he asked softly.

'Things. I can't remember exactly what.'

'Anyway,' he pointed out, 'I have sketched you so often . . .'

'Sketched, but never done a proper portrait.'

'I don't do many of those, you're aware of that,' he argued.

'So why Roxanne? Why her?'

'I've told you, she's a sympathetic subject. I empathize with her.'

'Oh I see! I'm not sympathetic and you don't empathize with me, is that it?'

Miles sighed with exasperation.

'*Do* you fancy her? Is that what it's all really about?'

'I do not fancy her, I swear. I like her, enjoy her company and find her easy to talk to. As do you. But I don't fancy her. You can be assured of that.'

India suddenly snatched up a cup and threw it against a wall, smashing it to smithereens.

'Feel better now?' Miles smiled thinly.

Her answer was to snatch up the saucer and hurl that against the wall as well.

'India, this is getting out of all proportion. You're being silly.'

She sucked in a deep breath. Now he was patronizing her.

'If you want your portrait done that badly then I'll be happy to oblige,' Miles offered.

'Like hell! That's the last thing I want now. I wouldn't sit for you if you went down on your bended knees and begged.'

Maybe he should go for a walk, Miles thought grimly. Let her cool off a bit. Or move into the studio? No, not the studio. He couldn't risk her following him and chucking things round there.

'Again, I'm sorry India. But you must have been imagining . . .'

'Imagining! That's what you always accuse me of,' she screeched at him. 'Like Hilary Catchpole, it was always my imagination.'

347

He'd had enough of this, Miles decided, rising.

'Where do you think you're going?'

'Out.'

'Where?'

'For a stroll.'

'It's dark.'

'That doesn't matter. Besides, there's a full moon.'

When he was gone India collapsed into a chair and sobbed. Was she being silly? Except she'd so set her heart on that portrait. Been so convinced . . .

If only she could be sure he really did love her. If only there had never been Hilary Catchpole.

'Fuck!' she swore and burst into floods of tears.

Chapter Twenty-Three

Roxanne had never seen Linnet in such a state. Her sister was beside herself. 'It can't be bad as all that, surely?' she queried.

'It is,' Linnet replied, shaking her head in despair. 'I just can't go on. I can't.'

'Kevern?'

'The man's a millstone round my neck, and he's going to be with me till my dying day. Which will be sooner than later the way things are.'

Roxanne went to Linnet and took her thin body into her arms. 'Doesn't he get out of bed at all?'

'Only to use the pot. Apart from that he simply lies there muttering and cursing and God knows what. I swear he's gone out of his mind. Completely round the bend.'

'Oh my darling,' Roxanne sympathized, stroking Linnet's lank and greasy hair that had recently become prematurely grey.

'And it's the farm as well. I tries me best, but it's too much for me. Even with Cara's help, and I don't know what I'd do without that girl, it's too much.'

'There there,' Roxanne murmured, thinking that Linnet had lost so much weight. There was nothing left of her except skin and bones.

'Are you eating properly?' Roxanne probed.

'I tries. But often a few morsels is enough.'

'You must eat more,' Roxanne chided.

'I got no appetite, that's the trouble. It's worry that's doing it. Worry about the farm, the crops, the beasts. Everything.' Linnet glanced up at the ceiling. 'The only thing I don't worry about is him up there. I just wish he would die.'

349

'We've got to get you sorted out, Linnet. You're on the verge of collapse.'

'It's all graft Roxanne, never-ending graft. From first thing in the morning till last thing at night. Graft, graft, graft!'

Roxanne pursed her lips in anxiety. It had been some while since she'd called on Linnet and the change in her sister both shocked and alarmed her. This was a woman close to the end of her tether.

Linnet began to weep. 'I ain't got the strength or fibre you have. I thought I did, but I haven't. And every day it all gets worse with me seemingly accomplishing less than the day before.'

'Do you have a hanky?'

Linnet shook her head.

'Where can I get one?'

'Upstairs, in me bedroom. Not the one I shared with Kevern, but the one across the landing.'

This was a surprise, something Linnet hadn't mentioned before. 'You've moved out of his bed?'

'I had to, Roxanne. I couldn't stand it no longer. His filthy fingers on me, him with his one leg grunting and heaving. It made me want to be sick.'

Roxanne could well understand that. 'You sit down and I'll get that hanky,' she replied.

Upstairs, Kevern's door was open. He was lying propped up in bed by several pillows. 'It's you,' he snarled when he saw her.

She stared hard at him, loathing him for what he was and what he'd done to Linnet.

He suddenly waved a hand at her. 'Fuck off! Get out my sight you bitch.'

'Nothing would give me more pleasure,' she answered calmly.

He snarled again, baring his teeth like an animal.

She found a hanky and took it back down to Linnet who was still crying. 'The man's a monster,' she declared.

'I told you, he's gone out of his head.'

'It mustn't happen to you,' Roxanne counselled, handing Linnet the hanky. 'Whatever your problems we'll overcome them together. There's nothing that can't be solved. You'll see.'

Linnet wiped her tear-stained face. 'I need to get the tatters in, but haven't the strength to plough.'

'Then I'll do it for you. What else needs done?'

Linnet reeled off a list of tasks.

'You're simply going to have to get a labourer,' Roxanne stated when Linnet reached the end of the list.

'Kevern won't budge on that. Says we can't afford one, and he's right. With me producing less and less, cash is getting tighter and tighter. I didn't even go to the market last Saturday because I had nothing spare to sell.'

Roxanne considered the business of the money. 'I'll pay for the labourer to begin with,' she proposed, holding up a hand when Linnet opened her mouth to protest. 'I insist, and won't hear any arguments to the contrary. I've done well out of my daffs this year and can afford it. And if we get the right man, which I'll ensure you do, he'll be paying his own way, and more, before long.'

'But what of Kevern? Remember what he said about still being head of the family.'

'There are ways to fix him,' Roxanne replied, steel in her voice. 'If he doesn't get out of bed that means he's totally reliant on you and Cara, for his food amongst other things. Just tell him if he doesn't agree, or causes trouble, then he can lie there and starve for his pains.'

She took a deep breath. 'And if the sod does get out of bed don't cook for him. Let him do it himself. Refuse point blank to do that or anything else.'

Linnet smiled. 'That's brilliant, Roxanne. Why didn't I think of it?'

'Maybe because you're too nice.'

'And you're *not*!' Linnet laughed.

'That's better.'

'You know,' Linnet mused, 'that's the first time I've laughed in . . . Well so long I can't even remember.'

'Would you prefer if I spoke to Kevern? Or will you do it yourself?'

'I'll do it myself. And you know what?'

'What?'

'I'll enjoy every minute of it.'

Now it was Roxanne's turn to laugh.

Linnet rose and stuffed the hanky into a pocket of the long white apron she had on. 'And there's no time like the present. The bugger's face should be a picture.'

'Which field do you want ploughed?'

'Strole.'

'I'll make a start on it right away.'

'Thanks, Roxanne.'

Roxanne kissed her sister on the cheek. 'And you must eat more. Force yourself if you have to, but eat more.'

351

'I'll try.'

'You won't just try, you'll do it.'

'Bully,' Linnet teased.

It took several weeks, but Roxanne finally succeeded in hiring a labourer by the name of Tod Ferrers to go and work for the Stonemans. Like Cara, he too was to prove invaluable.

'Well?' Miles asked.

Roxanne stared at the now completed painting, this her first sight of it. She was standing centre stage in front of a back drop depicting a London scene. The view was from the stalls so that the proscenium arch was included, bringing in red plush curtains on either side of the stage. The hem of her dress was swinging slightly, to reveal a number of frilly petticoats which Miles had added as she hadn't been wearing anything of the sort while posing.

'I don't know what to say.'

He frowned. 'You don't like it?'

'No, quite the opposite. It's taken my breath away. It's . . . fantastic and so lifelike that if the me in the painting suddenly burst into song I wouldn't be at all surprised.'

Miles relaxed and grinned. 'I must confess I'm rather pleased with it myself.'

'You have every right to be. I know nothing about art, therefore I can't comment on that level, but to repeat myself, for my money it's fantastic. A painting you deserve to be extremely proud of.'

'I've decided it'll take pride of place in my next exhibition. In fact I'll make it the centre-piece.'

Roxanne was thrilled. 'And when is this exhibition?'

'Shortly. A letter arrived this morning asking me to participate in a three-man show.'

'Oh Miles, that's wonderful. Where will it take place?'

'London again.'

'And how long will you be gone for this time?'

He shrugged. 'I don't know. These things vary.'

She gazed again at the painting, thinking how wonderfully he'd portrayed her, not just her features and form, but the essential her. Her very essence, her soul.

'I think this calls for a celebratory cup of tea,' he said. 'I'm afraid we've nothing stronger in the cottage.'

'Tea will be fine.'

She watched as he recovered the canvas which had yet to be varnished and framed.

'Thank you again for modelling for me,' he said.

'It was my pleasure.'

'Perhaps . . . if it wouldn't bore you too much, you might model for me on another occasion?'

'Any time you like,' she replied.

'In the daffodil fields I thought. Among the blooms.'

'Any time you like,' she repeated.

'It's settled then.'

Roxanne felt incredibly happy and elated as they left the studio together, the two of them chatting about his forthcoming exhibition.

'Roxanne! Roxanne!'

Roxanne paused in her hoeing and turned round to see India excitedly waving a paper above her head.

'What's up?' she demanded when India reached her.

'Miles has had a review in *The Times* which is most complimentary.'

Roxanne accepted the sheet of newspaper and began to read it. The review was indeed complimentary, and of considerable length, declaring Miles to be a young artist of great promise.

'You must be pleased,' Roxanne smiled when she finished it.

'I'm ecstatic, as I know Miles must be. This is his first ever major review.'

'Any news about when he's coming home?' Roxanne inquired.

'Late Friday. That's what he said in the note that came with the review.'

'Has he sold well?'

'That's the other good news, absolutely everything. Apparently your painting was the first to go.'

Roxanne was delighted.

'I was thinking, why don't we all get together at the weekend? A picnic maybe. The children would adore that.'

'How about down on the seashore? Then the children can have a swim. Or at least a paddle.'

'Wonderful!' India cried, clapping her hands together.

'I'll bring some goodies over with me and we'll go on from your cottage.'

'What day?'

'Sunday afternoon.'

'Perfect,' India agreed.

Roxanne glanced up at the brilliant blue, cloudless sky,

dominated by a fat, yellow sun. It was perfect mid-summer weather, an ideal time for a picnic.

'If this heat keeps up I'll have a paddle myself,' she said to India.

'We all can.'

Roxanne looked thoughtful. 'I'm becoming a bit concerned about this drought. It just seems to be going on and on. How's your well?'

'I don't know,' India replied slowly. 'I've never thought to check.'

'You'll probably find the level's dropped quite a bit. It happens when there's no rain over an extended period. My own has dropped to about a third of what it is normally.'

'Are you saying it might dry up altogether?'

'It is possible if this weather continues.' She glanced again at the blazing sun. 'If there isn't . . .' She gazed out over the field of broccoli they were in. 'I can say goodbye to this lot for a start. Though if the worst comes to the worst I'm lucky enough to be able to hand-water at least some of my crops from The White.'

'Oh yes, your stream.'

'It's never been known to dry up apparently.'

'You've got me worried now,' India declared.

'Well don't. You're always welcome to take water from The White whenever you like.'

'Thanks,' India replied, smiling her gratitude.

'Now about Sunday . . .'

They fell to discussing the details of their intended picnic.

'I'm just so disorganized. That's part of my trouble,' Linnet said.

'Then what you must do is draw up a plan, what's to be done, when and by whom. And you must keep to that plan. That way you'll know where you are at all times.'

Linnet stared at Roxanne. 'A plan?'

'Of course,' Roxanne replied patiently. 'A plan of all the chores, tasks, and the like. That'll stop you being so muddled.'

'It's a good idea,' Linnet nodded approvingly. 'I've been relying on Tod quite a lot, he's a dandy worker, don't get me wrong, but just not used to thinking for himself.'

'Why should he be when he's been taking orders all his life. There's a huge difference between that and being in charge.'

'Don't I know it!' Linnet sighed.

Linnet was beginning to put on some weight, Roxanne noted.

354

It appeared her sister was taking her advice and eating more. 'The other thing is,' Roxanne went on, 'I want you to go into St Petroc and have your hair done.'

'My hair done!' Linnet exclaimed, bemused.

'Quite frankly, it's a disgrace. Have it washed and cut. You'll feel a lot better afterwards.'

'I haven't got time for . . .'

'Make it!' Roxanne commanded. She then plonked several coins on the kitchen table. 'My treat. It's high time you got a bit of self-respect back and having your hair done will be the beginning.'

'Self-respect?' Linnet mused.

'That's correct. Something no-one should be without. I blame Kevern in the first instance, and your workload in the second. Whatever, you've let yourself go mentally as well as physically, which is going to stop right now.'

Linnet gathered the coins into her hand and gazed at them. 'I suppose I haven't taken as good care of myself recently as I might.'

'Things will change for the better from here on in, I promise,' Roxanne stated quietly.

'Know something?'

'What?'

'I felt dreadful when you arrived. Beaten, on my knees. Now I'm full of hope. Thanks to you.'

'That's my girl,' Roxanne approved. 'More like the sister I used to know before she married that monster upstairs.'

Roxanne took a deep breath. 'Now about that plan, get a paper and a pencil . . .'

When Roxanne came to leave Linnet was already transformed.

'The water's freezing,' Miles complained, having been cajoled by India to join Roxanne and the children paddling. Having taken off his shoes and socks, he'd rolled his trousers up to just below his knees.

'Don't be such a big softie!' Roxanne chided him, laughing.

'I'm nothing of the sort.'

'Oh yes you are, a big softie.' She turned to the children. 'What's Daddy?'

'A big softie!' they choroused in unison.

India lay stretched out on a rug, a parasol in the crook of her arm to shade her from the fierce sun, watching them. Should she go paddling? she wondered.

355

'Don't splash,' Miles warned Jonathan who, impishly, proceeded to do just that, scooping up several handfuls of water and throwing them at Miles.

Polly shrieked, thinking this game enormous fun made even funnier by her father's outraged expression.

'I said don't splash!' Miles roared.

Roxanne couldn't resist it. 'Why not?' she said, and repeated Jonathan's actions.

Miles held up his hands to ward off the water flying in his direction. 'Hell's bells!' he exclaimed.

'A little water won't hurt anyone,' Roxanne teased.

'Right then!' Miles began to retaliate, scooping up handfuls of water and chucking them first at Roxanne, then the children.

It developed into a battle royal with Roxanne, Jonathan and Polly ranged against Miles whose initial outrage had given way to glee at getting his own back.

Roxanne gasped as water hit her full in the face, temporarily blinding her.

'Serves you right,' Miles declared, chucking more which again hit her full in the face.

Roxanne staggered backwards and nearly fell, but, at the last moment, arms flailing, managed to maintain her balance.

She returned to the attack with a vengeance, scoop after scoop of water flying at Miles till his front was soaked.

India smiled to herself. She'd stay put, thank you very much. Nothing would tempt her into the sea with these shenanigans going on. Luckily they'd brought towels with them, though they'd need an entire change of clothes after this.

Polly was jumping up and down, completely over-excited.

Miles grabbed Roxanne and held her immobilized. 'Enough!' he yelled. His eyes bored into hers and suddenly he frowned, realizing the depth of his feelings. India had been right all along, he did fancy her. But more than that, it wasn't purely physical. It was emotional as well.

He abruptly released her, shaken by this revelation, and promptly waded ashore leaving Roxanne, feeling slightly bewildered, behind.

'It was a wonderful day,' India commented later that evening, glancing across at Miles, who was sitting opposite her, pretending to read an art journal, but really deep in thought. 'The children thoroughly enjoyed themselves.'

'Hmmh,' Miles grunted.

356

'I kept wondering, watching you and Roxanne in the water together . . .'

Miles suddenly eyed his wife keenly. Had she noticed something? That look on his face might have given the game away.

'She's so beautiful I can't understand why she has never married.'

Relief surged through Miles. 'I've no idea,' he muttered in reply, returning to his journal.

'Has there been anyone?' India probed. 'I thought she might have told you during one of your modelling sessions.'

Miles didn't glance up. 'I believe there was a chap once, but it didn't work out. That's all I know.'

'Odd for her to remain a spinster though. Don't you think? She must have had lots of admirers.'

'I've never considered it.'

Why did India keep prattling on about Roxanne? he inwardly fumed. Roxanne was the last person he wanted to talk about.

His earlier revelation had rattled him to his very core, and since then he hadn't been able to get Roxanne out of his thoughts. Even now, staring at his journal, he could see her face laughing, serious, teasing.

He was being ridiculous, he chided himself. He was a happily married man with two adorable children. Settled, content; a man who, despite the problems they had from time to time, loved his wife.

Or did he still? The Hilary Catchpole issue and all that had gone with it had certainly dented their relationship. But not to the extent that he would ever leave India. Roxanne or no, that was unthinkable, utterly out of the question.

But the fact remained that he felt as he did about Roxanne. How on earth had that happened? He had no idea. He'd been totally unaware of his feelings towards her until those few moments in the sea when he'd held her tight.

God, he thought, what a mess.

Luckily Roxanne didn't feel the same about him. There had never been a glimmer or spark from her on that score. She saw him as a friend, nothing more. If she had, well, that would have complicated matters, might even have necessitated another move.

This was just something he was going to have to live with, he thought grimly. It would be hard, yet would have to be endured. There was nothing else for it.

'We must have another picnic soon,' India said.

Miles didn't reply.

357

'Did you hear me?'

'If you like.'

'The five of us again.'

Did he want that? Of course he did. At the same time . . .

'Miles?'

'Whatever you say,' he answered, still not glancing up.

A few minutes later he excused himself, claiming that he wanted to sort out a few bits and pieces in the studio. The truth was he didn't want to speak about Roxanne any more.

Roxanne straightened up, and groaned. This hand-watering was back breaking, even for someone like her who was used to hard graft.

The drought hadn't abated, and the previous week her well had run dry, while the Careys' was almost empty. Thank the Lord for The White, she'd have been in serious trouble without it. At least some of her crops could be saved rather than suffering a total loss.

She gazed across at the adjacent field where Buster's cows were attempting to graze amongst the bleached grass. They looked dreadful, and it wasn't hard to guess why: lack of water.

Poor beasts, she thought, how they must be suffering. Unless Buster managed to get water from somewhere, they were doomed. She considered that. It would be a disaster for Buster, which didn't concern her at all, but what a dreadful way for those animals to die.

She thought that if Buster had been a reasonable neighbour she'd have gone round and offered him access to The White. But why should she after what he'd done to her!

Roxanne sighed as one of the cows staggered. It was literally on its last legs, might not even last the night.

Suddenly she made up her mind. Damn Buster, she didn't care a fig for him, but why should his animals suffer just because he was such a bastard! It wasn't fair on them.

What she wouldn't do though was go to his house; if she did that he might throw her offer back in her face. No, she'd have to circumvent the house somehow.

A letter, she decided. She'd write one later that evening and post it. Silly really, with him so close. But that was what she'd do.

She had a last look at the ailing beasts, then returned to her watering.

*   *   *

Roxanne answered the knock on her door to find Buster standing there, scowling.

'Do you mean it?' he demanded harshly.

'If you're referring to you using The White, then yes.'

His scowl deepened. 'Why? That's what I wants to know. You'll be wanting paid I suppose?'

'No money, Mr Buster. As for why, I'm simply not prepared to stand by and see animals like yours suffer when I have it in my power to help them. So, as I said in my letter, you can use The White until the drought breaks and wells fill up again.'

He grunted.

'Anything else?'

He turned and strode away.

Not even a thank you! she thought. But what else could you expect from a man such as Buster.

At least he'd accepted her offer. His stiff-necked pride hadn't stopped him doing that. Stiff-necked pride she had no doubt had been overcome by the alternative, crippling financial loss.

She closed the door again as he drove away.

India came up short when she heard the laughter emanating from Miles's studio where Roxanne was posing. How happy they sounded, and carefree. The session must be going well.

'You've got such gorgeous skin,' Miles declared from within. 'The trouble is it's so damned difficult to get the quality of it, its essence, just right.'

India frowned; something in Miles's voice disturbed her.

'Let me touch it, feel it. That might help.'

India's frown intensified. That was getting a bit intimate, surely!

'Ah yes,' Miles sighed a few seconds later.

Jealousy seized India. She'd never known him do that to any of his previous models. This was an entirely new departure as far as she was concerned.

Suddenly it dawned on her what had disturbed her about Miles's voice. There had been a mental caress in it that she recognized from their lovemaking.

'Oh that tickles!' Roxanne exclaimed. And they both laughed again, his a deep throaty chuckle.

India gnawed her bottom lip as doubt assailed her. She couldn't see what was happening after all. It might be completely innocent.

She glanced down at the tray and the tea she'd brought for them. Should she still take it in, or bring some fresh later?

'Tilt your head just a fraction upwards. It catches the light better like that.' There was a pause, then Miles added, 'Perfect.'

India bit her bottom lip, drawing blood. The way he'd said 'perfect' was not only a caress but croon of sheer pleasure.

He *did* fancy Roxanne. He'd lied! She was certain of both. His voice had given him away.

Hot tears spurted into India's eyes. How far had it gone between the pair of them? Were they already lovers?

What a fool she'd been to accept his denials. And what of Roxanne? How she must have sniggered up her sleeve at her, pretending to be her good friend while all the time carrying on with Miles behind her back.

Fucking bitch! she inwardly raged.

Thoughts in turmoil, feeling sick with a combination of jealousy and betrayal, she swung on her heels and strode away.

Roxanne woke to the sound of rain rattling against the window panes. The drought had broken at long last, she realized with relief. There had been times, of late, when it had seemed it would go on forever.

She could only pray that the rain wasn't a flash in the pan, for it would take a lot more than one downpour to revive the parched land. In the event her prayer was answered. The downpour was the beginning of a wet period which everyone in the area, particularly the farmers, greeted with rejoicing.

'Sleepwalking?' Roxanne repeated.

'As I said, last night. I found her wandering round the house.'

'Has she ever done that before?'

Miles shook his head. 'Not to my knowledge. I was about to wake her up when I remembered you shouldn't do that to sleepwalkers, so I took her by the hand and guided her back to bed.'

'And she never woke up?'

'No, simply lay down, closed her eyes and that was that.'

'Dear me,' Roxanne murmured.

Miles laid his palette knife aside and scratched his chin. He stared hard at the half-completed canvas in front of him, contemplating it.

He slowly shook his head. 'Buggeration!' he breathed.

'What is it?'

'I don't know. I just can't get it right somehow. The colours are wrong. The . . .' He trailed off in frustration.

360

'Maybe you should leave it for today? Think about it rather than continue painting.'

'Hmmh!' he sighed.

'Can I see?' she was teasing him, knowing full well what the answer would be.

'No!'

'All right, keep your shirt on.'

He crossed over to the window and gazed out. 'Imagine India sleepwalking. How extraordinary.'

'Did you tell her this morning?'

He shook his head.

'Why not?'

'It would only have worried her.'

'And what if she does it again?'

He considered that. 'I wonder if something's bothering her? Though I can't think what.'

'Could it be Jonathan going off to boarding school? She is his mother don't forget.'

Jonathan had been enrolled in St Aubyn's Preparatory School in another part of Devon that September; the fees were being paid for by India's father.

'That might well be it,' Miles said.

'It's only natural that she should be concerned. Jonathan is so young after all. It can't be easy for him to leave home at that age. Or for India to let him go.'

Miles returned to his canvas. 'I'll speak to her later, try and find out if that's what's upsetting her.'

Roxanne yawned, stretched, then resumed her stance. 'Another half hour and I'm off. I'm sorry, but I must. I've a farm to run don't forget.'

'As if I could,' he muttered, brow furrowed in concentration.

Roxanne smiled as she noticed he had a spot of paint on his moustache. Mention it or not? Not, she decided.

The spot of paint amused her for the rest of that session.

Roxanne's eyes opened wide with surprise when Buster appeared, driving a cart with a calf trotting along behind. Now what!

'Whooaa!' Buster commanded, and proceeded to tie off the reins.

'Good morning,' Roxanne said affably as he jumped down.

'Morning,' he replied gruffly, going to the rear of the cart where he undid the rope securing the calf.

'Tis for you by way of thanks,' he declared, handing Roxanne the rope.

She stared at the calf, a fine specimen if ever there was one. 'For me?'

'I won't be beholden to no-one.'

She smiled at him. 'I told you payment wasn't necessary.'

'No matter, I won't be beholden. Anyway, tis a small price to pay. I could have lost me entire herd if it hadn't been for you. As many did hereabouts.'

He shuffled his feet, looking decidedly uncomfortable. 'We're evens, eh?'

'Evens,' she agreed.

'Right then.'

'Mr Buster,' she said as he went to move away.

'What?'

'Is it truce between us?'

'Truce?'

'That's what I said, *truce.*'

He slowly nodded. 'All right, truce it is. You have my word on it.'

'And hand?'

He shook with her. 'And hand,' he repeated.

'Good, I'm glad. I like to be friendly with my neighbours, not in contention.'

'You shouldn't be running this place on your own. Tain't right.'

'You mean I should be married?'

'Twould be different if you was a widow woman. I could understand that.'

'But not a single lady setting up on her own?'

'Tain't natural.'

She suppressed her laughter, thinking that would upset him. He was only being honest after all. 'Does the calf have a name?' she asked.

He shook his head.

Roxanne had an inspiration. 'I'll call her Brocky.'

'Brocky?'

'After the broccoli your bloody goats ate.'

Buster threw back his head and roared with laughter. 'Tis good that!' he spluttered, smacking his thigh.

'Brocky it is then.'

He climbed aboard his cart. 'I was wrong about you, Miss Hawkins. You be all right.'

362

'Brocky,' he muttered, slapping the reins. He threw back his head and roared again as he drove away.

She'd have no more trouble from him, Roxanne thought as the cart receded into the distance.

The broken fence had finally, and permanently, been mended.

Chapter Twenty-Four

' "Woman Among The Daffodils",' Miles replied to Roxanne's enquiry. He'd really wanted to title the painting Beautiful Woman Among The Daffodils, but hadn't dared for a variety of reasons.

' "Woman Among The Daffodils",' Roxanne mused, staring at the now finished canvas.

'Has a nice ring to it, don't you think?'

It seemed rather unoriginal to her, but she refrained from saying so. 'Not bad,' she murmured.

He frowned. 'Does that mean you don't like it?'

'Not at all,' she replied quickly.

'I suppose *you* could do better?'

'I think the colours are brilliant,' she declared. 'So gloriously vibrant.'

That mollified him somewhat. 'I got them right in the end I feel.'

'No doubt about it.'

She shifted, viewing the canvas from a different angle. 'Why did you use a palette knife instead of a brush?' she queried.

'I don't know. That just seemed the right technique for this particular painting.'

'Well it's certainly worked. Though don't ask me why, I couldn't say.'

He was delighted that she approved. For some reason he'd been quite nervous about showing her the completed canvas. Perhaps because her approval was so important to him. He'd have been devastated if she hadn't liked it.

'The sea of daffodils,' she said.

'Pardon?'

'Your expression, that day you sketched in the fields. The sea of daffodils, that was how you saw them.'

'I remember,' he nodded.

'Why not . . .' She hesitated, thinking.

'What?'

'Better still, "The Daffodil Sea".'

'You mean as a title?'

'What do you think?'

' "The Daffodil Sea",' he repeated.

'It's different, memorable in my humble opinion. Of course what you title the painting is entirely up to you.'

' "The Daffodil Sea",' he repeated again.

'That's what I'd call it, but suit yourself. You're the artist.'

'It doesn't mention you though, the woman in the painting.'

'So? Is that important?'

'No,' he conceded.

'There we are then.'

When he didn't reply, or pursue the subject further, she left it at that.

Miles breezed into the room where India was busy on a water-colour and Polly was playing with her dolls. 'Roxanne's come up with a splendid title for the new canvas,' he announced.

India glanced at him, taking in his slightly flushed face and bright, sparkling eyes. Jealousy stabbed through her as it so often did nowadays at the mere mention of Roxanne's name. 'Oh?'

' "The Daffodil Sea". I think it terrific.'

'Has she gone?'

'Yes. Had to dash back to Cobwebs. She sent her regards and apologies for not saying hallo.'

India concentrated again on her watercolour, which was an external view of the cottage.

'Well?' Miles demanded.

'I think it's a fine title,' India said through gritted teeth.

'Isn't she clever! She got it from a comment I once made to her.'

India momentarily closed her eyes. How she now wished they'd never moved to St Petroc and met Miss Roxanne Hawkins. She regretted the move with all her heart and soul.

India laid down her brush and rose. 'I'll put the kettle on for tea.'

She left Miles, feeling mystified, as she swept from the room.

Roxanne came to the end of the letter and sighed. It was a letter from Miles in London. His latest exhibition had been an outstanding success, "The Daffodil Sea" having been acclaimed by the critics. Overnight he'd become the talk of the art world. The reviews he'd received, some of which he'd enclosed, were ecstatic in their praise. His name was made.

He'd sold everything he'd exhibited and commissions were flooding in, commissions for which he was going to be paid a great deal of money.

Roxanne laughed with delight, not only on account of his news but that he'd written to her personally to tell her about it.

She started at the beginning of the letter and eagerly read it through again, after which she devoured the reviews.

'That's right,' Roxanne said approvingly to Polly whom she was teaching to milk. 'Just gently squeeze.'

Polly watched the milk squirt into the bucket positioned at her feet. 'This is fun,' she declared.

Not so much fun when you had to do it day in day out, Roxanne thought. Then it became a chore, as were so many daily tasks on a farm.

'There you are!' India snapped from the shippon door, standing with legs akimbo and hands on hips.

'Look what I'm doing, Mummy!' Polly called to her.

'I can see what you're doing,' India replied crossly. 'What I want to know is why you didn't tell me where you were going. I've been searching high and low for you, madam.'

Polly stopped her milking. 'Sorry, Mum.'

'Come away from there this instant. It's home for you and straight to bed.'

'Oh India!' Roxanne breathed.

India whirled on Roxanne. 'I was worried sick, anything might have happened. She should have told me what she intended. And another thing, she comes over here far too often. She must be an annoyance to you.'

'She's no trouble at all, honestly, India. To the contrary she's good company for me.'

Polly crossed to her mother, a hint of tears in her eyes. 'Don't send me to bed, Mum, please?'

'Bed it is, and I'll have no further argument. It's time you learned you just can't go wandering off without a by your leave.'

'You might have guessed she'd be here,' Roxanne stated softly.

India had guessed, and found that all the more galling. Not only was her husband bewitched by Roxanne but it seemed her daughter was as well. Damn and blast the woman!

India grabbed Polly by the hand. 'Say goodbye now.'

'Goodbye Roxanne.'

'I'll see you again.'

'When and if I say so,' India declared curtly.

Polly was crying as India marched away, almost dragging Polly along beside her.

Roxanne stared after them in dismay, thinking that had been so unfair. All right, Polly had been in the wrong but her offence hardly merited such a severe reaction.

For the first time ever she found herself disliking India.

'You might as well not have bothered,' India declared, as she and Miles finished making love.

That surprised him. 'What are you talking about?'

'You weren't there. Your body was, but not your mind.' And she had a good idea where his mind *had* been.

'I'm sorry if that's how you feel,' he said softly.

'Well was it!' she exclaimed, her voice high and shrill. She turned her back to him and pulled the bedclothes tightly about her. Another humiliation, she thought bitterly.

'India?'

She pursed her lips and didn't reply.

'India.' She shrugged off his hand when he placed it on her shoulder.

'This is silly.'

She closed her eyes. Silly! Like hell it was. She'd been made love to by Miles too often not to know the difference.

'India?' he tried again, and again there was only silence.

India lay in a cold rage.

'Run the farms as a joint venture?' Billy Christmas frowned. He'd been asked over to the Stonemans to hear a proposal Roxanne had just put to him.

'With you in overall charge,' Roxanne added, glancing at Linnet.

'Tis a thought,' Billy murmured.

'With definite advantages to both sides. Think of the increased acreage for a start, and Linnet would have your help which she badly needs. I don't think she minds me saying she's just not cut out to run a farm. Even with the plan we drew up together she's still finding it difficult.'

'I'm hopeless,' Linnet admitted.

'What about Kevern. What does he think?'

'Sod Kevern!' Roxanne declared sharply. 'He's man of the house in name only, confined to bed as he is.' Kevern's surviving leg had deteriorated to the point where crutches were now out of the question. All he could manage was to use the pot and get back to bed again.

'The combined farms would be a more productive and efficient unit,' Roxanne went on.

Billy nodded; he could see the logic in that.

'Everything would be split straight down the middle which is definitely to your advantage,' Roxanne said. 'And Linnet would still be gaining, believe me. You both would.'

The more Billy thought about this the more it excited him. 'I'll need to think on't,' he replied cautiously.

'Of course. And if you want matters drawn up legally then Linnet's in complete agreement.'

''Tis certainly a thought,' Billy repeated.

'I'd be in your debt, Billy,' Roxanne smiled, a smile he returned.

How could he refuse now? Billy thought. He'd never been able to refuse Roxanne anything, particularly when she smiled like that. But he wouldn't be rushed, smile or no. Rushing into something was always a bad policy.

A week later he returned to the Stonemans' and shook hands on it with Linnet. The deal was struck.

The suggested legal agreement was drawn up soon afterwards.

India had been into St Petroc with Polly to do some shopping and returned to find a note from Miles saying he'd gone for a walk. On a whim she decided to take Polly and try to find him, the three of them could then conclude the walk together.

He often went to the clifftops, she thought, setting off in that direction, Polly skipping alongside.

'You look happy darling,' she commented to her beaming daughter.

'That's cause Jonathan will soon be home for his holiday,' Polly replied.

He was expected the following week and India couldn't wait to have him back. How she missed him. His careering round the cottage again would be a sorely needed tonic.

'He'll still want to play with me even though he's a big boy now?' Polly inquired, suddenly anxious.

'Of course he will.'

'It would be horrid if he didn't.'

'Don't you worry, Pol. Jonathan will want to play with you all right. And no doubt tell you all sorts of tales about St Aubyn's.'

Polly's beaming smile returned.

India stopped short when she spotted Miles, who wasn't alone, but deep in conversation with a female companion.

Roxanne, India realized, recognizing the woman. Was it an arranged meeting, or one by chance? Whatever, they were together and she would only be intruding.

How many meetings had there been like this? she wondered. Meetings she'd known nothing about. And if meetings had been arranged, where else other than out in the open? Cobwebs for example, where they could be quite alone, in comfort.

Were they lovers? Actual physical lovers?

A black depression almost overwhelmed her at the thought they might be.

'Mum, what's up?' Polly queried, staring up at India's stricken face.

'Nothing,' India heard herself mumble in reply.

She glanced at Polly. Had the child seen them, or not? She didn't think Polly had.

'We'll go this way instead. I have an idea we'll find Dad over there,' India said, pointing away from the clifftops. When Polly made no objection she knew she hadn't spotted Miles and Roxanne.

When they finally returned to the cottage Polly informed Miles that they'd looked and looked everywhere but hadn't been able to find him.

India pleaded a sudden blinding headache and took herself off to bed.

'Can I come in for a bit?' India asked Miles, hard at work on his latest canvas.

The last thing he wanted was to be interrupted, by anyone. 'Is something wrong?'

'No. I just fancied a chat.'

'About what?'

'Nothing in particular.'

He sighed. 'I'd rather be alone, India, if you don't mind. I need to concentrate.'

'Fine then. I'll leave you to it.'

'Oh India!' he said as she was turning disappointedly away. 'I thought we might ask Roxanne over for supper this Saturday. What do you say?'

She struggled to keep the anger from her face. Roxanne again, always Roxanne!

'If you like,' she replied quietly.

'Good. I'll pop over later and invite her.'

He could make time for Roxanne, she thought. But not her. *Not her!*

'That is funny!' Roxanne laughed. Miles had just related a humorous story about his last trip to London.

'And afterwards the same chap . . .'

They only had eyes for one another, India thought, staring at the pair of them. And that was how it had been all evening. When Miles spoke he was invariably addressing Roxanne, when she spoke it was invariably to him.

India felt she might as well not have been there.

When Roxanne laughed again India wanted to pick up her plate of food and throw it at her.

Miles and Roxanne were blissfully unaware of how much they'd excluded India.

India halted by some rocks, having come alone to the seashore, and sat down. It was the following morning, after that absolutely ghastly evening,

Perhaps she should take Polly and go away, she thought miserably. Anywhere, it didn't matter, just away from the cottage and St Petroc.

But she couldn't, she realized. She loved Miles too much to leave him. If she'd had proof of infidelity that would have been a different matter, but she didn't.

If only she had a magic wand she could wave to make Roxanne disappear; it would have solved all her problems. Except magic wands didn't exist in real life, only fairy stories. And what was happening to her was no fairy story, more like a nightmare.

She gritted her teeth and clenched her hands into tight fists at the memory of Roxanne's laughter, laughter that reverberated round inside her head till she wanted to scream.

She came to a decision. Something had to be done about it all. It simply couldn't go on as it stood, not if she was to keep her sanity.

She'd confront Miles, have it out with him. There was no other way.

She could still hear Roxanne's laughter as she purposefully retraced her steps back to the cottage.

'Are you having an affair with Roxanne?' India asked.

Miles stared at her, aghast. 'Am I *what*?'

'Having an affair with Roxanne?' India was surprised at her calmness.

'No I am not. Whatever made you think I was?'

'How the pair of you are together. It was quite disgusting last night. She could hardly keep her hands off you, or you off her.'

'That's nonsense!' he exploded, shaken to the core. So India had guessed about his feelings for Roxanne after all.

'Have you been to bed? Made love to her? I believe you have.'

'I swear India, on all that's holy, there's nothing going on. We're good friends, nothing more.'

Was he telling the truth? She couldn't be sure. Not after Hilary Catchpole. 'It doesn't come across like that.'

'Why does a man have to be conducting an affair with a woman just because they're friends,' Miles blustered, crossing to the decanter and pouring himself a brandy, more to give himself time to think than because he wanted one.

'It's all nonsense,' he muttered darkly.

'One thing's certain. I don't want her in my house ever again.'

'India!' Miles exclaimed, appalled.

'Never again,' India repeated.

'But you can't—'

'Oh yes I can,' India interjected. 'I can't stop you if you go on seeing her secretly, that's your business. But I want nothing more to do with her.'

'What about the provisions we buy?' Miles protested.

India laughed at the absurdity of that. 'You can continue buying them if you wish. Just don't ask me to go to Cobwebs.'

He gulped down his brandy and poured a second. 'You're making a mountain out of a molehill. Exaggerating the whole business.'

'Am I?'

'Yes, you damn well are.'

'Do you love her?'

'No I don't,' he lied. 'I love you.'

India's heart sank to hear the falseness in his tone, and in that

371

moment knew for certain she'd lost Miles to another. He might not realize it yet, but she did.

'I'll never leave you,' Miles said.

What did that matter when he loved Roxanne and not her? The calm that had possessed her up until then crumbled, to be replaced by fear and utter desolation. She wanted to rush to Miles, throw herself into his arms and beg him to love her again, for things to be as they had been before coming to St Petroc. For their marriage to be happy and secure once more.

'Not a single word of anything other than friendship has passed between Roxanne and I,' Miles stated.

Liar! she thought.

'Honestly India, not one word or action.'

She gazed into his eyes, smiling thinly and bitterly when he turned away from her, back to the decanter. Yes, she'd lost him all right, in his heart where it counted most.

'What went wrong between us, Miles. Was it me?'

'There's nothing wrong,' he replied harshly.

'I love you, and always will.'

'And I love you.'

Once, she thought. But no more. Now he loved Roxanne who'd stolen him away from her.

She then did something she'd never dreamt she'd ever do. She went to Miles and slapped him hard across the face.

'Sleep down here,' she declared.

'India!'

'I mean it. Down here. And I hope that slap hurt.' As much as you've hurt me, she added to herself.

'Jesus!' Miles swore softly when she'd gone. 'What a mess.'

Miles woke, and shivered. He was freezing. He glanced at the fire which had been ablaze earlier, but had now gone out.

He snuggled down and tried to get back to sleep, but couldn't because of the intrusive cold. He needed more blankets he thought, climbing out of his makeshift bed.

He lit a lamp and padded from the room into the hallway where he was instantly hit by an icy blast from an open outside door.

Now how had that happened? he wondered. He was certain it had been shut when he'd retired.

Then a horrible thought struck him. Burglar or burglars! And what if they were somewhere still in the house?

His first concern was for India and Polly. But before rushing to their respective rooms he armed himself with a brass poker. If anyone tried any rough stuff with him they'd regret it.

The door to their bedroom was also open. He paused, took a deep breath and entered. What he discovered was that their bed was empty, the covers thrown back from India's side.

A quick peek into Polly's room confirmed her presence and his suspicions. India must have gone sleepwalking again, which she'd done a number of times recently, only now it seemed she hadn't confined herself to the house.

He hurried off to slip on some boots and throw on a heavy coat, cradling one of India's in the crook of an arm.

He quickly located her. She was a little way from the cottage standing staring fixedly into the distance. As he'd feared she was clad in nothing more than her nightdress.

How long had she been out here? he wondered anxiously as he draped her coat round her shoulders. Some while he realized when his fingers brushed her bare skin.

As before, he didn't wake her. Taking one of her hands in his he said very quietly, 'Come along, my darling, we have to get you back to bed.'

She followed him without any resistance, as she always did. Hard frost crackled beneath their feet as they walked.

When they reached their bedroom he removed the coat and gently eased her on to the bed. When she was lying flat he tucked her in, thinking he should really rub her wet feet with a towel except that that might wake her. It was a quandary he partially resolved by patting her feet with the bedclothes.

Noting she hadn't used the stone hot water bottle he went to the kitchen where he boiled a kettle and filled it. He then slid it into bed by her feet, thinking that was the best place for it.

He stood staring down at her, worried sick. It was a bitter night, with a biting wind blowing, not a night to be out in only a nightdress. From now on he'd lock all the outside doors at night, he promised himself. He didn't want a repeat of this. In the meantime, had it affected her? Only time would tell.

Damn what she'd said about him sleeping on the couch, she needed his body heat. Surely she would understand when he'd explained to her what had happened. She knew that she'd been sleepwalking, as he had told her after the second occasion he'd found her wandering around.

He extinguished his lamp and crawled in beside her, pressing himself close.

Despite the bedclothes, hot water bottle and Miles, it was a long time before India began to get warm again.

The next day India was delirious. Eyes firmly closed, face and body streaming with clammy sweat, she babbling incoherently.

Distraught Miles swiftly dressed, his mind racing. The doctor clearly had to be summoned, but how? He couldn't leave India in her present state. The answer was obvious, Roxanne.

He roused Polly, explained that India was ill and what he wanted her to do. He then penned a note to Roxanne with which he dispatched Polly to Cobwebs. All he could now do was await the doctor's arrival.

Miles immediately ceased his pacing when a tight-faced Doctor Weeks entered the kitchen. 'Well?' he demanded.

Weeks placed his bag on the table. 'It's bad news I'm afraid. She has pneumonia.'

Polly started to cry. She didn't know what pneumonia was but could understand 'bad news' well enough.

Roxanne gathered the child into her arms. 'There there,' she soothed.

'I don't want Mrs Carey moved in her present condition,' Weeks went on. 'So she'll have to remain where she is.'

Miles made a dismissive gesture. 'I'll look after her, day and night. Just give me your instructions.'

'I've given her some aspirin and opened her window to try and lower her temperature. Apart from that we can only wait, and hope, for her to pull through.'

'She's a strong woman,' Miles declared. 'She'll fight it off. You'll see.'

'And of course I'll help in every way I can,' Roxanne stated.

Miles glanced at her, then back at the doctor.

'I only wish there was more I could do, but there isn't,' Weeks apologized with a shrug.

'Thank you for coming so promptly, doctor,' Miles told him.

'Miss Hawkins was fortunate to catch me at home. I was just about to set off on my early morning round.'

'Can I get you something, a cup of tea?' Roxanne offered.

Weeks shook his head. 'I'd better get on, I'm behind as it is.' He opened his bag and took out a small bottle of aspirins which he handed to Miles. 'Give her another two of those in four hours, if you can get her to take them which is difficult the way she is.'

'I'll manage,' Miles replied emphatically. 'And there's nothing more that can be done?'

'Nothing, I'm sorry to say.'

'Damn!' Miles muttered.

'Have you any idea how long she was outside?'

'None.'

'Whatever,' Weeks said. 'It was long enough to do the damage.' He closed and picked up his bag. 'I'll return this afternoon to see what's what.'

'Thank you, doctor.'

Weeks put on his hat, which had been beside his bag, and tipped the brim with a finger. 'Miss Hawkins.'

'Doctor.'

Miles escorted Weeks to the door, then came back to the kitchen where he found Roxanne consoling Polly, wiping away her tears while assuring the child everything would be all right.

'Tell you what,' said Roxanne. 'Why don't you take Bobby out and play with him. He'd like that.'

Bobby, who'd been lying quietly, eyes going from speaker to speaker, jumped to his feet, tail wagging, when he heard his name.

Polly brightened. 'I'd like it too.'

'Then off you go.'

'Come on Bobby! Come on!'

Bobby bounded after Polly who skipped from the kitchen.

'You'd better go to India,' Roxanne said. 'But in the meantime have you eaten yet? Has Polly?'

'Not for me, I couldn't get anything down. But Polly might.'

'Right then.'

'Roxanne . . .'

'What?'

He put a hand to his forehead. 'This is difficult, believe me. I appreciate your offer of help but can't accept it.'

She gazed at him in astonishment. 'Why not?'

'Because . . . of India, and last night. We had a terrible row about you.'

'Me!'

'It was all a misunderstanding. But, for some reason . . .' His voice faltered. 'India thinks there's more to our friendship than there is. In fact, she accused me of having an affair with you.'

'I see,' Roxanne murmured. This was awful.

'I assured her we weren't, but she didn't believe me. At least I don't think she did. She went off to bed on her own and told me to sleep on the couch.'

Roxanne didn't know what to say.

'Before she went she said she never wanted you in her house again. Not ever. She was quite adamant about that.'

'Oh Miles!' Roxanne breathed.

'Which is why I can't accept your offer of help. That would be going against her wishes and would be unfair. So it's best you don't come back here any more.'

Roxanne digested that. 'And you? Will I be seeing you?'

'I don't know, Roxanne,' he replied softly. 'At the moment all I can think about is India.'

'Of course.' That was perfectly understandable, she thought, rattled in the extreme.

'Is this why India has been so peculiar of late?' she asked.

'Has to be. Her suspicions must have been preying on her mind. And being so disturbed could explain the sleepwalking.'

The full implications of that hit Roxanne like a hammerblow. 'But it's all so utterly untrue. You and I that is.'

He nodded.

'Utterly.'

'Yes,' he agreed.

What could she do? Nothing in the circumstances. Perhaps when India had recovered she might listen to reason. Till then . . . well, all she could do was respect India's wishes.

'I'm sorry to be the cause of such an upset,' Roxanne apologized.

'A misunderstanding,' he repeated hollowly.

Roxanne gathered up her coat. 'I'll go then. Goodbye.'

'Goodbye.'

'And I hope everything turns out for the best where India is concerned, as I'm sure it will.'

'Thank you.'

Ouside a disconsolate Roxanne called Bobby to her side and returned to Cobwebs.

Miles sat by India's bedside, feeling completely wretched and tired beyond belief. His gaunt cheeks were unshaven, his eyes bloodshot. It was the third night since India had contracted pneumonia, a length of time during which he'd slept very little and her condition had remained unchanged.

Picking up a cloth he wiped her fevered brow, then laid the cloth aside. At least she wasn't babbling for the present, although she might start again at any time.

'You can do it, India, you can do it,' he whispered.

He sat back in his chair, trying to make himself more comfortable, and stared at her. They'd go on a holiday together, just the two of them, when this was all over, he thought. Jonathan would be at school and they'd make provision for Polly. A holiday that would aid her recuperation and bring them close again. He was still thinking about the holiday, and speculating where they might go, when he dozed off.

He knew the moment he opened his eyes and gazed at India that something was wrong. Her face was relaxed, devoid of sweat, while her body beneath the bedclothes was completely still. There was no rise and fall of breathing.

He hurriedly pushed himself out of his chair to sit on her bed. Her forehead, when he felt it, was cold. Nor was there any sign of a pulse either at her neck or wrist. Her wrist and arm hung limply in his grasp.

He knew then with certainty that the worst had come to pass. She was gone, dead. His India was dead. A great tidal wave of grief and remorse engulfed him, causing him to bury his head in his hands. 'Dear God!' he choked. 'Dear God!'

'Daddy, how's Mummy this morning?' Polly asked, standing framed in the doorway.

He glanced up at his daughter through eyes almost blinded with tears.

'Dad?'

He lurched from the bed, went to Polly and knelt before her. 'Oh my poor Pol,' he choked. 'My poor Pol.'

The funeral was over, the mourners beginning to drift away. Roxanne wondered if she should offer her condolences to Miles and the children, or not. During the entire proceedings Miles had studiously avoided looking at her, almost making a point of it.

She wouldn't, she decided. If he wished to ignore her, then so be it. He had his reasons which she could well understand, and sympathized with. She would withdraw, and stay withdrawn. If he wanted her he knew where she could be found.

Roxanne turned and walked away.

Chapter Twenty-Five

'Have you spoken to that artist chap recently, Roxanne?' Mary Scrivens asked, glancing at Roxanne over the box of daffodils she was busily filling.

Roxanne shook her head. 'Not for a long time I'm afraid.'

'They do say he's turned into something of a recluse,' Iris Morrish declared.

'His wife's death must have hit him real hard,' Mary added.

Roxanne paused to pull up the thin cotton gloves which had begun to slip down her hands. How long was it now since the funeral? Over a year. A year during which Miles had kept away from Cobwebs.

Sadness filled Roxanne as she thought about him. How she missed his company, his presence, his laughter. She'd only seen him in the distance, either walking or standing on the clifftops apparently deep in contemplation. Perhaps she should break the ice and go over and speak to him, ask how he and the children were.

No, she counselled herself. That would be wrong. If he wanted them to be estranged then that's how it would be, she wouldn't force herself on him.

'Tis been another grand crop this season,' Ella Pridmore stated to Roxanne.

'Excellent, I've no complaints.'

'And expanding all the time, eh?' Mary smiled.

'That's it,' Roxanne smiled in return.

She tried to put Miles from her mind as she got on with her bunching and boxing.

★ ★ ★

'Jonathan! Polly!' Roxanne exclaimed. 'How wonderful to see you.'

Bobby, recognizing his old friends, jumped up and down with excitement.

'Can we come in?' Jonathan asked.

'Of course. Would you like some tea? I'm afraid I've nothing else.'

'Not for me thank you,' Jonathan replied, stroking and patting Bobby, as was Polly.

'Nor me,' added Polly.

'It's been ages,' Roxanne said.

She found she was nervous as they entered the kitchen where she immediately got out a tin of biscuits she'd recently baked.

'How about one of these then?' she queried, opening the tin. Both children eagerly accepted a biscuit.

'I take it you're on holiday?' Roxanne said to Jonathan.

'So's Polly.'

'You're at school now!' Roxanne smiled, not having known that.

'I started in September. It's called Miss Bradley's and I love it there. The other girls are tremendous fun.'

'Good for you,' Roxanne approved. 'You don't mind boarding and being away from home?'

'No,' Polly replied quietly, her mood suddenly serious.

'I was sorry about your mum. That was tragic.'

Polly sniffed. 'We . . . think about her a lot. Don't we, Jonathan.'

He nodded.

'And eh . . .' Roxanne realized her heart was racing. 'How's your dad?'

'Painting like fury for his next exhibition,' Jonathan informed her.

'Oh?'

'It's in Bristol.'

'When?'

Jonathan gave her the dates which she mentally stored away.

'He took us to London during our last hols. We had a wonderful time,' Polly enthused.

'And does he know you've come over here?'

'Oh yes,' Polly answered. 'We asked, of course, and he said that was all right. We wanted to see you and Bobby.'

So he hadn't objected, Roxanne thought, wondering what to

379

make of that. Had he objected on previous occasions? She didn't think she could ask.

'Is he well?'

'He misses Mum,' Jonathan replied gravely.

'That's only natural.'

'We all do,' Polly added.

'Do you want to take Bobby out to play?'

'Yes please!' Polly responded eagerly.

'Then off you go.'

There were so many questions about Miles that Roxanne wanted to ask, but didn't feel she could pump the children in case they told Miles. But she would try to get a few further facts out of them before they went.

In the meantime, an exhibition in Bristol? That was interesting. Particularly as Bristol wasn't all that far away.

She'd love to view his latest work, she thought, considering the idea of visiting the exhibition.

She'd need someone to look after the animals mind, but that could be arranged. And she did need a break, she argued with herself. A few days in Bristol would be just the ticket.

Roxanne almost lost her nerve at the double doors leading into the gallery. What if Miles was there? Worse, what if he wasn't?

She gnawed a thumbnail, telling herself not to be so silly. As a member of the public she had every right to go in. And if Miles was there, well she'd just ignore him as he'd been ignoring her since the funeral.

Go on, she urged herself. Go on, move!

Taking a deep breath, she placed a hand on one of the double doors and pushed.

There was a middle-aged man behind a desk who smiled at her as she entered, and a man and woman studying the paintings.

The man behind the desk rose. 'Would you care for a catalogue madam?' he inquired.

'Please.'

She accepted the catalogue and flicked it open to discover Miles's name leading the other two artists that were being shown. According to the catalogue he had six paintings on exhibition.

She glanced about her, but there was no sign of Miles. Damn, she swore mentally, disappointed.

The first of his paintings she looked at was titled 'Fishing Boats, St Petroc Harbour'. There were two trawlers in the foreground, one with a dinghy at its side, and another off to the left in the mid-background. Half the painting consisted of St Petroc itself which he'd captured beautifully.

She took her time contemplating the paintings, slowly going from one to the other. She noted they all bore a mark indicating they'd been sold, which delighted her.

She was about to move on to the next artist when a voice behind her said, 'Hallo, I'm surprised to find you here.'

She turned to smile at Miles. 'Where did you spring from?'

'I was in the back and just popped out to have a word with Harold when I spotted you.' He pointed to the man behind the desk. 'That's Harold, the owner.'

'I'm in Bristol on business,' she lied smoothly. 'And suddenly remembered the children mentioning you had an exhibition on here. So I decided to drop in.'

'I'm pleased you have.'

Was he? she wondered. 'How are you?'

'Not bad, considering. Life goes on. And you?'

'Fine.'

He turned to his paintings. 'What do you think?'

'I particularly like "Fishing Boats, St Petroc Harbour".'

He smiled. 'Yes, I am quite proud of that. It was the first to be sold.'

'Which they've all been, I noticed.'

'Helpful to the bank balance, eh?'

He looked older, she thought. Considerably so. There were lines deeply etched on his face where none had been before. 'Was this exhibition reviewed?'

'Only in the local papers, not those in London unfortunately. But what they had to say about me was all complimentary.'

'That's good.'

He hesitated, then said softly, 'I saw you at the funeral. Thank you for attending.'

'It was an extremely sad day.'

'Yes,' he sighed.

She wanted to take him into her arms and comfort him, stroke his hair, absorb some of his hurt. 'Well, I'd better be getting on,' she declared instead.

'Where are you staying?'

'The Carlton. Expensive, but nice. I decided to spoil myself a little.'

He smiled thinly. 'There's no harm in doing that once in a while.'

'Exactly what I thought.'

381

'You had another grand crop this year from what I saw.'

'And more bulbs down. It's all working out well.'

'So . . .' he said, and trailed off.

'I'll be going then.'

'Thanks for coming.'

'My pleasure. Goodbye.'

'Goodbye, Roxanne.'

Well that was that, she thought as she walked away. Hallo and goodbye. She'd expected . . . hoped . . .

'Roxanne!'

She forced a smile onto her face as he hurried towards her. 'I was thinking, if you're still going to be here this evening why don't we have dinner together?' he proposed.

Elation leapt within Roxanne.

'If you're free, that is,' he added lamely.

'I'd enjoy that,' she replied. 'What time?'

'Eight. I'll meet you downstairs at the Carlton.'

'I'll be there.'

'Till then.'

'Goodbye again.'

'Goodbye.'

As she left the building she was wearing an expression of combined joy and self-satisfaction.

Roxanne was so nervous that her hands were shaking as she brushed her hair which she then folded and pinned up at the back. She didn't know why she should be in such a state, it was only Miles after all. Miles whom she'd thought about constantly since India's death. Miles whose company she'd missed so much.

And then a thought struck her which made her gaze at herself wide eyed in the mirror. Miles? she frowned. Had he come to mean more to her than simply being a friend? Certainly the thought had never crossed her mind while India was alive. But now India was dead had something changed within her, something that had been dormant all along?

Was that why she was so nervous? Why she'd really come to Bristol? Out of more than friendship. Because she was in love with him?

'In love with Miles.' She spoke the words aloud, amazed at how true they rang in her ears.

'In love with Miles,' she repeated, the shock making her go quite pale.

And she knew that it was true. Her heart told her so.

Damn, she thought in despair, their conversation was so stilted, awkward, to the point of embarrassment. It was her fault just as much as his.

'How's your veal?' he asked stiffly.

'It's lovely.'

'So's my steak and kidney pudding.'

Another silence, one of many since meeting up, fell between them.

'More wine?' he queried eventually.

'No, I'm all right.'

They were like strangers, she thought, with nothing at all in common. Damn it, what had happened to them! India of course. Her ghost lay between them like a steel barrier.

'Polly told me she's happy at school,' Roxanne commented.

'Yes.'

'A Miss Bradley's I believe.'

'That's correct.'

'It must be lonely without the children,' Roxanne smiled.

Miles lifted his glass and stared morosely into it. 'At times.'

'You should get that dog they always wanted.'

'Perhaps.'

'One similar to Bobby. It would be company for you while they're away.'

'Hmmh!'

Roxanne mentally sighed. This was dreadful. And so the meal dragged on.

Roxanne sat slumped in front of her mirror, bitterly disappointed by the evening which had been an unmitigated disaster. Miles had clearly lost all interest in her as a friend, regardless of anything else.

How ironic, she thought. It would be bad enough if she'd only been a good and close friend, but now she realized that she loved him, Miles had come to mean so much more.

Her head drooped in dejection as a profound sense of loss swept through her. It seemed she was always destined to be unlucky where men were concerned. Her fate was to remain a single woman, a spinster.

'Oh Miles!' she husked.

* * *

Roxanne paused in her hoeing to run a hand across her sweaty brow. Her mind turned to Linnet whom she'd visited the previous day.

Now there was a success story. The farm was fully productive again, everything running like clockwork. It was all thanks to Billy, of course. The pair of them joining forces had worked out wonderfully well.

She was about to resume work when she spotted Miles strolling towards the clifftops. They hadn't spoken since their evening in Bristol.

If he saw her he didn't wave and neither did she. She simply stared at him, thinking what a great shame it was that their relationship had ended as it had.

He stopped at the edge of the cliffs to gaze out to sea, and then it happened.

He suddenly threw his arms into the air, windmilling them around. And dropped from sight.

Roxanne stared in stunned horror. Throwing her hoe aside she galvanized herself into action, running as fast as she could for the spot where he'd disappeared.

She arrived there breathless to see that part of the cliff edge had crumbled, taking Miles with it. She peered over, dreading the worst.

But Miles hadn't fallen to the sand below. He was several feet down the cliff face clinging desperately to an exposed root system that he'd managed to grab. He looked up at her, eyes bright with fear.

'It just gave way,' he panted.

What to do? There wasn't time to return to Cobwebs for a rope, far less go for help, he simply wouldn't be able to hang on that long.

His scrabbling feet found toeholds, which gave him some support. He removed one hand from the root system and searched upwards for a higher grip.

Roxanne lay herself flat and reached down; it was only a few feet after all. Any further and he'd have been beyond her. 'Take my hand,' she instructed.

'What if I pull you over?'

'Shut up and do it!' she almost snarled.

His fingers curled round hers and their hands linked. All thoughts of her personal safety had gone, all she could think about was that she must save Miles. She dug her toes as hard as she could into the ground behind her.

384

'Come on,' she urged, pulling on his hand in hers.

Luckily for Miles Roxanne was used to hard physical labour and had the acquired strength that went with it; strength which now stood them both in good stead.

She continued pulling, gritting her teeth, as Miles inched his way back up the cliff face.

It only took a few minutes, but they seemed an eternity. Then Miles's hand made contact with the cliff edge giving him another firm hold and leverage.

His head appeared over the cliff edge, followed by his shoulders. Roxanne, now in a semi-upright position, heaved and threw herself backwards.

Miles slid over the cliff edge, his legs still briefly projecting into thin air, then they too were safe. Gasping, he collapsed beside Roxanne.

'Holy Mother of God!' he swore.

Anger, a reaction against what had happened, burst out of Roxanne. 'How stupid can you get, standing on the edge. You were nearly killed.'

'Don't I know it. If that root hadn't been there . . .' He broke off and shuddered.

'I hope you've learned your lesson and will never do that again,' she further berated him.

'You saved my life. I'd never have got back up again without you,' he stated softly.

'It was just fortunate I saw you go over. If I hadn't . . .' She too broke off, as a sudden vision of Miles's battered body lying crumpled on the sand below flashed into her mind.

'You saved my life,' he repeated.

'If that's a thank you, you're welcome,' she snapped in reply.

He took her hand and squeezed it. 'Are you all right?'

'Half frightened out of my wits, that's all.'

'How do you think I felt, and feel!'

His expression as he said that was so comical it caused Roxanne's anger to abruptly vanish, and her to sag with relief. 'Oh Miles!' she laughed.

He laughed also. 'I don't know why we're laughing, it certainly wasn't funny.'

'I know.'

His laughter died, eyes boring into hers. And suddenly, somehow, the barrier that had been between them was gone.

Roxanne realized it as well. 'Miles?'

'What?'

385

'Neither of us wanted India to die.'

'No,' he agreed quietly.

'And there was nothing between us for you to feel guilty about. We were both quite innocent.'

A strange expression came over his face. 'I wasn't totally innocent, I'm afraid. India was right . . . up to a point.'

Roxanne frowned. 'I don't understand.'

'She was right inasmuch as she'd correctly guessed my feelings for you.'

Roxanne went very still. 'What feelings?' she croaked.

He took a deep breath. 'This is very hard. For I know they're not reciprocated.'

'What feelings?' she repeated.

'I, eh . . .' He sucked in another deep breath. 'This might upset you. It . . .'

'Tell me,' she demanded.

'India guessed that I'm in love with you,' he stated in a sudden rush of words.

Roxanne's mouth fell open in surprise, her mind whirling. He was in love with her!

'Perhaps I shouldn't have said. Perhaps I—'

'And I'm in love with you,' she interjected.

Now it was his turn to look surprised. 'You are?'

'I think I must have been for a long time without realizing it. Then, earlier on that ghastly night in Bristol, the penny dropped. It just suddenly hit me.'

'Oh Roxanne,' he breathed, delighted beyond belief.

He took her into his arms, their lips meeting in what turned out to be a long lingering kiss that was tender rather than passionate. She sighed with contentment and peace when it was finally over.

'Say it again,' she urged.

'I love you.'

'And I love you.'

'With all my heart.'

'And me you, with mine.'

He kissed her again, then said, chest heaving, 'I'll walk you home.'

'I was hoeing.'

'Then I'll walk you there.'

They went off hand in hand, both somewhat dazed, and incredibly happy.

★　　★　　★

'How do you make them skip like that, Dad?' Jonathan queried, frowning.

'Watch again, I'll show you.' Miles skimmed another stone and succeeded in making it skip five times across the water's surface before vanishing into the sea.

'That's tremendous, Dad,' Polly complimented him.

'It isn't so difficult once you get the hang of it. Is it, Roxanne?'

'No,' she agreed, thinking what a wonderful time she was having with Miles and his family. This was the latest of a number of days they'd all spent together as the children were home from school for the summer.

'Let's see you do it then,' Jonathan challenged her.

Roxanne bent and searched for a flat stone, selecting one that should do the trick. Her stone skipped four times on a flat calm sea before disappearing.

'Now you try,' Roxanne said to Jonathan.

'Let me show you how to hold it,' Miles offered, squatting beside his son.

'You're terrific, Roxanne,' Polly smiled.

'Am I?'

'Oh yes! You can do all sorts.'

Roxanne returned the smile. 'You're pretty terrific yourself. And a good friend with all the help you've been giving me round Cobwebs of late.' It had been her idea that the children help round the farm, as it kept them occupied and meant she could keep an eye on them while Miles got on with his painting.

Polly's smile widened. 'Jonathan too. He's been helpful too.'

'Indeed he has, for which I'm most grateful.'

Miles glanced at Roxanne, noting the intimacy between her and Polly. How well she got on with his children, and they with her, he thought.

That would certainly make things easier for what he had in mind.

Miles groaned as his lips parted from Roxanne's. 'You taste delicious,' he declared.

'Like what?' she teased.

'I don't know. Nothing in particular. Just you.'

Roxanne closed her eyes, thinking how wonderful it was to be with Miles like this, his kisses causing her to drift off and feel as though she was walking on clouds.

'What are you thinking?' he asked.

'About you.'

'What about me?'

'How much I love you.'

'Oh Roxanne!' he breathed, tenderly stroking her neck, which he then licked.

The effect that had on her was purely physical.

He broke away, and leaned back. 'Will you marry me?'

'Of course,' she replied without hesitation. 'When?'

'As soon as it can be arranged.'

She considered that. 'Don't you think it's a bit soon after India? What will folk say?'

'It's long enough and they can say what they damn well please for all I care.'

She laughed softly, that was typical of him. 'And the children, what of them?'

'They adore you. Always have.'

'That might change when it's suggested I become their step-mother?'

Miles shook his head. 'I don't believe so. I'm sure they'll be delighted.'

'They mustn't think I'm trying to replace India. Even if I wanted to, which I certainly don't, I could never do that. Their mother will always be their mother, remembered, honoured and loved by us all as such. I'll simply be Roxanne, your second wife.'

He silenced her by placing a finger across her lips. 'Stop going on. It will be fine with the children, I know.'

She removed the finger. 'Then let's see the vicar and set a date.'

'I can hardly wait.'

She knew exactly what he meant by that. She felt the same way.

'I now pronounce you man and wife. You may kiss the bride.'

Radiant and glowing, Roxanne turned to Miles who took her into his arms. On either side of them, as page boy and bridesmaid, Jonathan and Polly smiled on, while in the congregation an overjoyed Linnet dabbed her eyes with a scrap of handker-chief. Outside, led by Billy Christmas, they were showered with confetti.

It was the happiest, most glorious day of Roxanne's life.

'I'll fetch ee a candle,' Kevin Staddon, landlord of the picturesque Stoke Canon Inn, said to Miles. Miles had just informed Kevin and his wife Sally that he and Roxanne were retiring to bed.

Miles had insisted on a honeymoon, saying he wanted Roxanne to himself for a while without children, animals, chores and the like to worry about. And so, neither wishing to go too far afield, they'd elected to remain in Devon at the pretty thatched village of Stoke Canon where they'd booked into the local inn. This was their first night together.

'Enjoy your meal?' Sally Staddon inquired.

'It was delicious, thank you,' Roxanne replied, thinking she couldn't have cooked a better one herself.

A loud laugh went up from a group of drinkers playing dominoes. 'More cider, my lover!' one of them called out to Sally, rising and waving an empty pot.

'They're a cheery bunch,' Miles commented, making conversation.

''Tis always the same with that lot. Cider and dominoes and a right good laugh. Salt of the earth they be.'

Kevin, who'd disappeared out the back, returned with a lighted candle set in a pewter holder. 'Here she is Mr Carey,' he declared, handing it to Miles.

''Tis a most comfortable bed you've got,' Sally smiled, it seemed to Roxanne with innuendo.

Roxanne felt herself redden slightly.

''Tis so indeed. Never no complaints about that bed,' Kevin added.

'Is there anything else you'll be wanting?' Sally inquired, moving away to take the empty pot.

'No, we're fine thank you,' Miles assured her.

'And don't worry about getting up at any special time. We'll serve breakfast whenever you appear,' Kevin said.

Oh God! Roxanne thought.

'Right,' declared Miles, taking Roxanne by the elbow and directing her towards the staircase that led upstairs.

'Good night now,' beamed Kevin.

'Good night,' Miles and Roxanne answered in unison.

'Do you think they know it's our honeymoon?' Roxanne whispered as they climbed the stairs.

'How could they. I didn't say anything. Did you?'

Roxanne shook her head. 'But his eyes were twinkling when he mentioned about there being no complaints about the bed and not getting up at any special time. And why bring up the bed at all!'

'Maybe they did guess. Perhaps we just look like honeymooners.'

389

Perhaps they did, Roxanne thought. How romantic, if embarrassing.

They arrived at their room and went inside where Miles placed the candle on top of a chest of drawers. He then turned to Roxanne and gave her a lopsided grin.

'Well Mrs Carey,' he said softly.

Mrs Carey! It thrilled her to be called that.

As it transpired the bed was extremely comfortable.

Miles sighed, and opened his eyes, 'Hallo,' he smiled.

'Hallo.'

'I'm starving.'

She laughed. 'I'm not surprised.'

'But not that starving,' he declared, reaching for her.

It was another hour before they finally appeared at breakfast after which they went for a long walk.

When they got back, they again, at Miles's suggestion, made use of the comfortable bed.

Chapter Twenty-Six

Roxanne had rounded the cows up from pasture and was now driving them back to the shippon for milking. Bobby, who'd become expert at the job, darted this way and that, keeping the cows together and heading in the right direction.

Roxanne wondered how Miles was getting on. He had started a new painting that morning in the studio they'd had built adjacent to Cobwebs. When she'd finished milking she'd drop by with some tea for a chat.

She frowned when a bushy bearded and heavily moustached man stepped out from behind a tree a little way ahead. A tramp from his appearance, after a free meal no doubt. Well, that was all right, no-one who came begging at their door was ever turned away empty-handed.

The man held his ground as the cows, tails swishing, ambled past.

This one really was in a state, Roxanne now saw as the gap between them closed. His clothes were rags, one sleeve of his jacket ripped along its entire length.

Roxanne wasn't worried that she might be in any danger from the stranger. Tramps occasionally did a bit of petty pilfering, but never offered violence of any sort. One who did would soon be hunted down and severely dealt with, as they were well aware.

The tramp stepped forward to confront her. Now would come the tale of woe and plea, she thought, stopping in front of him.

'Nice to see you, Annie.'

'*Annie!*'

'Don't you recognize me, princess?'

That voice, the face beneath the hair. It was as though a bucket of ice cold water had been dumped over her as recognition dawned.

'You!' she croaked.

'That's right, your old pal and partner, the one and only Harry Bright.'

Roxanne was thunderstruck, rooted to the spot, her mind numb with shock.

'Good dog that, I've been watching him,' Harry commented, referring to Bobby.

Roxanne swallowed hard. This wasn't possible. Harry here, in Devon, on her land.

'How did you know where to find me?' she asked at last, for he'd clearly been waiting for her.

'Ahh!' he smiled broadly. 'How indeed. Simple really, I came across your photograph in the newspaper. Quite famous your husband, isn't he?'

The photograph Harry had to be referring to was one taken of her and Miles at his latest exhibition in London the previous month. She had accompanied Miles to the opening and stayed on for several days before travelling back alone.

'The article with the photograph mentioned where you lived, or St Petroc anyway, which I recalled was where you came from. Once in St Petroc it wasn't difficult to trace your actual where-abouts,' Harry further explained.

'But . . . but your appearance?'

'Hard times I'm afraid. Very hard.'

'What about your act?'

He shrugged. 'Had to give that up. No point in going into the details, they wouldn't be of any interest to you.'

Evasive, and mysterious she thought, wondering what he'd been up to. 'And Elaine. The . . . woman you ran off with?'

'Long gone. Still dancing I believe, though not as young and pretty as she once was.'

He sized her up and down. 'Which I can't say about you, the pretty bit that is. If anything you're even more beautiful than I remember. Marriage must agree with you.'

Roxanne glanced after the cows which were continuing, with Bobby, on their way.

'I have to go,' she said.

Harry quickly grabbed her arm. 'Not so fast, Annie. Not so fast. Or should I call you Roxanne, as I understand you've gone back to that.'

'What do you want?' she demanded harshly. This was a nightmare.

'Your famous husband must be earning pots of money, being so extremely successful and darling of the art world. And as for yourself, you haven't done badly. An inheritance I believe?'

'How did you find out about that?'

'People talk, especially country folk. A word here, a word there, it wasn't hard to learn about your stroke of good fortune when auntie died.'

Harry released her. 'So, all in all, you and hubby are a fairly well heeled couple.'

It was cash he was after, that was obvious.

The amusement in Harry's eyes vanished to be replaced by a vicious, predatory gleam. 'Have you told your husband about you and me? That we lived together and that night after night I fucked you rotten.'

She winced. Put like that . . . 'Yes,' she breathed.

'Really?'

But her face had betrayed her lie. 'I don't think so,' Harry smiled.

'It's true,'

'Even if you have told him, which I doubt knowing you, I'll bet you haven't gone into all the sordid details. The little games we played, the positions . . .'

'Stop it!' she shrieked, beside herself. 'Stop it!'

'You love him then. This husband of yours?' The smile became a smirk. 'Of course you do. That's plain when you're together.'

'You've been spying on us?' she gasped.

'Observing I'd prefer to say.'

'You bastard!'

'How disillusioned your husband would be about you,' Harry went on relentlessly. 'And the neighbours and others in St Petroc, for I'd ensure they all got to hear about your past. You'd never be able to hold your head up again. Nor would Mr Miles artist Carey.'

She flew at him, intent on scratching his eyes out. But Harry caught her hands and held them fast.

'Calm down princess, calm down,' he said as she struggled violently in his grasp.

She tried to knee him in the crotch, but, with a low laugh, he easily warded her off.

'If you don't stop this right now I'll hit you. I swear I will,' he stated.

393

She ceased struggling, and gulped in air.

'That's better.'

He let her go. 'All I want is a hundred pounds.'

'A hundred!'

'A hundred and you'll never see me again. I swear that.' His expression became apologetic. 'It's a mean trick to play, I grant you. But you can see how it is with me. What I'm reduced to. And what's a measly hundred after all to someone in your situation? Nothing at all really. A drop in the bucket.'

'Hardly that.'

'A drop in the bucket,' he repeated firmly. 'You can easily afford a hundred. I know it.'

'And that . . . that'll be it?'

'On my sacred oath. Give me the money and I'll vanish for ever.'

Roxanne stared at Harry, despising, loathing him; emotions she did nothing to disguise.

'A week today, same time, same place. I'll be waiting,' Harry said.

'I understand.'

'I hope you do, princess. I sincerely hope you do,' Harry declared softly.

And with that he turned and walked away.

Roxanne felt sick. To think she'd once loved that swine, carried a torch for him. She must have been mad, stark raving mad.

One thing was certain. He would carry out his threat if she didn't pay up. There was no doubt about it.

And the effect on Miles and their marriage? She dreaded to consider that.

Miles laid down his brush, picked up a rag and wiped his hands. He then stood back and regarded the day's painting.

Not too bad, he thought. A good beginning. But that was it for now. He was tired and had had enough.

He found Roxanne sitting in the kitchen, ashen faced, staring vacantly ahead of her. 'You all right?' he queried with a frown.

She blinked, and focused on him. 'Eh?'

'I said, are you all right? You look as though you've seen a ghost.'

She choked back a hysterical laugh. He couldn't have been more accurate. That was precisely what she had seen. Not only a ghost, but a malevolent one.

'It's nothing,' she declared in a cracked voice, coming to her feet and brushing aside a stray wisp of hair.

He crossed to her in concern. 'Roxanne?'

'I said it's nothing!' she snapped. 'Didn't you hear me.'

He watched in amazement as she strode from the kitchen, banging the door shut behind her. This sort of behaviour was totally out of character for Roxanne. Something must have happened, something she didn't want to mention.

Was it him? Had he unknowingly offended her in some way? If so he couldn't think how.

Later, over supper, despite his repeated attempts to strike up a conversation Roxanne remained uncommunicative, answering monosyllabically.

In bed she said she simply didn't feel up to it that night. It was the first time she'd ever refused him.

'There you are,' Roxanne said, handing Harry a wad of fivers.

'You don't mind if I count it, do you, princess?' he mocked.

Her lips thinned in contempt as he slowly, methodically flicked through the notes. She couldn't wait for this to be over and him gone.

'It's all there,' he smiled.

'I've kept my part of the bargain. Now you keep yours.'

He stepped backwards and gave her an exaggerated, theatrical bow. 'That wasn't so painful now, was it?'

'I hope you burn in hell, Harry Bright.'

'Probably, dear heart. Probably.'

He stuffed the wad into his rags. 'Toodeloo!'

Profound relief washed through her as he strolled off. It had been worth every brass farthing of that hundred pounds to be rid of Harry Bright.

Every last brass farthing.

'Miles?'

'What darling?'

'Make love to me.'

He gathered her into his arms and stroked her hair. 'You mean so very much to me,' he whispered.

'And you to me. I think I'd die if I lost you.'

He found that amusing. 'Well there's no chance of that. At least, I hope, not for an awfully long time. I'm still relatively young and healthy don't forget, and plan to live for years to come.'

That wasn't what she'd meant at all, but he wasn't to know.

The nightmare was over, she told herself as Miles moved within her. They were safe once more. All was well again.

'What would you like to drink?' Miles asked Roxanne. It was Saturday, market day, and they'd decided to pay a quick visit to the King's Arms before returning to Cobwebs.

'A medium sherry would be nice.'

'Then a medium sherry it is.'

Miles glanced round the crowded bar, spotted a free table and escorted Roxanne over to it. When she'd settled down he went up to the bar to order.

Had she bought everything she'd intended to buy? Roxanne thought, ticking off various items in her mind. She'd meant to make a list but had never got round to it. Yes, she eventually decided, nothing had been forgotten.

She then wondered about Miles's latest painting, the subject of which he was keeping secret. He'd requested she knock at the studio and wait a few seconds before entering in order to give him time to cover the canvas. It had to be a portrait of her, she decided, being done as a surprise. Well, if it was, she wouldn't let on she'd twigged.

She gazed across at him, thinking how attractive he was. That lean, spare figure, the slightly gaunt cheeks set in a finely boned face. If she'd been a painter nothing would have given her more satisfaction than painting him.

'It'll be marvellous having the children home again,' Miles declared putting down their drinks. They were returning for the holidays the following week.

'Hmmh!'

'How's the sherry?'

'Lovely.'

He sipped his pint of beer. 'Your friend Ted Buster's over there. By the pillar.'

Roxanne glanced at the pillar in question, and sure enough there was Buster deep in conversation. She was about to return her attention to Miles when she spied Harry, glass in hand, staring at her.

Oh my God! she thought in horror. He was supposed to have left St Petroc. He'd given her his sacred oath he'd leave.

It was a different Harry to the tramp she'd paid off. His hair, moustaches and beard were now neatly trimmed and he was wearing a respectable suit.

396

Harry smiled, and saluted her with his glass.

Panic gripped her. She had to get out of here. What if he came over, spoke to her and Miles. What if he . . .

'I want to go,' she croaked.

'Pardon?' Miles queried in astonishment.

'I want to go. I've . . . got a sudden blinding headache.'

'But you were fine only a few moments ago.'

'I said it was sudden, didn't I? What's wrong, can't you understand plain English?'

Miles replaced his pint on the table. 'All right Roxanne, we're off if that's what you want.'

She hastily rose. 'It is.'

He took her by the arm and hastily guided her towards the door; she was walking so fast it was almost a run.

At the counter, Harry chuckled. Then he called the barmaid over and ordered himself a large Scotch.

'Why do you keep looking at the window?' Miles asked.

'Do I?'

'Every few minutes or so for the past half-hour. Are you expecting someone?'

'No!' Roxanne exclaimed sharply. 'No-one.'

Damn Harry Bright! Roxanne thought in despair. Ever since seeing him in the King's Arms she'd lived in dread of him popping up from somewhere, returning to tell Miles about their relationship despite the money she'd given him.

He'd confessed to spying on them, which was why she was continually glancing out of the window, half expecting to see his face leering in.

'Are you ill, Roxanne?' Miles frowned. 'You should have a word with the doctor if you are.'

'I'm not ill,' she muttered.

'You seem so nervous over the past few days. I've noticed that on several occasions.'

She put a hand to her forehead. If only she could get Harry out of her mind! Why hadn't he left the area as he'd promised! Miles was right, she was becoming a nervous wreck with worry.

Everything had been so wonderful until Harry's appearance. She and Miles couldn't have been happier.

'Would you like me to make you a cup of tea?'

She shook her head.

'What about coffee then?'

'Nothing Miles, thank you,' she replied tightly.

'If you're not ill is there . . . well, something bothering you?'

'No there isn't,' she snapped. 'Now will you please just let me be.'

'If you wish, darling,' Miles replied, now thoroughly puzzled. Roxanne retreated into herself, worrying, speculating.

Shortly afterwards she caught herself looking at the window again. If Miles noticed he didn't comment.

She'd known it would happen, had been waiting for it. And sure enough it did. This time Harry was leaning nonchalantly against the tree waiting for her.

'Hallo, princess,' he smiled.

'You promised . . .'

'I lied,' he interjected. 'Or, put it another way, I changed my mind.'

She knotted her hands into fists. 'What do you want this time?'

'Another hundred.'

'Another . . .'

'Life's a sod, isn't it?'

'Not life,' she hissed. 'You.'

He laughed. 'Christ you're gorgeous, Annie. Especially when you're angry. Your eyes spark fire.'

'How long is this going to go on for?' she demanded.

'I wouldn't ask. There's no point in giving you my word on that, not after breaking it. You'll just have to trust me.'

'Trust you!'

'What else can you do? It's either that or take the consequences.'

'I wish I'd never met you, Harry Bright. Oh how I wish it. I rue the day.'

'I like St Petroc,' he said. 'The people are extremely friendly. I might even consider settling here.'

She was appalled. 'You wouldn't!'

'Except I have a notion to move on. Itchy feet and all that. Another hundred would help me choose.'

Call him a bastard. Again? Why waste her breath. 'What if I went to the police?' she countered. 'I've got a suspicion you're in trouble with them already.'

'I wouldn't be the only one in trouble if you did. I might go down, true; but I'd drag you with me. You could count on that. Everything I know, everything, would come out. I'd see to it.'

Miles! she wailed inside her head.

'Believe me,' he added.

She sagged where she stood, beaten. She'd do anything to stop Harry disclosing her past to Miles. She couldn't bear to lose what was so precious to her, precious above all else.

'When do you want it?' she asked.

'Same arrangements as before. A week today, same time and place.'

'And that'll be the last. If I keep taking money out the bank Miles will soon find out.'

'That's your problem,' Harry replied. 'But this will be it. As I live and breathe.'

'All right then. Same arrangements as before.'

'Nice painting your Miles is doing. Brought back memories.'

Fresh alarm flared in her. 'You've been spying again!'

He wagged a finger. 'Observing, princess, I told you. And not a lot, just a little peek here and there. Seeing what was what.'

'You stay away from Cobwebs, you hear, Harry Bright!'

'I don't think you're in any position to be issuing orders. No position at all.'

Harry chuckled. 'You'd better get after your cows. I've done with you, for now.'

'A week today, don't forget!' he called after her.

As if she could, as if she bloody well could.

Roxanne was so distressed about her meeting with Harry that she forgot to knock on the studio door, but instead simply opened it and walked straight in. What confronted her brought her up short.

'It was supposed to be a surprise,' Miles admonished.

She stared at the canvas, a nude of her reclining on their bed.

'I hope you don't mind?' Miles queried with a smile.

Mind! No wonder Harry had said it brought back memories. Her, naked for all the world to see. If the situation had been different she might not have bothered, but as it was, she burst into tears and fled.

'Roxanne, what's wrong? I know something is,' Miles demanded later.

'Nothing's wrong.'

'Is it the painting? I don't have to finish it you know.' Then, hesitantly, 'Or we can keep it for ourselves. Neither exhibit nor sell.'

'It's not the painting,' she replied.

'But you were in tears. Ran off. Did you find it offensive? I appreciate I should have asked your permission, but it was supposed to be a surprise. One I thought you'd like.'

'Will you stop going on about a surprise. I'd guessed it was of me, though not a nude.'

'You'd guessed?'

'It wasn't that difficult. Why do you men all think you're so damned clever! You're transparent as glass most of the time.'

His pained expression told her she'd hurt him, instantly making her contrite. 'I'm sorry,' she whispered.

Miles shook his head. 'I just don't know what's come over you recently. Are you sure it isn't me?'

'No Miles, it's not.'

Her guilt lay heavily within her, knawing away like a rat at a rope. How she wished she could confide in Miles. But that was impossible, completely out of the question.

'It looked a fine painting,' she said instead.

'It will be, when finished, I hope. But again, that doesn't have to happen if you don't want. I can put it aside, or destroy it.'

She went to him and placed her hand on his cheek. How she loved him, achingly so. 'You finish it, Miles, with my blessing. I'll even pose for you if that'll help.'

'You will?'

'Of course. But not today, another time.'

Miles removed the hand from his cheek and kissed it. 'Dearest, sweet, adorable Roxanne,' he murmured.

He embraced her, holding her tight, feeling her heart thud against his chest. *Was* she ill? Had she already been to the doctor and been told she had something serious which she wasn't telling him about? Please God it was nothing like that.

'Now I'd better get on, I've the hens and pigs to feed,' she said, extricating herself.

The scent of her remained delightfully in his nostrils long after she'd departed.

'Ooops!' exclaimed Polly as the plate slipped from her hands to smash on the floor. She and Jonathan were helping Roxanne with the dishes. They were drying while she washed.

'Do you have to be so clumsy!' Roxanne snapped angrily.

'I'm sorry, Roxanne.'

'And so you should be.'

Polly glanced at Jonathan, who gave her a sympathetic smile. Roxanne had been simply awful since their return, bad-tempered, flying off the handle for absolutely nothing. They'd both agreed earlier that day that they'd be happy to get back to school.

Miles stared in dismay.

The spasm gripped Roxanne as she was forking hay. A nauseous, gut wrenching pain that caused her to gag, then bend over and vomit.

Three hundred pounds she'd now paid Harry, and still he hadn't gone. She knew that because she'd seen him the previous Saturday in St Petroc when he'd walked past, on the opposite side of the road from her and Miles.

How long was this to go on for? She couldn't keep paying him off indefinitely. It was only because Miles was relatively unconcerned about their finances, leaving most of it to her management in true artistic style, that he wasn't aware of the depletion in their savings.

What to do! Roxanne clutched her head. If only she knew.

A second spasm hit her and she vomited again.

Roxanne glanced up from her churning as a shadow fell across the dairy doorway. A neighbour dropping by? she wondered, knowing it couldn't be Miles. But it was no neighbour, it was Harry.

'Lovely day, isn't it?' he smiled. 'Though I have to say, not nearly as lovely as you, princess.'

'Get out. Go away!' she exclaimed.

Instead he came further into the dairy. 'What way is that to greet your ex-partner and one-time lover? Not very nice at all.'

'Get out Harry, if Miles . . .'

'Miles has gone sketching, I watched him go,' Harry cut in. 'Off he toddled, happy as Larry, with his sketch book sticking prominently out of his pocket, which is why I know his intentions. He'll be gone for hours, same as yesterday and the day before.'

'You shouldn't have come here. It's too dangerous. What if someone saw you?'

'Who?' Harry mocked. 'There's no-one about. I made sure of that. There's only you, me and the dog.'

Harry bent and rubbed two fingers together. 'Hallo doggy. Nice doggy.'

Bobby went to Harry who scratched him under the chin, then patted his head.

'I can't give you any more money. It's impossible,' Roxanne stated.

'Oh yes you can, and will. If you wish to keep your marriage and reputation intact, that is.'

'I've already given you four hundred . . .'

'Which I've spent,' he interjected.

'But how? That's so much.'

'Easy come, easy go. You'd be amazed. But then I've never been able to hold on to cash as you should remember.'

'This is ridiculous, beyond a joke,' she blustered.

'No joke, Roxanne, at least not for you. I want more money and you're going to provide it.'

'Please stop this, please?' she pleaded.

'Oh I will,' he answered casually. 'But not yet. Not quite yet. Not until I'm certain I've got all I can.'

She wondered what he was doing when he produced a short length of rope from his jacket pocket, but she soon found out as he slipped one end round Bobby's neck and tied it.

'I thought the mutt might be with you, so I came prepared,' Harry stated.

'Bobby won't give you any trouble. Not unless you attack me.'

Harry walked Bobby over to a metal hook set in the wall to which he secured the other end of the rope.

'Exactly,' he replied.

She dashed for the door, but Harry was too swift for her, blocking off her escape.

'I haven't been able to get you out of my mind, princess,' he declared. 'You're still so damned beautiful.'

She backed away. 'Harry, don't do anything stupid.'

'Stupid? I wouldn't call it that. You're hardly going to tell anyone, are you?'

'But I'm a married woman.'

'And I'm still a married man. So what?'

She retreated further as he advanced on her, his expression one she recalled only too well. 'Don't. Please?'

'We used to have great fun together, you and I, princess. Until it all turned sour when you became top of the bill as a solo.'

She attempted to dart round him, but he caught her and pulled her close. 'How about a kiss?' he breathed.

'Bugger off.'

'Only when I've had what I intend having. And I will. You can count on it.'

She twisted her head aside when he tried to kiss her. His response was to grasp a handful of hair and pull hard.

'You're hurting,' she gasped.

'Then kiss me.'

'No!'

'Kiss me bitch!'

There were tears of pain in her eyes as his lips clamped on to hers. She'd have bitten his tongue if he'd forced it into her mouth, which he wisely didn't.

His free hand was everywhere, touching, feeling, squeezing. Then he took hold of her blouse and ripped it open.

He soon freed her breasts, transferring his mouth to them.

She hit him as hard as she could and he swore when the punch landed. His reply was to slap her again and again, until he threw her onto the ground.

Bobby was going berserk, barking furiously and jumping up and down, but the rope, fully extended, held him at bay.

Roxanne couldn't believe this was happening. She struggled furiously but was no match for Harry who held her pinned. She sobbed when her skirt was yanked up round her waist and Harry began tugging at her underthings.

Then they were gone, leaving her fully exposed. She whimpered as he groped her.

'Not quite like old times, you were never reluctant then, princess,' Harry panted, making her ready for him.

'What the . . . !'

Harry froze for a second, then whipped his head round to find a disbelieving Miles staring at him in astonished outrage.

'Rape,' Roxanne croaked.

Miles bounded across the distance separating them and grabbed Harry, who somehow managed to slither out of his grasp. Quick as a flash Harry was off, racing towards the doorway.

Miles could see how shaken Roxanne was, but physically she appeared all right. 'The bastard isn't getting away with this,' Miles hissed, and set off in hot pursuit intending to bring Harry to book.

Harry was in a blind panic as he ran as fast as he could away from Cobwebs. A glance over his shoulder confirmed that Miles was after him.

What to do? Where to go? His fear was such he couldn't think. What he didn't want was to get into a fight with Miles, whose rage must be awesome after witnessing the scene in the dairy. Besides, fighting another man wasn't his style.

Miles gritted his teeth as he pumped his legs. Perhaps he should have stayed and comforted Roxanne, but if he had this would-be rapist would have got clean away. And the bastard was going to pay for what he'd attempted.

Miles was gaining on him, Harry realized. Shit! He'd hoped he could outpace Miles, but was unable to do so.

He veered to the left, and Miles followed suit, then he swerved to the right. His lips were pulled back in a wolfish snarl at the sound of Miles pounding along behind.

Then he remembered the narrow track from the clifftop that led to the beach below, a track he'd been up and down a number of times and knew fairly well. It would be a dangerous route to take at speed, but he was familiar with it where Miles might not be. If that were true then he could gain time and distance. And it was even possible, the track being so difficult and nasty, that Miles wouldn't follow, but let him go.

It was a chance, he thought, changing direction again and heading for the cliff edge. One thing was certain, he couldn't keep this up for too much longer.

The beginning of the track was almost in sight when he trod on the same piece of ground that had collapsed under Miles. He gave a startled cry of terror as the ground crumbled beneath him, pitching him into space.

Miles came up short, chest heaving, to stare at the spot where Harry had disappeared. He moved warily forward, crawling the last few feet, then lay flat to stare over and down.

It was an exact repeat of what had happened to him. Bulging-eyed, Harry was clinging for dear life to the root system he'd clutched himself.

'Help me, please!' Harry pleaded.

Miles hesitated. Why put himself at risk for a man such as this, someone who'd tried to . . . Don't be ridiculous! he chided himself. Of course he had to help.

Only that didn't happen, for the root system, previously weakened by Miles, now came away from the cliff face.

Harry screamed horrifically all the way down, the scream ending abruptly when he smashed into the sand below.

'Dear God!' Miles whispered.

'Harry dead?' Roxanne repeated, stunned.

'No-one could have survived that fall . . .' Miles broke off, and frowned. 'Harry? You knew him?'

Roxanne bit her lip. The last thing she wanted was to explain. But now, in the circumstances, there seemed nothing else for it. 'He was Harry Bright, my ex-partner from the halls.'

'Your ex-partner?' Miles breathed.

'And lover,' she added in anguish.

Miles's expression became grim.

'He's been blackmailing me. He turned up out of the blue threatening to tell you about me and him if I didn't pay him off, which I've been doing.'

'Blackmail!' That accounted for Roxanne's recent behaviour which had been so out of character and had mystified him.

'I only became his lover because I believed we'd get married. That's why I lived with him.'

'I see,' Miles murmured, shocked.

'Then he confessed that he was already married, after which he ran off with another woman.'

'Did you . . . love him?'

A thoroughly wretched Roxanne nodded. 'Very much. I would never have gone to bed with him, far less lived with him, if I hadn't.'

'And . . .' Miles swallowed hard. 'Do you still?'

'No, of course not. I love you with all my heart.'

She grasped Miles by the arm. 'Say it doesn't alter things between us? That you still love me as I love you.'

Miles was confused, bewildered, and did not know what to think.

'I couldn't bear you knowing about my past in case it made you feel differently about me, that I wasn't the virgin I pretended to be on our wedding night.'

Roxanne took a deep breath, forcing herself to go on, hating every minute of it. 'We had quite an active sex life, you see, which Harry said he'd describe to you, the sordid details as he put it. And not only you, all of St Petroc into the bargain.'

Miles knew only too well what the reaction in St Petroc would have been to that. 'Lucky I came back,' he said. 'I took the wrong sketch pad with me, one that's already filled. I came in here because I heard Bobby's barking and thought something must be amiss.'

Released, Bobby, hearing his name, vigorously wagged his tail.

Roxanne bent and patted her beloved dog. 'Good dog, good dog,' she smiled. Bobby's tail now thumped the floor.

'I stayed in the dairy because I presumed you'd return here,' Roxanne explained. Which was precisely what Miles had done.

Roxanne stood upright again. 'And it was the same place where you went over?'

'And the same root system. Only it didn't hold this time.'

Roxanne shook her head in amazement at this coincidence, and the irony of it.

'What I still don't understand is why he tried to rape you?' Miles queried.

'He said . . . He said he hadn't been able to get me out of his mind, that I was still so damned beautiful.'

Quite an active sex life . . . the sordid details. Miles blanched thinking about that and what those details might entail. 'I suppose I'd better notify the authorities,' he declared.

Roxanne was instantly alarmed. 'You can't do that. You mustn't!'

'But why?'

'We'd be connected to the body, and in the ensuing investigation who knows what might come out. No, better by far to leave Harry where he is. Let someone else find and report the accident. Being involved is just too risky. We've . . . *I've* too much to hide.'

'Hmmh,' Miles mused.

'Did anyone see you chasing Harry?' she asked.

Miles shook his head.

'Are you certain?'

'I can't be absolutely sure. Who could? But I certainly didn't notice anyone.'

'Then that's what we'll do. Leave well alone.'

Miles could understand the sense in this course of action. Roxanne had too much to lose for them to do otherwise. 'All right,' he agreed.

She put her arms round him. 'It's for the best Miles, believe me.'

A man dead, a man who'd been Roxanne's ex-lover, attempted rape, blackmail . . . It still hadn't all sunk in, Miles thought, returning Roxanne's embrace.

But whereas her embrace was warm and loving, his was cold, stiff and reluctant.

Chapter Twenty-Seven

Roxanne was jubilant as she drove Dingle back to Cobwebs. She was returning from St Petroc where she'd learned that Harry's demise had been accepted as accidental, which was true enough. No-one had come forward to report the chase which left Miles, and her, entirely in the clear. She couldn't wait to tell Miles.

She found him in the studio with his head in his hands.

'Miles?'

He glanced up at her, his expression wretched.

'What's wrong?'

He let out a long, heartfelt sigh. 'It's Bright, I keep thinking he'd still be alive if only I hadn't hesitated.' That was only part of the truth; he was also haunted by the active sex life and sordid details Roxanne had mentioned after Bright had died. His imagination had run riot, as he continually visualized all manner of goings-on between Bright and Roxanne. Images that made him want to throw up.

She knelt beside him. 'You mustn't torture yourself Miles.'

'But I could have saved him if I hadn't hesitated, for God's sake!' Miles interjected. 'Can't you understand that?'

'Maybe not, you can't be sure. And there was the chance he might have taken you with him.'

'Even though . . .'

'It isn't worth putting yourself through this,' she stated harshly. 'Harry was no good, scum. And he'd been trying to rape me, after all!'

'I know, I know,' Miles breathed, shaking his head.

'So stop it, here and now.'

He closed his eyes, and there she was, naked with a leering Bright crouching over her, her face contorted in ecstasy. Bright moving, Roxanne groaning.

'Can I get you some tea?'

'No, thank you.'

'Something stronger then?'

It would never be the same between them again, he thought. The confession of her relationship with Bright had seen to that.

Was he being stupid, getting things way out of proportion? He didn't know. But from the moment he'd walked in through that dairy door his life had been turned upside down.

And then there was India. He couldn't help but wonder if this agony he was going through was God's retribution for her death. If he hadn't fallen in love with Roxanne it would never have occurred.

Guilt lay heavy within him; guilt, disgust, and for some reason, fear. When awake his head was constantly spinning, his emotions stretched to breaking point.

'How's work progressing?' Roxanne asked.

'Not so well,' he mumbled in reply.

'I'll tell you what, why don't you take a break and we'll go for a walk together?'

'I don't think so,' he further mumbled.

She stared at him in consternation. 'I've got some good news.' She then proceeded to tell him about the verdict of accidental death that had been arrived at regarding Harry.

'Good. That's good,' Miles said.

She'd expected him to be more enthusiastic. 'So now it really is over and done with, finished.'

Was it? It might be for her but not him. 'I'd better get on if you don't mind.'

'I could stay and . . .'

'I prefer to be alone right now. I don't really want company.'

She felt totally rebuffed, as she had done so often of late. 'Miles, I love you,' she whispered.

He gave her a thin, twisted smile. 'We'll speak further later.'

When she'd left he picked up a brush and dipped it in his palette. When he came to apply the brush to canvas he noted his hand was trembling.

'You're not eating again,' Roxanne chided Miles. Picking at meals had become one of his new characteristics these days.

He laid down his knife and fork. 'I'm not hungry.'

'You'll make yourself ill if you keep on like this. You must eat.'

Miles shrugged that off. 'I'm going out,' he declared, rising.

Roxanne didn't ask if she could go along, knowing what the answer would be.

Suddenly she wasn't hungry either. She too rose and began clearing the table.

'Miles?'

He grunted.

'You haven't touched me since . . . you know.'

'I can't, Roxanne. Not yet.' He wondered if he ever would again, a question to which he had no answer.

'I want you so much, Miles. For things to be as they were.'

'I want something too,' he replied. 'I want to go away for a while.'

That stunned her. 'Go away. Where?'

'Tuscany.'

Roxanne sat bolt upright in bed. 'Tuscany. You mean Italy?'

'That's right. It's always been an ambition, a dream of mine, to paint there. The light is supposed to be amazing.'

Perhaps she should tell him, she thought. He might stay if she did. No, she decided. Let him do as he wished, that would be best.

'You wouldn't mind looking after the children during their holidays, would you?'

'Of course not. They can help me, they're both good at that.'

'That'll take care of them then. I won't have to worry.'

She was still stunned. This was so unexpected. 'When, eh, when do you plan to leave?'

'As soon as possible. I'll see Jonathan and Polly, explain in person. Then travel on from there.'

'And how long will you be away for?'

'I've no idea.'

She lay back down again and pulled the bedclothes up to her chin. Then she placed the palms of her hands on her stomach.

'You will manage?' he queried softly.

She bit back an angry retort. 'I did before we married, and can again.'

'Thanks, Roxanne.'

He would come back, she assured herself. If not for her then for the children. He'd never abandon them.

The following day he began making preparations for his trip.

* * *

'Goodbye, love,' Miles said as the train drew into the station.
'Goodbye.'

'Don't wave me off. I'd rather you left now.'

'You will take care. And start eating properly again. Please?'

He kissed her lightly on the lips. 'I promise. Now off you go.'

She walked away, not looking back, wondering bleakly if he'd return before she gave birth to his baby.

410

Chapter Twenty-Eight

Roxanne strolled through a great sea of waving, golden daffodils. She was tired, exhausted after what had been her most successful season yet. She was also huge, as she was eight months pregnant.

The children, Jonathan and Polly, had been wonderful during their Christmas break, toiling with her and the others in the fields and dairy when bunching and boxing.

She stopped and rubbed her stomach, wondering for the umpteenth time if it was going to be a boy or a girl. She'd have given anything for Miles to be home again for the birth, but so far hadn't received a single letter from him since he'd left.

She sighed, thinking a lie-down was what she needed for her aching legs; it was a luxury she could afford now that specific blooms had been cut and dispatched. The remaining flowers were earmarked for bulbs which, at the appropriate time, would be dug up and then left above ground to ripen before being gathered and either replanted or sent to Covent Garden.

What a magnificent sight, she thought, gazing out over the daffodils, wishing with all her heart that Miles was there to share the moment with her.

She missed him so desperately and worried about lying by herself night after night in their bed, with Miles, off painting in Tuscany, so very far away.

She was about to turn round when she spotted a figure walking towards her. It was a man, though at that distance, she couldn't make out who.

The man halted, stared at her, then raised an arm and waved.

The breath caught in her throat as recognition dawned. Tears of joy came into her eyes as she returned the wave. What she'd been praying for all this long, lonely time had finally happened. Miles was back.

He broke into a run, arms pumping at his sides. She would have raced to meet him but couldn't because of her condition.

'Roxanne!' he yelled. 'Roxanne!'

Now he was cleaving his way through the undulating yellow sea, his face clearly discernible, his expression one of sheer delight.

'Roxanne!'

'Miles!'

He came to a sudden stop to gaze at her in astonishment. 'Good Lord!' he exclaimed.

'Surprise!' she called out. 'We're going to have a baby. You and I, my darling. A baby.'

She could hardly see through her tears as he quickly closed the gap between them. Then she was in his arms, his eager lips on hers, their tongues entwining.

When the kiss was finally over he gently wiped away her tears. 'I had no idea,' he breathed.

She drew the warm smell of him deep into her lungs, shivering slightly. 'Because I didn't tell you.'

'You knew then, before I left?'

She nodded.

'Sweet Roxanne, sweet, sweet Roxanne.' He wiped away more tears, and lightly, lovingly kissed the damp patches on her face.

'How are you?' she husked.

'Better.'

'Truly?'

'Truly,' he assured her. 'I've come to terms with my hesitation on the clifftop.'

'And . . .' She paused. 'Everything else?'

'Yes,' he confirmed firmly. '*Everything.*'

'Oh Miles!' That single word thrilled her beyond belief. She couldn't have been more happy.

'There was a little church in Tuscany where I used to go. And there I found peace at last.'

He drew her even closer, she laying her head on his breast. She sighed as he stroked her hair.

'I'm home for good,' he said. 'I'll never ever leave you again.'

412

'I love you so much,' she whispered.

'And I love you. And always will.'

He kissed her again, the dark days between them gone, only light and laughter ahead.

Then, hand in hand, they set off through the flowers.